The Pride's Claw

INDIGO LEO MAX

DEDICATION

For the late Indigo

-

I dedicate this book and the name I pen beneath to your memory.

May the pastures of your after life stay ever green, and the skies above stay ever friendly.

ACKNOWLEDGMENTS

To my wife and confidant —
Thank you for being my strongest ally and most devoted proofreader. Without your patience, insight, and unwavering support, I would never have finished this journey.

To my beta readers —
Thank you for taking time from your busy lives to read, critique, and share your thoughts. Working with you has been both an honor and a joy.

To my readers —
It is my sincerest hope that you find meaning in the journey you're about to begin.
May your travels take you far, and your dreams carry you farther still.

CHAPTER 1 - WHAT'S THAT SMELL?

"Hey.. What's that smell?"

"Schnozzle is free."

Sigh … "Can't you be helpful just this once Reaper?"

"I'm a little busy here Cynthia, this thing didn't come with an extra set of paws."

"You don't have to drop it to tell me what that smell is!"

"Don't you think I'd tell you if I knew? You're the one that wanted this ridiculous thing. Tell me again how it's supposed to make our evening more fun? It's not exactly intended for males."

"I thought you'd enjoy watching me use it. Besides, It was on sale."

"You thought I'd enjoy watching you straddle a donkey-sized vibrator? What am I in this scenario — hyena bait?"

Cynthia sighed, "Can we just get it inside and figure out what that rutting smell is Reaper? I'm getting hungry!"

Reaper grunted with strain, struggling with the unwieldy box. "You have the keys … could you unlock the door? It's the one with the lion thingy on it."

"This one? Oh, that's tails! Where can I get one of these?" Cynthia asked, her ears perked in curiosity.

Reaper shifted the box awkwardly from paw to paw. "I

7

don't know, some weirdo gave it to me at the clinic last week … said something about pride or whatever. Would you just unlock the door? This thing is heavy."

She fumbled with the key, then slid it home, twisting until a satisfying click echoed. "Sorry, go ahead." The smaller raccoon anthromorph wrinkled her nose and covered her muzzle as the rank, chemical-tinged scent intensified. "Ugh, that's foul! What's going on inside your apartment, Reaper?"

Reaper rolled his eyes and growled with frustration as he maneuvered the box through the doorway. "Oh, I remember!" the larger raccoon exclaimed sardonically. "I was staging the scene of your murder last night and had to get the scent of your ruthole just right!"

He grunted as he set the box down in the middle of his studio apartment. "Itchy balls, that thing is heavy!"

Flicking an ear, he cast his gaze around the room, his eyes locking onto a particularly unusual-looking apparatus. "Rutting hell, I knew I shouldn't have left Richard out."

What could only be described as science experiments lined the apartment walls and every available counter. The noise of the city, muffled through early 19th-century factory windows, cast shifting shades of green and blue across the floor of the cluttered space. Dust glittered and spiraled in lazy, sunlit motes, drifting like tiny galaxies suspended in the air. The apartment was a large third-floor studio, constructed inside the remnants of a textile business. It sat within what had once been the Garment District of New York City. Before corporations absorbed the fractured remains of the United States in the late 22nd century, this district had been populated by powerful fashion empires. Now, the same streets pulsed with the neon heartbeat of casinos and other similarly indulgent, decadent industries.

A comfortable-looking (if messy) bed formed the centerpiece of the space. Its frame was rough-hewn natural wood, the sort that suggested it had been cobbled together by Reaper himself. Just beyond it sat a small sofa, tucked at the bed's foot and blanketed in discarded clothing and other detritus. There was little room left for additional seating. Past the sofa, a nook just wide enough to house a holo projector stood across from a small coffee table, which was buried under clutter. Drink packs (bag-like, lightweight liquid containers) dominated its surface. Reaper's preferred poison, alcoffee — alcohol-spiked coffee — mingled with a few energy and fruit drinks that claimed what little free space remained.

Something chittered in the corner, catching Cynthia's attention. Small, furry, and fast, the creature twirled … or perhaps rolled … in a wild yet oddly graceful dance, its motion a blur of fur and playful chaos.

Reaper! What is that?!" Cynthia squeaked.

"Hmm? What is what?" He followed her gaze to the corner and spotted the creature still twirling — or something. "Oh, that's just Richard, my pet ferret. I got him last week. I think he knocked over one of my bio experiments … they don't smell very good when decanted."

"A ferret? Like a real ferret? I thought they were illegal to keep as pets."

Reaper grinned. "Yeah, they are. I won him in a bet. I was gonna set him free once I could get out of the city. Meanwhile, he seems perfectly content destroying all my experiments."

Reaper crouched and began collecting the scattered pieces of the broken experiment. A small glass beaker (once filled with a bluish fluid) had fallen to the floor, its stopper resting a few feet away. The apparatus that had supported it was now bent and twisted, skewed at an angle that must have let the beaker slide from its perch.

Reaper plucked the stopper from the floor and pressed it back into the beaker's neck. After a quick adjustment to the apparatus, its angles still off, he nestled the container back into its rightful place.

Cynthia placed the bag of ursine food she'd brought with them on the counter, then began untying the knot at the top. "I'll get our food ready while you clean that up. Do you want any river sauce with your salmon?"

9

"That would be nice, thanks. Do you want to watch some sitcoms while we eat?"

"What's a 'sit-vom'?" Cynthia asked, ears flicking curiously.

"It's sit-com," he corrected, carefully enunciating sit then com. "It's a type of entertainment humans enjoyed for many years after inventing television. It fell out of popular use three or four generations after the internet was invented. I know one you might like — it's based right here in Manhattan."

Cynthia continued unpacking the food, refolding the containers into flat surfaces similar to synth-paper plates. "Sounds great! But... can you set my toy up for me tonight? I'm really looking forward to trying it out."

With a shrug, Reaper patted the mess on the floor with a nanofiber towel. "Let's see how things go ... I might just decide to take care of you myself. Then you won't need your toy."

The attractive female grumbled, then rolled her eyes. "You promised, Reaper."

"I know, but I didn't expect to run into that tailhole client of yours tonight. He's lucky I didn't break anything else. I don't have much patience left for extracurriculars tonight."

Cynthia sighed, recalling the evening's events. "Yeah ... sorry about that. I guess he thinks he owns me. I've never seen anyone move like you did tonight; I almost felt sorry for him," she said, rubbing her elbow and shaking her head.

Reaper shrugged again, then spread his paws. "It's not your fault — I just wish you had better taste in clients. That guy had it coming."

Without comment, she gathered their meals and padded toward the couch. Once there, she paused. "Your apartment is a mess, Reaper — how are we supposed to sit with all this clutter?" she asked, gesturing toward the coffee table while twisting her whiskers with annoyance.

Reaper swished his tail and continued blotting the mess with the towel. "Just sweep the drink packs off the table ... the cleaner bot'll grab them. I usually clean it myself, but things've been a little feral lately. There should be enough space on the couch if you scootch the laundry over."

Paws full, Cynthia daintily cleared the drink packs with a foot-paw while balancing on the other. Her ear gave a flick of mild irritation as she set the food on the table and made room for herself on the couch before sitting down to enjoy her meal. "Okay, how do these sitcoms work? Should I just ask Squeakers to bring sitcoms up?"

Having finished wiping the last of the liquid from the cabinet, Reaper wadded up the synth-paper and tossed it into the recycler. "No. There are almost no living copies in the ether. I had to make duplicates of the holo chips they keep at the community library. I think they might have the last remaining full sets anywhere." He reached into the cold food storage and pulled out an alcohol-spiked coffee. "Would you like alcoffee or boysenberry wine?"

"Wine sounds great. Do you have any glasses?" she asked, knowing full well he didn't.

The male growled low. "You do that on purpose, don't you?" he asked, glancing sidelong at her as he plucked the wine pack from a shelf, tossed it to her, then flicked her off.

She smiled innocently, deftly catching the drink from the air. Having seated herself in the small space on the sofa, she glanced around. Haphazard stacks of clothing and clutter towered nearly to her shoulder, reinforcing her earlier point about the mess.

"You're not going to make space for me too?" Reaper asked incredulously, sighing with exaggerated drama. "Must I do everything myself?"

Cynthia laughed. "You made the mess, you clean it! Besides, there's plenty of room for me in your lap, big boy — come be my seat."

With a sigh, Reaper leaned over to clear a space next to her, tossing a pair of shorts in her direction.

Cynthia gasped as the shorts landed squarely on her snout, wrapping themselves like a veil and making her look absurdly ceremonial.

Reaper chuckled. "Serves you right — cheeky little vixen!"

"Ugh! That's disgusting, Reaper!" She growled, her expression incredulous.

"Oh relax, they're clean! I just bought them new a few days ago. Besides, I thought you liked having your head between my legs," Reaper chuckled, inserting a chip into the holo projector.

The scene on the holo display opened to an outdoor setting. A sofa sat directly in front of what appeared to be a Roman-style fountain, lit from below. Upbeat music was accompanied by a light sequence that played fore and aft of the setting. Water cascaded from the fountain's peak in long, flowing arcs, landing in the wide pool at its base. The shot suddenly jumped closer, as three women, followed by three men, began to pop into existence on the sofa one by one. The scene continued to shift, objects and people blinking in and out of existence in time with the music. The characters danced through the spray, weaving around the fountain with exaggerated energy, each movement hinting at personality traits.

Reaper sang along with the tune, hugging Cynthia and grinning stupidly. All the while, she stared at him incredulously. "I really like this series — I once spent an entire week doing nothing but binging it and drinking alcoffee. My neighbors weren't very nice to me after that."

"Do you think it was the song?" asked Cynthia, beginning to enjoy the tune herself.

"Could be? I guess not everyone enjoys hearing the same song repeat every twenty-two minutes, morning until dusk, for five days straight." He chuckled, taking a sip of his alcoffee. "This show reminds me of life at the clinic with Leliana and Minka. The two of them are always whispering about things they don't want me to hear — Minka constantly trying to get into my pants, or Leliana going on about her latest date... I swear she's trying to stir something in me by talking about dating outside her species."

Cynthia eyed Reaper. "Why would she care about your opinion of her partner choices?"

Reaper fell quiet and stared at the floor for a time, letting a few moments pass as the sitcom played out in front of them. The ethereal screen hovering before them showed a girl in a wedding dress rushing into a coffee shop, visibly distressed. Several of the same characters from the intro scene now sat on the same sofa, turning to notice the bride as she entered.

"I shouldn't have said anything," Reaper sighed.

"It's a little late for that now, isn't it?" she asked, leaning closer. "Tell me!" she exclaimed, her breath warm as it tickled the fur along his neck.

"Can you keep a secret?" Reaper asked, shifting uncomfortably.

"Of course I can — my career depends on it." She winked and smiled as she sipped her wine. "Mmm, this is really good... Anyway, who could I tell that would care?"

Reaper shrugged and nodded. "Good point. Well..." He hesitated. "I sorta rutted her a few weeks after I started working there. I don't know why I did it ... something just came over me. Next thing I know, I've got my paws under her skirt and I'm taking her to town."

He drew a deep breath. "As soon as we finished, I told her it was a mistake and left. We never spoke about it again. So now I guess she feels like I should feel something for her. You know?"

Cynthia gasped. "Reaper! You rutted your boss and expect her not to feel some kind of way about that?! The poor girl's probably been torturing herself ever since, wondering what she did wrong."

She shook her head, muzzle scrunching into a deep scowl. "You really are an idiot sometimes, you know that?"

Just then, Richard appeared at their feet — flitting and curling around their ankles while chirping happily. He nudged Reaper's ankle, as if echoing Cynthia's thoughts, then hopped up and nestled into her lap. A short silence settled over the pair as the sitcom continued on the holo screen hovering before them. In the scene, a young woman sat alone, clutching her wedding dress as she watched a couple exchange vows on a glowing television. "Aww, but Joanie loved Chachi — that's the difference," she murmured,

13

pressing the dress tightly to her chest.

Silence filled the space between them, stretching several minutes. Each took quiet sips of their drink, as though the motion provided comfort. Richard continued to nuzzle Cynthia's paw contentedly, while distant horns and sirens blared outside Reaper's apartment. Meanwhile, the sitcom played on, undisturbed.

It was Saturday, August 2nd, in the year 2352. Reaper and Cynthia now lived in the modern-day United Corporate Americas, 160 years after the fall of the United States government to ultra-powerful corporate entities. Anthromorphs (originally genetically altered humans pioneered by Diggercorp) now represented 15% to 18% of Earth's population. Anthromorphs, or 'anthros' for short, had since developed multiple population centers of their own. The variety of anthro species was nearly as numerous as Earth's original biosphere. Capable of sexual reproduction among like species (and occasionally among adjacent ones), anthro populations continued to climb. Cynthia and Reaper were third-generation, sexually reproduced anthromorphs, both residing and working in New York City.

"We shouldn't rut other species, Cynthia — you know how I feel about that. I couldn't just lead her on, you know?" Reaper sighed, resigned. "Honestly, I feel bad about the whole thing. And Minka doesn't make it any easier either — I swear, otters are hornier than a wild elk during mating season."

He rubbed his chin thoughtfully. "I kinda screwed everything up pretty good, didn't I?"

Cynthia lightly caressed Reaper's thigh, nodding slowly. "We all make mistakes — but you really need to give that poor girl some closure. She deserves that at least." Her gaze drifted back to the sitcom for a moment as she thought. Then, reminded of something, she turned to him again. "You said some weird lion gave you that trinket at the clinic? Why did he do that?"

"Oh. That guy... He came in all banged up. While I was treating him, he acted really suspicious, wouldn't answer any

14

questions about what had happened to him. Just kept complimenting me on my stitch work and said he could use someone like me. When I finished, he gave me that trinket and told me to look on the back if I ever wanted to do something else with my life." He took a long swig of his drink, then shrugged. "I meet a lot of really odd people in my day-to-day. Comes with working at a free clinic, I guess."

The conversation trailed off as they continued to enjoy the ancient sitcom as it played out on the holo projection. Richard snuggled into Cynthia's lap, and the three enjoyed the comfort of a typical evening. Leaning over, Reaper lightly kissed Cynthia's cheek before they began to eat their meal. As he did so, Richard quietly hissed at him — as though Reaper had just committed a personal slight against the tiny mustelid's dignity.

Their meal was a blend of various fresh fruits and richly seasoned meats, sweet sauces clinging to the cuts in glistening drizzles, typical of ursine fare. They ate in companionable silence, letting the moment stretch, until the sitcom finally drew to a close. One character asked, "Hey, what's with you?" as another paused dramatically in their apartment doorway and answered, "I just grabbed a spoon."

***

As the credits of the third episode played, she reached for the remote, but Reaper intercepted her, gently plucking it from her paw. He leaned in close, inhaling the soft, floral trace of her shampoo, before pressing a warm kiss just behind her jaw. "I think that's enough for now, don't you? Come on — I want to show you something."

Hopping down from Cynthia's lap, Richard glared at Reaper and huffed, then scurried off to his corner in protest. "Just let me grab us a few more drinks first," Reaper called as he rose.

"Aww, I was really getting into this sitcom thing!" she huffed, but complied eagerly, a faint tingle snaking down her spine courtesy of his kiss.

"I know, but I think you'll like this too. Besides, I think it's time we had some time together — without the distractions." He grinned at her, then trotted to the cold food storage to grab their drink packs. Finally, making his way to the apartment door, he paused and held out his paw to her. "Ready?"

She nodded, hopping up from the sofa, then striding over to him. She was lithe and graceful, naturally attractive in the drowsy blue-green hue of the evening light that spilled through the apartment windows. Her tail was a fluffy bottle brush with alternating black and white stripes that swayed gracefully with her hips as she walked, catching Reaper's attention as she drew near. He couldn't help but admire her beauty with a quiet sense of wonder, knowing his species wouldn't exist if it weren't for humans meddling with their own genetics. In a strange sort of way, his kind represented a leap in both scientific and spiritual understanding. He, and his attraction to a genetically unique species created no more than seventy-five years ago, were nothing short of a miracle. Four hundred years ago, the humans of Earth could never have guessed that Reaper would exist, let alone that he would be sapient.

These thoughts drifted through his mind as he opened the door. He insisted Cynthia pass into the hallway first and let his eyes wander to her rump while she gracefully complied with his request.

"Follow me," he said, grasping her paw, then heading toward the elevator.

As they walked, he pulled his com from his pocket and launched an app. Once inside the building's elevator, he pushed the door-close button, then began to fiddle with his com. A soft ding eventually echoed from the panel, and the elevator began to move.

"What did you do?" Cynthia asked, fixing him with a concerned look.

Grinning, Reaper shrugged. "I've sent us to the maintenance floor."

"Why would we want to go there?" she asked, her

16

expression shifting to interest.

"That's how we get access to the roof, obviously," he replied, a sly smile stretching across his muzzle.

Moments later, another ding came from the door as it opened onto an apparently unoccupied floor. Various machines whirred and hummed as they walked past. Ducts and plumbing dominated what had once been open floor space. They crept through cramped pathways with little room for passage. A few turns later, they approached a door with a small plaque that read "ROOF" in boldface lettering.

Approaching the door, Reaper began to manipulate controls on his com once again. A barely audible click followed a second later. As he grasped the door handle, he reached for Cynthia's paw once more. "After you, beautiful."

As she stepped inside, the echo of the slamming door startled her in the relative quiet. Glancing backward, she saw Reaper following close behind, then peered forward again to see an empty stairwell stretching upward into the shadowed gloom.

"Almost there," he chimed, then led her up several flights of stairs — each flight turning back on itself in an endless upward spiral.

They were both out of breath by the time they reached the top, only to find another door waiting for them. This time, Reaper simply reached out and pushed it open, guiding Cynthia forward. "After you, miss," he said, holding his paw out invitingly.

Stepping through the doorway, the first thing she noticed was the breathtaking view of the Garment District from above. Colorful lights and displays lined the streets, stretching out on both sides. Several penthouse gardens shimmered in the distance, bathed in soft light, highlighting the lesser-known qualities of the district, the ones typically reserved for the most exclusive social circles.

Cynthia gasped. "This place is tails! But... are we even supposed to be up here?" she inquired, her eyes sparkling with glee and wonder, tail swaying excitedly.

Reaper strode forward and took her paw in his, leading her to one corner of the roof. Hidden behind a walled section was a small garden opening into a secluded patio area, complete with a table, chairs, and several potted plants. Vines crowded the entry, obscuring it from the rest of the rooftop, and a floral sweetness filled the air, tickling her nostrils and stirring her curiosity as she stepped inside.

Her mouth fell agape at the sheer unexpectedness of the scene. As they approached the table, Reaper pulled out a chair for her. When he beckoned for her to sit, the warm lighting in the space accentuated his angular, masculine features — a visual reminder of the raw presence he carried so effortlessly. Suddenly feeling flushed, Cynthia timidly accepted the proffered seat, almost embarrassed by her own sudden shyness.

Smiling, Reaper observed her in silence for a moment before speaking. "When the maintenance crew found me nosing around up here, they were none too pleased. But they came around in time."

He waved his paw at the hidden garden surrounding them. "I made a deal with them, if they let me build this garden, I'd let them use it whenever they like... except when I bring my date."

He glanced at her and winked, then plucked the drinks from his pocket. Opening one, he handed it to her, then did the same for himself. Finally, he seated himself across from her and produced a small electric candle. With a flick of the switch on its base, a soft glow bloomed, and he placed it in the center of the table between them.

"This is amazing, Reaper! I never would've pegged you for such a romantic," she sighed, leaning back into her chair and looking up at the sky as it began to reveal the moon and stars. "This place reminds me of a little garden I found as a kid. My old neighbor kept it hidden at the end of our alley, and would let me visit — as long as I helped tend to it."

The moon, a waxing gibbous, hung low in the eastern sky, casting a gentle silver sheen over the growing shadows. "I really miss those days sometimes," she added, glancing toward him.

"I'm glad you like it. I come here when I need to let my burdens go. That — and when I want to impress pretty females," he commented dryly, casting a sideways glance toward Cynthia. "You know... so I can get myself under their tails."

Cynthia didn't take the bait. She only nodded with a slight shrug. "I'd do the same if I were in your shoes. In fact, I feel my tail beginning to raise this very second."

Reaper suddenly barked with laughter, then leaned in to plant a kiss on her cheek. "You're always so quick-witted — sometimes you catch me off guard."

Cynthia giggled and grinned, then her expression softened. Her eyes found his in the dim light, contemplative. "Where do you want to be ten years from now?"

She straightened and took a sip from her drink pack. "Honestly, I feel like my life never really went the way I'd hoped it would … you know, with everything that's been going on." She sighed, then leaned forward. "Do you think we're going to be okay, Reaper? I mean… is the world going to be okay?"

Sobering, Reaper stared at her in silence. The sudden shift in mood made him pause, his gaze drifting, unfocused, toward the streets below. City lights flickered on like fireflies as the day's bustle slowly dimmed. He took a long draw from his drink, ruminating, then placed it on the table and leaned back. "Honestly? I'm not sure…"

He sighed, rubbing his chin. "If you'd asked me a few years ago, I'd have said I was going to save the world — one miracle at a time. But that was before all this started happening... Now it feels like we're all on rails, all throttle and no brakes — just barreling toward the end of the line."

He reached forward and took her paw in his. His larger paw engulfed hers as he gently rubbed the velvety pad at the base of her palm.

She nodded. "I guess… But still, even if I could, I wouldn't want to be a working girl for the rest of my life. I think I'd like a family of my own one day. A good, strong male and a couple cubs to call my own." She hesitated, watching him caress her paw in his own before lifting her gaze to meet his. "W-why do you pay for me, when you could have me for free, Reaper?"

Reaper's heart sank. He gave a small, uncertain shrug, her unexpected vulnerability catching him off guard. "I'm sorry, Cynthia. I didn't mean to upset you. I just wanted to share something special with you... I know how hard you work, and how difficult it can be."

He glanced at her and sighed quietly. "I wish I could be optimistic like you, but I get the feeling we're doomed to something completely out of our control. I just ... I feel like the world doesn't want us here anymore, and I'm just trying to make the most of what's left, you know?"

Reaper watched her finger the embossed lettering on her drink pack as silence settled between them. Then, haltingly, he continued, "I think you'd make a wonderful mother, Cynthia. I mean — if things were different — I think I could see us being something other than... this."

She nodded, her expression softening before his eyes. "Sometimes it's easy to forget that our relationship is only..." She hesitated. "Professional. You're the only client who treats me like a real person. Thanks for bringing me up here, Reaper. You're one of the good ones."

A long silence stretched between them as they both stared into the distance, uncertain what to say next.

As if on cue, music began to drift up from one of the apartment windows below, a popular romantic ballad. The tension between them eased. With one swift motion, Cynthia drained her drink and tossed the empty pack onto the table before rising to her foot-paws. She held out a paw to him and swayed her hips in a slow, rhythmic tease. "It's time you work your way under this tail, sir."

Without a word, Reaper rose and took her paw in his, tugging her close with a firm, confident pull. His free paw wrapped around her waist, sliding down the curve of her back until it rested on the soft swell of her rump. He gave a gentle squeeze, then stole a kiss.

They danced in silence, swaying to the rhythm as the city lights pulsed below. Unspoken thoughts and unshed confessions flickered between their eyes, each movement pulling them deeper into the moment — and into each other.

Finally, he turned her hind end toward the table and stepped in, forcing her to stumble back until he had her pinned between his body and the table's edge. His paws were firm, but gentle, exploring her from nape to nether. He tugged lightly at the curves of her body with measured, deliberate purpose.

His paw slipped lower, squeezing her once more before his fingers crept into the cleft of her butt. Her cheeks parted slightly under his touch as he gently tugged, then slid his paw upward along the curve. Reaching the base of her tail, his fingertips stroked the sensitive skin just above her tailhole, where her tail met her spine. She gasped into his ear as his finger drifted lower, tracing dangerously close to her quivering ring.

His thumb curled around the other side of her tail, deftly loosing the clasp that secured the skirt's tail loop. Freed from the skirt's constraints, Reaper slipped a paw beneath — only to discover she'd worn nothing underneath. He sighed softly, leaning forward to bury his muzzle in the curve of her neck, while his paw found her already-moistened nether lips, gently rubbing the slick folds.

With sudden ferocity, his teeth clamped down on the tender flesh of her neck as his other paw slid to her backside. He cupped her opposite cheek while she gasped, supporting her as he withdrew his fingers from her slickness. In one smooth motion, he lifted her onto the tabletop, parting her legs before him, then stood still, looming above her. His manhood strained beneath his jeans until Cynthia finally reacted, reaching to undo the clasp. She fumbled with the buttons hurriedly, while he unlatched his own tail loop.

Her sweet, musky scent drifted into his nose as he eased her skirt back, revealing her hips — and the tender mound between, with lips already glistening. He let Cynthia free his cock from its confines while he worked to open her blouse.

21

Soon, her bra slipped free, and her pert breasts rose into view. They were both breathing heavily now, deep, urgent breaths as though it were their first time all over again.

Each of their paws began to roam, greedily tracing fur, curves, and heat, exploring one another with rising hunger.

Finally freed from his jeans, Reaper's swollen member sprang forth, throbbing with heat as the denim puddled around his ankles. Leaning in, he caressed her left breast, his thumb circling her areola as he kissed her deeply, pushing her backward until she lay flat against the table. As her back met the surface, their drink packs and assorted clutter clattered to the floor. When he reached to clear the rest, she gasped — his tip had nudged her softness, hot and heavy between her thighs.

Once more standing, Reaper paused to admire her from above. The dim evening light kissing her short gray chest and belly fur, accentuating stiff pink nipples. Glancing down at his engorged manhood, Cynthia could see him throbbing, just inches from her glistening folds. His large, furred balls rising slightly with each heaving breath.

Reaching forward, he slid his paws up along her inner thighs, fur brushing fur, until his right paw stopped, thumb resting just above her clit, nestled in the dark, silken tuft crowning her mound. His other paw moved to her hip, anchoring her as he eased his own body closer, his hips pressing close with slow, gathering tension.

She felt his manhood begin to part her slick, wettened lips, the movement agonizingly slow, deliciously deliberate. At the same time, his thumb swept downward, the pad grazing her swollen clit before beginning to trace short, slow circles, each one sending a fresh jolt of heat through her core.

Slowly, he pushed himself into her, the deliberatc movement stretching and filling her deliciously. Each added inch seemed to beckon him deeper, her tight, welcoming warmth wrapping around him with every pulse. "Pan, you are so wet... I love knowing that you want me inside you like this."

Cynthia purred low, her breath catching softly in her

22

throat as she relaxed against the tabletop — her head resting mere inches from the building's edge as they coupled. Gently, he lifted her legs up and back, fully exposing her slick, trembling folds as his hips met hers. He let himself rest for a moment, his cock fully sheathed inside her. His hilt and balls gently ground into her labia, the swollen heat of her sex pressing against him in pulsing waves, as he savored the sensation of her warmth flowing into him.

The sounds of the city surrounded them like a comforting blanket of anonymity as he began to move. Their steady rhythm began to build with the tempo of the music below, the sounds of passion muffled, fading with the sun as the night wrapped them in its darkening embrace.

CHAPTER 2 - FILTHY, YIFF!

Dim light filtered through the apartment windows, casting muted, meandering shadows across the cluttered floor.

Snick...

A figure toiled just out of focus, digging, scrubbing, maybe even scraping with tiny, insistent claws?

Snick...

With a groan, Reaper rolled over, peering toward the far side of his now-empty bed. He exhaled sharply, finding himself alone again — aside from the ever-troublesome ferret. Noting the odd noises behind him, Reaper called out, "Dick, what the rut are you doing?"

Snick...

Reaper leaned over the edge of the bed to glare at Richard. "Listen, I didn't appreciate having to clean up my experiment after you knocked it over. That one actually mattered, and now I've gotta start all over. You set me back at least two weeks, you little terror."

Snick...

"Hey! Did you hear me? Quit licking the carpet ... that's where you spilled it!" Reaper grabbed a pillow and flung it at the ferret. It missed, thumping down right atop the stained patch he'd been licking.

A stream of excited dooks erupted from the ferret as he danced away, tail wagging in triumph. Then, with exaggerated calm, he plopped onto the floor and — Reaper could swear — shrugged.

Sitting up, Reaper rubbed the sleep from his eyes. "Did you just shrug?" he muttered, yawning. "Listen, you troublesome little rodent ... do that again and I'm sending you down the trash chute. I've got enough credits bleeding out as is, and that stuff wasn't cheap."

The ferret, suddenly contrite, slunk off to his corner and curled around one of his battered toys, sullenly eying Reaper like a scolded child.

Reaper stood, immediately aware of the heady traces of Cynthia's scent still clinging to his fur — along with other, stickier reminders of the night before. His coat was matted in places, disheveled from hours of passion. He glanced toward her side of the bed, a rumpled mess of covers as if she'd fled in a rush. He shook his head and gave a rueful shrug. *Did she say she loved me? What was that about? Aren't there rules against falling for a client?*

Reaper sighed and stripped down, baring his frame to the cool air. His anatomy, a seamless fusion of human and procyonid features, was slender but muscular, standing at a modest five feet tall, typical for his variation. A soft layer of short fur covered him almost entirely, with bare patches around his eyes, mouth, nose, ears, and groin. His coat bore the markings of his wild ancestors: a dark, mask-like pattern over his face, gray-black fur across his limbs, and lighter gray-brown tones cloaking his chest and loins — classic counter-shading. His fingers and toes ended in thick, black keratin claws, flattened into humanoid nail beds but sharp enough to mean trouble in a fight. His tail, like Cynthia's, was full and plush, a striped bottle-brush of black and gray ending in a white tip.

His eyes were an uncharacteristically bright green — piercing, almost hypnotic — rarely failing to catch the attention of a potential mate. The otherwise smooth continuity of his pelt was interrupted in several places where

25

old scars broke through, the most prominent one running from brow to temple just above his left eye, a prize claimed in a brutal knife fight. A skull and crossbones cold brand marred the fur on his left shoulder blade. His manhood, another curious blend of raccoon and human anatomy, was nearly indistinguishable from a human penis when erect. It only extended for mating and urination, retracting while flaccid into a pseudo-sheath nestled above a particularly dense patch of fur near his scrotum. Unlike humans, Reaper had two pairs of nipples, one set just below the lower edge of his pectorals, and another further down his abdomen, both mostly hidden beneath his short, gray-brown coat.

Beginning his morning ritual, Reaper padded toward the washroom, tossing his used clothing onto the overflowing pile in the corner of his bedroom. "Squeakers — start my morning. Full shower, please." At once, the shower kicked on, dispensing a jet of warm water alongside the pulsing riff of upbeat metal music.

"Playing station 'Morning Rock.' Shower on. Drying booth ready," the disembodied voice replied as Reaper closed the washroom door behind him with a quiet *click*.

Reaper stepped into the shower, letting the steaming water soak his fur from head to toe ... the heat sinking deep into his muscles, relaxing him. He leaned his forehead against the tile wall, letting the spray drive rivulets down his body as he reflected on the strange tangle of his life. Something still felt... missing. As his mind wandered, memories of the previous night crept back — Cynthia's scent, her moans, her warmth. His sheath stirred, manhood engorging at the thought. *What would it be like,* he wondered, *to be mated for real? A family? Cubs?* He scoffed, shaking his head. The idea felt far away, even foolish. There were too many broken things inside him to think of fixing someone else's world just yet.

"Cleanser," he murmured. Seconds later, a stream of thick, foamy lather sprayed from a nozzle, coating his fur in a cool, silky layer of procyonid-specific cleansing formula. He grabbed his polyflex scrubbing brush from its holster and

26

worked the bristles into his coat in slow, deliberate circles, driving the cleanser deep into the roots of his fine fur. Grooming, for most anthros, was a drawn-out affair, their dense coats made thorough cleaning an intensive task. A full-body cleanse wasn't something they did daily, unless they'd worked out... or had sex.

Reaching down, Reaper gave his sheath and balls a thorough, methodical scrubbing before returning the brush to its holster. "Rinse," he called out, and the foam began to wash away. As the warm spray rinsed his coat, he began to sing along with the driving rhythm of the music. He scrubbed the brown, flowing hair atop his head — a curiously human feature retained by most anthros from their genetic origins.

"Come to think of it ... I don't think I've ever met an anthro with male pattern baldness," he mused aloud, brow quirking.

His observation wasn't just anecdotal, anthros didn't go bald. Diggercorp had solved that problem back during the early phases of anthro development. In their quest to perfect the genetic blueprint, they'd quietly cured male pattern baldness — along with several other nuisances. *For the low, low price of 99 credits a month, you too can have a full head of hair!* he thought dryly.

With his coat fully rinsed, Reaper stepped out of the stall and into the sonic drier — a full-body device built to wick moisture from an anthro's coat without frizzing or damage. The machine thrummed to life, enveloping him in vibrating pulses of warm air. He kept singing along with the song, fur rippling under the dryer's breeze. " — opens her eyes — sets in — before the doctor can even close the door..."

He dressed quickly after finishing in the sonic drier, donning his favorite outfit: tattered jeans, a tight white T-shirt, and a canvas belt. Reaper styled his hair in a punk-like mess, deliberately tousled, with just enough gel to hold it against the morning breeze. Finally, he slid on a pair of dark sunglasses and adjusted the two earrings on his left ear. One (a silver loop) hung low on the outer edge, while the other (smaller and subtler) clung higher, halfway to the tip.

"I'm looking pretty damn good today, Squeakers," Reaper chuckled to himself, fully expecting silence.

"Yes, sir. Very fetching, as always. You are nearly out of hair gel and cleanser ... shall I place an order?" replied the disembodied voice, its inflection subtly amused.

"I hope that wasn't sarcasm, Squeakers. You know how fragile my ego is." He smirked, adjusting his belt. "Order more cleanser. I'll grab gel later — once I can load your account again."

Reaper tugged on his combat boots, then slung a worn leather jacket over his shoulders. Before heading out, he scanned the apartment and spotted Richard curled up in his toy pile. "Remember our talk this morning, Dick. Behave yourself."

He slammed the door behind him and descended the stairwell three flights, boots thudding against steel steps. In the lobby, the building's guard lounged behind a reception desk. "Ayo, Reaper! You hear about the races tonight?"

"Hey, Charlie! Yeah, I heard the snow leopard's in again. She's been showing up more lately — but I've still got my creds on Rico," Reaper replied, stepping up to the counter. "You want me to place anything for you?"

Charlie shook his head. "Put mine down for the new girl yesterday. She's gonna wipe the floor with your boy — and damn, she's easy on the eyes, ain't she?" He chuckled, waggling his brows.

Reaper rolled his eyes and headed for the exit. "I'm not into cross-species, you perv. Later, Charlie!" he called over his shoulder, stepping into the street and turning left down the sidewalk toward the bodega on the corner.

Charlie muttered to himself, shaking his head as the raccoon disappeared down the sidewalk. "Damn 'coons and their weird inter-species hang-ups... I'd stuff that kitty silly..."

Reaper trotted past a cross-section of early risers, humans and anthros alike. A shy young lady looked away, a tiny mutt barked with wild energy, and a hybrid couple jogged in sync down the boulevard. The scent of breakfast drifted through the air — smoky meats and fried starches teasing his nose. As he stepped into the bodega, he spotted a squirrel anthro behind the counter, busy grilling vegetables and turning an especially aromatic sausage on the griddle.

He scanned the specials scribbled in marker across the sneeze guard. "Can I get one of the sausage and mushroom rolls when you get a chance?" he asked, eyeing the seasoned hard-boiled eggs. "And a couple of those too, please."

The squirrel gave him a dry glance, flipped two eggs into a paper sack, and dropped the steaming roll on top. "Forty-five credits," he muttered, holding out the scanner for Reaper's chip.

Minutes later, Reaper was striding down the sidewalk, halfway through his breakfast roll. A familiar female raccoon leaned against a post as he passed. "Hey, sweetie... remember me? In the mood for some company tonight?"

Mouth full, Reaper simply waved her off and kept walking, chewing absently. He remembered her — they'd shared a night after one of his harder shifts at the clinic.

Just then, he remembered his chat with Charlie and pulled his com from his pocket. "Message Sal — ask if he's got the odds on tonight's races."

A soft chime came from his com: *Sal: Rico 1000, leopard girl -120. Your credit's looking rough, though. Boss is starting to notice.*

Reaper shook his head and muttered, "Just float me another 2k. When Rico wins, you can take it all. Last time — I swear."

"Hey, asshole!" A harsh voice cracked the morning calm.

Reaper turned, and across the street, a disheveled male stumbled toward him, face a mess of blackened eyes and a nose split wide. Blood crusted around his nostrils as he half-jogged across the lane.

"I know it's you! You're the filthy yiff who sucker-punched me last night!" Just behind the shouting man, another figure calmly finished a pastry, tugged their hat low, and slipped into the shadowed mouth of an alley.

"Get back here! I'm gonna cut your filthy tail off!" the wounded man raged, his voice hoarse and cracking with fury.

***

Festival-goers crowded around vendor stalls, the rich aromas of grilled meats, fur musk, and sweat thick in the air. Music, bodies, and shouting voices collided in the narrow lanes of a metro district gone wild. Alcohol flowed freely, and most patrons were well past tipsy. A volatile, electric vibe charged the square where Reaper and Cynthia stood.

"Come on, you know you belong with me, Cynth. Ditch this filthy yiff and come with me. You know you want me up under that cute little 'coon tail of yours!" The larger human shoved between them, his hand shooting out to grab Reaper by the scruff.

Reaper's face went still, flat as stone. He spoke quietly. "Kindly remove your hands from me so that you may leave with them still attached."

The man turned his attention to Reaper, barking out a laugh. "What do you think you're gonna do, ya mangy mutt? She's my little 'coon, ain'tcha Cynth?"

A feral grin split Reaper's muzzle. His canines bared — sharp, deliberate — as he locked eyes with the male. A low growl coiled in his chest. "I asked you nicely the first time, trusting you weren't as stupid as you look. Shall I assume that you are, in fact, exactly that stupid?"

The man's expression darkened as his grip tightened. "I'll show you — oof!"

In a heartbeat, Reaper was free, a blur of movement. His elbow drove into the man's face with a wet crack of breaking bone.

The male reeled, hands flying to his face as blood burst from his nose, eyes welling up in watery confusion. Reaper calmly stepped back to Cynthia, slipping his paws into his pockets. "We should probably go. He'll be a little hot when he regains vision ... sorry for screwing up our night."

30

Cynthia slid her arm through his and shook her head, her voice calm but edged. "You didn't ruin anything. My ex-client here did. Let's go have fun somewhere else."

As they turned to leave, Cynthia cast the man one final glance. "Our business has come to an end, Chad. Don't bother calling after me again."

With that, she lifted her chin and swished her tail, each step radiating quiet satisfaction. The ambient lights caught the sleek sheen of her fur as she and her partner melted into the crowd, their silhouettes swallowed by motion and color, leaving the gibbering man alone in the noise.

***

Reaper paused, eyes narrowing slightly as he lifted the cuff of his pant leg — revealing the twin hilts of throwing knives sheathed just above his ankle. "I suggest you forget about the whole experience before you make things much worse for yourself, Mister Willdorf."

Reaper paused again, lifting an eyebrow. "Mister Chad Willdorf. Married to one Tess Willdorf, with whom you share a daughter, and a stepson who just so happens to be a raccoon mix ... Now, I understand you like flirting with my kind, Mister Willdorf. But I'm sorry to say, you're just not my type. Please — have the day you deserve, Mister Willdorf."

Reaper let the pant leg drop, obscuring the blades as he turned and walked off without another word. Behind him, Willdorf stood frozen, jaw slack, then turned and stumbled off, muttering under his breath.

A faint vibration in his pocket pulled Reaper's attention back to Sal. He fished out his com and read the message: *Sal: Done. You'd better hope Rico wins. I can't protect you if he doesn't.*

Reaper grumbled under his breath and stuffed the com back into his pocket.

One last glance over his shoulder confirmed Willdorf had wandered off — still muttering, still broken. Reaper shook

31

his head and turned toward the clinic ... until a brief flash caught his eye from the alleyway. He squinted at the moving shadows, ears twitching, but when nothing emerged, he shrugged and moved on.

He reached the clinic some time later. Taking a deep breath, he steeled himself for the day ahead, then pushed the door open. He was immediately greeted by an attractive young fem otter anthro who bounced with enthusiasm, her wide smile radiant. "Good morning, Reaper! How are you today?" she chirped, her cheer unshaken.

"Hi, Minka. I'm fine — you're in good spirits as usual," Reaper chuckled, offering her one of the eggs he'd picked up from the bodega. "Got these just up the street. Want one?"

The smaller fem grinned wide, then turned aside with exaggerated shyness. "Oh! You're such a sweetheart. When are ya gonna let me take you home so I can thank you properly?" she teased, winking and wagging her hips in a playfully sultry rhythm.

Reaper laughed, adopting a mock air of modesty. "In the name of Pan, you're a cheeky one. You, of all otters, should know we must wait until our wedding day for such activities!"

Minka giggled, plucking the egg from Reaper's offering paw and popping it into her mouth. Just then, a graceful figure rounded the corner — an attractive cougar whose rich brown facial fur deepened to a dark chocolate hue near the tip of her muzzle. She peered intently at a chart as she approached.

"Morning, Reaper. Minka stocked rooms two and three for you," she began, glancing at him briefly before continuing. "We're a little low on suture kits, but the autoclave's working again ... so we can probably reuse a few if needed. We should get a restock by the end of the day, but try to stretch what you've got."

The cougar paused, her gaze shifting between them before she scowled. "Minka, stop fraternizing with the help — it makes him flush and act stupid."

Mouth agape, Reaper planted a paw on his hip. "I'm

standing right here!" he protested, shooting the cougar a dirty look before clicking his tongue. "And you're one to talk — surely you remember when we first started working together."

***

"Ouch!" Leliana barked, pulling away, "You're on my tail!"

"Sorry, I've never done this with a cougar... your tail's longer than I'm used to," Reaper admitted, quickly easing his weight off her pinned appendage. "It keeps going places I don't expect, stop moving it so much!"

"I can't help it, stupid! I'm feline, you're triggering my piloerection reflex. Maybe learn a little more about cats, huh?" Leliana wiggled her rear at him, challenging. "Now get under my tail and quit fumbling, would you?"

"Well, if your tail wasn't smacking me in the face and darting into places it doesn't belong, maybe I could!" he complained, gently sliding his paw from her flank down to her hip.

He watched another tremor ripple through her tail. "It's awfully cute though."

He continued to stroke her fur, flexing his claws and dragging them lightly along the grain. "Does it feel good when I touch you like this?"

Leliana shivered, her hips swaying as waves of heat coursed through her lower belly. "It'd feel better if you'd quit teasing me. I'm trying to get a cute raccoon to rut me, and all he wants to do is play with my tail!"

She arched her back, lowering her front half onto the bed while keeping her rear lifted high. Her claws dug into the synth-paper coverlet draped across the exam table as she pressed back into Reaper's hips.

Reaper grabbed hold at the base of her swaying tail, using it for leverage as he rubbed the throbbing tip of his girth along the slick length of her vulva. Gently, he slid himself against her soft folds, from her sensitive button to her inner fourchette, letting his tip savor the silken heat before continuing. Again, he slowly buried himself partway into her, the velvety tightness of her body drawing him deeper as she loosed a quiet gasp. The sound shot a jolt of pleasure through his core, and her wetness, already clinging to his fur, made the differences in their physiology unmistakably clear as his girth stretched her entry.

He huffed and slowed his movement. "Itchy balls, you're tight. Have you ever taken a 'coon before?" Reaper murmured through clenched teeth, her radiant heat and growing excitement tugging him deeper with every slow pulse.

She gasped again as his tip nudged deeper, her head shaking in impatient pleasure. "Shut up and focus on rutting me," she growled, pushing her hips back into him, her voice thick with heat.

A low growl rumbled in the raccoon's chest as her inner walls welcomed him further. That velvety, liquid warmth sent a shiver racing up his spine, his claws flexing against her hips in primal appreciation.

"Pan help me, you're big though…" she moaned, her voice quaking with breath. "Just go slow, okay? — Oh Pan!" Her body trembled beneath him as she tried to adjust around his stretching presence.

Without another word, Reaper guided her back against him, driving deeper as her scent and sex cloaked him in a primal warmth. A jolt of self-awareness hit him hard as he glanced down — his paws were locked on either side of Leliana's hips, his cock buried to the root inside her. The visual of her stretched around him, that contrast of fur and flesh, momentarily stole his breath. He couldn't believe it. He was rutting his new boss. It felt so impossibly right … and yet, so undeniably wrong.

She loosed a quiet, low moan as he pushed to the hilt, his hips meeting the base of her tail. A warbling growl rolled from her throat, and a shudder rippled through her coat, neck to tail, waves of pleasure cascading along her spine like electric fire.

Her scent, her fur, the rhythm of her movement — it was all alien to his instincts, yet each detail gripped him with a magnetic intoxication. She wasn't just his boss, she was the feral embodiment of everything he wasn't supposed to want.

She wasn't the kind of female he'd be expected to bring home — not a raccoon, not one of his own. His family would raise their brows, maybe worse, if they knew he'd knotted a beautiful cougar instead of a proper procyonid. Would they see it as failure, a sign he couldn't catch a girl of his own kind? Just the imagined scowl on his mother's face sent a tremor down his spine. *Was it true? Was Leliana less worthy simply because she wasn't a 'coon?* Or was he lying to himself, using her as a fleeting distraction to dodge deeper questions? The doubt tangled in his thoughts like vines.

Reaper shook the doubt away, dragging his mind back to the present — where his cock was buried to the sheath in Leliana's heat. She squirmed beneath him as he held firm, savoring the wet, velvety warmth engulfing him while his paws roamed the soft curves of her body. Then, instinct surged. Reaching forward, he seized the tuft of fur below her scalp in one swift motion. His fingers curled into her scruff, gripping hard, and he thrust into her with primal intent.

Leliana half-growled the moment he gripped her scruff — the response immediate, instinctual. Her slickness doubled, drenching his already soaked shaft as fresh heat dribbled down his balls. The growl deepened, turned menacing, and she ground her hips against him with fierce, urgent rhythm. Her expression froze in a mix of tension and pleasure, tail hoisted high, swinging in slow, serpentine arcs like a flag of surrender and dominance all at once.

Reaper exhaled sharply — had he been holding that breath? He couldn't be sure. All he knew was the throb in his loins and the hot slickness dripping from his sac. Her walls clenched with every serpentine flick of her tail, urging him to move. Still, he held position, fully sheathed, watching her expression morph from irritation to feral hunger. A growl, sharper, angrier, erupted from her throat as her hips bucked into him. He gazed down, transfixed, as her body writhed beneath him. Her sex, snug and stretching, began to slide forward, her labial fur rippling in hypnotic waves as she fought his grip with wild energy.

"Ggrrrff!" Leliana barked, her voice laced with defiance. Her rigid posture dissolved into open impatience, tail now whipping in sharp, irate strokes. "FFfffuck me!" she groaned, slamming her hips backward with a force that rattled Reaper's balance. Her claws dug into the table covering as she began wrenching herself from his grasp, breath ragged, punctuated by growls. "Finish... what... you... started!" she demanded, thrusting her rump so hard into his hips that he had to grab her waist just to stay mounted.

Reaper gasped, scrambling to recover his perch. "Holy Pan — you're feral!" he panted, driving himself into her with renewed force, eager to reclaim dominance. Their breath mingled in ragged cadence, each grunt matched by a wet slap of hips and dripping desire. Her tail lashed again, and this time, he caught it, clamping his jaws down just below the tip. Leliana squealed, a shocked tremor wracking her frame as his teeth found their mark and he claimed her body in full.

His grip on her hips tightened as his climax built — that swelling, throbbing inevitability crashing against him with each thrust. Leliana's grunts matched his rhythm now, raw and deep, growing louder with every piston of his hips. Then, her body bowed like a drawn string, her head dipping low as a guttural moan tore from her chest. Her walls clamped down, nearly pushing him free, and he knew — she was cumming. His pace didn't falter as her juices spilled, coating his balls in a rush of liquid bliss. Her moan turned into a shuddering cry that nearly drowned his senses.

His climax hit like a thunderclap, white-hot and overwhelming. Reaper's body stiffened as pulse after pulse of his thick seed flooded her depths, his hips jerking with every wave. He held her tight — feral, unrelenting — grinding into her as his orgasm spilled out in greedy pulses. Her surprised cry barely reached him. Growling low, he released her tail from his mouth only to grab it again, this time at the base, and pulled her flush to his hips, burying every inch as his knot surged with release.

He moaned as the final surges of pleasure rocked through him, waves of heat, each pulse of his cock emptying another thick dose of seed into her spasming depths. He remained buried inside her for what felt like an eternity, the base of his shaft still engorged, keeping her plugged. Only when the pressure grew too much did it begin to force itself out, a slow, warm trickle of mixed fluids dribbling down her thigh. They stayed like that, locked in feral stillness, the air heavy with their scent, breath rising and falling in quiet, uneven rhythms.

"Wow," Leliana huffed, breath catching in her throat as Reaper finally let go of her scruff. Her back arched slightly, spine rippling from the lingering aftershocks as she shifted beneath him.

"'Wow' is a word for it," Reaper muttered, his voice thick, guttural. A grunt followed as he finally, reluctantly, pulled free — his shaft sliding wetly from her heat, a tender drag that left them both gasping.

Leliana gave a soft gasp as his tip slipped from her with a faint, slick sound. Their combined slickness immediately began to trail down the insides of her thighs, staining the synth paper below in slow, warm droplets. She stepped carefully, lifting her paw-like feet to avoid the mess, backing toward the counter with quiet grace. Reaper watched her move, her lithe form trembling slightly with every motion.

Reaper reached the counter just as she neared it, plucking a few tissues from the dispenser. He stopped her gently with a paw at her hip, then crouched slightly, dabbing at the mess between her legs with slow, deliberate care. His thumb traced the edge of her thigh, the gesture almost reverent as he admired the soft slope of her rump, the slight twitch in her tail. She didn't protest, only exhaled, steady and low.

He finally turned away, dropping the used tissues into the biohazard bin. For a moment, he just stood there — staring at it blankly as the weight of the moment settled into his chest. That hadn't just been sex. That was raw, instinctual, feral in a way that bypassed words. It was the most intense, most intoxicating rut he'd ever experienced ... and the most confusing.

It had only been minutes ago that she'd told him his flush was cute — the way he wore embarrassment so openly. Then, as if surprised by her own words, she'd blushed fiercely and bolted, claiming she needed the restroom. But Reaper had followed, suspicion mingling with curiosity, and found her slipping not into the bathroom, but into one of the empty exam rooms. That was how this had started.

And now, here they stood — breathless, sore, and utterly altered. Whatever line had existed between them before, it had been obliterated. This wasn't just heat. This was tectonic, a shift in something deeper neither of them could name yet.

"Sorry... I have to go," Reaper said, too quickly, too quietly. He dressed in a flurry of motion, zipping, buckling, pulling on layers with uncharacteristic haste. Then he slipped out the door with barely a sound, leaving only silence in his wake.

Leliana eased onto the edge of the bench, her legs trembling faintly, and stared at the door long after it had closed. Her ears twitched. Her breathing slowed. And for a long, long moment, she sat there — stunned, silent, and utterly dumbfounded.

***

"I seem to recall a time when you said something about me that ended up embarrassing you more than it embarrassed me. If memory serves — you ran off to the restroom to hide your shame!" Reaper clapped back, though regret hit him the moment the words left his muzzle.

Leliana shifted her weight from one hip to the other, blinked once — slow and unreadable — then turned and walked away without a word. Her heeled shoes clicked sharply on the tile floor, each step punctuated by the sensual sway of her hips. Her tail moved like a trained viper, elegant and deliberate, keeping time with her stride like a symphonic conductor, the tip flicking with practiced precision at each downbeat. She remembered — that much was clear. Their meeting, and everything that had followed.

With a sigh, Reaper's gaze dropped, lingering on Minka for just a breath. "Thanks, Minky... I don't know what I'd do without you." He offered her a small, tired smile, then turned and moved quickly in Leliana's wake. There were patients to tend to ... but there was also something far more complicated trailing just out of reach.

***

"There — all set. How does that feel?"

"Feels okay, thanks doc. Like I was saying, that crazy bird bit me for no reason! I was just walking near the park and — WHAM! — wacky yiffer was taking chunks outta my leg!"

"You're the third bird-related injury we've had today ... we're almost out of suture kits." Reaper offered a tired smile as he held out his paw, gesturing toward the front desk for the middle-aged, overly chatty rat anthro. "Right this way, Mr. Roder. Minka will take care of you up front."

"Minka! Mr. Roder is all set, but he's gonna need help with the antibiotics," Reaper called out in a singsong voice, delivering the line like a pitch from a holo ad.

"There's something up with the birds today ... First bird anthros, now wild ones?" Reaper muttered under his breath, watching Mr. Roder wave cheerfully on his way out the door.

***

Inspecting the young dalmatian's left ear, Reaper couldn't help but notice how her blouse hung just a little too loosely. A ruddy pink nipple peeked out at him from beneath the fabric, subtle, unintentional, yet unmistakably there, as if offering a shy hello. "Last I heard, they've just begun evacuating the newer coast cities. It's starting to happen again."

39

"Really? And we keep moving farther from the sea — without moving at all!" she huffed, her frustration spilling out in an animated burst that caused her blouse to shift, exposing just a bit more of that pink temptation. "I just don't get it. How can they not know what's happening?"

Reaper screamed internally — Itchy balls, I need to focus!

"You're still hearing okay in this ear though?" he asked, forcing himself to redirect his attention as he leaned toward her other ear.

She gestured casually toward her other ear. "Mostly. The balloon popped on the opposite side. That ear wasn't really pointed that way either."

Reaper sighed and gave a helpless shrug. "It's definitely a weird one. There are a bunch of theories, but the one that makes the most sense to me is the 'phantom rogue' hypothesis. Basically, some massive object is out there, creating enough tidal force to move Earth's surface liquid — oceans, rivers, everything. We just can't see it, and nobody knows why... or why it only affects certain regions."

He finished examining her ear and leaned back slightly. "There's always been impossible riddles to solve, I guess. Anyway, this ear looks fine. We'll have Minka get you started on a steroid pack to help the other one heal up."

The young dalmatian stood and followed Reaper into the hallway, her expression shadowed with concern. "Japan was bad enough... but now it's flooding more of Eurasia. The polar bears — even the anthro ones — are nearly gone. It's all so terrifying. Makes me break out in hives just thinking about it." She patted at her dress, searching a side pocket. "Here — I hope you like these. I love them, but I really shouldn't eat so many. They'll make me fat."

Smiling warmly, Reaper accepted the candy from her paw and gestured toward the front desk. "That's very sweet of you, Miss Elena — thank you. Minka over there will get you checked out. Just remember to keep that ear clean and rinse it with the cleanser once a day, okay?"

***

"Yes she does! Every time she shows up, she asks for *Reaper* and spends the whole appointment swooning while he's feeling her up!" Minka cackled, her voice bright with mischief as they worked their way through the clinic's end-of-day cleanup. "She's been trying to get you to rut her for *months*, Reaper. Why not give the poor girl what she wants?"

Reaper shook his head, tugging another sanitary wipe from its dispenser with a faint sigh. "She's just a hypochondriac. Let it go, Minka." He turned to wipe down a nearby counter, though his eyes couldn't help but flick toward Leliana. "Besides, Leliana's the one who attracts the *real* stalkers. Just look at what she wears to work."

"That's her *uniform*, Reaper. We all wear the same thing," Minka giggled, lobbing a used synth towel at him before shooting a playful glance toward Leliana.

"I'm just saying, who'd bother getting under *my* tail when you two are out here soaking up all the attention?" he quipped, catching a fleeting smile on Leliana's face as she turned slightly away. He smiled to himself, nodding with quiet affirmation. *Cynthia must be right. She's waiting for me to make another move… but why wait so long?*

"Oh, stop it, Reap. Every fem that walks through those doors ends up swooning over *you*!" Minka declared with a wink, subtly tipping her chin toward Leliana — who, whether by choice or coincidence, still had her back turned to them.

A brief silence settled over them as they continued tidying up, the soft ambient hum of the clinic their only companion. As she moved closer to discard a towel, Minka let her tail gently trail across the back of Reaper's arm — just long enough to register.

Feeling the soft brush of her fur, Reaper glanced down, then followed the line of sensation back to Minka's teasing tail. He turned to face her just as she smiled up at him. "You *still* haven't let me thank you for breakfast," she purred. "It's happy hour over at Schmitt's … can I tempt you with a

41

drink?"

Reaper's whiskers twitched thoughtfully. With a soft sigh, he began gathering his things. "Thanks, Minky... but I'm not feeling too hot. Mind if I take a rain check?"

"Aww, I get it ... But if you *do* change your mind, I'd be happy to help you feel better," Minka offered with a cheeky grin and a wink as he slipped out the door.

Reaper chuckled, waving lazily as the clinic door slid shut behind him. "I'll keep that in mind! Thanks for understanding. See you tomorrow." As he rounded the building's front corner, he shook his head, his thoughts drifting back over the day. *Pan knows I wish I could give that silly otter what she wants... She'd probably be a riot in bed. If only she were a raccoon...*

CHAPTER 3 - THIS IS IT, DICK.

"In other news, chaos erupted in Queens late last night as street racers and their crowds brought traffic to a standstill across multiple intersections. Though dispatched quickly, law enforcement was unable to reach the scene in time to catch the pilots. One storefront sustained heavy damage after a racer lost control and plowed into the building. Several injuries were reported. The pilot, allegedly known as Rico, was among those rushed to the hospital in stable condition. Now for the weather: expect partly cloudy skies…"

Reaper's attention drifted from the glowing holo display as a knot of dread twisted in his gut. He could be in serious trouble. Shaking it off, he forced himself to focus, paws deftly navigating the controls of his holo PC. Abstract symbols and flickering data danced across the projection, an overwhelming mosaic of stylized text and cryptic graphics. At its center, a dark gray interface pulsed steadily, the focal point of his effort and intent.

In the periphery, fragments of data flashed, evidence of a concealed database hidden beneath layers of code. "I think this is it, Dick!" Reaper hissed, excitement rising. "Diggercorp thinks they can bury their secrets, but I've got news for them." The ferret, perched like a lazy gargoyle in

the corner, tilted his head ever so slightly at the name —
Diggercorp.

A chime cut through the projector's hum. A small cube
labeled 'SAL' materialized in the corner of the display.
Reaper swiped it away, too focused to deal with distractions.
It blinked out of sight, only to reappear seconds later. *Shit.* He
sighed, this time swiping it upward. The cube expanded,
morphing into a translucent window that hovered in front of
him, Sal's face flickering into view. Before the other could
speak, Reaper blurted, "I can have the money in a few days,
just give me a little time, okay?"

"I don't have any time to give, Reaper," Sal replied, voice
flat, eyes hard. "The boss knows how deep you're in." His
image flickered slightly as he reached offscreen, the tension
palpable.

"I'm sorry, Sal — I thought Rico was a sure thing. It had
to be fixed or something." Reaper's voice was tight,
panicked. "What can I do? I can get you ten grand by
tomorrow, is that enough?"

Sal shook his head slowly, grimly, then tapped a device
out of frame. "You owe the house two-fifty-seven, Reaper.
Ten K won't even get you to the starting line. The boss wants
two hundred by end of tomorrow."

"Two hundred K? Are you feral?" Reaper's voice
cracked. "There's no rutting way I can get that kind of cred
by tomorrow!"

His ears rang, panic rising like steam in his skull. His
breath quickened, shallow. *It's worse than I thought.* He
swallowed hard. *I gotta find a way out, but how? I can't drag
my family into this. Even if they had that kind of money, it'd
be too dangerous.* No. He'd dug this pit. He had to climb out
of it on his own.

"Look, Reaper, this is me being generous," Sal said, tone
heavy. "You're a good 'coon, and I like you. But there's
gonna be a target on your head — if there isn't already. Get
your tail in gear before it's too late."

"I'm sorry for the trouble, Sal. I'll try to make it right… I
gotta go." He severed the connection without waiting for a

reply, slumping into silence as the holo dimmed. For a long time, he sat staring into the void, the weight of his future pressing down like a lead blanket.

"Well, Dick… this time I've really stuck my paw in the salted cucumber," Reaper muttered.

He turned back to the interface and keyed in a final set of commands. The screen shimmered, then bloomed into a ghostly animation of a skeleton key sliding into an old-world padlock. With a metallic click, the lock turned and vanished. "Got 'em," he whispered. "Now… time to save my own tail."

Continuing to manipulate the shimmering holo interface, Reaper saved his progress with Diggercorp's cracked database before pulling up several new panes, dark squares littered with numeric figures, each one denoting banked quantities of credits. Most displayed balances in the low thousands. With a flick of his paw, he conjured another object — a consolidated ledger — and began dragging the figures into it one by one. *Not enough to clear the debt… but maybe enough to disappear for a little while,* he thought grimly.

"Well, Richard, there's nothing for it," Reaper muttered, eyes locked on the dwindling figures in his financial interface. "Time to leave this life behind or lose my tail trying. I know *when* I have to run… now I just need the *where.*"

His thoughts were interrupted by a sound, faint but distinct, like a muffled scream echoing from the windowed wall. Brow furrowing, Reaper crossed to one of the clearer panes and cracked it open. Voices rose in the distance, rough and hostile, carrying from the alley across the street. Several large anthro figures had surrounded a lone, slender female. *Is that a deer?* The aggressors looked like wolves or some other large canids, their posture unmistakably threatening.

Without another thought, Reaper spun toward the door, snatching up his med kit and holstering a pair of throwing knives. He shrugged on his leather jacket for good measure — it would not stop a bullet, but it might turn a blade.

45

Bursting from the apartment, he crashed through the stairwell door and pounded down the steps, clearing three at a time. He nearly collided with the evening guard at the lobby. "Sorry! Someone's in trouble, alley across the street!" he shouted over his shoulder as he bolted past.

After checking for traffic, Reaper sprinted across the street and ducked behind the corner of the nearest building. He peeked around the edge, pulse racing, and spotted her. The deer stood alone now, her back and left side partially turned toward him. Her attackers had fled, their silhouettes vanishing down the far end of the alley. Breathing hard, Reaper stepped cautiously into the open for a better look.

Reaper's breath caught in his throat. Now bathed in the soft glow of the overhead security light, the deer's beauty was undeniable. She stood hunched slightly, still turned to the side. Her white sundress fluttered around her knees, decorated with a simple pattern of buttercups and primrose. A pale pink scarf clung delicately to her shoulders. For a moment, Reaper forgot why he was even there. She looked like a dream, or a ghost.

Snapping back to reality, Reaper hesitated, unsure if she was hurt. He began to approach slowly, paws half-raised in a peaceful gesture. She straightened slightly, and he caught the soft sound of a sniffle as she wiped at her face with the back of her hand.

"Miss — are you alright?" Reaper asked, his voice gentle as he extended a paw.

One of her large ears swiveled in his direction, catching the sound. She straightened, still not speaking, and calmly dusted herself off as if nothing had happened. Then, without a word, she spared him a brief glance over her shoulder, unreadable, before turning away and walking off.

"Miss?!" Reaper called again, more uncertain this time… but she was already moving, quick steps carrying her down the sidewalk and out of reach. Maybe she thought he was just another predator. Reaper took a step after her, then stopped. He watched in silence as she disappeared into the city's shadows, the sway of her elegant silhouette seared into his mind.

He stood there, eyes fixed on the corner where she vanished, unmoving until the lingering scent of her had all but dissipated. At last, Reaper exhaled and gave a small shake of his head, shoving his paws deep into his pockets as he trudged back toward his apartment.

His thoughts spiraled, dragging him inward as he stepped off the curb — completely unaware of the rushing traffic. Horns blared. Vehicles swerved. A torrent of curses rained down from angry pilots as he barely dodged death with each near-miss. *She was beautiful... but what the hell happened? Why did she just turn and walk away?* So many questions, and no answers, echoed in his head as his paws carried him safely, and miraculously, back to his building.

By some miracle, he made it to the building without becoming a stain on the pavement. Shoulders slumped and mind still tangled in that alley, Reaper shuffled through the automatic entry. The building's night guard, John, stared at him with wide eyes, clearly having seen his street-dancing spectacle.

Just as he passed the kiosk, a thought struck him. Reaper paused, turned, and asked, "Hey John — if you see a deer girl pass by, could you let me know? She had on a white sundress, walked down the alley across the street, seemed shaken. I think she might be in trouble, but she bolted when I called after her."

John nodded slowly, flipping open his log and scribbling a quick note. "Yeah... I've seen her before. Think she lives a few blocks down." He made a flinging gesture with two fingers, flicking a data tag toward the nearby holo node. "That still the right com for you?"

Reaper shook his head, flicking his wrist in a downward toss. "No — use this one. I'm heading out for a while and won't have access to my primary line. And John, don't give it to anyone. Especially if someone shows up looking for me. Trust me, you'll *know* when you see them." Another subtle flick of his paw transferred a small bribe to the guard's personal tip jar. Without waiting for acknowledgment,

Reaper turned and ascended the stairwell, tail twitching behind him.

As he climbed the stairs, Reaper replayed the moment again and again. *Maybe she didn't hear me... or maybe she just didn't care.* But those eyes, deep and knowing, hadn't looked past him. They had *seen* him. *Seen through* him. He clenched his jaw. *I've got to find out who she is.*

When he reached his floor, Reaper found his apartment door still ajar — exactly how he'd left it in his rush. He stepped in cautiously. "Richard? You still here, bud?" The door clicked shut behind him as he scanned the room. A soft rustle from the ferret's preferred corner answered his question. Reaper let out a long breath and leaned against the door. One less crisis for today.

Refocusing on the storm still hanging over his life, Reaper headed for the closet. He dug out his bug-out bag, along with a larger suitcase, and tossed both onto the bed. With methodical urgency, he grabbed clothes from the couch and drawers, stuffing in essentials — tools, data sticks, old credentials. The act of packing was both routine and sobering.

"Squeakers — com Cynthia," Reaper muttered, still packing as the AI chimed in acknowledgment.

"Requesting audio com with Cynthia," the smooth voice replied. A sequence of soft digital chirps filled the room, waiting for a connection.

After a few beats, the chirps cut off, replaced by the familiar voice of Cynthia, soft and surprised. "Reaper! I wasn't expecting to hear from you for another week. Everything alright?"

"Hey Cynth," he said, exhaling hard through his nose. "I've found myself in a bit of a salted cucumber... any chance I could crash at your place for a few days? I know it's a big ask. I wouldn't call if it wasn't important."

A long silence stretched between them as Reaper stuffed another shirt into the suitcase, each second compounding the weight in his chest. Finally, pausing mid-fold, he spoke again, more hesitant this time. "I understand if you can't. I'll

48

figure something else out," he added, belated and unsure.

"No, it's alright. Just… unexpected," Cynthia replied, her voice now colored by a quiet concern. "Is everything okay? Should I be worried?"

"Everything's fine, you don't have to worry," Reaper lied smoothly, his voice only slightly too quick. "Pipe burst in the unit above mine. Whole place is a mess, just need to get out for a few days while they dry it out." He fell silent after that, heart thudding. *Did she buy that?*

"Oh! Itchy balls, that sucks, Reaper. Yeah, of course you can stay — but only if you bring my viby," she teased, then gasped. "Wait… it didn't get wet too, did it?"

Reaper rolled his eyes, whiskers twitching as he gave his head a dry shake. "It's fine. Safe and dry. Hopefully it'll still fit in the ridekick." He exhaled through his nose, tone softening. "Can you send your location? I can probably be there in a couple hours. Thanks, Cynth. I owe you one."

"I'd say you owe me *two*, at least," she giggled, the sound light and familiar. "I'll com you my location right now."

"Tails! See you soon, Cynth." He waved to end the call, the holo interface collapsing into itself. With a deep breath, Reaper turned back to his room and resumed gathering what remained of his scattered life.

***

Finally zipping the bag closed, Reaper brushed his paw clean against his pant leg, casting a final glance around the apartment. With a curt nod, he strode over to his holo PC. A flurry of practiced gestures summoned the interface, his fingers dancing over the translucent deck as he selected a sequence of glyphs only he understood.

One by one, the scientific instruments lining the room flickered and powered down, their hums trailing off into silence. The holo display darkened, then flashed one final image — a stylized mushroom cloud blooming in fiery amber before bleeding into a smoky crimson. Then, nothing. The absence of sound crashed into his ears like pressure, the sudden stillness making his fur bristle. The familiar noise had been part of the background of his life for so long that its vanishing felt like a death. With a slow, heavy sigh, he turned toward the apartment door.

Just as he reached for the door handle, Reaper stopped short — a groan rising in his throat as he remembered Cynthia's "one condition." The damned viby. How was he supposed to haul that thing without looking like some overgrown deviant lugging around a fetish chest? His eyes scanned the room for a solution, and landed on the dusty old fold-up hand cart leaning in the closet corner. Perfect. He snatched it up, snapped the lift plate horizontal, the wheels folding out with a familiar clack. Extending the handle, he fashioned it into a scaled-down mover's dolly, then slid the oversized toy's box onto the plate and covered the whole thing with a sheet that had seen better decades.

He tilted the cart back, testing its balance before muttering under his breath, "This should do — thanks for making it awkward, Cynth…"

Reaper stacked the last of his essentials atop the awkwardly-concealed viby, then dragged the cart to the door. Before opening it, he turned — pausing to absorb the view of his cluttered, dim apartment one final time. So many memories, and yet… so little life. He let the silence hold him there, honoring the reckless path that had carried him this far — the gambling, the near-deaths, the intoxicants and conquests. *How the yiff do I have a medical license?* He smirked bitterly. *Barely passed the boards… guess it's lucky they don't require psych evaluations. Probably wouldn't have made it past the first question.*

His gaze swept across the room — the now-black holo PC, the heap of used clothes, the tangled mess of half-built projects and lived-in debris. Finally his eyes settled on the pale green hue of the windows. Beyond them, a cityscape of forgotten promises — buildings just like his, crumbling echoes of a metro that once hosted the world's elite. Now, just another tomb for ambition.

Outside, the ever-present thrum of traffic, sirens, and grinding machinery echoed through the concrete canyons — a city eternally repairing itself, never quite finished, never quite fixed. It struck Reaper that his life wasn't so different. An endless loop of patchwork and maintenance. Always on the verge. Always leaking.

His gaze finally landed on a trio of serum vials and a slim virtual tablet — his life's work in portable form. *Almost forgot the most important damn thing.* He snatched them up, tucked them under his arm, and turned to the door. One last look. One last breath. That flutter in his chest returned — not fear exactly, but the sharp pang of leaving behind the known. Of walking into a new storm, unsure if it would shelter or destroy. *Better not get my hopes up,* he thought, stepping over the threshold.

Finally, he made his way through the lobby, slowing as he neared the front kiosk. The night guard glanced up, catching Reaper's eye. "Hey — sorry about earlier," Reaper began, voice low but earnest. "I forgot to ask… could you get Charlie to keep an eye out for the doe too? It's really important."

John nodded, offering a warm grin. "Sure thing, Reaper. Want me to send him your travel address too?"

"Yeah — please do. And, uh… maybe forget you saw me leave. I'll make it worth your while. Same goes for Charlie."

"No problem, boss. Lips are sealed. Safe travels, friend — have a good trip." The guard's voice followed Reaper as he pushed through the building's main doors and stepped out into the neon blur of the night.

Lifting his com, Reaper hailed a ridekick and waved one last time to John before stepping up to the curb. Moments later, the sleek, humming vehicle pulled to a stop — its pilot barely concealing his skepticism as he clocked the sheet-draped cargo. No offer to help. No words. Just a blank stare. Reaper grunted and wrestled the awkward load into the craft's belly compartment, finally dropping the last of his bags inside. With a weary exhale, he slammed the hatch

51

closed — the sharp *clunk* echoing like the end of a chapter.

***

Some time later, Reaper hopped out of the ridekick, slipping the driver a few extra credits in silent apology for the absurd luggage. He gave a helpless shrug while tugging the awkward box free. The pilot watched him with mounting suspicion.

Satisfied, Reaper ducked into the nearest alley and wove his way between the sleek, early twenty-third century housing units. His eyes stayed sharp over his shoulder. He had long suspected he was flagged on at least one list somewhere, and he wasn't about to lead trouble straight to Cynthia's door. He had taken no chances: multiple drop-offs at different locations, always on foot between blocks, always through side alleys and narrow paths.

Each time he hailed a new ridekick, the same pilot showed up, expression souring with every loop of the absurd cat-and-mouse routine. By the fourth pickup, the pilot didn't even bother looking at him — just popped the storage hatch and stared dead ahead. Reaper had to respect the silent professionalism, if not the enthusiasm.

By now, Reaper felt confident the only tail he had was a grumpy ridekick pilot, and that guy clearly wanted nothing more to do with him. He slipped from the final alleyway just a few houses down from Cynthia's place. The street lay hushed under the thickening twilight, quiet in that carefully curated way only premium residential districts could afford. He didn't notice the shadow watching him from across the street.

A few quiet moments later, Reaper reached Cynthia's door. He tapped the glowing call button beside the frame and waited, glancing around as he stood. It was nicer here than he expected: manicured hedges, whisper-quiet air filtration systems, homes with clean lines and soft perimeter lights. Not bad. He could get used to this, if he lived long enough.

The door swung open with a soft hiss, revealing Cynthia's

beaming face. "There you are! I was about to send out a search drone," she teased, offering him a glass of dark red wine already sweating with condensation.

Reaper shook his head and took the glass, his ear flicking. "Sorry I'm late. Had to make a few detours... new ridekick every time."

He followed her inside, the soft lighting and quiet hum of the climate control wrapping around him like a blanket. "Thanks for this, Cynth. I really owe you."

Cynthia turned, eyes glowing as she shut the door with a practiced flick of her tail. "You sure do — and you can start by hauling my toy to the bedroom. You're gonna help me set it up. Then you're gonna help me use it."

Reaper barked a laugh, the sound echoing off her polished floor. Behind him, she locked the door, hips swaying, tail twitching like a lure. "I suppose I deserve that," he muttered, already grinning.

CHAPTER 4 - SHADOW.

Yawning, Reaper opened his eyes to the unfamiliar contours of a new ceiling, the soft chime of his com alarm gently stirring him from a surprisingly deep slumber. For a moment, he blinked in confusion, disoriented by the warm sunlight tracing lazy lines across the wall. Then came the birdsong outside the window, sharp, bright, alive. It tugged a faint smile from him. A soft tickle teased his inner thigh. Lifting the blanket, he discovered Cynthia's tail coiled gently around his leg like a velvet ribbon. Her sleeping face, so close, so still, bathed in that warm morning light — it stirred something tender and primal deep in his chest.

A subtle sound from another room briefly drew his attention, but then the memories hit like a breaker flooding with current. Yesterday's events surged back to him: the mystery of the doe in the alley, her haunting eyes and silent retreat; the quiet grief of abandoning his home; the ache of leaving behind the cluttered comfort he'd known for years. That cloying paranoia, like a shadow pressed to his back, had hounded him down every stairwell and alley. Then came the softness of the evening — Cynthia's arms, the hush of her laughter, the comfort of her body next to his. He'd slept beside her, wrapped in warmth, sweat and silence. And now, somehow, he felt whole, if only briefly.

He stayed still, eyes fixed on the ceiling, mind churning. The last few days had been chaos in motion, barely contained and constantly threatening to overflow. Should he have called his mother? She might've had the means, or known someone who did. But dragging family into this mess would've been a mistake. Even if they could help, they'd never be safe. And work? That ship had sailed. If Sal's people had any brains, they'd already have eyes on the clinic. Leliana and Minka didn't deserve that. Hell, they didn't even know the danger they were in. He should've warned them. He still could. Maybe.

Then came a memory — strange and sudden. The lion. That eccentric bastard with the trinket. Reaper hadn't thought of him since. The lion had said something cryptic, to check the back if he ever wanted to get in touch. Reaper had dismissed it then, figured it was a scam or some delusional mystic's sales pitch. He'd pocketed it without looking, and somehow, later, it had wound up clipped to his keychain. He never remembered doing that. That alone made him curious again. What if the lion hadn't been bluffing? What if there was something real there?

Reaper gently scooted away, carefully unwinding Cynthia's tail from his thigh so as not to wake her. She looked utterly at peace, the kind of stillness that came after full-body bliss. His gaze shifted toward the absurdly large vibrator they'd christened the night before, and he stifled a laugh. The expressions she'd made when it first kicked on — that gasp, that desperate grind — replayed vividly in his head. No wonder she was out cold. He'd lost count of how many times she came. Thankfully, he'd had the foresight to throw a towel under the thing, though it barely helped. In the end, she'd collapsed into sleep while he quietly cleaned up the flood.

Reaper slipped from the bed, moving with practiced quiet. He eased the bedroom door open, stepped into the hallway, and let it shut behind him with a soft click. The home was still, morning light slanting through the blinds, warm and golden. His nose twitched — no coffee. That would have to change. In the kitchen sat a neglected coffee maker gathering dust in one corner. He rummaged through drawers and cabinets until he found a single pod: french vanilla. He wrinkled his nose. Figures. With a sigh, he slotted it into the machine and made a note to himself: *Buy real coffee. None of this flavored shit.*

As the coffee machine chugged and hissed behind him, Reaper leaned on the counter, deep in thought. Going back to work at the clinic was out of the question, too many eyes, too many risks. But... the clinic. He straightened suddenly. *Yiff!* He'd left gear there. Equipment, vials, personal items — things he couldn't afford to lose. "Rutting salted cucumber," he muttered under his breath. "Guess I know what I'm doing today." The machine gave a final sputter, and the mug filled with vanilla-scented mediocrity. He sniffed, grimaced, and took a reluctant sip. It'd do. As the caffeine hit, he focused on the more pressing problem — not *what* he'd left behind, but *how* to get in and out without drawing heat. That meant timing, stealth... and maybe a little luck.

***

Reaper slipped into the ridekick, garbed in the blinding green jogging outfit Cynthia had let him borrow. The kind of distraction that could double as camouflage if he played it right. He gave the pilot an address a few blocks from his old stomping grounds, careful not to make his trajectory obvious. With the way things had spiraled lately, he wasn't taking any chances — not with the kind of heat he might have drawn. He had the driver drop him in a no-man's-land: far enough from the clinic to avoid suspicion, but not so far that it looked deliberate.

When the craft touched down, he hopped out with forced casualness, waving the pilot off and slipping into a slow jog. He kept his ears pricked, eyes flicking to mirrored surfaces and quiet doorways. Any tail worth their claws wouldn't be obvious, but Reaper knew how to read the rhythm of the street. Ducking into a side alley, he followed a zig-zagging path through narrow back streets, the scent of old trash and oxidizing metal guiding him closer to the clinic's rear access.

Eventually, he spotted the squat silhouette of the clinic's back entrance. Drawing his com, he flicked through the security interface and let the retinal scanner read his eye. A muted click told him the lock disengaged. With one last glance over his shoulder, he slipped inside, ears flattened and body tense.

The sterile corridor stretched ahead, the hum of lighting panels overhead barely masking the sound of his claws ticking against the floor. He turned toward the storage wing, slipping into the supply closet with a careful push of the door. It clicked softly shut behind him. Here was the clinic's lifeblood: rows of stainless steel shelving stacked with medkits, scanners, surgical packs — and more importantly, bio-samples. Near the back wall loomed the cryo-safe, its matte surface marked with warning labels and fingerprint smudges.

That fridge had become his secret vault. Months back, he'd slipped several of his own vials in — genetic samples, tailor-coded for experimental regrowth and immune enhancement. Early tests looked promising. Too promising to trust them to rot at home in a second-hand cooler. The clinic's cryo-safe, with its clinical chill and no-questions-asked inventory, had become their refuge. He'd mislabeled them carefully so no one else would know.

He moved quickly, scanning the shelves until his eyes locked on a compact cryo-transport cube, its silver shell slightly scuffed but intact. A heavy-duty clasp kept the clamshell lid sealed tight, and a soft-blue UI blinked on one of its panels. He tapped a command. The lid popped with a faint hiss, revealing four cylindrical recesses surrounded by a low-humming coolant array.

Turning to the cryo-safe, Reaper entered his personal access sequence and leaned into the retinal scanner. A soft chime followed by a sharp warning echoed through the room:

"Caution. Contents dangerously cold. Use appropriate PPE."
He snorted softly. *Yeah, yeah. I get it every time.*

The cryo-safe's internal carousel began to rotate behind the frosted viewport, its vials ghosting past like spectral bullets. When it stopped, he grabbed the cryo-tongs from a magnetic hook, popped the door with his free paw, and let the arctic vapor spill across the floor in pale plumes. He reached into the haze, the tongs clinking against glass before securing the first vial. He slipped it into the cube's port, then repeated the process — two, three, four vials, all loaded, all intact.

Once done, he sealed the transport cube and gave the cryo-safe one final pat on the door before resetting it to idle. No trace. No sign. Just like he was never there.

Satisfied, Reaper tapped the cube's UI. A soft whir followed as the refrigeration cycle activated. He placed the device on a nearby shelf and gave the room a quick sweep. That's when his eyes landed on the corner relic: a dusty old 2D PC, the kind rarely used anymore except for secure offline logging. A thought sparked. He padded over, pulled up a stool, and sat. His paw pads hovered over the keyboard for a moment, then settled into position with the practiced touch of someone who didn't trust touchscreens for everything. Time to do a little cleanup… and maybe leave behind a digital ghost or two.

Some minutes later, after fumbling through the outdated controls of the terminal, Reaper finally located the employment database. The screen flickered with dull green light as he scrolled through his profile — shifts, credentials, logged cases. All of it had to go. He began erasing his digital footprints with careful precision, his pawpads tapping out silent goodbyes to the life he'd just torched. Once satisfied the system held no trace of him, he logged out and slipped from the storage room with a quiet exhale.

He peered around the edge of the door and spotted Leliana's familiar silhouette drifting down the corridor toward the clinic's front. His heart gave a soft thud. Stepping fully into view, he called out, voice low but urgent. "Leliana

— hey, is Minka around? Can you both come over here?"

She stopped dead, eyes wide as her head snapped toward him. "Reaper?!" Leliana rushed to him, brows knitting into an anxious scowl. "Where have you *been*? You just disappeared! You had us scared out of our tails!"

"Leliana? What — who's there?" Minka poked her head around the corner, her eyes lighting up like synthlamps. "Reaper!" she squeaked, bounding forward. Her whiskers twitched adorably as she reached him. "You're okay! We were *so* worried. Pan's tail, what happened to you?!"

He lifted both paws, motioning for silence. "I'm sorry," he said softly, ears folding back. "I got into some trouble. I couldn't risk dragging you two into it. I'm only here to grab a few things — then I'm gone."

Their faces — confused, wounded, aching — hit him harder than he expected. He could see it in their furrowed brows and half-parted lips: they wanted to help. Leliana finally stepped forward, her voice a hush. "Can we do anything… at all?"

Reaper shook his head slowly. His gaze softened as it lingered on her lips — a flicker of their impromptu tryst flashing through his mind. "No," he whispered. "It's not safe for either of you. Pretend I was never here. If anyone comes looking, don't let them scare you." He stepped in close. Leliana stiffened for a breath, then melted into his arms as he embraced her. Over her shoulder, he met Minka's gaze, then leaned in to whisper into Leliana's ear.

A low purr rumbled from her chest, her muzzle nuzzling his neck as though trying to memorize the warmth. Her blush painted her cheeks in soft heat, her defiance finally fading into reluctant understanding. Reaper pulled back, holding her gently by the shoulders, staring into eyes that had once made him forget everything. When her gaze dropped, he tilted her chin up with a single pawtip. Their eyes locked. He nodded once, the sadness behind his smile impossible to hide. Then he stepped away, leaving a hollow space in his chest.

Stepping around Leliana, Minka stared up at him in disbelief. A sheepish grin slowly spread across Reaper's face as he regarded her. "I'm going to miss you, Minky." Slowly approaching him as he spoke, her eyes darkened and began to glisten. Her usual plucky spirit was replaced with something akin to fury. Taking a cautious step back in surprise, Reaper opened his mouth to speak, but was silenced as she pounced on him. Minka's legs wrapped around his hips, her lips fusing to his, his eyes opening wide in shock. Having never kissed the energetic little otter, it was his turn to melt — the sensation of her astonishingly soft lips sent shivers up his spine. His eyes closed slowly, leaning into her, a nearly inaudible, involuntary moan escaping his throat.

Unwrapping her legs from around him, she released him from the kiss. Her eyes stayed locked on his as she hopped to the floor. "That was for never taking me up on all those times I tried to thank you!" Resting her paws on her hips, she gave him a stern glare. "I can't believe you'd just up and leave without saying goodbye!"

"I couldn't, Minka. It isn't safe. But I'm here now. I took a huge risk coming here, though." Placing a paw on her arm, he slid it down until it rested just above her hip. "For what it's worth — after what you just did, I'm starting to regret never letting you have your way with me."

Suddenly, Leliana released an exasperated harrumph, throwing them a petulant look.

Ignoring her, Minka's expression brightened with mischievous glee. She giggled, wiggled her hips. "You have NO idea." Then her expression sobered as she pulled out her com. "Maybe we can get together some other time. Are you still using this address?" A gasp and disapproving tongue-click sounded from Leliana.

Stepping back, Reaper shook his head. "No — I can't give you my address. They could use you to find me. It's too dangerous, Minka."

Grumbling, she rubbed her chin, then nodded to herself. "Here, give me your com. This way you can contact us when it's safe." She entered both her and Leliana's contact info, then handed it back with a grin and a sidelong wink toward the cougar.

Leliana just stared at her, disarmed. How had the little otter found out about her and Reaper anyway? Thinking back, the way she'd reacted to his whisper probably made it obvious. Dammit. She really needed to work on her poker face.

Turning for the door, Reaper drew in a breath. "I'll miss you both. Please be careful. Okay?"

Stepping forward, Leliana's mouth opened, then closed — her expression unreadable except for the heartbreak that lived in her eyes.

Bounding to her side, Minka waved with a bright, teary smile. "Take care of yourself, Reaper. Com us as soon as you can, okay?" Her paw gently rubbed Leliana's back.

"Thank you, Minky. I will." His gaze shifted from the otter to the cougar — the look on her face lingering in his mind like the memory of a kiss. "I'll miss you too, Lel. Thank you for everything." He turned for the door. Sunlight poured in as he stepped through the portal.

Minka called after him through the closing door, "Love the outfit, Reap! The sweatpants really accentuate your figure!"

He chuckled, but didn't look back.

***

True to his cover, Reaper resumed his jog in the direction he'd originally come from. Though now carrying the cube-shaped machine, anyone watching would've guessed he'd made a stop. Several blocks later, his ears perked at the quiet *shuff* of movement, his eyes catching a silhouette watching from the shadow of a high-rise alleyway. Pretending to check a non-existent fitness tracker on his wrist, Reaper jogged past, every nerve on high alert.

The figure moved slowly at first, stepping out of the gloom — tall, clad in dark slacks and a hoodie that concealed rounded ears. Without speaking, the shadow began jogging in the same direction as Reaper. Whether he was interested in Reaper's destination or just coincidentally headed the

61

same way, it didn't matter.

Reaper picked up the pace, turning left at the next alley intersection to break line of sight. After a block, he checked again. The figure was still tailing him, matching speed. He turned again, sprinting now, no longer pretending to be just out for a run. Behind him, the shadow closed in.

At the next turn, Reaper veered left and dove behind one of several dumpsters lining a building wall. Back pressed to the cold metal, he held his breath, cursing himself for leaving his knives back at Cynthia's. Carefully setting the cube down beside the bin, he steeled himself.

Seconds later, the figure skidded into the alley, slowing to a walk, scanning. Just then, a burst of motion drew both of their attention — a trash bot emerged from a concealed alcove, its rotors buzzing as it floated toward the dumpsters.

Reaper struck.

Pain lanced up his arm as his fist connected with the figure's jaw. The hood slipped back to reveal the angular, sharp features of a male black panther, tall and broad-shouldered, probably late twenties, and a full head taller than Reaper. The feline staggered back a step, growling low in his throat.

Reaper shifted into a ready stance, feet apart, paws raised. "Why were you following me, Shadow?"

The panther hissed and clutched his jaw. "I'm going to hurt you for that, 'coon. You know why I'm here. You owe my boss a lot of money. I've come to collect — one way or another."

Reaper narrowed his eyes. "Maybe. But your boss wouldn't get a single cred even if I had it. He's not a good person, Shadow. I would've paid him if he'd given me the chance. But it's too late now. Sending you only made my decision easier."

He backed away slowly, never breaking eye contact, sliding one paw toward the wall to steady himself. "I don't want to fight you, cat. Turn around. Tell your boss you never saw me. You walk, and we both forget this happened."

The panther's snarl deepened, paw dropping from his jaw

as he resumed his slow, predatory approach. "You know I can't do that. Especially not after that sucker punch. You got lucky — now I'm going to make you regret it."

Still stalking forward, the panther straightened his back and puffed his chest, putting on a show of dominance, or at least trying to mask the sting still ringing in his jaw. He flicked imaginary lint from the hem of his shirt, feigning boredom.

Then lunged.

Reaper twisted aside with fluid precision, ducking beneath the grab and slamming a tight jab into the panther's oblique, low and just behind the ribs. *Whump.* The cat let out a sharp gasp and staggered sideways, unleashing a string of vicious curses through bared fangs.

Snarling, the feline wheeled to face him again, crazed heat in his glare. His lip curled back to reveal sharp ivory teeth as he resumed his advance. Reaper exhaled through his nose and retreated with controlled steps, ears flicking as he hunted the alley's soundscape for opportunity. Then he heard it — the rising *whirr* of the trash bot returning on its route. Industrial model. Reliable. Predictable.

As he moved, Reaper opened his arms, paws raised, furred palms up, placating. "I told you I didn't want this fight, Shadow. Tell me what it'll take to make you back off."

The cat didn't break stride. "I told *you* — my paws are tied, 'coon. You're either walking with me or I'm dragging you back in a bag."

Reaper's ears tilted toward the returning *whirr.* The bot was close now. Still backing, he reached slowly into his jogging suit pocket. The panther's gaze dropped, tail lashing once as his body tensed. Reaper lifted his other paw. "Easy. Just my com. I wanna show you something."

He pulled out the burner com and tapped the app — the disguised override he'd once used to unlock the rooftop hatch back at his apartment. To a casual glance, it looked like an old-school holo-still viewer. Swiping through with intent, he turned the screen toward the feline. "Here. Look. You'll get it once you see it."

The panther squinted, suspicion knotting his brow. "What am I looking at? Some kind of bookshelf?" He looked back to Reaper, clearly unimpressed.

"Closer. You'll see." Reaper stepped nearer, thrusting the screen toward the cat's face, voice lowered into a silky calm. "Right... there..."

The panther growled low, stepped into his space, and locked eyes. "Enough of your games, 'coon. You're—"

WHRRR-BOOM!

The trash bot burst through the upper-level portal like a metal ghost. Its sudden roar and downward surge caught the feline's attention for just a fraction of a second — all Reaper needed.

With a leap born of desperation and training, he snapped forward. His foot connected hard with the panther's jaw in a rising arc, *crack!* Then his paw snagged the trash bot's maintenance handle. The bot beeped in surprise, struggling to stabilize as it gained altitude with Reaper awkwardly clinging to its underside. The wind rushed around him, fur fluttering wildly as the alley fell away beneath.

Below, the panther crumpled onto the cracked pavement, groaning and clutching his muzzle as his eyes rolled from the shock.

Reaper pocketed his com with a flick of the wrist, then reached for the trash, paw darting toward the recessed hatch on its underside. Fingers brushing over the tangle of emergency tools inside, he pulled free a roll of multi-use quack tape, standard-issue repair adhesive, then dropped to the surface.

The panther groaned, still stunned, struggling to push himself upright. He'd barely made it to his elbows when Reaper grabbed his arm, yanked it backward, and shoved the cat muzzle-first into the pavement with a heavy grunt.

"You should've walked away," Reaper growled.

The cat thrashed, earning himself a hard kick to the uninjured side just above the kidney. He gasped and froze, hissing between clenched teeth.

"Stop struggling," Reaper warned, his voice low and

64

grim. "I gave you the easy out. Now we're doing things the hard way."

Standing with a foot planted squarely between the panther's shoulder blades, Reaper seized both of the cat's wrists and cinched them tight with the tape — layer after layer binding the panther's thick limbs until the struggling subsided. Moving to the ankles, he repeated the process, taking no chances.

Somehow, despite the scuffle and the bot's interruption, the alley remained mercifully silent. No alarms. No curious onlookers. Just the hum of distant traffic and the faint click of Reaper's claws against the concrete.

He crouched beside the feline, now blinking groggily but aware. That same burning defiance still shimmered in the cat's yellow eyes. "I didn't want to do this," Reaper said quietly, his voice calm but edged in warning. "You're doing your job, I get it. But I meant what I said — next time, I won't be so gentle."

He pulled his com from his pocket, tapped the screen, and snapped a still of the bound panther. "Now I've got a request. Go back to your boss. Tell him I was polite. That I asked — *asked* — to be left alone. No games. No lies. Just a raccoon trying to walk away. Tell him if he thinks about sending someone else, I'll stop being polite."

He gestured again, fingers flicking across the com screen. A chirp confirmed the credit transfer. "This is for the shirt. And a stiff drink. You'll need one. In two hours, that still and your location go to your boss. Don't try to follow me."

Reaper stood, tail flicking once as he stepped back toward the bot and retrieved the cube from where he'd hidden it. "Best of luck, Shadow."

Without another glance, he turned and resumed his jog, the cube cradled under one arm. His other paw lifted in a casual wave as he rounded the alley corner and vanished from view.

Unseen across the street, half-concealed in shadow, a second hooded figure watched Reaper disappear — then quietly pulled their hood lower and melted into the darkness.

***

Waving lazily at the ridekick pilot as the craft pulled away, Reaper adjusted his grip on the cryo-cube, the cool surface damp against his paw pads. His borrowed jogging outfit was ruined, mottled with dark stains from his fight with the panther, most of them still tacky. He'd tried to wipe them away with little success. They weren't blood, but they might as well have been — the memory of each strike, each dodge, was etched into every smudge on the synthetic fabric.

As he made his way down the familiar block, his thoughts drifted unbidden to his mother. He hadn't called her. Hadn't even sent a message. Every instinct told him to reach out, to hear her voice if only for a moment. But the smart part of him, the part that knew what came next, told him that was a luxury he couldn't afford. Not now. Not when someone had already been sent to drag him in. He'd risked enough bringing Cynthia into this. Leliana and Minka too. He couldn't make the same mistake with his family.

Not again.

With a heavy breath that trembled in his throat, Reaper resigned himself to silence. She'd be safer not knowing, even if it gnawed at him.

Arriving at Cynthia's home, he keyed open the door and slipped inside, his tail brushing the frame before the door clicked shut behind him. "Cynth? You here?" he called out, thumbing the lock.

Her voice purred from deeper in the apartment. "I'm in the bedroom. About time you got back. How'd it go?"

Reaper looked down at himself and grimaced. "Let's just say I owe you a new jogging set. I ran into a few… technical difficulties."

A husky laugh echoed back. "They never fit me right anyway. Come in here — I want a look."

Following the sound of her voice, Reaper pushed open the bedroom door to find her sprawled luxuriously across the bed, entirely nude save for the smile she wore and the half-finished glass of wine in her paw. Laid out beside her were a handful of toys, artfully arranged like an exhibition. Her tail flicked once behind her, slow and inviting.

His grin spread immediately. He set the cube down on her dresser, peeled off the ruined shirt, and began undoing the pants with one paw as he stepped closer to the bed.

"What have we here?" he murmured, voice low as his finger pad ghosted over the polished handle of a black leather flogger. "Does this mean you've been naughty while I was out?"

She raised her brows and took a slow sip of wine. "Not naughty. Just appreciative. I thought I'd return the favor from last night."

Her legs parted in a slow, fluid motion as she nodded toward the flogger. "That one's my favorite. Really gets the juices flowing — if you know what I mean."

He plucked it from the bed and weighed it in his paw, giving it a thoughtful swish through the air. "I've got a pretty good idea," he said, stepping closer, his grin darkening with anticipation. "But I think I'll need to test that theory to be sure."

CHAPTER 5 - THE IRON SCENT OF BLOOD.

Looking out the window opposite him, Reaper sipped from a chipped ceramic mug emblazoned with the words *I came, I saw, I forgot my underwear"* in bold, irreverent lettering. Wisps of steam rose from the mug, curling upward to tangle with golden shafts of morning light slanting across the breakfast counter and floor. Specks of dust danced lazily through the beams, giving the whole scene a tranquil glow.

Opposite the window, Reaper lounged at the edge of the counter, eyes fixed on the garden beyond. A feral squirrel was busy stashing nuts beneath a gnarled oak, its twitchy movements oddly calming. Cynthia's garden was an organized tangle of perennial shade bloomers, evergreen shrubs, mossy bricks, and last year's leaves, all softened by the persistent veil of dew clinging to every surface. In the shaded hollows, low mist hovered like the breath of an ice dragon sleeping just out of sight.

His com buzzed near his left paw. A soft vibration. A holo popped up from Charlie:
She just walked by. I think she's going to the bodega on the corner — the one you like so much.

Reaper snapped upright. *Tails — I almost forgot!*

Another ping:

She's headed back the way she came. I think she's going into The Arbor Building. She's using the alleyway to get to the back.

Then, a third:

Pretty sure I saw her on the roof during my break a few days ago. I bet she lives in the greenhouse up there. Some of the windows are painted over now.

"Reply to Charlie," Reaper murmured, dragging the com closer. "Can you confirm she lives up there? I'll head that way as soon as I can. I owe you."

He tried not to feel like a stalker, tried to frame it differently in his mind. *Concerned citizen*, he told himself. *She might be in danger. She might be lost.* Maybe she was running too, just like him. But deep down, he knew better. It wasn't just concern. It wasn't just the mystery. It was those eyes … he couldn't shake them. And the worst part? He wasn't even sure he wanted to.

Another ping:

Just saw her walk from the roof door to the greenhouse — she's definitely doing something up there.

Reaper tapped his com and checked his credit balance. After a moment's consideration, he swiped a few hundred credits into Charlie's account.

"Reply to Charlie: Please keep this quiet. Delete our messages if you can — just in case someone comes sniffing around about me. Consider the credits your silence bonus. You haven't seen me. Thanks again, Charlie."

His fingers lingered on the com for a moment. Trust was a dangerous thing to buy, and an even more dangerous thing to misplace. But Charlie had always been a decent guy. Hopefully, that was still true.

Draining the last of his coffee, Reaper thumped the mug onto the counter and glanced down at it.

"That's got to be a double entendre," he muttered, lips twitching despite himself.

He chuckled softly, pushing his chair back with a quiet scrape. "That's definitely something Cynth would do…"

69

Speaking of Cynthia ... He padded toward the bedroom where he'd left her slumbering nearly an hour ago, her tail draped across the sheets like a silk ribbon forgotten by morning.

Time to wake her with a little treat ... he mused, the corner of his muzzle lifting in a slow grin. *Maybe some breakfast too.*

***

Both satisfied in more ways than one, Reaper and Cynthia sat side by side at the breakfast counter, the remnants of sourdough toast, strawberry preserves, fluffy eggs, crisp bacon, and Reaper's own decadent hollandaise sauce scattered across their plates. Wiping his muzzle with a napkin, Reaper sighed, tail twitching lazily beneath the stool as he cast a fond look toward Cynthia.

"That was delicious. Thank you," he murmured with a grin.

She blinked at him, brow furrowing. "What do you mean? I didn't cook. You did."

He chuckled, collecting the plates. "I wasn't talking about the food." A sly glint danced in his eyes as he shot her a wink.

"Reaper!" she gasped, giggling and turning slightly pink beneath her fur. "You're so naughty!" Her voice dropped with mock indignation. "You're welcome though — you weren't so bad yourself. Your food, I mean."

Their shared laughter filled the kitchen, warm and fleeting. But as the moment passed, so did Reaper's smile, fading like morning mist in the rising light. He turned toward the sink, shrugging slightly as he turned on the water and began rinsing the plates.

"I'm gonna have to leave soon."

She joined him, standing quietly at his side, reaching for the faucet to help rinse. "I thought you might say that." Her voice had softened. After a pause, she looked up at him, her ears angling forward with worry. "What's really going on,

Reaper?"

He glanced at her, then away again, ears folding low. "The less you know, the better. I just ... I need to leave town for a while. Maybe longer."

Cynthia stilled, her paws hovering over the sink as her gaze hardened. "Why would you do this, Reaper? You come here, make me feel like this, then just up and leave?" Her voice cracked. She backed away from the sink, leaning against the counter, her tail drooping low. "You can't just use people like that."

Reaper stepped toward her quickly, ears flattening. "I didn't mean for it to happen this way, Cynth. I swear. I just needed somewhere safe to disappear for a bit, and you were the first person I thought of. I knew I could trust you. I didn't plan on ... this. But it's not nothing to me. I like you. A lot."

He reached for her, gently placing a paw on her arm. "This ... us ... it's real. I just ..."

She stepped back again, a small sob slipping past her lips. Her shoulders slumped as she wrapped her arms around herself. "Rutting tailhole," she whispered. "I knew something was up the second you asked to borrow that yiffing jogging outfit. And then you came back looking like you'd gone ten rounds with a dump truck." Her voice wavered, her eyes narrowing as she grabbed a towel to dry her paws, tossing it carelessly onto the counter. "So what now, huh? What do you expect me to do?"

Reaper shut off the water and pulled a chair out, offering it to her with a slow, sincere motion. Sitting across from her, he met her eyes — his own dark with sorrow, but tempered by something steadier. Pride. Resolve.

"Cynth ... short of my mother, you're the toughest sow I've ever known. Honestly, if I thought I had any business raising a family, you'd be my first pick. But as it stands, I can barely keep myself from falling apart." His paw drifted up to the back of his neck, rubbing absently as his gaze dropped to the floor. "I'm sorry I dragged you into this mess. I shouldn't have led you on. It's just ... it felt good, you know? To

71

pretend I was something else, someone normal, even if it was only for a little while."

A crooked smile crept onto his muzzle as his eyes met hers again. "Besides … you're absolute fire in bed, and you damn well know it."

Her modesty briefly abandoned her as a soft giggle escaped, her cheeks coloring beneath her fur. "Guilty. But you were the one eager to dive into my toybox. You think a sow can just forget a boar who knows how to work a flogger?"

His grin faltered into a dry, sardonic look. "You'll survive. There's gotta be a million better boars out there — ones who won't leave you with blood on your sheets and a target on your back. I'd rather you be safe with one of them than hunted down because of me."

That last line hit like a slap. Cynthia's ears perked sharply, her smile vanishing as alarm flooded her features. "What is that supposed to mean? Reaper — seriously — what the yiff is going on? Who's chasing you?"

With a long breath, he pushed his chair back and stood, sliding it in without meeting her gaze. "I have to head out for a while. Not sure when I'll be back." He hesitated a beat longer, voice quieter now. "Please … don't wait up."

***

"Reaper? We've got an abdominal injury — possibly a stabbing. He's losing a lot of blood. Stable for now, but you'll need to examine the wound and get him stitched."

Reaper turned toward Leliana's voice just in time to see her wheeling a lion anthro into exam room three. The lion looked far too alert for someone bleeding out — he was chatting about the weather like they were at a garden party.

Grabbing his cap and gown, Reaper raised an eyebrow. "Did you sedate him?"

Leliana shrugged as she guided the chair to a stop. "Of course. He's resistant. I can dose him again if you think it'll take."

The lion's demeanor changed instantly — his golden eyes flaring with alarm. "No! Please — no more! I'm fine, really. I just need to go." He tried to rise, and Leliana immediately braced him, struggling to keep him in the chair.

"He's lightheaded from blood loss," she grunted. "Move it, Reaper!"

Reaper rushed forward and pressed the lion back down with a steady paw. "Easy, big guy. You've sprung a leak. Let me patch you up, and you'll be on your way. But I need to know what I'm dealing with. What happened?"

The lion hesitated, then relaxed slightly at Reaper's touch, his voice dropping. "I slipped. That's all."

Reaper wasn't buying it. He met the lion's eyes, catching a flicker of recognition in them. "That's a clean slice, not a fall. If I had to guess, I'd say stab wound."

Blood slicked his glove as he probed the edges of the wound — a sharp two-centimeter slit in the lion's lower left abdomen.

"Leliana's got fluids going, but you're going to need blood." He turned his attention to the lion, "Do you know your blood type? Do you consent to transfusion?"

"A-positive. Feline, if you've got it. O-neg will do." The reply was fast — too fast.

Reaper scanned the lion's frame, noting the old scars layered beneath the tawny fur. Deep cuts on the limbs, thin slashes on the back — someone who'd seen more than a few fights.

"This ain't your first rodeo. Look — I don't care how it happened. But I need to know how deep it went. What kind of blade?"

The lion's ears twitched. "Switchblade. Fifteen centimeters. I caught it here." He lifted a bloodied paw, showing a slashed palm.

"Pan-damnit," Leliana swore, rushing for supplies. "Why didn't you say anything about that?"

"You need lessons in knife work," Reaper muttered, reaching for the wound. "This is going to suck."

With a breath, he drove a gloved finger into the wound,

73

fishing carefully for debris or shrapnel.

The lion growled through gritted teeth, straining beneath Reaper's firm grip. "Argh! Rutting hell, that *hurts!* Why didn't you numb it first?!"

"Because there's clearly something in your system messing with the sedative's uptake," Reaper shot back, not missing a beat. "I wasn't about to risk stacking another cocktail on top of that."

Satisfied the blade hadn't nicked any vital organs, Reaper withdrew his bloody finger, stripped off his gloves, and snapped on a fresh pair. "Leliana, call Minka in when you go for the blood." He pivoted toward the surgical tray, already tearing open a sterile suturing kit.

"You're feral, you know that?" the lion said between breaths, his voice a mix of pain and begrudging admiration. "Why are you here instead of on a fleet ship? You've got field med stamped all over you."

With a shrug, Reaper clamped a curved needle in a pair of forceps. "Tried that. Didn't work out. I have a problem with idiotic orders. Stop squirming."

The door whooshed open just as he finished his prep. Minka entered, sliding a mask over her muzzle. "How can I help, Reap?"

"I need an extra set of paws to close this up." Reaper reached for a tongue depressor, wrapped it in med tape and gauze, then reinforced it with another layer. "Stick this in his mouth. He's still fully aware, and I doubt he's done being difficult. Hold the wound closed for the first stitch and help me manage bleeding from there. Got it?"

A spark lit in Minka's eyes — the adrenaline she lived for. Nodding, she took the makeshift bite stick and held it out to the lion. "Bite down hard and try not to move. Reaper's rough, but he knows what he's doing."

Minutes later — and after a storm of snarled expletives and muscle tension — the room settled into silence. All three were slick with sweat, peeling off their gloves like battlefield veterans at the end of a skirmish.

Minka and Leliana gave weary nods and exited the room

without a word.

Standing over the lion, Reaper cocked a brow and smirked. "That could've gone smoother."

Still catching his breath, the lion laughed weakly and shook his head. "I *knew* your kind when I saw you. You're one of those damned thrill junkies. Of course you enjoyed that."

Then, as if remembering something critical, the lion fished around in a pocket. After a few seconds, he produced a small metal disk engraved with a lion-and-crossbones. Holding it out with a blood-stained paw, he locked eyes with Reaper.

"I could use a medic like you. Look on the back — when you're ready for a change."

***

The memory of the lion — his strange composure, the blood, and the cryptic offer — came flooding back as Reaper crested the top of the stairwell, his chest heaving with exertion. Sweat matted the fur at his neckline, and his arms ached from hauling his bags all the way to the roof of The Arbor Building like a fool on a mission without a plan. Dropping his gear with a *thud* just outside the rooftop entrance, he stared silently at the side of the greenhouse, its windows painted over in rough strokes of privacy green. He didn't know what he was hoping to find — or even what he'd say — but his gut told him this was the next move. Even if it made no yiffing sense.

***

An ancient bonsai stood as the solemn centerpiece atop a low wooden table — its twisted, contemplative form illuminated by a warm, overhead light that cast gentle shadows across the serene space. Cypress beams stretched overhead, holding parchment-colored ceiling panels that seemed to glow softly in the ambient warmth. In each corner,

75

delicate lanterns dangled on slender cords. One wall was formed entirely of shoji, the classic Japanese paper screens, while another featured yukimi-shoji, the kind with inset windows meant for snow-viewing. Against the third wall, a graceful wooden bench met handcrafted shelving, softly lit from behind to highlight its curated treasures: delicate porcelain, minimalist pottery, and freshly cut cherry blossom stems arranged with near spiritual care.

Beyond the windows, the world opened into a hidden sanctuary — a private Japanese garden bordered by a towering cedar plank fence. Precisely pruned bushes flanked a winding stone path, while a koi pond cleaved the garden's symmetry in half. Its placid surface mirrored the soft light, broken only by ripples from golden fins beneath. Stepping stones crossed the water, and around them, the gravel had been raked into perfect concentric patterns, hugging large mossy stones and ancient timber like a meditation in form.

Aside from the quiet, stifled sobs carried on the midday breeze, the garden was utterly still.

Near the calligraphy scrolls hung on the fourth wall, behind a standing shoji blind, a young deer anthro sat curled into herself. The tears had been flowing for some time now, tracing down the velvety softness of her cheeks as she stared into the garden beyond the glass, aching for something unreachable. Her sobs eventually faded into silence, save for a shuddered breath as she brushed at the damp fur beneath her eyes.

She wore a pale blue gown of lotus silk — its soft sheen clinging to her like moonlight, whispering over her curves in seductive folds that offered no room for deception. A matching shawl clung to her shoulders, though it did little to conceal the bluish bruise marring the fur above her left elbow. Even so, she was radiant — ethereal — with large, luminous eyes framed by dark lashes and ears tipped in cream, twitching at every breeze and shift of sound. The palest fur lined the shell of her ears, curling inward like petals.

She stood slowly, folding the shawl tightly around her as

76

she drifted from the room. Sliding the shoji door aside, she stepped into the hallway, the tile cool beneath her cloven hooves, which moved silently over the stone. She headed toward the kitchen, the quiet purpose in her steps barely veiling the weight in her chest.

Some chamomile might help.

At the sink, she filled the kettle, watching as the bruise darkened at the edges — a slow bloom of violets and grays beneath her fur. Tugging the shawl tighter, she placed the kettle on the burner, hiding the blemish away once more.

Moments later, seated with a warm cup of tea, she found herself staring again at the mark. Her fingers hovered, grazing the skin with hesitant pressure. Her expression shifted — the tears gone, replaced by something sharper, colder.

She reached for her com.

With a few practiced swipes, a holo display flickered to life. "VOICE ONLY" flashed across the screen in pale blue letters.

Her voice was soft, but steady. "Rina? It's Dusk. How are you? How are Marcus and Lily?"

"Dusk! Pan, I haven't heard from you in forever! We're doing great — how have you been?" Rina's voice crackled through the line, bright and buoyant, carrying the same musical cadence as Dusk's but laced with a brightness her own had long since lost. "Is something wrong with your com? I'm only getting voice."

"I've been well."

The reply was soft — too soft. Dusk didn't acknowledge the question, her voice dropping to a hush, thinned by restraint. "I just … missed your voice."

There was a shuffle from Rina's side, then the muted click of a door latching. Ambient noise faded. "Dusk? Is everything okay?"

The silence that followed was heavy. A single tear carved a slow path down Dusk's cheek. Rising from her seat, she moved to the kitchen window, eyes scanning the misty garden beyond. Her fingers hovered over the bruise again, tracing the pain with familiar reverence.

"May I visit?"

***

"What were you thinking, Dusk? You made me look like a fool in front of the president tonight!"

The suite bathroom door slammed hard enough to rattle its hinges as the towering man emerged, half undressed and visibly fuming. He yanked his shirt off with a dramatic sweep, his broad chest rising and falling with rage. A head taller than Dusk, his presence filled the room — imposing, volatile. She barely reached his shoulder, her delicate build paling in comparison to the sheer force of his body.

"Hun, you're drunk," she said gently, her voice a wisp of calm trying to anchor them. "I didn't mean to upset you. I just thought we were having fun."

Her gaze fell to the floor, ears dipping back as her fingers anxiously worked the hem of her silk gown. She didn't need to see his expression to know the look on his face.

"Don't tell me what I am!" he snarled, his voice cracking into vitriol. "You're the rutting reason I drink! I can't believe how stupid you are sometimes. Why the hell would you think that was okay?"

With a sudden motion, he slipped off his trousers, pulling the belt free with a hiss of leather. The pants fell forgotten to the floor. The belt dangled from one hand — not idle, not innocent. Just waiting.

She flinched, her voice barely above a breath. "I'm sure he'll forget by morning … don't worry so much, dear. Come to bed — we can talk it over in the morning, okay?"

But his eyes had already turned — wild, glassy, unmoored. "Only a rutting idiot deer would say something that stupid! I've spent twenty years clawing my way to this point and you blow it all in five damn minutes!"

The room echoed with his rage, but she no longer heard it. Her mind slipped free, disassociating from the storm, retreating down well-worn neural paths … back to the

78

moments that had brought her here.

***

Draped in an exquisitely tailored designer gown that clung to her curves like flowing water, she moved through a sea of wealth and silent judgment. Her arm nestled lightly in the crook of the man beside her — tall, commanding, polished in a midnight-blue suit — the one who had brought her here, yet seemed blind to the eyes that followed her every step.

The men's stares were voracious, territorial; the women's, laced with disdain, suspicion, or icy curiosity. The servants, quiet and practiced in their deference, regarded her with a sort of shared sorrow. She wasn't the only anthro present, but she was the only one not in uniform. That distinction drew attention like blood in the water.

Her escort moved with practiced charm, leading her from one knot of power brokers to the next. They barely spared her a glance before diving into rehearsed conversations, handshakes, and false laughter. More than once, she felt fingers brush her flank or trail along the small of her back as strangers "passed." The women clung to their husbands' arms like statements, but never acknowledged her. Curiosity shifted swiftly into hostility. She existed only on the periphery of their elite world — seen, judged, but not engaged.

The hors d'oeuvres passed her by, trays of gold-leaf delicacies and crystalline flutes of champagne offered to others with surgical precision. She didn't reach for them. She didn't need to. Her purpose tonight was presence — to be seen, measured, and misjudged. To absorb the ugliness behind their civility and meet it with quiet poise. Beneath the disdain, she felt a perverse satisfaction in how much she unsettled them.

Somewhere in the crowd was the one they called *The President* — not of any nation, but the de facto emperor of a sprawling criminal empire that spanned the inner colonies.

His influence whispered through government corridors and echo chambers of corporate boardrooms. The man at her side, her so-called partner, was nothing more than a syndicate ambassador, a link between old-world power and new-world profit.

Among these predators in polished shoes and evening gowns, anthros were still seen as novelty or nuisance. She knew the looks. She knew the game. She had not come for him. Not for the man whose arm she clung to. She had come for her own reasons. To observe. To listen. To remember. The man handing out business cards didn't realize every contact he made tonight was already a dead end. He didn't notice the way they dismissed him, or the way they watched her when his back was turned.

This was her first time stepping into his world — the first time he'd let her see it without a veil.

He'd mentioned the gala in passing days ago. "It's just a formality," he said. "The President's little August ball."

But August meant more to her than parties and power plays. August — five years ago — was when everything had changed.

***

"Are you even listening to me, you stupid deer?!"

His voice tore through the room, dragging her violently back to the present. Her breath caught in her throat, but she lifted her hands slowly, stepping forward with forced calm.

"I'm sorry, dear. He just kept asking questions … I thought maybe a little humor might lighten the mood." Her eyes dropped, her voice a whisper wrapped in a fragile giggle. "I thought you'd find it funny."

He approached with the belt dangling loosely from one hand, every step calculated, measured — stopping just within range.

"Your job is to stand there, shut the fuck up, and look pretty. And you — you tell him I like to be pet like some godsdamned German Shepherd? What the fuck is wrong with

80

you?"

A stifled laugh broke from her lips, unbidden. Her hands rose defensively, trembling. "It was just a joke! I swear I didn't mean—"

A sudden flash of light — pain splintering across her face like glass. Her vision fragmented in shards of color. Her balance failed. Her cheek burned like fire.

He grabbed her arm, squeezing hard enough to bruise, shaking her as spittle flew from his mouth with incoherent rage. The words lost shape. His voice became thunder. The moment became endless. Another blow followed — her ears rang.

Her mind shattered inward.

She wasn't here anymore.

She was at her high school graduation. Her mother crying, her father snapping photos with a proud, shaking hand. Balloons. Applause. The moment she thought the world might actually love her back.

Her gown tore as he yanked it violently, seams ripping across her fur. The silky fabric clawed her flesh like angry hands. She didn't fight. She barely moved. He wasn't hitting her anymore. His breath changed. The air thickened. The intent was different now.

He shoved her against the wall. Cold. Impenetrable. Her shoulder blades scraped wood. Her knees buckled.

And her mind drifted again.

To Fridays. Apple pie. The scent of cinnamon drifting through their apartment. Her mother humming softly, coring apples with the skill of a seasoned baker. Dusk peeling the skins beside her. Her mother always switched the audio to Dusk's favorite song. They'd sing together. Laugh together.

She could smell scotch and synthetic tobacco as his breath rolled hot over her neck. The tears came as instinct, not choice. His body pressed against hers in rhythm. She gasped with each violation, his grunts timed like a metronome to her undoing. Somewhere inside of her, she tasted blood.

Then another memory. Her father met her at the door every Friday with a bag of golden delicious apples. His timing always perfect. He'd smile and say, "You ready for magic?" That pie had been more than dessert. It had been safety. It had been love with crust and sugar.

Now, the only thing warm was the bruise blooming across her cheek — and the hollow shell her body had become, performing its grotesque ritual for a man who would forget all of this by the morning.

She could feel it — the nearness of his finish. Every disgusting breath rasping against the back of her neck. The hot sweat dripping onto her fur in thick, bitter beads.

At some point he had dragged her to the bed, her body limp, face buried in the comforter she'd laid out with care that morning. Now it reeked of him; liquor, smoke, and exertion. His fingers gripped her scalp like talons, driving her head down as if her shame alone could absolve him.

She let him. She let him punish her. For what? For that Friday — the one time she'd skipped apple pie and line dancing to go see a holo with a boy whose name she couldn't even remember.

They used to dance while the pie baked. Her and her parents, that silly ancient style called line dancing. Mom would pour something she affectionately called *watermelon wine* from the old cooling unit. They still jokingly referred to as a fridge, swearing it was a sacred Friday ritual. They'd cue up *The Watermelon Crawl*, twirling through the kitchen, knocking elbows and laughing until their sides ached. Those nights had meant something — a sanctuary carved from the bones of a world that resented their very existence. Friday was the one time of the week they weren't just anthros, they were a family.

A strained grunt from behind snapped her back to the present. He drove himself against her rump with one final thrust, grunting, his weight crushing her as his climax pulsed through her like a sentence passed. His hand still clenched her hair like it might hold together what was left of his pride — but it was fading fast. His grip weakened, the anger seeping from him in shallow, wheezing exhales. He slumped against her, spent and slurring breath, a pathetic weight against her spine.

Her fur was slick with his sweat, her breath caught in the stench of his mouth: scotch, smoke, and stale arrogance. She didn't move. Couldn't. Tears slipped silently down her muzzle, soaking the comforter, carving wet lines through her cheek fur.

She remembered the smile she wore that night. The smile she had worn walking home from the holo. Her first kiss — that awkward, fumbling moment that left her giggling as she climbed the stairs to their apartment. Still wearing the glow of new affection.

That smile died the moment her key touched the lock.

It was already ajar.

Music spilled into the hallway — her mother's favorite playlist, upbeat and warm, still humming softly. But beneath the scent of cinnamon and apple ... the scent of something darker clung to the air. Metallic. Wet. Wrong.

The door creaked open at her touch, revealing her home ... and the blood that had drowned it.

Pools of it — impossibly red. Fresh. Coagulating. Reflecting the glow of the kitchen light like broken mirrors.

***

She didn't know how long she'd been lying there. Time had twisted, broken apart into flashes of ceiling, muffled sound, and the lingering burn of salt-streaked fur. When he returned to the room, she stirred — slowly — the motion deliberate. Her limbs ached, but she moved anyway, rising like smoke from ruin.

His gaze slid over her as she wiped the remnants of her tears away, not with shame, but resolve.

He sneered, gesturing toward the bathroom with a flick of his wrist. "Go take a shower. You stink."

His words bounced off her like dust. She walked past him, unflinching, and moved toward the closet, gathering what little she needed. The weight of silence between them grew heavier as she turned toward the door.

83

"What? Did you hear me? Where the fuck do you think you're going?" he barked, spreading his arms wide in mock confusion.

Still, she said nothing. Still, she walked.

At the threshold, she paused. Her eyes caught the bedside table — the ruin of that gown, crumpled like broken wings. A shiver snaked up her spine, a cold, controlled fury detonating deep in her chest.

"Hey, idiot! I'm talking to you! Where are you—?"

Her ear flicked. That was all he got.

She bent to retrieve her com from the wreckage of the dress, slowly, deliberately. And for a moment — as she bent, the shredded remains of her womanhood exposed — she let him see. Let him stare into the aftermath of what he had done. The mark he'd left.

Their eyes met as she stood.

And then she walked past him, head held high, a goddess cloaked in defiance.

He froze, confusion creeping over him like a fog. Then rage. He lunged after her, hand snapping forward to seize her arm in his crushing grip.

The crack was deafening. Followed by a scream that split the room in half.

He staggered back, howling, his right forearm bent grotesquely — bone jutting through skin, glistening and raw. Shock widened his eyes as he stared at her, not understanding, not believing.

She simply looked down at where his hand had touched her — and brushed it off like dirt.

Her voice, cold as a surgeon's scalpel: "Next time, that'll be lodged in your gray matter. You've got maybe twenty minutes before the blood loss takes you out. Better hurry."

She turned toward the door.

Paused.

Glanced over her shoulder.

"Oh — and thanks for introducing me to the President. The UCA boss of the Alpha Syndicate, right?" She grinned faintly. "The same Syndicate dedicated to purging people like me."

She let the silence sit.

"You didn't just ruin your career, sweetheart. You declared war on your future."

He stammered, eyes bouncing between her, the broken dress, the jagged bone protruding from his arm. "H-How? How did you do this? Who are you?!"

She shook her head, already walking away, her hooves silent as snowfall on tile.

"And to think … you called me stupid."

CHAPTER 6 - PERSEVERANCE.

"Of course you can, Dusk. You know you're always welcome. Why don't you come by around six? I should be home by then — I'll have dinner ready for us."

Rina's voice was warm, concerned, and impossibly familiar. Just hearing her steadied Dusk's trembling spirit. A weak smile touched her lips, a ghost from a time before her world turned desperate.

"Thanks, Rina... See you then."

The connection closed with a soft chime. Dusk stood motionless, staring out the window for what felt like ages. The dried trail of a single tear clung to her fur, a reminder of grief not yet spent. Then, as if something deep inside her finally exhaled, she turned from the sunlight and padded toward the bedroom.

The room was a mess — shadows of last night still draped across every wrinkle in the bedspread, every misplaced item. She avoided the mirror and went straight to the closet, her hooves muffled against the floor as she crouched low, pushing past shoes and boxes until her hand landed on old leather.

She pulled it out slowly: travel-worn luggage from a better time. The time she and Rina had roamed free.

Unzipping one of the outer compartments, she reached in — and felt it.

Her katana.

She drew it from its saya in a single fluid motion. The steel glinted coldly in the dim room, its edge pristine, waiting. Her eyes, too, now glinted with steel. Without a word, she slid the blade back into its sheath and set it gently atop the bed. Packing began — methodical, controlled, precise.

From a low cabinet near the bed, she opened a drawer lined with delicate scarves — pastel silks and satins folded with obsessive care. Her hand dove through the layers, bypassing the decorative to find something sacred.

A kerchief — dark blue. Wrapped around something rectangular and solid.

She unwrapped it slowly, reverently. A photo frame lay inside, its simple edges aged but polished. Behind the glass: a picture of two deer — smiling, radiant, in love. A pregnant doe stood with a buck's hand over her belly, her features so close to Dusk's it might've been her reflection in another time. Their smiles held the kind of love that burned so brightly, the world never seemed dark.

She traced a claw over the doe's curve, her breath catching.

"I found him... I finally found him, Mom. It took five years, but I found that rutting carcass..."

A sob slipped free. A tear splashed on the glass, distorting her father's image until she wiped it gently with the edge of a kerchief.

"Sorry, Daddy... I didn't mean to cry on you."

She smiled faintly, then let it fade.

"I'm going to finish this now. I'll see you soon."

She wrapped the photo back in silk like a relic and placed it carefully in the suitcase.

One last thing.

Her eyes dropped to her hand. A golden band clung to one finger — its shine still flawless despite everything it had witnessed. She stared into it, not at the ring itself, but at the warped little reflection of herself inside.

She didn't like what she saw.

With slow precision, she slipped the ring off and watched the distorted image vanish. The tiny gold circle spun once in her palm, then descended toward the carpet, vanishing into the shadow beside her feet.

***

Her holo com chimed softly just as the ridekick approached — a sleek hovercraft gliding soundlessly to a stop in front of her. As it settled, the vehicle's hull shifted hue, flowing from a muted burgundy to a calming sky blue, the soft shimmer of reactive paint responding to her proximity. Dusk checked the incoming message with a quick swipe, confirming the pilot's identity and arrival.

She offered a curt, polite wave as the cabin door hissed open.

Sliding into the seat, she leaned forward slightly, her tone flat but courteous. "No need to drop me on the roof. Lobby entry is fine."

"Tails! Thanks for choosing RideKick today," came the chipper, pre-programmed voice of the pilot. "Would you like a refreshment? We have grass juice, maple bark soda, or a selection of species-neutral beverages —"

"— No," she interrupted gently, turning her gaze to the window. "Thank you. Just... please activate the privacy screen. I'm exhausted."

Without hesitation, the pilot nodded and reached for the control console. A soft hum emanated from beneath the floor as dark-tinted privacy panes rose up around her, seamlessly enclosing her seat in a cocoon of silence and shadow.

"Of course. Enjoy your rest, ma'am. Tap the com button if you need anything," the pilot's voice replied — now hollow, distant, its tone reduced to a filtered echo as the final pane sealed the chamber.

Leaning her head against the side of the window, Dusk watched the world slip by outside — the skeletal remains of upstate New York scattered like a memory half-forgotten. Old buildings, skeletal tree lines, moss-covered structures long surrendered to time... it all drifted beneath her as the hovercraft carved its silent path through the open sky.

***

Dumbfounded, he stood frozen, eyes fixed on the young doe's retreating form as she disappeared into the distance. Just minutes earlier, Avery had pinged her com, letting her know he was waiting in the lobby. He'd planned everything: street food near Central Park, a walk through the shaded garden paths, maybe even one of those guided hoverbike tours.

Pan, her eyes... they were beautiful. But this time, they looked different. Sad. Hollow.

What the hell just happened? Was it the bike tour? Maybe deer anthros couldn't ride — rut, why didn't I check that first?

Avery tapped out a message on instinct, fingers trembling.

Avery:

Dusk? Was it something I said? Are you okay?

The com chirped almost immediately.

Operator:

Error: Message not sent. Com address invalid. Please verify the recipient's ID or contact your provider for assistance.

***

The ancient maglev train quickly outpaced the crafts crowding the interstate highway. Dusk watched as the reflection of the sky blue craft reflected in the train windows. A tiny facsimile of her face stared back at her, flickering and shrinking with each passing car as the train arced away.

***

"We're not sure yet, ma'am. The preliminary report suggests they were professionals. Highly skilled — and very well funded. We believe they used sophisticated weapons, possibly even experimental tech. We still can't explain how the limbs were severed so cleanly..." The detective shifted uncomfortably, his words trailing off as he shrugged weakly, visibly unsettled by what he'd just said.

Dusk paced in tight, furious strides, then spun to glare at him, his last words carving themselves into her memory. "So what — you have no idea who killed my parents? Then what the rut is the point of all this? You've turned my life inside out with your damn questions and rutting searches, and now you're telling me you don't even know what killed them?"

The detective spread his arms in a sheepish, helpless motion, shifting his weight from one foot to the other. "Of all the theories floating around, the Alpha Syndicate one holds the most water. We found links between your parents and The Pride — a pirate organi —"

She slammed her fist down on the counter, cutting him off. "I know what The Pride is, detective! What I don't understand is how the hell you could suspect my parents of working with them. They were the kindest, most decent people I've ever known. They were not pirates!"

He rubbed the back of his neck, letting the silence stretch as he stared down at the floor. Finally, he exhaled and turned toward the door.

"I should go. I'll stay in touch." His voice had lost all energy, all authority. "I left a box of their belongings on the entry table. And... thanks for the tea."

Pausing in the doorway, he didn't look back — just stared at the doorframe as if it might offer him some wisdom he didn't have.

"For what it's worth, Dusk... it frustrates the itchy balls out of me too. I will find out who did this. I promise."

***

The hovercraft jolted hard to the left, yanking Dusk from her thoughts. She looked up in time to see the pilot wrestling with the controls, narrowly avoiding a reckless vehicle that had veered too close. A string of expletives tumbled from the pilot's lips, her eyes flicking rapidly across the driver display.

A moment later, the tinny comm crackled to life, unnervingly calm. "Apologies for the turbulence, Miss. Just a bit of spirited traffic. Nothing to worry about."

***

Wiki-holo after wiki-holo blurred past her furious swipes. "How can there be so little on the Alpha Syndicate?! What am I missing?!" Her voice cracked with frustration. With a sharp slam of her fist on the countertop, her teacup jumped — then clattered — and finally shattered as she swept her arm across the surface, sending it flying. Fragments of brittle ceramic burst across the floor. The holo display flickered, inverted, the wiki's citations now displayed in chaotic, upside-down order.

"Rutting hades! None of this makes sense! Who did this?! What did I do to deserve any of it?!"

With a ragged scream, she yanked the holo-projector from the table and hurled it against the wall. Sparks spat from its casing as it cracked apart. Her knees buckled beneath her. Collapsing to the floor, she slumped against the chair, sobs wracking her body in violent pulses. The dam she'd held shut for days finally burst — anger, grief, guilt, despair — all flowing in one incoherent flood.

When the worst of it had passed, and the tears stopped just long enough for her to breathe, Dusk's gaze turned toward the box the detective had left. It waited silently on the entry table like a final verdict.

With trembling hands, she lifted the lid. Inside — fragments of a former life. Folders of paperwork, salvaged documents from the ruins of her family's home. A few framed photographs. A familiar stuffed deer, dulled with age.

And something odd — a strange little figurine.

Curious, she lifted it gently.

It was a round-headed toy, the face pale and serene, stylized with butterfly-wing artistry around the eyes and muzzle. Crimson paint framed the mask like a hood, the kanji characters "忍耐" — perseverance — rendered in delicate silver strokes beneath the nose. Curved accents painted the surrounding face with artistic flourish.

Turning the figure over, her brows knit in confusion.

Etched into the base were tiny letters:

"Forever in your debt. — Haku. P.S. Should you ever return, my new address is below."

Below the inscription, a sticker had been affixed. A line of kanji, followed by what looked like a street name and business title.

Dusk blinked, staring down at the figure, the lines of her expression softening into something unfamiliar — something between bewilderment and fragile hope.

***

Glancing down at the 2D time display on her com, Dusk noticed she still kept Japan Standard Time and Eastern Time side by side — a habit she'd never bothered to break. Her gaze drifted from the screen back to the window, where scenery blurred softly past in hues of green and stone. Her thoughts meandered, weightless, drifting with the ride as she daydreamed — half-present, half-lost.

Outside, the world transformed by degrees. Neatly trimmed hedgerows and modest homes gave way to gated estates, each property more extravagant than the last. The soft sprawl of suburbia began to recede, replaced by the shimmering facades of luxury hotels, towering high rises wrapped in glass and chrome. Sculpted gardens framed the entrances of the ultra-wealthy, their opulence reflected in gold-tinted windows.

Even in her haze, Dusk unconsciously registered it all —

the subtle transition from comfort to grandeur, from lived-in charm to curated perfection.

***

Sitting at the table opposite the lawyer, she stared blankly at the paperwork splayed before her.

"You became the trust's beneficiary immediately. The funds from both insurance policies will funnel into the account. Your monthly distribution will adjust — as noted at the bottom of the last page. The firm will continue to manage the trust until you reach the age of twenty-five, or complete an undergraduate degree, whichever comes first."

The lawyer, a greying ram with gentle eyes and a calm baritone, smiled warmly as he slid a pen toward her writing hand.

"I was named executor of your parents' estate well before you were born. They were among the most thoughtful and compassionate souls I've ever had the privilege to know. I'm deeply sorry for your loss, Dusk — the world is dimmer without them. I know this can't bring them back, but they left you this so that you'd never have to walk the road alone, so that you'd always be cared for."

***

Stepping off the train, Dusk scanned her surroundings for any hint of direction. The long journey had left her exhausted, her shoulders heavy with the weight of fatigue, yet a pulse of nervous energy danced beneath her fur. For the first time in her nineteen years, she'd set foot outside New England. And now, here she was: Tokyo. The city shimmered with unfamiliarity. Lights brighter, smells sharper, the bustle more frenetic than even New York City.

Both cities carried history on their shoulders, but Tokyo's roots stretched back millennia — nearly five thousand years before the foundations of New York had ever been imagined. Both were ocean cities, shaped by salt air and commerce, but in this era, their seaports served little more than tourism. Cargo had taken to the skies. None of these facts filtered into Dusk's conscious thoughts — her senses were too overwhelmed by the sheer magnitude of motion, noise, and color around her. Anthros, humans, androids, and even ferals wove through the station in a chaotic ballet, barely noticing one another. In the haze of it all, she focused on one goal: finding a hotel for the night.

Climbing the narrow stairs leading up from Hatchobori Station, she emerged into Tokyo proper — the city that would be her home for the foreseeable future. The late summer air tasted electric, and a thousand smells battled for dominance on the wind. Though her parents' trust fund could support her comfortably, her visa status was less flexible. She could only stay if she was actively studying or working.

Applying for the visa had meant hard choices. University in Japan was expensive, far beyond her monthly disbursement. That left two options: take out loans, or work. Not knowing yet what she wanted to study, she'd chosen the latter. But jobs for nineteen-year-olds were limited... unless she exploited a loophole.

Art had always come easily to her. A natural extension of her empathy, it was how she processed emotion. She'd painted murals, drawn sketches for shops and friends, even created a watercolor scene of her high school's mascot — a lioness cloaked in cloud and school colors — that still lingered above the gymnasium doors. It had taken her days, fits and starts, mistakes and corrections, but it had made her feel seen. Whole. Useful.

Now, as she walked the streets of Chuo City, the dazzling storefronts and neon kanji signs sparked an idea. Maybe she could offer her skills here. Signs could always be brighter, more evocative. She made a mental note to visit the shop owners.

A soft buzz vibrated at her wrist. Glancing down at her com, a green overlay flashed: *Chuo City* — and below it, two blocks ahead, *Hinata Hotel*, marked in glowing orange.

Turning down a narrow street lined with mom-and-pop

shops and late-night cafés, she let the tension in her shoulders slip just slightly. Her eyes glimmered with hope, and a small, determined smile found its way to her muzzle.

This was the beginning — and she was walking straight into it.

***

"Sumimasen, sensai..." Dusk enunciated carefully, her accent heavy and uncertain. She bowed stiffly at the waist, ears twitching with tension. Without waiting for a reply, she bowed again — deeper this time, pressing her palms together in humble supplication. "Please forgive my poor Japanese. I saw your dojo, and I would like to learn from you. Will you accept me as your student?"

The red panda — thick with muscle, his frame compact and broad — leaned heavily on a polished bamboo staff. It served as both cane and symbol of authority. His sharp eyes narrowed as he scrutinized her from head to hoof, lips already drawing downward into a dismissive frown.

Seeing the skepticism flare in his gaze, Dusk pressed forward, her voice gaining conviction. "Sensai, I'm willing to do anything you ask. I've wanted to train with you since the moment I saw your dojo. I will work hard — I want to make you proud!" Still kneeling with her hands pressed together, she risked a fleeting glance upward, only to quickly avert her gaze again under the heat of his stare.

"How do you even know of me, little fawn?" His voice was a low growl. "You're nothing more than a newborn, and clearly just another stupid American. Why should I help you?"

She hesitated, the words catching in her throat, then finally spilled out — soft but resolute. "You're right, sensai. I am just another stupid American. But I want to be better. I want you to teach me how not to be stupid." She bent lower, folding herself as far as she could, arms lifted in deference above her head.

There was silence, broken only by the soft pad of his

95

steps. He was circling her now — slowly — his staff tapping occasionally on the tatami mats. She didn't move. Her heart pounded like a drum in her chest. Then — a feather-light touch on her left shoulder.

What followed struck like lightning.

A jolt of energy surged through her nerves. Her limbs gave out instantly, collapsing her into a heap on the floor. Her ears rang, her breath gone.

"Your first lesson — never turn your back to your opponent." The stick slammed down mere centimeters from her muzzle. She winced, eyes wide as she looked up at him towering over her.

"D... Ow... I mean, my name is Dusk, sensai..." she croaked, still stunned but forcing herself upright.

With a grunt of acknowledgment, the red panda gestured toward a back door. "Rina — please show our new student to the dressing room. Give her a gi. Once we're done here, take her to get one of her own." Then he turned his crimson gaze back to Dusk. "I hope you came prepared. Rina will be your sparring partner. She's very skilled. I doubt you'll ever match her. Good luck."

"Spar... Sparring partner? But I don't even know how to fight yet!" Dusk's eyes widened, dread creeping into her throat.

A figure filled the doorway — another white-tailed doe, almost Dusk's mirror in height and frame, though slightly more compact and toned. Her gaze — cold and sharp — cut through Dusk like a blade. Is that... contempt?

Before Dusk could react, her world inverted. The breath fled her lungs in an instant as she hit the mat, flattened by a blow she hadn't seen coming. Above her, Rina stood astride, looking down with a smirk.

"She's cute, Master Haku. Did you pick her because we look alike?"

Thwack!

Rina yelped as Haku's staff struck her squarely in the ribs. She stumbled, lost her balance, and crumpled beside Dusk, groaning.

Blinking through the pain, Dusk turned her head just enough to meet the doe's glare — a mix of pain and loathing simmering behind those familiar eyes. Her chest ached. Her pride even more so.

"...Nice to meet you too," she muttered, eyes drifting toward the ceiling.

***

"How many times am I going to have to best you before you figure it out?" Rina sneered, standing tall with her bamboo staff raised triumphantly overhead. "You can't beat me!"

Dusk groaned as she rolled onto her side, fur matted with sweat and dust. Every joint ached, her lungs burned, but she forced herself up — again. Her knees wobbled, tail twitching erratically behind her as she squared off against the smug doe across the mat.

"As many times as it takes for me to beat you." Her chest heaved with every word. "Now shut up... and fight!"

With a wild cry, she launched herself forward, hooves thudding against the tatami as she charged. But just as she closed the distance, *snap* — Rina's staff appeared like a phantom, its tip halting Dusk's momentum a hair's breadth from her muzzle.

Staggering back, Dusk's breath caught in her throat.

Rina spat at the floor near Dusk's hooves, her scowl venomous. "Master was right. You'll never be good enough to beat me." Her eyes flicked over Dusk's exhausted body — the tremble in her stance, the bruises beneath her fur — with cold derision. "You're just a weak little fawn."

Turning away, Rina's tail flicked with finality. "Give up. You're useless. Just go back to wherever you came from, and stop wasting my time."

***

Rina stumbled back, a sharp gasp escaping her as she

clutched her side. "Pan, where did that come from?! Did you suddenly grow some talent overnight?" She winced, rubbing her rib as her sharp gaze traced over Dusk in wary appraisal.

Dusk didn't move to press the advantage. Her grin widened instead, ears perked and tail flicking with pride. "A deal's a deal. You agreed — if I got past your defense twice in one day, you owe me lunch."

For a tense moment, Rina stood silent, her posture unreadable. Then — unexpectedly — she turned her back, extending one hand toward Dusk. "Fine... Teriyaki or sushi? Give me your *bo*, I'll put it away."

Dusk exhaled in relief and stepped forward. As she handed the staff over, their fingers brushed — just a fleeting contact, but enough to spark a pause in them both. Rina hesitated, eyes flicking toward Dusk with an unreadable expression. Dusk caught the glance, her breath hitching slightly, and quickly averted her gaze.

"I... I like teriyaki," she murmured, her voice softer now, fur brushing across her cheek as she lowered her head.

***

"So then, Master Haku accidentally brushed my nip, and his face went crimson!" Rina cackled, barely containing herself as she recalled the moment. "I had him on the floor a second later. It's the only time I've ever gotten past his defenses. You should've seen his face when I helped him up!"

The two does dissolved into giggles, the warm aroma of green tea curling between them. Their knees nearly touched beneath the low table. Despite the laughter, their eyes lingered — just a second too long — and silence crept in as their giggling softened.

Dusk cleared her throat, ears tilting slightly back. "Rina... Did I do something wrong earlier? I didn't mean to make you uncomfortable, if I did."

"No, no!" Rina's voice pitched high with panic before dipping into a breathy laugh. "You didn't do anything wrong,

I promise. I just..." She looked down, her hands tightening around her teacup. "Will you promise not to get weirded out if I tell you something?"

Dusk's ears lifted, a sheepish smile curling her lips. "I think I already know what you're going to say..."

Her voice softened, barely above a whisper. "I've been feeling it too... even though you've tried to hide it, I've known since we first met."

***

The hovercraft's horn blared sharply — a low, resonant *WHAARRM* — as another craft swerved recklessly into their lane. The pilot flailed in the display window, pantomiming an impressive string of expletives, complete with exaggerated gestures and wild ear flicks.

Dusk blinked, then chuckled softly, watching the silent little drama unfold with growing amusement. The tinny approximation of the pilot's voice returned over the intercom.

"Apologies again, Miss — traffic's *absolutely feral* today. Please accept a complimentary drink before disembarking!"

In the display, the pilot shook his head violently and appeared to launch into another tirade — still unaware the feed was live. His hand movements grew more theatrical, his muzzle clearly shaping words that didn't need audio to be understood.

Dusk giggled, her shoulders shaking slightly as she turned back toward the window, brushing a hand across her lips to stifle the smile. Some things, even in a future like this, never changed.

***

Rina peeked into the room, her expression drawn with concern. Dusk's sobs were muffled — but not enough. Silently stepping inside, Rina closed the door behind her with a gentle *click*. She brought a hand to her muzzle, uncertain.

"Dusk? Are you alright? What's wrong?"

Wiping a tear from the edge of her cheek, Dusk shook her head, her voice quiet and tight. "I'm okay... I was just thinking about Mom and Dad. I still miss them — sometimes it just hits me."

Rina's eyes widened. Without hesitation, she rushed to Dusk's side, wrapping her arms around the doe in a warm, protective hug. "Dusk... you've never mentioned them before. What happened?"

Dusk sat frozen for a moment, staring at the floor, the air between them thick with unspoken weight. When she finally spoke, her words came fast, detached — as though rehearsed in silence too many times.

"They were murdered. By the Alpha Syndicate. It happened just over a year ago... I think they were tied to The Pride before I was even born."

***

Finally, the hovercraft glided to a graceful stop before a modest wrought-iron gate. Twin stone walls framed the entry, and beyond them, ancient oak trees loomed — their broad branches clawing at the sky like living spires, obscuring the estate nestled beyond. Shadows wove between trunks like whispered secrets, veiling the early 22nd-century home in an eerie, dignified hush.

Dusk waved faintly to the departing ridekick before stepping through the slowly parting gate. The sheer scale of the oaks alone was awe-inspiring — their bark furrowed with time, their roots thick as sleeping beasts. The estate itself lay cloaked in silence, regal and unreachable. As she approached the door, her bags hit the flagstone with a soft thud, just as she reached up to knock — everything changed in a heartbeat.

The door flung open, and she was engulfed in a bone-tight embrace. "Pan, it's so good to see you, Dusk! I've missed you so much!" Rina's familiar scent — wild cherry and woodsmoke — filled Dusk's nose. Before she could respond,

100

her bags were snatched up, and Rina was already leading her inside. "Come on in! Marcus and Lily are off on a father-daughter weekend. They won't be back until Monday — we've got the place to ourselves!"

Relief unfurled in Dusk's chest as she followed, her footfalls swallowed by the grand home's plush interior.

"Dinner's nearly done," Rina said with a playful glance over her shoulder. "We'll eat in the kitchen — then I'll show you your room."

In the sweeping kitchen — a room lined with granite counters and glowing under warm pendant lights — Rina poured them both a glass of wine. They sat at a small table tucked against a wide window, the city flickering in the distance.

"To old times and good memories," Dusk murmured, her smile tinted with melancholy. Rina echoed the sentiment with a soft clink of glass.

Dinner was modest but artfully prepared: a nut salad over ryegrass, rhubarb ribbons glistening alongside finely shredded carrot. Their conversation ebbed and flowed easily — centered on Marcus, on Lily's brilliance, on the joys of penthouse living. Dusk kept her own trials at bay, nudging the focus toward Rina, savoring the comfort of her voice and the familiarity of shared laughter.

Time moved gently until Dusk's gaze slid toward the kitchen window — her hand curled beneath her chin, her ears slackened with quiet fatigue. The events of the past few days — the heartbreak, the revelations, the rage — began to crush her chest again.

Noticing, Rina scooted closer. Her hand found Dusk's knee — soft, grounding. "Dusk? You okay? You kind of vanished for a second."

Turning toward her voice, Dusk's eyes met hers — and in that instant, something raw and electric passed between them. A spark from a long-buried ember. Her breath caught. Without thinking, she raised a hand, brushed her fingers through the fur behind Rina's neck, and gently pulled her forward.

Their lips met — softly at first, then with a sudden heat — years of unspoken ache flaring to the surface. For a moment, the world stood still, wrapped in warmth and memory.

Then, Rina gasped. Her lips broke away, her chest rising in stifled tension. She shook her head, her voice cracking. "You know we can't go back to what we once were, Dusk... I'm *married* now..."

Her eyes sharpened with sudden clarity — and panic. Dusk recoiled slightly, realizing the kiss she'd stolen. "Oh Pan... Rina, I'm so sorry. I don't know what came over me..." Her hands flew to her face, trembling, and as she did, the bruises beneath her fur became starkly visible — mottled blooms of violet and ochre staining the pristine white of her forearms.

Rina gasped audibly, her chair scraping back. She lunged forward and grabbed Dusk's wrists, inspecting them in horror, turning them gently but insistently. "What the itchy balls happened to you, Dusk?!"

Dusk flinched at the contact, gently slipping her wrists from Rina's grasp. Her eyes dropped to the floor, voice soft. "I... He... I embarrassed him. Last night, at the party. I made him look like a fool — in front of the president. The Alpha Syndicate's boss, no less." She gave a hollow laugh. "He didn't even know who he was."

Rina's head snapped back in disbelief. "Wait — what did he do to you, Dusk?!"

Still not meeting her gaze, Dusk exhaled slowly. "He ignored me the rest of the night. Then, once we got home... he snapped. He screamed, then..." Her voice caught. "He forced himself on me. I... I broke his arm and left. That's why I'm here. I needed... somewhere safe. I missed you, and I thought maybe..."

She trailed off, wrapping an arm protectively over her bruises.

Rina stood frozen, mouth parted in stunned silence. Her ears twitched as if trying to catch up with the torrent of words. Then, softly — "You... met the Alpha Syndicate boss? Face

102

to face? Dusk, are you insane? What could you possibly have said to piss him off that badly?!"

A slow grin tugged at the edge of Dusk's lips, the fire rekindled behind her tired eyes. "He asked me what I liked most about my date. I told him I liked how easy he was to train. That he wore a dog collar I got him — and loved to be pet like a German Shepherd."

Rina's eyes widened, and a moment later, she burst into laughter — loud, wild, and uncontainable. "You can't be serious?! Pan, Dusk, you are *out* of your mind! You're lucky he didn't gut you on the spot!"

Dusk's smile didn't falter. She met Rina's gaze evenly. "I'd like to see him try."

Then, with a sigh, she stood from the table, stretching her arms high above her head. Her voice softened. "Hey... do you remember those old movies we used to watch together? Think we could watch *Howl's Moving Castle*?"

***

"Here's the apartment I mentioned — the future penthouse once renovations are complete. We also own the rooftop garden above. They're not starting work until next year at the earliest," Rina said as she unlocked the door. The lock clicked, and the door creaked open beneath her hand. "I thought maybe you could stay here in the meantime, while you get back on your hooves. What do you think?"

The air inside hit them like a damp cloth — thick with mildew and aged paper, tinged with something like worn leather and dust-choked vents. The apartment was cramped, clearly a late twenty-third century renovation, and the years had not been kind. Floor-to-ceiling panes in anodized aluminum frames faced the blank brick wall of a neighboring building, letting in light but little else. Beneath their hooves, the stained concrete floor bore the weary, softened trails of foot traffic — gray paths where the once-amber finish had been scrubbed away by time and lives now gone.

Dusk hesitated, ears twitching as she took it in. Still, she

103

managed a small, brave smile as she turned to Rina. "I could probably make this work... Did you say there were other units on this floor? Maybe one with a street view?"

Rina giggled and shook her head. "Most of the others aren't fit for a broom closet. That's part of why the whole floor was so cheap — it's basically a fixer-upper nightmare." She wandered toward the window, nose wrinkling at the uninspiring view. "But! The roof's incredible. Come on — I've got plans for a meditation space and a little herb garden. It'll be tails once I get it cleaned up."

Later, the two of them climbed the narrow stairwell that led to the roof. Rina's bushy tail flicked in excitement as she gestured Dusk forward. At the top stood a dented steel door — graffiti scrawled across it in a half-dozen languages, the chain lock clinking as Rina unlatched it.

"I think you'll love it," she said, beaming. "This place has a vibe. I've always wanted to do my morning stretches up here."

The door groaned open. A gust of rooftop air slipped past them — cool, carrying hints of rust, old iron, and rooftop gravel. Thirty feet ahead, set like a forgotten jewel atop the city, stood an elderly greenhouse — no, a conservatory. Its panes were mostly covered in grimy green-gray paint, though a few allowed slivers of pale light to pierce through. The frame, ornate wrought iron in floral scrollwork, curved upward in a gothic arch. At its base, a weather-worn red brick foundation held the entire structure above tiled flooring that had faded with sun and age.

Curious, Dusk padded forward, hooves clinking softly on tile. She pulled open the rust-framed door — and gasped.

The interior felt like stepping into a dream halfway remembered. Dust motes danced in the beams of filtered light. Two battered leather chairs, one tipped over, flanked a small circular tea table — a chess set sat half-finished on its surface, the pieces frozen mid-battle. A chaise lounge rested along the eastern wall, opposite a forgotten easel that leaned near a cloth-draped partition. Other shapes — mysterious, possibly broken — lay buried beneath black plastic sheeting along the back wall.

Spinning slowly to take it all in, Dusk extended her arms, eyes shining. "This is perfect. Can I stay here?"

Rina raised an eyebrow, her tone more amused than dissuading. "It's a little run down, don't you think? Wouldn't you rather take the apartment downstairs?"

Shaking her head with an eager flick of her ears, Dusk turned back toward the conservatory, her voice filled with quiet reverence. "There's something about this place... it feels like home. I could fix it up — give it life again. It just feels right, Rina. Please?"

Her grin blossomed with mischief and joy as she stepped toward her friend, arms wide, tail flicking playfully behind her. "Come on! You know you can't resist me when it's something that makes me happy."

Rina sighed — long, theatrical — but the smile that tugged at her muzzle betrayed her fondness. As Dusk wrapped her in an enthusiastic hug, Rina rolled her eyes and gave a resigned little nod. "Fine. But you're doing the cleaning. And I get veto power on any weird décor choices."

CHAPTER 7 - ON TOP.

Her tail had always made sitting an awkward affair, a quiet struggle humans had never even considered until generations after her kind were engineered into existence. Dusk's was shorter than most: an understated nub, hardly noticeable to anyone but another anthro deer. Her mother used to coo over it with a pride that made young Dusk blush, treating it like a unique little charm. Over time, she'd trained herself to curl it protectively around her rump whenever she sat, more out of habit than necessity. Only recently had public seating begun to accommodate tail-bearing bodies: curved cutouts in restaurant chairs, cushioned nooks in hotel lounges, ergonomic hollows at stadiums. A belated courtesy in a still-clumsy world.

Now seated cross-legged on her meditation mat in the southeast corner of the Arbor rooftop, one cloven hoof tucked over the other, Dusk exhaled slowly. The city's ambient hush surrounded her. Her tail, pinned awkwardly between the mat and her rump, twitched with discomfort. The position was better than most, but it still didn't feel natural. Deer were never meant to sit like primates. A part of her always felt... exposed. Lewd, even. With her tail flattened, it was as if she were mooning the nether gods with the soft fur beneath her dock. She knew it was irrational, but the feeling remained, made worse by how raw her awareness of her body had become since the kiss. Since *Rina*.

She shook her head, huffed, and tried again to sink into silence.

Sleep had eluded her that morning, Rina's guest bed no match for the ghosts in her heart. Memories, soft, sharp, slow, had pressed against her mind until she'd surrendered. Dawn had barely tinted the sky when she spotted the penthouse key on the nightstand. Rina must have placed it there before leaving her to rest. Dusk had taken it gently, like accepting a parting gift. The previous night played in her mind like broken cinema: the tour, the rooftop, the moment their lips had touched, and the long walk back to the estate.

Her lips still felt warm where they'd met Rina's.

Embarrassed and uncertain, she'd gathered her things and scribbled a note before slipping away. *Thank you for everything. Please come visit.* A gentle hope lingered in those last three words, one she didn't dare unpack just yet.

***

"See? I told you! You'll never be good enough to beat me, little fawn! Just give up!" Rina barked, teeth bared in triumph as she shook her bo staff and rose back to her hooves, breathing heavily.

Dusk didn't answer, didn't flinch. She bent to retrieve her own staff when *crack!* Pain burst through her hand like fire. She bit back a scream as Rina's staff slammed down, snapping across the knuckles of her right hand. Her breath hitched. The sharp, nauseating sting told her everything: her index knuckle was out of place.

Eyes watering, she reached again, dodging the second blow. The bo staffs collided with a thunderous *crack*, the sound ringing through the rooftop like a gunshot. Dusk dropped low and slinked back, keeping her body coiled and compact, left hand clutching her right. With a grimace, she seized the crooked finger and yanked. *Pop.* Her sharp yelp

107

echoed, but the joint reset cleanly.

She rose again, her stance steady now, both hands on the staff. Her eyes, locked onto Rina, were no longer those of a student.

"What? Not gonna fight back?" Rina jeered, circling slowly. Her hooves scraped against the floormats, tail flicking with impatience.

Dusk said nothing, letting the rhythm of breath guide her. Every testing strike Rina made met with calm deflection, no wasted movement. But she still felt Rina reading her footwork, her posture, her uncertainty.

Then... something else.

Her eyes kept dropping, not to Dusk's stance, not to her hands. Her muzzle. Her chest.

What is she watching for?

The realization settled like a pebble into still water, spreading through her. A flicker of recognition, no, of amusement, danced at the edge of her mouth.

The smirk didn't go unnoticed.

"What the rut do you have to be smiling about? Are you stupid or something?" Rina snapped, her voice a raw rasp of nerves and ego.

Dusk's smile vanished.

Rina pressed, sensing a nerve. "That's it, isn't it? You're a moron. Too stupid to take your rutting trash and leave. That it?"

She never saw the strike coming.

Dusk moved, a blur of motion, rage, and trained instinct. Her staff sang through the air, a barrage of strikes cascading in rhythmic fury. Rina staggered back, stumbling beneath the pressure. The speed, the precision — this wasn't the Dusk she knew. This was something primal. Elemental.

Blow after blow landed: ribs, thigh, elbow. Rina couldn't keep up. Her defenses faltered. The edge of the staff struck her flank and she folded in pain. Her bo slipped in her grip, then flew from her hand entirely.

And still, Dusk didn't stop. Tears streaked her cheeks. Her eyes, wide and feral, burned like wildfire as she advanced.

Rina raised her gaze, breathless, heart hammering against her chest. *She's going to kill me.* And pan... *she's magnificent.*

"I concede!" Rina gasped, dropping to her knees and clutching her ribs. "Please!"

"Rut you, coward! I thought I wasn't good enough to beat you?!" Dusk roared, her breath ragged as she advanced, staff poised to strike again.

Rina curled tighter on the floor, her body folding into itself, her ribs tender, her breath hitching with each pulse of pain. She shielded her sides with trembling arms, tail pinned beneath her in a tangle of sweat and hurt. Her ears flicked once, then flattened entirely.

But Dusk didn't stop.

With a savage growl, she raised the staff high overhead, her hands white-knuckled, her silhouette backlit by the dying light. Her chest heaved. Her stance shook with the promise of a fatal blow.

She froze.

Time held its breath.

Something in her eyes shifted, the feral haze giving way to clarity, to horror. Her arms trembled as the staff hovered in place... and then, with a heavy exhale, she let it fall. The bo clattered softly to the floor, landing between her hooves.

Her breath slowed. Her arms slackened. Dusk stood there, haunted, staring at what she'd nearly become.

Rina peeked up cautiously from beneath the crook of her arm, ears twitching, lips parting into a crooked, pained grin. "Ow..." she groaned, eyes glinting despite the pain. "So you *can* fight after all..."

Dusk blinked. The red drained from her vision as guilt rushed in. "Rina!" she gasped, darting forward and crouching beside her. "I'm so sorry, I don't know what came over me! Are you okay?!"

Rina winced as she took Dusk's outstretched hand, letting herself be pulled gently to her hooves. "I'll live..." she muttered, trying and failing to stretch. She hissed through her teeth. "But you are definitely buying lunch *this* time."

109

A flicker of her old smugness returned as she winked at Dusk. "Come on. Before I collapse and you have to carry me."

***

"What was that?! Are you serious right now? You're not even trying, Dusk!"

Rina's growl was punctuated by the sweeping arc of her staff. It caught Dusk low, hooking around her ankles with a deft snap. Her right hoof tangled with the left, and she pitched forward.

But Dusk planted her staff just in time, halting her descent mere inches from the mat. With a breathy grunt and a heave of her toned limbs, she rose again, then launched into a wide, arcing swing.

This time, she didn't retreat. She danced.

Rina blinked.

Dusk's body moved with a newfound elegance, her movements flowing like water, each step folded into the next in graceful, controlled rhythm. Hips pivoted, shoulders dipped, her bo staff twirled like a brush painting arcs of air. Was that... ballet?

The tempo built, seductive and confident.

Rina's stance faltered, hooves squeaking softly on the mat as she adjusted, eyes fixed on Dusk's mesmerizing motion. Her jaw slackened. The staff in her hand dipped just slightly.

Then came the strike.

Dusk lunged, her bo slicing toward Rina's unguarded side. The red-furred doe gasped, barely catching the blow in time. The impact jarred her arm, shooting pain up to her shoulder. She hissed through clenched teeth, stumbling back.

"Rutting yiff, Dusk!" she growled, rubbing her arm. "How did you switch like that?"

Dusk just winked, the glint in her eye equal parts triumph and tease. Her staff continued to spin, hips swaying to the

110

beat of some silent melody. She moved like a song in motion: deliberate, unreadable, devastatingly poised.

Each of Rina's counterattacks was met with an effortless parry. Dusk flowed around her like wind through reeds, all motion and grace. She wasn't fighting; she was performing.

And Rina?

She was watching her hips.

Again.

She barely saw the leg sweep in time to *feel* it.

Her hooves went skyward. A grunt escaped her lips as she crashed back onto the mat. And before she could recover, Dusk's staff plunged down, thunking into the mat mere inches from her temple.

Leaning lazily on it, Dusk grinned down at her. "With you, I don't even have to try."

Rina blinked, still winded.

"You're too busy staring at my tail end to remember defense." Dusk's voice turned mockingly sweet. "You used to be able to hide it. Now? You're practically drooling. You're supposed to be teaching me, not trying to rut my brains out."

Giggling, Dusk reached down and clasped Rina's hand, helping her up with practiced ease. Rina's blush was immediate, her russet cheeks flaring crimson as she stared at the mat beneath their hooves.

Without a word, she turned to stow her staff.

"It was that obvious, huh?" she mumbled, tail flicking low in embarrassment.

Dusk followed silently, pausing just behind her. As Rina reached back to grab Dusk's staff, she turned — and froze.

Dusk stood less than a hare's breadth away. Her presence filled Rina's vision: tall, radiant, breathing slow and deep. Her soft-furred breasts hovered just between them, the heat of her body pressing lightly against Rina's chest.

Rina's breath caught. Her eyes moved, hesitant at first, from Dusk's chest, then up… lingering on the soft curve of her lips, and finally locking onto those deep, shining eyes.

They stared.

111

A long moment passed in silence, thick with electric possibility. Both of them were breathing harder now, but neither pulled away.

Rina's whiskers twitched.

Dusk tilted her head slightly, not enough to lean in, but enough to tempt the idea.

Drawn to each other with magnetic inevitability, their awareness of the world around them slipped into dim irrelevance. The quiet rustle of fabric, the whisper of breath, all muted by the growing storm inside.

Their fingers found one another first, tentative, then eager. The fine hair along their wrists parted like delicate grass in a breeze, revealing the lighter roots beneath. As their fingers glided and curled, the fur folded and fell back into place, a soft fan of motion that faded into contact. Their hands clasped fully, instinctively, the web of digits lacing tight as warmth bloomed where fur met fur.

Their breaths mingled, short, uneven exhalations infused with anticipation. Warm air puffed in soft bursts, brushing past the taut whiskers of their muzzles — each breath a caress, each movement fanning the tension between them.

Pupils dilated. Hearts pounded. Their cores surged with heat, not lustful yet, but pulsing with a raw, unspoken yearning.

They leaned forward, slowly, noses brushing in a tender nuzzle. Dusk's hand rose to Rina's cheek, the pads of her fingers tracing along the plush curve of her jawline, grazing downward toward the warm hollow of her neck. The contact was delicate, reverent.

Then, at last, they surrendered.

Their eyes fell closed. Their lips parted.

The kiss was slow at first, exploratory, reverent. A hum of hunger rose in one of their throats, barely audible, a tremulous sound born of both relief and desire. It might have come from either. Neither knew which.

It didn't matter.

They sank into each other fully, wrapped in the whispering silence between heartbeats.

***

The dawn's light filtered softly through the blinds, casting warm amber stripes across the small bed where Rina and Dusk lay, limbs woven together in quiet reverence. Their breathing was slow, steady, the sort of calm that follows surrender. The scent of passion lingered faintly in the air, a subtle blend of warmth and fur and breath, still fresh from the intimacy they'd shared only moments before.

Fingers traced along flanks and arms, gentle, wordless caresses that spoke of affection deeper than anything their lips had yet confessed. Cradled in the afterglow, they spoke softly, whispers shared skin to skin.

Rina's hand rose to Dusk's cheek, her thumb brushing the delicate fur beneath her eye. Her gaze searched Dusk's face, hesitant but needing to know. "What are you really doing here, Dusk?" she asked, her voice low but direct. "You begged Master Haku as though you couldn't live without his training, but you rarely apply yourself. What's really going on?"

Dusk didn't answer immediately. Her eyes dropped to where her finger idly traced circles along Rina's bare arm, watching the fur shift gently beneath her touch. Then, slowly, she rolled over, taking Rina's hand in her own, and stared at the ceiling. Her gaze drifted somewhere far away, somewhere past the light and safety of this room.

"A year ago..." she began, her voice barely above a whisper, "my parents were murdered. In our apartment. I... I found them. The police never figured out who did it. They couldn't even determine how."

Rina remained silent, her breathing stilled. A faint gasp caught in her throat, but she didn't interrupt.

Dusk's voice wavered, the trembling edge betraying the tears welling behind her eyes. "They said the wounds were... strange. Too clean. The detective thought it might've been some kind of experimental weapon. Something only the Alpha Syndicate could get their

113

claws on. But he couldn't prove it."

A tear traced down Dusk's temple, catching the morning light. Rina moved to catch it gently with a thumb, stroking the soft curve of Dusk's cheek.

Dusk sighed long and deep, then continued, her tone quiet and   haunted. "When they cleared out the apartment, the detective returned some of their belongings. That's when I found it: a Japanese doll. Handcrafted. There was an address on the bottom. Master Haku's address. That's why I came. He's involved somehow. I know it."

Rina sat upright, her hand tightening around Dusk's. Her voice   dropped   to   a   near-whisper. "Master Haku once told me the Yakuza weren't to be trusted. Said they had dealings with the Alpha Syndicate. That they even gave their own up when it suited them."

Dusk turned to face her, the look in her eyes raw, desperate, a plea for truth she hadn't yet dared to speak aloud.

***

"Block with your left, you're leaving that side exposed!" Haku's voice was firm as his staff cracked sharply against Dusk's left hip, twice. He struck again. "See? You're favoring your right too much. Move faster, little fawn!"

"Oooff! Yes, Master!" Dusk danced backward, disoriented, the sting radiating through her flank. She pressed a trembling hoof to the spot, leaning on her staff. "I keep losing focus, Master… May we take a break?"

Grumbling under his breath, Master Haku slid down onto the mat. He crossed his legs, cradling his staff across his lap. "Ten minutes," he decreed. "Then we continue."

Dusk nodded gratefully and seated herself before him, her hands still shaking. She couldn't help but observe him: posture taut, muscles lean, still commanding even in repose. The red panda's ears stood straight atop his crown, white and perfectly triangular, dark tufts inside giving them depth. His

114

amber eyes flickered with intelligence and something fierce when he wished, a spark she'd seen once before. His fur was immaculate, black, white, and burned crimson braided into a regal topknot. A single scar traced down his left cheekbone, the only imperfection in an otherwise noble visage. Thin braids framed his face, lending him the bearing of ancient warriors.

Curious, she let her gaze drift to a white spiral tattoo on his flank, a striking emblem modulating against his charcoal fur. "Master... may I ask something?"

He blinked, shifting his gaze to Dusk's. A quizzical arch of his brow appeared. "You don't usually ask permission first. What's on your mind, little fawn?"

Dusk hesitated then tilted her head, nodding toward the tattoo. "I don't mean to offend... but I'm curious about that spiral. I've heard rumors, but I don't know if they're true."

Master Haku's gaze dropped. Silence stretched before the soft rustle of his shift in seat signaled the end of his contemplation. Finally, he exhaled. "Many rumors are rooted in truth. That spiral... it's a reminder of the mistakes I once made. The masters I once served betrayed what was sacred to our kind, and I bear the mark of my complicity. No more questions."

Dusk absorbed this, uncertainty twisting in her chest. *As I suspected... he's Yakuza. And not low rank. But how did he escape that world?*

She opened her mouth to press further. "But master, I don't understand, why should the Yakuza matter to our kind? They aren't even related to the Alpha..." She was cut off as Haku suddenly rose.

With lightning speed, he hurled a wooden training sword toward her.

"SILENCE! You will not speak of that swine in my dojo!"

Dusk gasped and instinctively caught the blade mid-air. She scrambled upright, readying herself, heart pounding, as Haku advanced, staff raised, and the dojo's silent walls held their breath.

***

As the morning dew gathered along the conservatory's unpainted glass panes, it formed trembling droplets, each one catching the early light before sliding downward, tracing arcs like glistening analogies of shooting stars. Their trails shimmered across grime-streaked surfaces, marking time in slow, liquid descents.

Standing in the doorway of the small glass-and-wrought-iron building, Dusk stretched languidly, her lithe limbs extending into the crisp morning air. Her breath rose in soft clouds as she surveyed the ruin within. The once-elegant interior, all quiet craftsmanship and botanical intention, now lay buried under years of neglect. Dirt, clumps of brittle plant matter, shattered ceramic, and unnamed detritus carpeted the floor. The tile beneath, pale white with black inlaid patterns, peeked out from beneath the filth, fractured and dulled with age.

The structure itself was intimate, measuring roughly fifteen feet wide by twenty deep, its graceful curves and Victorian geometry hinting at a bygone elegance. Opposite the doorway, a modest brick partition divided the front from a utility space in the rear. Behind it, to the left, a deep porcelain sink sat beside a wide drain basin, both coated in sediment and rust stains. To the right of the partition, a set of rough-hewn wooden shelves leaned precariously under the weight of time. A narrow door, its paint long since peeled, led outward from this cramped alcove, opening toward the rear of the conservatory.

A small, tea-stained table rested off-center in the main room, flanked by two chairs. One had toppled long ago, its torn cushion hosting remnants of insulation and dried grass. The other, still upright and oddly dignified, bore the scrappy remains of a rodent's nest hidden just beneath its seat. The air held a thick, earthy scent: decay, old roots, aged wood, and the sharp tang of ammonia.

Curious, Dusk crouched and peeled back a brittle sheet of

116

plastic covering a nearby stack of forgotten objects. Beneath, she found weathered wooden doors, relics from an age before bio-locks and nano-mesh, before retinal scanners replaced door locks. Their grain and carved panels whispered stories of hallways and rooms long erased from memory.

She rose and crossed to the rear entrance, gently pushing it open. The sweep of her motion stirred a rain of dust motes, and the door creaked loudly, protesting its long disuse. Kicking aside the debris gathered at its threshold, she stepped into the gust of cool air that surged through the opening, crisp and clean, heavy with moisture and the scent of nearby gardens. Letting go of the door, she watched it swing wide and slam into the wooden shelving with a hollow thud. Her fur fluttered in the breeze, hair blown back as she closed her eyes and smiled. That sudden gust, sharp, honest, alive, reminded her she was still here. Still breathing. Still standing.

To her left, a toggle switch jutted from the wall. She flicked it up, and a single overhead fixture flickered before casting a thin, yellow glow across the conservatory's innards.

"Okay," she said, planting her hands firmly on the tiled threshold. "Time to make this hovel into a home."

Turning to the right, she spotted a broom tucked between the shelves and the brick partition, its bristles curled, handle worn smooth. On the shelves beside it: a hammer, a roll of quack tape, a frayed length of rope, a razor knife, and a battered pair of gloves. The items seemed almost staged, as though someone had expected her, and left behind just what she might need.

Taking the broom, Dusk set to work. Dust and dead leaves swirled as she swept the dirt and clumps out through the open front door. As she worked, the floor's intricate design revealed itself. Inlaid ebony tiles coalesced into an elegant mosaic: a stylized setting sun, rays unfurling outward like a corona of light. It had once been beautiful. It would be again.

The day prior, Rina had told her she could use anything

117

she found in the penthouse or on the rooftop to make the conservatory into a home. Dusk had already begun forming ideas, and the discarded doors and the thick plastic sheets covering them were suddenly full of possibility. The tools she'd discovered on the shelving were primitive by modern standards, but they'd do for now. At the very least, she reasoned, she needed somewhere to sleep, meditate, wash, and, though far less glamorous, do her business. She'd noticed a weathered sign just beyond the conservatory, affixed to the exterior wall: *Restroom.* She'd check that out later.

With most of the larger debris swept into piles, she leaned the broom against the front wall and stood quietly, scanning the space with calculating eyes. Her gaze caught on the pile of plastic sheeting, thick, cloudy, and heavy, draped over the wooden doors. One hand reached out to gather it, her claws sliding beneath the edge. An idea sparked. That basin near the sink — the mop-sink — might just serve as a shower floor. If she could keep the water contained, the place could be made to function.

Unfolding the sheet revealed its true size, at least ten, maybe twelve feet long, doubled over itself like a massive tongue of ebony skin. When unfurled, it spread wide across the floor, curling at its edges and climbing partway up the brick walls. Dusk's tail flicked with approval.

Shoving the sheet aside for now, she moved to the stack of old doors and selected one that looked mostly intact. Gripping it at the base, she hoisted it upright. The door wobbled before thunking loudly against one of the conservatory's wrought-iron roof trusses. Dusk's ears twitched from the sound, but a grin tugged at her lips. The truss could act as an anchor, a skeleton for this living space. Leaned against the trusses, these doors could become partition walls.

She dragged the door to the back corner, to the small alcove with the basin and sink. With a bit of maneuvering, she managed to slide the door vertically into place, the bottom corner snugged just behind the basin's lip, the top

118

resting against the truss, and the middle braced neatly by the hand sink. It was crude, but solid. And functional. Her tail flicked once as she stepped back, admiring her work.

Some time later, she had propped a second door opposite the first, on the far side of the basin. Lacking the bracing geometry of the sink or truss, the door swayed, and then, with a hollow clatter, fell inward against the first panel. Dusk groaned, rubbing her brow. She needed a way to stabilize it, but how?

Her eyes drifted across the conservatory, then toward the back wall — and that's when she saw it. Tucked beyond the structure, half-obscured behind overgrown ivy and a faded stack of old crates, was another doorway. A rusted plaque above it read: *Mechanical.*

Her ears perked immediately. She padded toward it without hesitation, the tips of her hooves whispering across the broken tile. If there was anything useful — hooks, brackets, wire, fasteners, even old mounts — it would be in there.

Heart quickening, she reached for the handle and hoped it hadn't rusted shut.

Pushing the door open, Dusk cautiously peeked inside. Darkness met her gaze, pierced only by the soft glow of a few brilliant pinpricks of light, red and green, scattered like stars across a wall of steel. The ambient hum of machinery met her ears, low and constant, vibrating faintly through the palms of her hands. The light seemed to radiate from metal faceplates embedded in the far wall, each one a sentinel in the dark.

She reached instinctively to the left, claws brushing against a familiar shape. *Click.* With a flick, the room flooded with sterile, electric light.

What she saw drew a quiet whistle from between her teeth.

Directly ahead, the entire back wall was an expanse of industrial hardware, steel-gray electrical panels, each one marked with aggressive caution decals. *DANGER — HIGH VOLTAGE.* They lined up like armored shields, cables slithering from beneath them like veins. To her left, the room stretched a good twenty feet farther, ending in a clustered wall of controls and machines she didn't recognize. Some bore foreign characters, others mere code numbers. The scent of ozone and old metal clung to the air like a second skin.

Turning toward the wall beside the entrance, her gaze lit upon what she'd been hoping for: a long, dust-covered workbench. The bench was cluttered with a chaotic but promising mix, scattered tools, coiled wires, jars of screws and bolts, small metal parts in various states of decay. Her tail gave a hopeful flick.

She stepped closer, eyes scanning the mess with purpose — and paused as her breath hitched softly.

There, nestled in a dark foam tray, was a black case stamped with words that sent her heart skittering:

SYNTHETIC MULTITOOL.

Pan, she thought with a grin, *don't jinx it now.* Flipping open the latches, she slowly opened the lid. Inside, cushioned neatly, sat an ergonomic grip handle connected to a cubic housing. Three color-coded dials adorned its sides: red on the right, green at the front, and blue on top. Sleek, clean — it was old, but clearly high-end.

Next to it, she found a small, transparent jar filled with what looked like silvery sand. But it wasn't sand, not exactly. Each grain was a perfect, shiny cube, about a millimeter across. Dusk held it closer, turning it slightly in the light — they shimmered like starlight in mercury.

She closed the case carefully, grabbing several long zip ties from the bench and tucking them into a pocket. Heart buoyed with excitement, she trotted back to the conservatory, her footfalls brisk, mind racing with plans.

Inside, she set the case on the lip of the sink and opened it once more, her eyes glimmering with anticipation. Unscrewing the jar, she inhaled the faint scent of lubricant and synthetic oil. Then, taking the handle in her hand, she gave the trigger a gentle squeeze.

With a soft hum, a holographic projection bloomed into the air above the cube, a faint green sheet appearing like a pane of ghostly glass. Turning the handle, she found a panel illuminated with several interactive icons and three-dimensional templates. She selected a slim cylinder with a tap of her claw, a perfect virtual drill bit.

Before her hovered a softly glowing rod, one centimeter wide and four long, suspended midair in gentle rotation. A perfect simulation of her selected bit.

With practiced care, she set the multitool aside and lowered the second wooden door, propping it against the first. That brought the top edge into easy reach.

Grasping the handle again, she moved the holographic cylinder toward the top of the door. As she hovered it near the wood, the cylinder extended, slipping ghostlike through the surface. She leaned to the side, checking that it had penetrated completely.

Then, she exhaled and pulled the trigger.

A sudden high-pitched whine cut through the silence.

Dusk flinched, ears twitching toward the sound. The open jar of shimmering micro-cubes had begun to sing. A wisp of smoke curled upward from its mouth, ghosting like incense. But instead of dissipating, the smoke coalesced and glided toward the door she'd marked moments ago. As it neared, the haze resolved into a cloud of suspended metallic grains, thousands of tiny reflective cubes drifting with eerie precision.

They gathered around the spot where the holographic cylinder had pierced the wood. The hum from the jar intensified as the swarm began to orbit in a tight circle, each grain moving faster, forming a silver blur. Then wood dust sprayed outward in a perfect spiral. The sound was like a swarm of wasps dancing on sandpaper.

In under five seconds, the hole was bored through cleanly, as smooth as if it had been lathed by hand.

Dusk's eyes sparkled. "Pan…" she whispered, admiration edging her breath.

She repeated the process twice more: two identical whirlwinds of micro-blades sculpted twin holes beside the first. Three perfect openings, equidistant. Satisfied, she lowered the door and dragged one of the chairs closer.

Standing on it, she fed zip ties through the holes and fastened the top of the door securely to the iron truss above.

Tug. Solid. She smirked, tail switching with satisfaction.

Next, she unfurled the plastic sheet. The stiff material crackled as she wrapped it over the top edge of the newly mounted door. Securing it in place with long strips of tape, she doubled over the upper corners for strength. Another piece was hung across the opening between the doors, an improvised curtain flap. And finally, using an old staple gun she'd found earlier, she drove staples through the taped plastic for good measure.

The curtain rippled gently in the draft like a breath, her new sanctuary slowly taking form.

Luck, or perhaps fate, rewarded her again. Coiled near the sink's base, she discovered a garden hose, still functional, with a rusted but intact sprayer head. Dusk hoisted it over the truss, guiding the hose across the ceiling and fastening the sprayer to a beam that bisected the shower space. It wouldn't be luxurious, but it would work. It would be hers.

She stepped back down, brushing her hands on her thighs, admiring the strange, satisfying comfort of a space slowly transforming into something livable.

Then — *THUMP*.

The building shuddered slightly. A harsh *squawk* followed, raw and jarring.

Dusk's ears flattened, heart kicking into high gear.

Cautiously, she crept around the partition wall, eyes scanning for threats. Her gaze shot to the open front door, and there, stumbling back into view, was a bird. But not just any bird. It was massive, easily three feet tall at the shoulder, covered in mottled, slate-gray feathers. One wing dragged slightly behind it. She saw no immediate signs of damage, save for a smudge high on the glass, one of the few unpainted panes near the conservatory's peak.

It must've flown into the window.

Dusk stepped forward slowly, fur bristling down her arms and neck. She sniffed the air: just feathers, dust, adrenaline. But as she turned to check the wall for damage, she caught a

122

flicker of motion from the corner of her eye.

The bird was closer.

Its posture had changed.

It was stalking her.

"Oh no you don't..." Dusk muttered, slowly retreating toward the door.

Then it lunged.

The creature shrieked, wings exploding into motion as it launched forward. Talons scraped against the concrete, beak wide, and before she could react, it sank its curved beak into her forearm.

Pain lanced through her body. "AAAH!" she cried out, her voice cracking.

Reflexively, she brought her knee up and shoved the bird away, narrowly dodging another strike from its talons. She spun, yanking the door open and slamming it shut behind her as she stumbled back into the safety of the conservatory.

Breathing hard, she leaned against the door, clutching her wounded arm. Blood oozed through her fur, painting crimson streaks along her white coat. "What the *yiff* was that all about?!" she gasped, staring at the faint outline of the bird pacing outside.

Back inside the comfort of the building, she crossed to the sink and ran cool water over her arm. The sting made her wince, but the relief of cleaning the wound overtook the pain. As the blood ran clear, she noticed something nestled in the shadowed corner of the counter: a dull, cube-shaped object.

It was an audio cube.

Curious, she wiped her hand dry, tapped the power button on top then dabbed nano bandage on the wound.

A pleasant synthetic voice chirped to life: "Greetings. Please select your preferred assistant. You may choose from Alexis, Bert, Squeakers, or Wolfgang."

Nodding, Dusk answered the disembodied voice softly, "Squeakers, please."

"Thank you. How may I help you?" The voice replied in a soothing, subtly synthetic tone, a voice she hadn't heard in years. After so long living with a human, it tugged at something deep within her. A trace of nostalgia crept into her smile. "Play local news, then classical, please."

Satisfied with her patch job, she wandered over to where her bags still sat, just to the right of the door. Retrieving a granola bar and a warm bottle of water from her pack, she pulled the chair back to the tea table and flopped into it with a tired thump. As she tore into her first meal of the day, the audio cube filled the space with grim, grainy reports.

"Flooding has worsened in the southeastern regions of the Russian territories, displacing thousands and permanently scarring much of the land. Rescue operations are underway, though efforts are hampered by ongoing water surges. UCA troops deployed nearby have begun evacuating civilians using both passenger craft and industrial lifters…"

Dusk chewed silently, eyes on the floor as the bleakness continued.

"… Tent cities and temporary shelters are now operating well beyond safe capacity. Volunteers, not officials, are coordinating most food and housing efforts. Meanwhile, UCA coastal fishermen are experiencing catastrophic losses. Nearly forty percent of the continental shelf now lies exposed. Receding ocean tides have stranded hundreds of vessels in thick silt beds. Declining fish populations are exacerbated by environmental displacement and —"

The voice paused. "… Ornithological researchers also report erratic migratory behavior in multiple avian species. Some birds have grown aggressive, even hostile. Here's Cindy Fowl with more…"

A sigh escaped her. Dusk stood slowly and set the empty wrapper on the table. "Next program, please."

The cube's reply was immediate, its digital transition seamless, as the first notes of a gentle string ensemble spilled into the air, curling like steam through the dusty, sun-warmed space.

Some hours later, Dusk stood beside her latest creation, a makeshift bed built with the same innovation as her shower. Four doors had been arranged to form a stable rectangular frame. Two stood upright, secured to the trussing above. Two more rested on their sides, completing the box. Atop this structure, she'd laid a final flat door, now topped with salvaged cushions stripped from the tattered chaise lounge. A light blanket and a small pillow, both freshly aired and beaten free of dust, gave the whole assembly a surprisingly inviting charm.

By now, the sun had begun to dip below the horizon. A soft, amber light slanted through the unpainted pane on the back wall, dust motes turning gold as they drifted.

Dusk crossed the room toward the front door. The air had grown close, warm, almost stale. Remembering the earlier attack, she cracked the door slowly, peering out. The rooftop was empty. No sign of feathers. No clicking talons.

With cautious confidence, she pushed the door wide. Cool evening air rushed in, sharp, sweet, and edged with the scent of rain on sun-baked brick. She stood in the doorway for a long moment, eyes raised. The grainy indigo of twilight was just beginning to overtake the sky, blurring the line between day and night in soft strokes of ink.

Her tail flicked once, slow and thoughtful.

She was alone... but for the first time in days, the solitude didn't feel empty.

Returning to the soft solitude of the conservatory, Dusk slipped into her evening wear, a loose tunic that clung gently to the curves of her fur, and climbed into the makeshift bed she'd so carefully crafted. Lying back, she tucked her hands behind her head, her gaze drifting upward through the freshly cleared glass panes.

Above her, the sky unfolded like a living tapestry. The darkness deepened, woven with threads of violet and deep indigo, while scattered stars flickered to life like nervous fireflies. As she hummed a quiet, nameless tune to herself, streaks of blue, green, and violet began to arc across the sky, meteors casting momentary flames before vanishing into the ether.

Her breath caught as she watched them fall, trailing tails of light through the cosmos. Some primitive part of her mind stirred, uncertain whether the sight should fill her with awe...

or dread. But even as the thought took shape, her eyelids grew heavy. The sky blurred, the stars melted into softness, and sleep, gentle and absolute, claimed her before concern could.

CHAPTER 8 - JUST A LITTLE HEAT.

Why do I keep getting distracted like this!? Pan, I only kissed her once. Why can't my hormones understand that?

Shifting uncomfortably, she tried to concentrate on her meditation, but was failing miserably. Suddenly, her nether region throbbed, the memory of a particularly sweaty session with Rina intruding with full sensory assault.

Itchy balls, I need to get a grip! Ever since that asshole...

She sighed, the heat in her belly dissolving as her thoughts drifted toward her ex.

Though she'd never loved him, she had enjoyed sex with him for a time. Human men were different, less harsh than the bucks of her kind. Unlike her species, they were *thick*. She'd only been with a few cervid partners: Rina, and two bucks whose names she couldn't recall. One had barely lasted fifteen seconds; though thicker than the other, they were both generally unsatisfying.

Their scent, on the other hand... *Pan, their scent!*

They might've been lackluster in bed, but their primal musk and ferocity nearly made up for it.

She'd had two human partners, both male. The first, Jacob, had been amazing in bed. She'd sometimes thought of him even while still with her ex. Female anthro deer were naturally smaller than humans, but their sexual anatomy followed different proportions. Dusk wasn't particularly small for a doe, but something truly special happened when she took Jacob inside her.

She'd slept with other species too: a rabbit couple, a female fox, a male raccoon, even a one-night stand with a wolf. Each had been unique in their way, but if she were honest, Jacob still topped the list. The raccoon had left an impression too; he'd done this thing with his tongue…

"Agh! Just stop!"

She huffed in frustration and shook her head, trying to snap out of it. That's when she realized her midsection was uncomfortably warm. Moisture slicked the inside of her thighs, enough that she knew she'd need to change.

"Get it together, Dusk!" she whispered angrily to herself.

She stood, then stared down at her yoga mat, a glistening mark betraying her failed attempt at serenity.

***

Struggling, Rina shifted uncomfortably, trying to prop herself up on her elbow. The bed, not quite spacious enough for the both of them, made the movement awkward. Grumbling, she stared down at Dusk. "We just finished rutting and you're already talking about this again?" Gently, she dragged her finger up Dusk's arm, over her shoulder, then down in a slow glide to her breast. "Do I need to go down on you again so you'll shut up?"

Dusk giggled, shaking her head, a soft moan escaping as Rina leaned down to nip teasingly at her breast. The suckling pull sent shivers racing down her spine. Dusk arched her back, then moaned again, a little louder. Without warning, she felt Rina's fingers sliding between her thighs, grazing the slick heat of her folds, brushing her clit in a single, featherlight pass. A gasp burst from her lips, and she instinctively reached to still Rina's exploring hand. "Wait…"

128

Just as she began to speak, Rina dipped two fingers inside her, drawing a helpless moan from her throat.

"No, Dusk. You're obsessed," Rina murmured, voice sharp with conviction. "You have to let it go. You need to spend time thinking about something else. Doing something, or *someone*, else." She punctuated each phrase with a deeper thrust, silencing Dusk's protest with sensation.

Seizing the moment, Rina rose up, turned herself smoothly around, and straddled Dusk's chest. Lifting her leg over, she planted her knees to either side of Dusk's torso and leaned back, lowering her hips until her glistening sex hovered just above Dusk's muzzle. She didn't have to wait long to see if she'd won.

***

"Yiffing hell..." Reaching down to pluck the yoga mat from the ground, she shook her head at the glistening patch marring the normally dull surface.

The cool morning breeze tousled her hair as she stood. It was then she noticed a heavenly scent tickling her nose. She moved to the edge of the roof to peer down at the street, her stomach growling. Nearing the corner of the roof, she could see a bodega with its door propped open. She hadn't eaten much the day before, and her stomach voiced its protest with a gurgle. That decided it: food came first.

Turning around, she noticed the area she was standing in felt unexpectedly cozy. The mechanical room's back wall stood ten or twelve feet from the raised edge of the roofline, leaving a small open area in between. *I could build a little garden or meditation space here. Maybe that could help me stop thinking about sex every time I sit on this rutting mat...* she complained to herself as she inspected the area.

Grumbling again, Dusk made her way back to the conservatory to change, and to clean the mat where she'd so generously accentuated its texture.

Minutes later, having donned fresh undergarments, her favorite sundress, and a silk scarf, she made her way to the

129

stairs. Hoping the bodega had some breakfast items suitable for vegetarian anthros, she trotted down the steps, hooves clacking lightly, humming a playful tune.

Inside the building elevator, she checked her com for new messages. As expected, she found a few threatening notes from unknown addresses, presumably the work of her ex. She ignored them, then noticed a message from Rina:

"It was good to see you again. I was sorry to see that you'd left so early yesterday, but I understand your eagerness to start your life again. I'll try to visit in a few days... P.S. I missed you. Take care of yourself, little fawn."

The elevator door slid open. She sighed quietly, slipped her com away, and stepped out. A young man in a cheaply made uniform sat behind the reception desk, half-slouched, nose buried in his com. The screen showed a three-dimensional version of an ancient puzzle: small colored blocks of various shapes fell from the top. With casual flicks, the man gestured to shift or rotate them, slotting each into place as the pile rose.

He barely glanced up. He offered no greeting, nodding absently.

She waved meekly as she passed, heading toward the lobby doors.

Just short of the exit, she hesitated. Her hand hovered near the handle. Those hateful messages lingered in her mind, tightening around her gut like a band. It might be safer to avoid being seen; her ex likely had people watching by now.

With a subtle pivot, she retraced her steps, moving past the distracted guard once again and toward the back exit.

Dusk might normally avoid dark alleyways or rear doors out of caution, but her training had taught her a hard truth: shadows were safer than light when you didn't want to be found.

She pushed through the rear door and stepped into a narrow alley. Dumpsters lined either side, their dented bodies slick with years of grime. The stench hit her instantly, a violent wall of hot fish oil, spoiled meat, and sour vegetables.

Her muzzle twitched. Apparently, her neighbors had a serious seafood addiction.

Holding her breath, she turned left, following the tight corridor toward the corner of the building. Another turn revealed a narrow path cluttered with debris: discarded packaging, shattered glass, the occasional crumpled takeout box speckled with sauce and fly eggs.

Despite her efforts to remain unseen, an apparently homeless wolf slouched against the wall to her right. His fur was mottled, matted in places. He watched her briefly, eyes half-lidded, then averted his gaze. Still, she felt it — his attention trailing her like a thread pulled taut. Or maybe it was just the alley's shadows playing tricks on her nerves.

Reaching the street, Dusk quickened her pace. She looked left. Then right. Then turned the corner toward the bodega.

The morning air teased her nostrils, thick with the scent of city grime and morning indulgence: smoke, yeast, cured meats, doughnuts, sweat… and something more.

No. I know that scent…

Wolf. Specifically, a male wolf. Probably the one she'd just passed.

It tugged at her memory — something feral, something sharp. Something recent that set her fur on end… and her thighs on fire.

I wonder what he's been up to? Maybe he'd want to—
Pan! I'm thinking about sex again!

Anthromorphs were a unique group when it came to social constructs. Given that Diggercorp was technically their maker, the concept of "God" never fully fit into their sociocultural DNA. Instead, they chose symbolic figures, characters who aligned more closely with their species' values and instincts. Pan, the Greek god of fertility and wildness, found a natural home among anthro society.

He quickly earned the dubious title of "first curse from an anthro's muzzle."

But of course, none of this actively crossed Dusk's mind as she pressed onward. Her focus narrowed. She didn't need to rut a stranger. She didn't need to let this scent soak into

131

her fur like sweat and pheromones. She just needed—

Food.

Not fantasies. Not alleyway heat. Not strangers' breath brushing her neck.

Just food.

What should have been an ordinary morning was quickly turning into a minefield of absurd, unbidden sexual urges.

In her distracted state, she failed to notice two additional canine anthros. They stood about fifteen yards behind her, near the opposite corner of the passage she'd emerged from. Ears alert and postures casual, they watched with interest as she made her way to the bodega. One gestured subtly to the other, but neither moved to intercept her.

Crossing the street and stepping inside, Dusk was instantly enveloped in the heavenly scents of sesame and yeast. Leaning over the sneeze guard, she pointed at the fresh bread, some cheese, a bowl of hummus, then plucked some pita chips from a shelf behind her. She grabbed a carrot soda from the cooler near the register and smiled at the cute squirrel behind the counter.

Hmm, I've never fooled around with a squirrel before. Maybe they feel nice under tail?

Her ears twitched in embarrassment as the thought crept in. She flushed, then shook her head violently, as if to fling the fantasy away by force.

Pausing, she closed her eyes and tried to regain her composure.

Confused, the squirrel repeated the cost of the items, his paw extended with practiced boredom. Fumbling, she handed him her credit chip, praying he hadn't noticed the flush burning beneath her cheek fur.

Seconds later, she was storming out of the bodega, huffing and mumbling under her breath. Frustrated, she resolved to stay on the roof the rest of the day, never to so much as *glance* at another male again. Not so much as a sniff. Turning into the alleyway, she failed to notice the canines from earlier. Their ears perked as she passed, and their eyes tracked her every step. Quietly, they fell into motion, following close on her heels.

Her head down, she was startled when a low, gravelly voice rasped out: "Hello love. I see you've returned! And you've brought us a tasty morsel as well!"

Her gasp broke the stillness. She stopped sharply, hugging the bag of groceries to her chest as she twisted to her left. The two canines from before stood just a few paces behind, their grins smug, their eyes sharp. Spinning back to her right, she found the source of the voice — the slouched wolf from earlier. He was standing now, that same crooked grin on his muzzle, eyes gleaming with feral curiosity.

"Don't worry little fawn, we don't want your salad greens. Your old man sent us to... in his own words: 'return the favor.' If you know what I mean?"

At the mention of her ex, Dusk sobered, clarity snapping into place like a blade sliding home. Calmly, she studied her surroundings while edging toward the center of the alley. Speaking quietly, she began to lower the groceries to the ground.

"I don't want any trouble. Walk away. Forget you saw me and no one will get hurt."

With that, the canines burst into laughter, the two to her left slapping one another's backs.

Snap.

Her patience shattered. She let a kick fly at the canine closest to her left, scoring a direct hit to his genitals.

"I said walk away!" she screamed.

Without pause, she lunged, her palm slamming into the wolf's throat in a motion nearly too quick to follow. The two injured canines stumbled back, stunned, as Dusk whirled to face the third.

Unphased, the last canine took a bold step forward, directly into an open-hand slap that cracked through the alley. The impact snapped his head to the side, his body crumpling against the wall with a grunt.

Seconds later, the trio retreated, tails tucked tight. The wolf who had stood before her clutched his throat, groaning hoarsely as he staggered off, one paw at his neck. He croaked something unintelligible and vanished around the corner.

She stood trembling, fur on end, fists clenched, chest heaving.

Eventually, she bent to retrieve her groceries, hiking them onto her right hip, her fingers twitching with leftover adrenaline. As she brushed the dust from her dress, a voice drifted in from the alley behind her.

She froze mid-motion. One ear swiveled toward the sound.

It was a young male, definitely anthro, and definitely not one of the canines. His voice carried an accent she couldn't place, low and cautious. Then his scent followed: musky, earthy, edged with the bitter sting of coffee… and something else.

Sex.

That's… mine.

The realization hit her hard. Her heart pounded. Her core clenched. Cheeks flushed, her breath caught in her throat as heat swelled low in her belly. She turned her head slightly, just enough to see.

A raccoon anthro. Handsome. Dressed plainly, a med kit in one hand, the other stretched out toward her in concern.

Her thighs twitched. Need flared, sudden, raw, and undeniable.

She spun away fast enough to make her scarf flutter.

This is getting ridiculous! You can't just rut a random stranger, you stupid doe!

Her knees buckled slightly.

It's just hormones! Just ignore it!

She repeated it like a mantra, trying to calm the storm building inside her.

Hormones!

The heat slicked her thighs again. Her tail lifted involuntarily.

Ignore it!

The raccoon called after her again, concern in his tone.

She didn't respond.

Bolting for the building's back entrance, her steps frantic,

134

she vanished into the shadows of the doorway.

I'm gonna have to do something about this... I just hurt three strangers and all that did was make me hornier. Even now I want to turn back for that yiffing raccoon!

She sighed hard through her nose, heaving the door open and rushing inside. The thought of rutting someone new after being with the same male for so long sent a fresh thrill up her spine. The temptation gnawed at her, raw, immediate.

She imagined slipping back into the alley. Stepping in close. Breathing him in. Sharing breath. Letting him take her. Turning. Lifting her tail. Offering her folds, hot and honey-slick, to his whim.

WHAT?!

She gasped, stumbling as she reached the elevator. Her heat throbbed viciously now. *Focus,* she begged herself, pushing the call button with a trembling hand. Her fingers drifted from her chest to her abdomen, almost unbidden. When the elevator chimed open, she rushed inside, her breath sharp and uneven, smashing the button for the penthouse.

She didn't make it to her floor before giving in. Pressing back against the wall, hips rolling, breath ragged, she hitched up her dress, letting her fingers slide beneath the damp silk. Her breath hitched. Her knees quivered. The pressure of her need consumed her, and as the elevator ascended, she chased release with frantic, desperate strokes.

Her body jerked — one, then twice more — until she sagged against the panel, fur flushed, gasping.

Two additional releases later, she sat panting, legs splayed and fur mussed, at the edge of the bed. To say the least, her ecstasy had been spectacular. The first, having echoed shamelessly through the elevator walls, had left its slick, undeniable mark on the floor. Feeling both guilt and embarrassment simmer in her chest, she'd wiped it away with an old cloth she'd found just outside the elevator. She'd then tossed the evidence into the garbage chute and bolted back to the conservatory.

Her second and third orgasms had drained her utterly, leaving her legs wobbly, her body flushed, but her mind

135

finally still. Lucid again, her instincts dulled at last, clarity crept back in, cold and merciful, riding the cooling tide of post-release calm.

Suddenly parched, she was reminded of the hunger she'd tried to ignore earlier. The release, both physical and emotional, had sharpened her appetite into something primal. She padded her way to the sink, washed her hands and muzzle, then returned to the tea table to finally enjoy her long-delayed breakfast. As she sat, chewing thoughtfully, she let the silence settle around her and decided, quietly, firmly, this would be her new beginning.

"Squeakers, classical music please."

A cheerful chime echoed from the back room, followed, inexplicably, by late-twentieth-century rock.

"...Maybe not *that* classical," Dusk muttered under her breath with a smirk.

Having finished her meal, Dusk returned to cleaning the conservatory. She removed the remaining unused doors, keeping a few for future projects, then swept up the last of the dust and debris. As she looked around, she found the room now felt a little too open, almost exposed. She missed the sense of containment, the small sanctuary she'd started to create.

Making her way to the mechanical room, she retrieved the drop cloths she'd spotted the day before. The heavy, canvas-like sheets would be perfect for adding some much-needed privacy.

Returning with a bundle under her arm, she got to work hanging the cloth around her bed, using zip ties and old hooks already mounted on the iron trusses. When she finally stepped back, she grinned. The result reminded her of a four-poster bed, draped in soft curtains, the space now cozy and intimate. With a playful spin, she performed a pirouette and giggled.

For just a moment, she felt like a princess, and this, her secluded royal chamber.

With a self-mocking curtsy, she swept the curtain aside and stepped through to sit on the edge of her reimagined bed.

It was warm. Personal. Safe.

Looking across the space, Dusk decided a workspace would serve her well. A desk, and maybe a pinboard, for her notes and plans. Using the remaining doors and the synth multi-tool, she constructed a broad desk in the front corner of the room, directly opposite her bed. Next to it, she placed the easel she'd found earlier, propping a large rectangle of synth-board insulation onto it. She pressed a few nails into the foam and pinned the framed picture of her parents to the upper left corner. Finally, as a tangible reminder of her purpose, she set the little Japanese doll beside the frame, its painted eyes forever watching.

She hung more of the drop cloths across the open partition wall, creating a curtained entry to her shower nook. Sunlight streamed in as she scraped old paint from more panes, golden warmth returning to the room with each stroke.

In the corner, tucked behind some stacked boxes, she retrieved the old chess set she'd packed the pieces in the day before. Gently opening it on the tea table, she arranged the worn but charming pieces in their standard formation, restoring the table to its original glory.

Stepping back, she took it all in: her new sanctuary. A place that was hers alone.

And for the first time in a long while, Dusk felt... home.

***

In an effort to be as quiet as possible, Dusk gently pulled the door toward her while she manipulated the latch. Shrouded in darkness, few details revealed themselves as she opened the door partway, then slipped inside. She turned, slowly easing the door shut behind her, the light wood settling into the jamb before she released the latch. Despite her hard, cloven hooves, she crept silently across the plank flooring of the small room.

Through the shadows, a sliver of moonlight cast itself across the floorboards. Near the center of the room, it illuminated a desk, pale silver pooling like breath held in the

137

dark. Beside it stood a file cabinet, a small lamp perched atop its metal frame. She pulled at the handle of the topmost drawer but it didn't budge. The drawer caught just before opening, stuck fast. Jiggling the handle, she applied more force, but it refused to move. Frustrated, she released the handle and turned to the desk instead. She slid open the nearest drawer. The cavity lay shrouded in gloom.

Pulling her com from her pocket, she whispered, "Flashlight on."

The darkness fled before a white beam, revealing a cavity filled with paperclips, scissors, and other office supplies neatly arranged in a tray. She pushed the tray aside and rummaged beneath it and to the edges, hoping to find a key to the file cabinet. Coming up empty, she moved to the next drawer. Like the first, it held clutter, similar in contents but slightly disordered. She reached in, brushing aside items, when a voice near the door said:

"If you're looking for the sake, you're three years too late."

It took Dusk half a beat to register the voice. Master Haku had slipped in unnoticed, his presence landing like a dropped feather. Her ears flicked forward, then twitched in opposite directions as the shadows stirred around her.

She slowly withdrew her hand and stood to her full height, bowing at the hip. "I am sorry, Master… but I am not here for sake…"

The moonlight caught Master Haku's face as he moved closer. His eyes, sharp as obsidian, locked onto hers. A click sounded, and suddenly, the lamp atop the file cabinet flared to life, flooding the room with light.

Dusk flinched instinctively, lifting one arm halfway to shield her eyes. The sudden illumination cast harsh angles across the walls, throwing her shadow long and animal behind her. The silence that followed hung heavy with the unspoken.

She squinted, forced to avert her eyes.

"If you are not here, rummaging through my office for sake," he said, his voice low and calm, "then what are you

138

here for?"

Standing straight again, her gaze downcast, she blinked away the brightness as her vision adjusted. Silence settled. Gathering her thoughts, she inhaled slowly.

Leaning in, Master Haku's voice curled around her like smoke. "At your convenience, little fawn. Why did you interrupt my rest with this little treasure hunt? Hmm?"

She turned toward him and bowed again. "I am sorry, Master... but I am not who you think I am."

Straightening, she took several steps away from him, then pivoted to face him directly. Her posture became composed, back tall, chin up, expression unreadable.

Her voice was steady. "I believe you knew my parents. I've come here because I need to know why they were involved with you. I need to know why you were helping the Yakuza, and how my parents were connected."

His eyes narrowed, studying her. The subtle cues of her form sharpened into familiarity. The delicate arch of her muzzle. The short tail. Those eyes, a deep blend of chocolate and coffee.

A whisper escaped him. "Pan... I don't know why I couldn't see it before. You have her eyes... and her stubby tail."

He hesitated, staring at her, disbelief softening the lines of his face. "But how... how did you find me?"

"I found a daruma with the kanji for *perseverance* painted on it," she said.

"It had your contact information on its base. When my parents were murdered... that was one of the few things that survived. Untouched."

He began to pace, stopping in his tracks at the word *murdered*. The air thickened. Their gazes met, hers unflinching, his cracked with realization.

She nodded slowly as the weight of her words settled across his shoulders. "They're gone. And I need to know why."

Reeling, Master Haku backed toward the nearest wall, his posture faltering as he leaned into it, eyes growing distant and unfocused.

"What do you mean, *murdered?*" he asked, his voice rough with disbelief, weariness immediately etching his features.

Sighing, Dusk returned to the desk. She pulled out the chair and offered it to him, her movements slow, careful. "They were murdered in my childhood home about a year ago. The investigators had never seen anything like it. Most of the apartment was destroyed, but not like a robbery. This was deliberate. Almost personal. The only things left untouched were in a floor safe, and the contents of the refrigerator."

As silence pressed between them, Haku stared at the floor. His head drifted side to side, a quiet denial shaking through his frame. He whispered something unintelligible, then rubbed his chin, brows cinched with worry. His gaze finally lifted to meet hers, his amber eyes glassy, tears welling at their edges.

"What have you done, Dusk…?" He stepped back, catching his breath.

"Never mind. You can't stay here. You should have told me long ago. They will have been watching you…" His voice frayed, unraveling fast. His eyes darted left, then right, then back to hers.

"They may have used you to find me. *Pan*, I hope I'm wrong. You must leave immediately!"

Her eyes widened. Dusk leaned forward from her perch on the desk's edge. "Master? I *can't* leave now. I need to know what happened! I need to understand why the Alpha Syndicate murdered my parents! I need to know how *you* were involved!"

Agitated, Master Haku rose abruptly, tossing the chair aside with a sharp clatter. He strode toward her, his steps brimming with frantic energy. "You have made a grave mistake, little fawn. We are all in danger. You must leave. Take Rina with you."

Spinning away, he stormed toward the file cabinet, unlocking it with a sharp twist. He yanked open the bottom drawer and rummaged through it, muttering curses under his breath. Finally, he pulled free a laser pistol and a small stack of credit chips. Setting the pistol on the desk with a sharp click, he extended his paw toward Dusk.

"Take this. It should be enough for you and Rina to live on for a few months. You're done here. You're banished from my dojo. I don't want to see you again." His voice cracked, but he pressed on.

"I know why you're here. No good can come of this, Dusk. I beg you — let it die with your parents."

Dusk shook her head slowly, refusing the credits. "No, Master. Please, keep it. I have more than enough to survive. Please… just help me understand."

A tear slipped from her eye, carving a path to her cheekbone as she reached toward him. But he stepped back, shaking his head with finality. "They saved me. That's all I can tell you."

His voice dropped to a hush. "Please, just go. Protect Rina. Protect yourself."

Without another word, he turned and strode from the office. The door slammed shut behind him, his final words echoing like a blade left hanging in the air:

"Do not seek me again."

***

With a sigh, she continued scraping paint from a front-window pane in the conservatory. Opposite the desk corner, she carved out a slightly oblong, waist-height window. Nearby, a cylindrical device perched atop a three-legged stand caught her eye. Sparks of light danced along the cylinder's surface, flickering as the sunlight struck its narrower end.

Leaning in, she peered through the freshly cleared section of glass, then turned her head slightly to the left, closing one eye in focus. In the distance, she spotted a symmetrical, rectangular glass tower. Near its top, a stepped configuration formed a broken mosaic of green and brown shapes, with

141

pale blue sky behind them — architecture half overgrown, half pristine.

She stepped back, gently lifting the tripod setup and sliding it closer to the wall. Bending forwards, she repositioned the assembly near the doorway, turning the cylinder to the left.

Peering to her right, she noticed a small, two-dimensional holographic projection flickering at the edge of the desk. In it, a simulation of a building's top floor spun into view: a rectangular structure surrounded by greenery, with a wraparound balcony embraced by plant life.

CHAPTER 9 - IF WISHES COULD FILL A WELL.

Her breasts yielded beneath her hand, their supple curves molding to the arc of her fingers as though sculpted just for her. Tilting her wrist, she let her thumb graze over the taut nipple, coaxing a ripple of invisible tremors. Tiny, downy fur near the areola stood on end as she gently pinched, rolling the hardened peak between thumb and forefinger with exquisite care. A quiet moan escaped her partner, her body arching into each new, concentrated sensation.

Holding her breath as she moved from one sensitive nub to the next, she struggled to maintain control, the weight of desire pressing against the wall of her restraint. Rina reached out reflexively, craving to return the caress, but a sudden, involuntary gasp left her lips as heat bloomed in her core.

Slowly, deliberately, she drew closer, her breath brushing along Rina's thighs like an electric current. Her muzzle dipped lower, lingering just inches from her lover's glistening sex. She hovered, a devoted pollinator, drawn by instinct to the nectar of her mate. Her tongue parted her lips, tentative and reverent, until she made contact with the slick petals of Rina's heat-swollen folds.

Rina's hips bucked as a sudden surge of pleasure wracked

her, forcing her to sit up slightly, fur ruffling as if bracing against a storm. Through the haze of arousal, she caught Dusk's eyes, locked on her from just above her mound. They pierced her like obsidian knives, anchoring her in place, flaying her open in more ways than one.

Then it began: waves of sensation cresting and breaking inside her, relentless and liquid. Her folds parted, then clenched, undulating with maddening slowness. Anticipated or not, the first contact of Dusk's tongue still startled her, and she gasped, each pulse of pleasure dragging her closer to the brink. Her sex, slick with need, grew wetter with every deliberate stroke. Dusk lapped at her steadily, unhurried, claiming her inch by inch.

A low purr of satisfaction vibrated in Dusk's throat as she dragged her tongue from the base of Rina's entrance to the aching nub at the apex. Her lips curled into a muted grin, eyes still fixed on her prey. One hand traced Rina's side, kneading the soft fur along her waist before gripping her thigh, pushing her legs wider apart with a gentle but insistent strength. Rina lay bare beneath her, trembling, her breath broken into short, shallow bursts.

The other hand slipped lower, trailing along the inside of Rina's thigh, pads brushing against the fevered flesh. Her touch circled the flushed opening, teasing, spreading the slick folds until her fingers finally pressed inward, finding Rina's heat with a slow, penetrating glide. She moved in time with the rolling buck of Rina's hips, never breaking contact with her tongue, each motion building on the last like a rising symphony.

Rina cried out, her voice caught somewhere between moan and whimper as Dusk's lips closed around her engorged clit. Her lover's tongue curled beneath the hood, teasing side to side, then drawing the peak fully into her muzzle. The sudden intensity slammed into Rina's core, and she clutched at Dusk's head, fingers threading through her partner's fur, nails catching for just a moment as raw pleasure surged through her.

She was being filled, stretched, and licked all at once, a

144

triple assault that shattered her composure and scattered her thoughts like leaves in a storm. Her tail quivered against the sheets, her breath now ragged and uneven.

Above her, Dusk moaned into her work, hips rising instinctively, offering herself to the imagined lover looming behind her. Her sex glistened in the low light, moisture trailing down the curve of her inner thigh. Her tail lifted, flagging wantonly, brushing back in unconscious invitation. Her scent, ripe and demanding, filled the air like pheromonal smoke. She needed to be taken. Claimed. Her body radiated that demand without shame.

Then, sudden and searing, light flooded the space, catching her in mid-motion. Dusk squinted, muzzle twisting as her eyes struggled to adjust. Heat from the beam warmed her face, almost cruel in its intensity.

All around, gravel crunched underfoot.

Figures loomed just beyond the blinding glare, silhouettes shrouded in harsh illumination, their whispers hushed and incomprehensible.

She tried to ask what they wanted, but no sound came. Her throat locked tight, her body frozen beneath the crushing weight of fear. Her eyes flicked toward her lover only to find the familiar form unraveled, transformed into a mass of writhing, inky creatures, serpentine and slick, their eel-like bodies folding into one another in an impossible tangle of motion and shadow. Their voices hissed like air escaping from a dozen punctured balloons, each whisper stitched from static and breath.

Startled, she gasped, ripping herself free of the dream's paralysis, and found her breath ragged, chest heaving as she stared up at the glassed ceiling of the conservatory. Midday light poured in through the high canopy, blinding in its intensity, scattering across the room in shimmering beams. Turning her head, blinking past the dazzle, she tried to reorient.

The dampness between her thighs remained, a lingering echo of heat and contact that refused to fade. Her body still tingled, sensitive and half-clenched in the memory of

145

pleasure. The dream came rushing back — phantom lips, imagined breath, that unbearable yearning made real again.

She let her fingertips slip downward, sliding between slick folds into the molten heat. Her eyes fluttered closed, pulling the ghost of Rina back with each gentle stroke. For a moment, she was no longer alone. She chased the ghost of that intimacy, her breath catching, her body tightening, until the tremors overtook her again. Then silence. Sobbed breath. The high, bright ceiling above. The familiar hollowness.

Another climax, and with it, another vanishing. Another lover gone, her cheek now streaked with tears not from release, but from aching remembrance.

Later, she sat in bed, staring at the holo-still projected near the corner of her room.

The image shimmered with light interference, but the subject was crystal clear: Rina, grinning, her arms stretched wide, standing before a breathtaking panorama of green-cloaked mountains. Her medium-brown coat was partly exposed between fitted cargo shorts and a snug black crop top. A wide-brimmed canvas hat rested over her head, with her ears poking through slits at the top, the chin strap hanging loose between her breasts.

Dusk extended a hand toward the projection, fingertips ghosting through Rina's cheek. The holo fluttered, pixels distorting briefly, then correcting.

She hadn't heard from Rina since the day after she'd left for the arbor site. Not a message. Not a visit. Just that still silence, thick and unrelenting. Dusk stared, her pulse slow, heavy. She summoned the last message again, her nails twitching slightly as she scanned it for meaning. She read it once. Then again. And again. There was something missing. Something left unsaid. The tone was restrained, the language too careful.

It felt unfinished.

She thought of sending a reply. Just a few words. Maybe a voice snippet. But the idea caught in her throat like thorns. It would be like dropping a bottle into a black sea, hoping it would surface somewhere, someday. That pain, raw and biting, clawed behind her ribs.

Her mother's voice echoed in her head: *"If wishes could fill a well, no one would ever go thirsty."*

With a bitter exhale, she swiped the message away. The holo collapsed into nothingness.

She sat up slowly, wiping a tear from her cheek. The air touched her bare fur, cool against her nipples, which tightened in the draft. She'd forgotten her nudity. Shrugging, she wrapped the rumpled bed sheet around herself, tugging it snug against her chest before walking barefoot across the smooth floor toward the low tea table.

On the table, remnants of her earlier lunch sat untouched. She picked up a piece of torn bread, biting into it absently while her gaze drifted toward the desk — and the wall behind it.

The makeshift bulletin board was crowded now, every inch of the synth-wood surface covered in pinned two-dimensional stills. Captured on synth paper, the images flickered slightly in the light, their surfaces reacting faintly to motion and heat.

Several stills showed a well-dressed male figure, his posture sharp, the cut of his clothing expensive. In one, he stood on a penthouse balcony, framed by the city skyline. The corners of that image blurred, tinted with a greenish hue, the same color as the coating on the conservatory windows.

Other images revealed a patchwork of lives: laborers mid-task, a laughing child, a tall red-haired woman in a sleeveless top, a housecat sprawled on a brickwork ledge, and an elderly couple clutching each other's hands. Each still bore a printed timecode in the upper right corner.

Interwoven between them, sometimes overlapping the edges, were handwritten notes, a flurry of observational fragments.

One note was scrawled next to a still showing the man dining alone behind tinted glass. The angle was oblique, captured at distance:

"9:15... orange juice – did not drink... coffee... muffin (blueberry?)... banana... 9:27... kisses redhead... hand

147

between redhead's legs... departs... redhead seems distressed."

Dusk narrowed her eyes at the note, her tail flicking once, sharply.

Beneath the calm, the pulse of something larger stirred. Observation had become a habit. But this was something else.

A scatter of sleek components, clearly belonging to a plasma rifle, rested atop Dusk's makeshift desk. Each piece had been laid out with meticulous care across a rubberized mat, flanked by cleaning cloths, solvent droppers, and a worn bristle brush. Nearby on the floor sat the open carrying bag where she kept her katana. Nestled inside were several power packs and a compact laser pistol, its metal frame catching a glint of morning light.

Chewing the last of her bread, Dusk let the sheet fall from her shoulders, padding across the room and settling onto the low stool in front of the disassembled rifle. The cool air kissed her fur, but she barely noticed, her focus shifting into the clean, quiet discipline of weapon maintenance.

She picked up a slender, barrel-like composite tube, then a bulkier housing bearing a telescopic optic and shoulder pad. With practiced ease, she slotted the slender barrel into the main chassis, the faint click of magnetic locks confirming a proper fit. Already, the rifle's silhouette began to take form.

Above the barrel, she slid an optical module into place, then leaned forward to peer into the viewfinder. At its center, a glowing holographic arrow hovered just above a small rectangular reticle, an upward point guiding aim with quiet menace. Below the primary assembly, she fitted a heavy grip module, its base housing a twin-pronged trigger and actuator plate. The extended bulk of the power housing jutted forward into a rectangular cavity, its flanks recessed with circular indentations, finger-shaped, ready to lock or release.

Dusk plucked one of the power packs from her bag, its metal surface cool against her hand pads. She slid it into place just ahead of the grip. With a sharp click, the circular detents locked tight. Turning the rifle sideways, she checked a small display screen embedded into the stock, just aft of the grip module.

A vertical row of bar-shaped indicators filled the left side of the screen. To their right, a "12" glowed inside a small circular glyph: fully charged.

Nodding, Dusk pressed her thumb into one of the release points. The power pack disengaged with a satisfying click. She returned it to her bag, gave the rifle one last visual inspection, then slid it carefully inside beside her katana.

Bending to zip the bag, the mid-morning sun bathed her hindquarters, the warmth on her fur a gentle nudge reminding her she still needed to wash and dress.

Showering was always an ordeal. Dusk's coat, short, dense, and soft, made rinsing simple but drying a challenge. For anthros, it was a known burden; full-body fur made traditional showers time-consuming, especially without access to a sonic dryer. Normally, she would have used a sonic bath, but her modest home had no such luxury yet. And today, as usual, time wasn't a gift she could afford.

Instead, she focused on the essentials, scrubbing her most-soiled parts with vigorous, well-practiced strokes: armpits, hands, thighs, tailbase, and sex. The rest, she left to a perfumed bodycloth she rubbed gently across her flanks and spine.

Stepping from the misty alcove, she snatched a towel from a hook and began patting herself dry, mindful of the grain of her fur. As she ran the towel between her legs, a low sigh escaped her. The lingering ache of her heat stirred again, faint but persistent.

Her seasons had always hit hardest around this time of year, but nothing like this. This heat had been unruly. Unrelenting. It clung to her skin, haunted her dreams, pulled at her thoughts even now. No medical warning, no signs of imbalance. She suspected the turbulence of the last few weeks — emotional, physical, even hormonal — had simply pushed her into overdrive.

Shrugging off the thought, she tossed the towel aside and padded back into the main room, fur slightly damp but

149

already fluffing at the edges.

She dressed quickly: a pair of well-worn cargo capris, snug across her hips and easy to move in. A dark button-up blouse followed, its fabric soft against her chest, sleeves rolled halfway up her forearms. She cinched a black handkerchief around her neck, tying it at the front, then reached for a faded cap. Her ears slipped effortlessly through the ear-holes at the top, and she tied her hair back into a low bun beneath it.

As she finished lacing her boots, her ears flicked instinctively, swiveling toward the conservatory's rear alcove. The cap's special cut allowed full ear articulation, and she paused, alert. No sounds yet. But something in the air caught her attention.

A shift in pressure. A change in rhythm.

She straightened, hand brushing near the bag where rifle and blade waited in silent readiness.

***

Still panting, Reaper stood in the stairwell doorway, framed by the industrial steel and concrete behind him. The conservatory in front of him looked like something out of a dream, or a bad aesthetic decision. The kitschy greenhouse, all tawny-green panels and mismatched seams, sat awkwardly on the rooftop. It looked more like a neglected art installation than a functional structure meant to let in sunlight.

Overhead, a flock of birds burst into the air, their shrieking wings casting restless shadows that danced over the greenhouse glass. Something about the way the shadows shifted made Reaper's fur prickle.

He caught his breath, but the real unease gnawed deeper. Why was he here? Why had he followed her?

How could he explain this to anyone else, even to himself? Was he stalking her? Was this even her home? And if it was, did that make it worse?

Why was he so drawn to this doe? So captivated that he'd

followed her across districts, all the way to this rooftop?

Was it curiosity? Lust? Or some twisted sense of responsibility?

His breath steadied, but his heart continued its fluttering rebellion.

Was he supposed to find other species attractive? Was that the real problem? Did it matter?

He'd already come this far. Maybe there was no harm in checking if she was okay.

He whispered under his breath, ears twitching. "Salted cucumber, this is stupid… Just leave and forget about it…" But even as he said it, his legs carried him forward. He turned left, moving toward the front of the greenhouse, the structure looming closer with every step.

Inside, Dusk paused, ears already pointed back as a faint scraping noise cut through the morning stillness.

A wrongness slithered through her gut.

She finished tying the handkerchief at her neck with deliberate calm, then stepped lightly toward the desk where she'd left the razor-edged utility knife and solvent bottle. Her hand hovered above the table, casual, practiced. She forced her ears to rotate away from the sound, using her other senses instead: air pressure, scent, vibration through the floor. Something was out there.

Without hesitation, she spun, one hand sweeping the knife up in a fluid motion.

"Who the rut are you, and what do you want?!"

Her voice cracked across the greenhouse like thunder.

Reaper stopped mid-step, several yards from the entrance, arms raised instinctively in confusion and alarm. His ears flicked, tail twitching behind him.

"Uhh… hello?.. I — uhh, I mean… You…" He winced. "Itchy balls, you caught me off guard. Can I… start again?"

He took a breath, tried to stand straighter.

"My name's Reaper. Miss? I tried to help you the other day. At least, I think it was you… I just — "

He trailed off, paw rubbing the back of his neck, eyes lowering like a guilty pup.

151

Inside, Dusk's ears flicked again. That voice — familiar. A raccoon. That raccoon. Her stomach dropped.

What the rut is he doing here?!

Annoyance flared, mixing violently with alarm. She turned her head slightly to track the sound in front of her, backing away apprehensively as the shape of her would-be assailant resolved from the shadows.

A tall, nasty-looking rat anthro had entered the greenhouse behind her. His fur was mottled, uneven, and clung to his bones like a moldy coat. In one paw, he held an ancient revolver, leveled squarely at her chest.

Dusk's knife didn't waver.

"You filthy rutting trespasser!" she snarled. "Who the yiff do you think you are? You break into my home and threaten me? I'll slice you open and let your guts decorate the floor!"

The rat said nothing. He advanced a step, slow and deliberate, the grin on his muzzle revealing yellowed teeth and something hungrier behind his eyes.

Outside, Reaper's eyes went wide.

"I — wait, what?!" he blurted, taking a step back in confusion. "The stairwell door was unlocked! I thought — I mean — if you didn't want anyone up here, you'd lock it, right?!"

His voice cracked, tail bristling with the sudden realization that this was no longer just a misunderstanding or awkward apology.

Something had gone very, very wrong.

Growling with frustration, Dusk's ears flicked and swiveled, struggling to track the chaos. That stupid raccoon just wouldn't shut up, even as the rat with the revolver edged her backward, her hands instinctively lifting in slow defiance. Each step brought her closer to the conservatory's front entrance. Then, from the corner of her eye, she spotted another figure slipping in through the rear door, shadow against shadow.

Her heart sank.

They weren't random. This was a coordinated intrusion. The way they moved, the silent efficiency — they were

Yakuza.

Sent by him, no doubt. She'd been expecting more harassment, yes. But this was escalation.

Reaper tilted his head, opened his mouth, then promptly shut it again, the tension finally registering. "Miss? Are you still there? I can leave if that's what you prefer. I just..."

Still holding the knife leveled at the rat's throat, Dusk snapped, "Would you shut up?! I didn't leave the door unlocked, you idiot!"

Her eyes didn't leave the gun, but she flicked them across the intruder's strange features, still unable to place the rat's gender. "I've been dealing with this dung-eating freak pointing a gun at my chest! The yiff must've picked the lock!"

Reaper gasped and made to rush forward, but didn't get far. A powerful paw clamped down on his collar, yanked him backward, and spun him around.

He blinked into the sunlit silhouette of a large, imposing figure: a panther, thickly muscled and grinning with jagged teeth. "Not so fast, rutting yiff," the feline snarled. "You and I have unfinished business."

From inside the greenhouse, Dusk sighed with exhausted disbelief. "What now?!"

Outside, Reaper squinted, temporarily blinded by glare. His breath caught as the shapes surrounding him resolved: half a dozen figures emerging from shadows and rooftop structures. They moved like ghosts, but they were clearly armed, except the panther still gripping his collar.

And Reaper knew that face.

A voice barked from behind the panther. "Release the 'coon and put your paws up, cat."

The unmistakable whine of a charging energy weapon rose behind the words.

The panther hesitated. Reaper didn't. He raised his paws slowly, head turning just enough to take in the broader trap.

"Uhh..." he muttered, voice half-shout. "I think we have a problem..."

Back inside, the rat with the revolver gestured

aggressively, motioning Dusk toward the door as its partner flanked her from the other side. She flicked her eyes between them, judging angles, timing, outcomes. None of it was good.

This was a losing hand.

With a growl of pure resentment, she dropped the knife and kicked it away. The rat barked something guttural, then jabbed the gun toward the exit.

With slow, deliberate movements, Dusk reached behind her, released the latch, and pushed the door open.

She stepped backward into the daylight, ears forward, hands raised.

"Oh, now you think we have a problem?" she bit off, dripping sarcasm. "What gave it away, captain obvious? The guns? The home invasion? Or the moron raccoon babbling like a cub in a blender?"

She stopped beside Reaper, still staring straight ahead as the Yakuza filed out of the greenhouse before her, their weapons leveled at her chest like hunting lasers on a pinned target.

Next to her, Reaper shrugged, lips twitching in a smirk. He glanced sideways at the panther still holding him, then down, grinning wider.

"Oh! Hey there, kitty. Didn't I tell you not to follow me? Your fuzzy little nuts must've grown since the last time I put you down." He paused, glanced lower again. "Hmm. Never mind. Still haven't dropped. Huh, buddy?"

The panther snarled, lips peeling back. His claws tightened on Reaper's collar and he shook him roughly.

"Shut up, you rutting yiff!" he snapped. "I should kill you where you stand! I was stuck in that alley for seven hours before someone finally found me!"

Looking just past the shadow, Reaper locked eyes with a towering anthro: a hyena, broad-shouldered and battle-scarred, his fur a sun-bleached mottling of tawny and gray. The hyena cleared his throat and spoke, voice smooth and just on the edge of dangerous.

"Ahem… Did I not just tell you to release the 'coon? I

won't ask again, cat."

The panther blinked, seeming to finally register the full extent of the figures surrounding him. His muzzle opened, closed again, then opened once more in sputtering confusion.

"I… Wait — who the yiff are these people?!"

"Yakuza," Dusk answered coolly, eyes never leaving the two still approaching her. Her posture remained tense, her weight shifted slightly toward the tips of her hooves, tail low but twitching.

The panther's ears folded back. "Oh, Naraka!"

In a blur of motion, he dropped Reaper like a sack of vegetables and took a hasty step backward, paws up and empty.

Dusk shook her head, one brow arched. "No. The Naraka are far more dangerous than these mangy thugs."

The big feline glanced toward her, brow furrowed, then turned to Reaper and tilted his head, a silent, furrowed expression that practically asked: What the hell is she talking about?

Reaper only shrugged.

Soon they felt it: a low, unnatural thrumming that settled in their chests like a subsonic warning. It didn't seem to come from anywhere, yet vibrated through the air, a bass rumble without a source.

Reaper's ears twitched, and he scanned the edge of the rooftop. There, opposite the conservatory, the air shimmered. Warped heat? No — a distortion. The light bent unnaturally.

He watched with rapt curiosity as the surrounding colors swirled and bent. Soon the phenomena began to resolve, straight lines emerged, darkening and sharpening into focus. The fluid shapes steadied, and the shifting haze coalesced into the outline of a hovering craft, like a ghost rising from the depths of some unseen world beyond the material.

Sleek. Angular. Flat black.

The craft rose, fully de-cloaking, bobbed as it lifted above the rooftop, revealing its undercarriage. The rumble grew sharper, higher-pitched, as if the air itself were being carved.

Blocking out the skyline behind it, the machine's surface gleamed like obsidian etched with light-absorbing hexes. On one side, a flag unfurled on a digital display: radiating purple and black stripes, with a polished circular emblem at its center. Crossbones framed a lion's head, metallic, regal, and unmistakable.

Reaper gasped, the memory snapping into place. That keychain. The polished trinket the feral lion had handed him not long ago. It was the same damned emblem.

Dusk sighed and shifted her weight, finally lowering her hands to rest on her hips. Her patience had been worn paper-thin.

"What the rut is happening now?!" she muttered, watching her two former captors gape at the sky like starstruck cubs.

Reaper's grin returned in full force. He pointed, even though Dusk was only a few feet away.

"I think it's that feral lion!"

At that moment, red dots flared to life, targeting lasers sweeping across the rooftop. Every weapon-bearing figure was painted in seconds, except for Reaper and Dusk.

There was a beat of stunned silence.

Then confusion.

Then realization.

Yakuza eyes widened. One slowly lowered his weapon. Another snarled, turning to the floating vessel, now hovering like a silent predator.

Dusk noticed the lasers on her captors' chests, and her temper snapped. She flung her arms skyward.

"WHAT FERAL LION?! And for that matter, who even are you?! Why do you keep talking to me? Why am I suddenly surrounded by feral nonsense?!"

Reaper spun to face her, exasperated and clearly enjoying himself.

"Okay, first — *slow down* — you just asked four questions at once. Second, turn around!"

156

He gestured grandly to the massive hovering craft behind them.

"Who else am I supposed to talk to, huh? The plants?! And third — you're welcome!"

Her mouth fell open. Dusk turned toward Reaper, hands planted firmly on her hips, tail twitching behind her in exasperation.

"I'm welcome?! You showed up here, no doubt hoping to get under my tail, then all of these rabid voles show up, and I'm the one who should be grateful? For what?!"

She jabbed a finger at his chest, eyes flaring. "Listen to me, you feral little trash panda, I didn't ask — "

Reaper's cheeks flared red beneath his fur as he spun to face her, ears twitching, both hands flapping outward with heated offense.

"Trash panda?! LITTLE?! Who are you calling a trash panda, you overgrown brown-nosed ru — "

A booming voice interrupted them both, loud, low, and amused. The sound originated from a deep-voiced male, broadcast over the gunship's loudspeaker, now hovering just above rooftop level.

"Ahem... Sorry to interrupt your lovers' quarrel, but we're under a bit of a time crunch. Dusk. Reaper. You two stay where you are, we'll have you safe in a moment."

A beat of silence.

"The rest of you — do not move."

Everyone froze.

The panther, sensing his opportunity, bolted toward the stairwell, but he barely made three strides before his muscles locked. With a twitch, he seized up mid-run, then crumpled face-first onto the gravel with a sickening thud. A wet stain spread across his pants as his limbs spasmed violently. Mouth agape in a soundless scream, he rolled to his side, drooling and convulsing.

Reaper sighed, arms crossing slowly. He shook his head, disappointed but not surprised.

"What is it with you? Are your ears too small to follow a simple command?" He turned, gesturing at the gunship

157

without looking.

"You heard that, right? He said 'don't move,' right?"

Dusk glanced sideways at Reaper, rolled her eyes, and muttered, "Both of you are idiots…"

Then her brow furrowed. "Wait. How the yiff does he know my name?!"

The voice from the gunship returned, ignoring her entirely. "Now that we've completed our demonstration, the rest of you may place your weapons on the ground. Move slowly. If you make the wrong move, the tracking AI will do the same to you as it did to your friend."

A brief pause.

"Once you've done that, slide them away with your feet."

Without hesitation, the Yakuza complied. In practiced, synchronized movements, they knelt, gently laid their weapons on the gravel, then nudged them away with slow, deliberate kicks. A dozen red targeting dots remained fixed on their chests and throats as they stood, paws raised, fur bristling with tension.

"Thank you for your cooperation," the voice continued, cheerful now. "Now that everyone's calmed down, we're going to play a game."

A few exchanged glances. No one moved.

"Starting with the Yakuza nearest the stairwell: when, and only when, I ask a question or issue a command starting with 'Simon says,' you will do as instructed. Is that understood?"

The Yakuza near the doorway — a tall canine with one ear chewed off — twitched, clearly unsure. He nodded quickly.

"Ah-ah!" the voice scolded. "I didn't say Simon says! What did I just say about only following instructions that begin with Simon says?"

The Yakuza froze, eyes wide, lips parting as realization hit. He stood rigid, mouth now trembling with unspoken apology.

The voice chuckled. "Now you're getting it. Simon says… smile."

158

The canine's attempt at a grin landed somewhere between a grimace and a sob. His jaw trembled as his eyes began to glisten, lower lip wobbling.

He was terrified — and smiling.

Laughter erupted from the gunship's loudspeaker, deep and feral, followed by the sound of someone being hushed in the background.

"Shhh! Ahem... Now, where were we? Oh yes! Yakuza number one, you may leave now."

All eyes snapped to the canine nearest the stairwell. He stood trembling, unmoving.

The voice continued, sing-song and cruel. "Very good, Yakuza number one! Now here's how this works. When Simon says so, you will turn, walk calmly to the stairwell, and leave this building. Do not collect your weapon. Do not return. This goes for all of you."

A pause.

"Simon says — is that understood?"

The Yakuza all nodded in unison, a silent ripple of obedience.

"Excellent!" The speaker chirped. "Simon says, Yakuza number one, you may leave."

Snickers followed from someone off-mic.

Without hesitation, the chosen Yakuza turned and walked, shaky but quick, toward the stairwell. The moment he was out of sight, the footfalls turned into a sprint. Behind them, the panther still lay twitching, moaning, and babbling nonsense to the gravel beneath his cheek.

The game continued, round by round, until all but one had departed. That unlucky soul tried to move too early and crumpled mid-stride, body seizing like a dropped puppet. He was dragged away, slumped and unconscious, by one of his fellows.

And then the rooftop fell silent.

Only Dusk, Reaper, and the half-conscious panther remained.

The gunship shifted, rising vertically, then pivoting mid-air with a hiss of compressed air and magnetic plates. It floated just beyond the roof's edge, turning to present its sleek port side, the matte-black hull adorned with that stylized purple-and-black striped emblem. A hatch slid open some feet behind the cockpit windows to reveal the a lion standing in the opening, mane tousled by the ship's downdraft.

Reaper's eyes lit up. His grin returned like it had never left.

"I knew it was you!" he shouted over the hum of the ship. "Are you healing okay? Also... how the rut did you know I was here?!"

Dusk stepped forward, fur rippling in the wind, her arms crossed tightly beneath her chest.

"Yes! How the yiff did you know I was here? How do you know my name?! And who the rut even are you?!"

Without missing a beat, she turned and jabbed a finger toward Reaper. "For that matter. Who the yiff are you?!"

Reaper opened his mouth to protest, but the lion lifted a paw in a calming gesture.

"Please," the lion said, voice now unamplified — calm, deep, and rich with command. "We have little time. My name is Captain Gyata. I serve with The Pride. This is my lander-slash-gunship, and I also command a frigate, the Claw, currently waiting for us in low Earth orbit."

He gave them both a look. Not aggressive, but firm.

"I have a proposal for each of you. But we can't stay here. Please. Come with me, and we'll discuss it safely aboard the Claw."

Dusk blinked, jaw clenched tight. She looked at Reaper. Then back to Gyata. Then again to Reaper, her ears angling forward with suspicion.

"How do you know this guy?"

Reaper shrugged, raising both paws in mild surrender.

"Couple weeks ago, he stumbled into the free clinic I was working at. Nasty knife wound. I stitched him up, cleaned the infection, and before I could finish a full sentence, he bolted."

Reaching into his pocket, Reaper produced a dull-metal

keychain and held it out. "Left me this. Figured it was just a trinket. Turns out it's a signature."

Dusk stepped forward, narrowed her eyes, and took the keychain between two fingers.

She studied the etched lion crest, then turned slowly to the gunship's hull, matching the symbol with the one painted on its side. She blinked, ears twitching. It was a perfect match.

Turning back to Reaper, then up to the lion standing above them, she exhaled hard through her nose.

"I don't even know this 'coon," she said, voice flat with disbelief. "You expect me to just hop in a gunship with both of you?"

Nodding solemnly, Captain Gyata stepped off the gunship and onto the rooftop, the wind from its engines fluttering the hem of his long coat.

"No. I don't expect you to trust me. But since your parents were murdered, it's been part of my duty to help look after you. I made a promise, Dusk."

He lifted one paw, pointing steadily toward the building and the penthouse she'd been watching for days.

"I'm sorry. But I cannot allow you to carry out your plans for the man in that building. There's so much more at stake than you know."

His voice cracked slightly as he stepped closer.

"Please, I beg you. I swear on your parents' afterlives, I'll explain everything — once we're safe."

Dusk froze. Her ears snapped upright. Her breath hitched.

Her eyes widened at Gyata's mention of the man — the target — she'd been watching so carefully. The bastard. The one she'd planned to silence.

But then her expression shifted: eyes narrowing, posture straightening. She stared at Gyata, scrutinizing his face as if seeing it for the first time.

"How... how do you know about him? About what I was planning?"

But even as she spoke, the answer came to her.

Of course he knew.

161

Of course The Pride would be watching. The Alpha Syndicate, its boss, the city's political rot — they were all connected. Her parents hadn't just been dissidents; they'd been thorns. Strategists. Freedom fighters. It all fell into place.

She clenched her jaw. Stupid doe. So naïve. You thought you were alone?

They've been watching you this whole time.

Before she could respond, the sound of rustling gravel snapped them all to alert.

All eyes turned as the panther — still twitching — managed to roll onto his side and groaned, attempting to stand. Gravel shifted beneath his claws as he staggered to his feet, eyes wild, breath wheezing.

Then he bolted.

Or tried to.

Again.

He got about five steps toward the stairwell before his limbs locked up mid-stride. His back arched. Eyes rolled. A strangled, airy moan escaped him before he dropped — flat on his face. Again.

He convulsed. Moaned. Soiled himself. Again.

Gyata turned, brow lifting in quiet disbelief as he looked from the trembling cat to the other two.

He gestured vaguely toward the twitching mass on the ground.

"…Why does he keep doing that?"

There was a beat.

Reaper and Dusk locked eyes.

And for the first time, perfectly in sync, they both burst out laughing — bitter, tired, and entirely unplanned.

Then, in unison, they shrugged.

CHAPTER 10 - BIG BROTHER.

"Sorry, Papa. I wanted to be here sooner, but a truck overturned on the bridge. How are you feeling?" The deep voice faltered, its owner's tongue tripping over the foreign syllables.

"Anya told me I must visit you alone today. She made it sound as though she wanted to give us time — but I think she is just depressed."

Boris's eyes opened slowly, peering up at the anthro standing at his bedside. His lids, heavy with exhaustion, struggled to lift. He attempted to sit up, smiling weakly as he blinked the haze of sleep away. "Anya will take time to accept it, Yuriy. Please forgive her."

As Yuriy helped him upright, Boris gestured toward a nearby chair. "Sit, my son. You know you don't need to speak Russian for my sake. Anya and I taught you English, and I know it flows easier from your tongue. Besides, I understand Ursine as well."

Sighing, Yuriy sank into the chair, switching to English. His baritone carried a low rumble, like distant thunder. "I know, Papa. I just want you comfortable. Your native tongue feels truer to you. I'm sorry I do not speak as well as you."

Boris shook his head vigorously, his brow furrowing as

the motion evoked a dull of pain in his temple. "Don't be sorry, you big furball. Your mouth was not shaped to speak the mother tongue. Perhaps after this life, you'll return as a human — then maybe you'll master it. But for now, I remain proud that my son honors me as he does."

His expression softened, a flicker of warmth lighting his weary eyes as he extended a hand to pat the young bear's broad shoulder.

Yuriy said nothing, simply holding his father's gaze. The huge anthro dwarfed the chair, his body pressed against its narrow wooden arms. Though not yet fully mature, he already stood an astonishing seven and a half feet tall. His coat gleamed white and dense, the fur catching the dim light like snow under a pale moon. He was every inch the son of proud arctic bear stock, his size alone commanding attention wherever he went.

"It wasn't so long ago that I found you starving and alone. Do you remember?" Boris's voice drifted with memory.

"You were large even then — nearly taller than me, and only ten years old. I'll never forget Anya's face when she first saw you. She could hardly believe you were real. And then, when you tried to greet her—" He chuckled hoarsely, coughing into his fist.

"She decided that very moment, at just six years old, that it was her mission to teach you proper Russian."

Yuriy's ears burned, his pale muzzle tinged with embarrassment at the memory. He recalled how his tongue stumbled clumsily over the formal greeting, the sounds collapsing into awkward growls.

The northern tribes had long since retreated into isolation, their Ursine dialect serving for daily speech. Few bothered with human languages anymore, environmental collapse having driven them deeper into the wastes. Yet even as a cub, Yuriy's hunger for knowledge was fierce. He collected words as other bears collected meat, pawing through scraps of paper, books, or anything legible he could find.

"I remember, Papa. Anya never stopped making it her mission to help me fit in. I don't know what I would have done without the two of you."

His heavy paws rubbed against each other as if seeking warmth. "When I was separated from my birth parents, I thought I would die in the north. But you found me. I thank you — and the heavens — for caring for me ever since."

Boris gave a rueful shake of his head. "I did nothing a kindhearted soul would not do."

Silence stretched between them, broken only by the faint hum of medical machinery. Their thoughts drifted across shared years and fragile memories. Finally, Boris spoke again, his voice subdued. "When we found you, I feared the captain would order me to leave you behind. The mission was already strained — supplies dwindling, two months from port. I tried to argue you'd be useful aboard, but he refused to listen. In defiance, I smuggled you into my quarters, teaching you where to hide. For an entire week I gave you my rations, until my weakness betrayed me. It was Polina who finally began to ask questions."

Sitting quietly, Yuriy listened as Boris spoke, his attention pinned to every word. Boris tilted his head, offering his son a faint smile. "Maybe I never told you this — but once Polina discovered you, she persuaded the crew to share portions of their own rations. Almost all of them defied the captain's orders just to keep you alive. You and your sister have been my everything since Anya's mother passed. I could not have managed it without that crew — and I could not have managed it without you."

A puffy redness swelled across his cheeks as Boris's eyes began to glisten. "All the years since we rescued you have been the best of my life. I couldn't have kept going without your shoulders to lean on."

Yuriy shook his great head and rose from the chair, stepping to the bedside. He folded his paw carefully around Boris's hand, the pads rough yet trembling with tenderness. "No, Pa... you could have done it better without me. You had Anya to look after. I only made things harder for you."

Boris cut him off with a sudden, firm squeeze of his hand — startling in its strength. "Don't say that. I miss the days

165

when we ran the boat together. You were so good at finding fish, I could never have done it without you. And the way you could fix anything you could get your paws around… Saints, I still don't know how you wriggled into those tight little spaces. But you always got us running again when I thought we were finished."

Yuriy shifted uneasily, torn between pride and sorrow, his paw tightening around his father's fragile grip.

Boris smiled again, though a strange lilt crept into his tone. "You were never meant for us, son. Your eyes were always on the stars. You loved talking about the spaceship you'd own one day — a polar bear in space! Honestly!"

The laugh that should have followed broke into a cough. Boris straightened with effort, waving Yuriy back even as his son leaned forward in concern. The lines of his face looked deeper to Yuriy now, carved like stone, each crease carrying a melancholy finality.

Yuriy's gaze fell to the hand resting in his paw. Once broad and strong, Boris's hands had been marked with thick scars — testament to a lifetime of labor. Now the skin hung slack, the blue veins standing like cypress roots breaking through thin soil. His hand trembled with every cough, cold against the warmth of Yuriy's paw.

It all came rushing back. Three months ago, Boris had first complained of fatigue and the weight that slipped from him day by day. At first, they had believed it only a cruel bout of flu, waiting for recovery that never came. After a month, Anya had convinced him to see a doctor. But by then it was too late. A week later, he had collapsed carrying groceries to their apartment. Yuriy still remembered the shock of finding him dazed and sweating, and the panicked dash to the emergency ward.

The diagnosis had landed like a blow: cancer, already too far spread. Treatments might prolong him a year, no more — but at the cost of draining every coin they had saved. Boris had only shaken his head, asking the doctor to leave. Then he had looked at Yuriy — and in that silence, Yuriy had begun to understand what the world expected of him.

166

Boris's voice drew him back to the present. "You always spoke of the early space heroes as though they were your friends. You told Anya and me about Yuri Gagarin and Valentina Tereshkova… and even those early Americans."

His lips curled slyly, a glint of mischief lighting his eye as his coughing faded. "Buzz Lightyear and Louis Armstrong!"

Chuckling softly, Yuriy flashed a toothy grin and rolled his eyes. "You know that's not their names, Pa! You always make silly jokes about the Americans, but they were only doing their jobs — just as ours were."

Yuriy had always defended the American astronauts with surprising zeal. His admiration for the early explorers of space had never been bound by borders or flags. Since cubhood he had looked to the sky, tracking the satellites as they glided past, their hulls catching the light of the distant sun. Sometimes he caught sight of frigates or cargo haulers drifting through orbit, their exhaust plumes flaring against the charged arctic gases above. Those sudden blossoms of artificial aurora still thrilled him — a new sky-fire born of fusion engines.

Even now, with his frame towering into adulthood, he felt he belonged up there among the stars. He dreamed of casting off in a vessel of his own, or signing on with some vast corporation to mine the bones of asteroids. In his youth, Boris had fanned those flames by bringing him model kits of famous ships. Yuriy would spend hours hunched over each one, thick paws surprisingly nimble as they set every piece with care. His small room had become a shrine of scale models, lined wall to wall with pristine, assembled craft — each one loved as though it were real.

He realized with a start that he had drifted into silence, lost in reverie. Returning his attention to the bed, he saw Boris sliding lower, his breath hitching. A ragged cough tore through him, bending his frame forward. The fit grew harsher, and before Yuriy could move, a nurse burst between them, brisk and commanding.

She scolded sharply, one finger stabbing toward the

oxygen tube lying slack on Boris's chest. "Your blood oxygen levels are dangerously low! You cannot remove this tube."

Huffing, she lifted it back into place, guiding the forked tips into his nostrils.

Boris complied, wheezing as she monitored the readout. She instructed him to breathe deep, again and again, until the alarms softened. Satisfied, she swept from the room in a practiced flurry, though her eyes flicked toward Yuriy with suspicion before the door clicked shut.

Boris let out a hoarse laugh, nodding faintly toward the door. "It seems you've gained an admirer."

He winked, then waved Yuriy back into his chair. His voice dropped to a sigh, carrying the tremor of something final. "I'm ready to see my Sofia again, Yuriy. She was so beautiful... I wish you could have met her. I see so much of her in Anya, it breaks my heart. She will grow to be just as wonderful as her mother... perhaps more."

Hours later, the sound of coughing pulled Yuriy from a shallow, unrestful sleep. The room was dim, lit only by the cold glow of medical instruments. Boris looked ghostly, his pallor like wax in the faint light.

Yuriy rushed to his side, paw outstretched. "Pa? Can I help? Do you want me to call the nurse?"

Boris shook his head slowly, lifting a trembling hand. When he drew it back from his lips, the palm was streaked red. He wiped it absently on the sheets, leaving a vivid stain that jarred against the sterile white fabric.

Yuriy's breath caught. He seized Boris's wrist gently, turning the hand upward. Blood bloomed across the creases of his palm, dark against the pale skin. Fear sharpened in Yuriy's eyes, his instincts urging him toward the door to summon help.

But Boris's other hand caught him weakly by the arm. Yuriy turned back, finding his father's gaze fixed on him — pleading, urgent.

"Stay..." Boris rasped, struggling to shape the words. "We don't have long." His lips worked dryly before he

168

flicked his eyes toward the glass of water on the tray at his side. With a faint gesture, he whispered, "I need your help…"

Quickly, Yuriy reached for the glass. His massive paw dwarfed the fragile vessel as he lifted it, careful not to crush it in his trembling grip. Tilting it toward his father's lips, he watched Boris sip, each swallow strained, each breath shallow. A cough threatened to rise, but Boris forced it back, throat working hard.

When he pushed the glass away, his eyes clung to Yuriy's, sorrow flickering across them before softening into a gaze full of quiet adoration. Then, with a weary sigh, he slumped against the pillow, eyes drifting up to the ceiling's dim glow.

"Please… look after Anya," he whispered, voice thready.

"Take her away from this place. Give her what I could not. Keep her safe… let her destiny be brighter than ours, Yuriy."

Slowly he turned his head. His eyes brimmed with tears, trembling as they sought Yuriy's face. A soft sob broke from him, barely audible. "Will you do this for me, son?"

Yuriy's throat closed around the words he longed to speak. He could only nod, again and again, tears streaking down his white fur. He grasped Boris's hand in both of his, pressing it close, unwilling to let go.

Boris held on with surprising force, fingers curled as though clinging to life itself. His grip carried urgency, desperation, but beneath it, a final trust. Yuriy met his gaze, understanding, and whispered through the ache in his chest, "Yes, Pa."

His voice shook, but pride steadied it.

Boris's grip loosened. His hand slipped from Yuriy's paw, falling limp against the sheets.

The silence that followed roared. Yuriy's ears rang, drowning out the hum of machines, the soft hiss of oxygen, the muted night beyond the window. The world seemed to tilt — and in its stillness, he knew.

***

Keys in paw, Yuriy stood motionless at the door for what felt like hours. His breath came uneven, fogging faintly against the wood as he leaned forward. Sniffling, he dragged his paw across his face, but the gesture only matted the tears deeper into his fur. With a frustrated growl, he dropped his paw back to his side, pressing his forehead against the door. A sob tore free, low and muffled, leaving him trembling — helpless, defeated.

How will I tell Anya? The thought burned through his skull. *Why is everything so painful?*

The sudden click of the latch jolted him. He staggered back, shoulders hunching, head bowed in resignation as the door creaked open. Through the narrow crack, Anya's face appeared — wide-eyed, fragile.

"Yuriy? Why are you—? …Yuriy?…" Her voice broke, catching on the question she could barely bring herself to form.

"Is it Papa?"

Yuriy's throat locked. He couldn't raise his gaze, couldn't give her the mercy of an answer. He stood there, mute and shaking, as though the truth weighed too heavily on his chest to speak.

Her questing words, an eternal loop in his mind — *Is it papa? Is it papa? Is it papa?… Is it…*

His vision blurred again, tears spilling freely. Through the shimmer, he saw her vanish from the crack of the doorway. The door drifted open on its hinges, slow and inevitable, as his tears pattered to the floor beneath him.

***

Moscow was far larger than Yuriy had ever imagined. After selling most of their belongings, he and Anya had boarded the Trans-Siberian hover-rail in Khabarovsk. Even at high speed, the journey had stretched nearly ten hours. To

Yuriy, it seemed impossible that such vast emptiness still lay between the remote town of his childhood and this sprawling metropolis.

They stepped down from the train into a vast glass terminal. Its ceiling arched high above them, latticed spires of glass and steel curving together like the ribs of some titanic creature. Through the transparent roof, shadowy silhouettes of passing craft swept overhead, their masses briefly veiling the gray sky. Moscow stirred and shifted beyond, a living city preparing for the evening.

The closing hiss of the train doors pulled Yuriy's ears back. The latch clicked, sharp against the cavernous acoustics. Anya, brushing grit from her jacket, and tilted her face up toward him.

"Did you contact the apartment manager already?" she asked, voice casual but carrying a thin undercurrent of worry.

Mentally switching gears, Yuriy flicked open his com, scanning for messages. "About an hour ago, but no reply yet."

He gestured with a raised paw toward a nearby pavilion thrumming with activity. "Are you hungry? That place looks promising. We can eat while we figure out our next step."

Soon they had settled into a corner table, shielded by the bustle. Yuriy offered her a small smile as she fussed with her bag. Extending one claw, he nodded at it. "Pass it here. I've got space. How's your stomach? Still giving you trouble?"

She handed it over, half-shrugging as she checked her com again. "It's better now that we're off the train. But yeah... I'm starving."

He chuckled, tucking the bag behind him, then tapped at the menu. "They have tacos. You can't resist tacos."

Anya giggled, her eyes brightening as she picked up the slim display menu. For a moment Yuriy simply watched her, content, ears tilting to the soundscape around them — the wheeled rattle of luggage, the murmur of languages, the occasional clatter of utensils. Snatches of conversation drifted past. And, as always, wandering eyes found him.

171

Some looks lingered with curiosity, others with unease, a few with open disinterest. Children were the boldest; more than once in his life, tiny hands had reached for his arms or legs, eager to sink fingers into the thick, snowy pelt that made him so conspicuous.

He had long since learned to dress in ways that concealed most of his fur. A coat, long sleeves, muted colors — the fewer reminders that he was not like them, the less likely strangers were to treat him like some exotic pet.

"I really like it here," he said at last, his voice low but hopeful. "Feels like our luck is about to turn."

Anya didn't look up, eyes still scanning the menu. "Yeah. It seems nice so far. Warmer, at least. And the food looks good."

Her reply carried more politeness than conviction.

Yuriy tried to hold on to his optimism. He turned back to the menu, a flicker of genuine hunger stirring as he spotted a salmon filet plated with roasted vegetables.

The rest of the day slipped past in much the same rhythm — simple, necessary tasks filling the hours. By evening he had finally reached the apartment manager, who agreed to show them the unit in the morning. They found a modest hotel nearby, paid for a single night, and collapsed into their room. Yuriy fell asleep almost instantly, exhaustion dragging him under as soon as his head met the pillow.

The next morning, they met with the apartment manager — a wiry man whose brusque tone was matched by an acrid scent that made Yuriy's nose wrinkle. He guided them through the unit with practiced indifference. The apartment itself was spacious enough, with tall windows and serviceable fixtures, but the walls carried every echo. The thrum of nearby traffic seeped in constantly, joined by muffled voices and the faint clatter of cookware from the surrounding units.

Friends had assured Yuriy that city noise faded into the background with time, but as he stood there, ears twitching at every intrusion, he wasn't so sure.

Later that day, Yuriy made his way to an interview at a

hovercraft garage only a few blocks away. The air there was thick with machine oil and hot metal, a scent he found grounding, almost comforting. The garage manager, however, seemed far less interested in Yuriy's knowledge of machines than in the sheer bulk of his frame. His questions circled back again and again to lifting, hauling, and "how much weight those shoulders of yours can handle."

It wasn't the role Yuriy had hoped for. Still, when the offer came, he accepted. The job promised steady work, and perhaps in time he could prove himself with a wrench instead of just raw muscle. For now, stability mattered most. Anya needed a chance to finish her schooling, and Yuriy would shoulder whatever he must to give her that chance.

***

Working at the garage had turned out to be duller work than Yuriy had hoped. In the three years since he'd started, the mechanics occasionally let him lend a paw on a craft, but most of the time he was moving crates of parts, hauling power plants, or keeping the floor spotless.

Only when the shop was shorthanded was he trusted with real repair work. Still, he gained experience on several models of hovercraft, though the title of *mechanic* remained just out of reach.

With Anya's graduation looming, his thoughts had shifted more and more toward the cost of university. His wages at the garage wouldn't be enough. If he wanted his sister to have the future she deserved, he'd have to find another source of income.

The garage had introduced him to all manner of characters, but none so persistent as Ivan — a wiry, fidgety stoat who owned far more hovercraft than one creature could reasonably need. Ivan was a regular, rolling in with some new upgrade request or damage from a race, and much to the irritation of the other mechanics, he always asked for Yuriy specifically.

The mustelid rarely left Yuriy to work in peace. He paced,

173

gestured wildly, and filled the air with chatter, while Yuriy mostly grunted or nodded. But Yuriy didn't mind him. Ivan tipped generously, and his stories — tall as they were — carried an infectious energy.

Today was no different. Ivan hovered just behind him as Yuriy adjusted the intake manifold of the stoat's prized Mojave speeder. The American-built craft gleamed in metallic red, its panels trimmed in sleek lines of black and gold — the kind of machine that demanded attention both in the hangar and on the streets.

"I won this beauty off some blowhard who thought he could beat me in his own craft," Ivan boasted, voice sharp with amusement.

"You should've seen his face when I left him choking on exhaust." He chuckled, the sound quick and mischievous.

"Course, afterward he claimed I cheated. They all do. Sometimes I even hire muscle just to pry them out of their cockpits." He leaned closer, eyes glittering. "And maybe I *did* rig the race. Who cares? All's fair in illicit street racing, right?"

Yuriy only nodded absently, ears angling toward the words but paws steadily at work. The manifold's O-ring kept slipping from its groove as he tried to set the airspeed sensor. With a rumbling sigh, he tore a strip of masking tape, pressed the O-ring into place, slid the sensor home, and cinched it tight. A quick tug freed the tape, leaving the seal firm.

"Ha! Clever!" Ivan slapped his shoulder, bouncing on his toes. "See? That's why I like you, big guy. You think with your paws."

He grinned, teeth flashing. "Tell me, Yuriy… you ever think about making some extra credits? Because I could use a mountain like you."

Rubbing his chin, Yuriy gave a slow shake of his head. "I don't think so. I'm a mechanic, not a bodyguard."

Ivan only laughed, flicking his com. A sharp chime in Yuriy's device announced a new contact. "A mechanic? Please. They've got you cleaning floors here. I have something else in mind. Why don't you come by the club

174

later? We can talk in private."

***

On his way home from the garage, Yuriy's com chimed with a new message. It was from Ivan. Reading it, his ears pricked with curiosity.

Ivan:

Come see me, I have another job for you.

Ivan almost never called him on weekends. In fact, he usually teased Yuriy for working Saturdays and insisted he use the time to rest. If he was summoning him tonight, it had to be something important.

Ivan's work had kept Yuriy afloat. With the stoat's help, he'd been able to pay Anya's college tuition and even set a little aside. The jobs weren't always the most savory, but Yuriy told himself they were harmless enough — moving hovercraft from one shop to another, running quiet deliveries, or simply standing at Ivan's side during tense negotiations. His sheer size was usually deterrent enough. Ivan carried a plasma pistol, but he much preferred not to draw that sort of attention.

On his way to the club, Yuriy tapped out a quick message to his sister. *Sorry, Ivan needs my help tonight. Won't make it home for anime night. We can do it tomorrow if you're up to it. Love you, sis.*

Her reply came almost instantly, as if she'd already been typing.

Anya:

Awww! I was really looking forward to tonight's episode! You better not have to work tomorrow! Love you more, see you later furball!

Yuriy smiled faintly as he pushed the club door open, her words glowing in his com. They had been watching anime together every Saturday for years, ever since he had shared his favorite series with her as a cub. Canceling their ritual gnawed at him, the guilt sitting heavier than usual.

Inside, the bar was nearly empty. He slipped onto a stool

and lifted a paw in greeting to the arctic fox tending the counter. Silvia returned the gesture with a bright smile, her fur catching the neon glow overhead. She poured tonic, honey, and a squeeze of lemon into a tall glass, sliding it smoothly across to him. As he took it, her fingers lingered against the back of his paw.

"Hey, sweety. Ivan'll be out in a minute — finishing some paperwork." She winked, lips curving into a playful smile, before sauntering away with deliberate sway. Yuriy's eyes betrayed him for an instant, catching the flick of her hips. Heat rushed to his ears. Guilt stabbed through him, and he jerked his gaze back down into the drink.

"Yuriy!" Ivan's voice rang out from the side doorway, rough with laughter. "Quit gawking at Silvia's rump and get back here, ya big yiff!"

Yuriy flushed scarlet beneath his fur as Silvia glanced back. With a sly grin, she lifted her tail, resting her paws on her hips before giving her rump an exaggerated wiggle. Ivan chuckled, clearly enjoying the display. Mortified, Yuriy mumbled a quick thanks for the drink and hurried after the stoat.

Ivan was already seated in his office, a smirk still curling his muzzle. He tossed a sleek fob onto the desk. "She's got a thing for big guys like you. Why haven't you gotten under that tail yet? Eh — never mind."

He flicked a second object onto the desk — a credit chip that clinked against the fob. "I need you to take the blue craft in the back to Slavin's shop. It's a little hot, so be careful. Here's your payment. Take Silvia somewhere nice after."

Yuriy shook his head, scooping up the chip and the fob. "She's not interested in me. And… you've never sent me to Slavin's shop before. Is there anything else I should know?"

Ivan's smirk faltered, replaced by something harder. He swiped at his com, the location data chiming into Yuriy's device. "Clueless about females, that's what you are."

His tone sharpened. "Anyway, Slavin doesn't know you're coming. Don't let him see you. He's a big yiff like you, only brown instead of pearl. I told him the drop would be on the side with the clown graffiti. Leave the craft, fob under the seat. That's it."

Leaning forward, Ivan fixed him with a pointed stare. "Don't let him see you. You're not even supposed to know his name. Send me a message when it's done — and then delete that contact. Got it?"

"Got it." Yuriy gave a short nod, then turned, broad shoulders brushing the doorframe as he left Ivan's office. His heavy paw lifted in a parting wave before he strode down the hall.

Silvia was waiting near the bar, her eyes catching him as he passed. He tried to offer her a polite smile, lifting his paw in a shy farewell, but couldn't quite hold her gaze.

Her grin spread wide, teasing, her tail swaying in a slow, deliberate rhythm. "Bye, sweety," she chimed, her voice ringing with a bell-like sweetness. She lifted her paw in a languid wave, hips rolling as she leaned on the counter. "Come back soon."

Yuriy's ears burned as he ducked his head and pushed through the club door, the echo of her voice following him into the night.

***

Startled by the vibration at his side, Yuriy rolled over on the couch and blinked at his com.

[Today - 04:02:55] - Urgent Message - Ivan: *We have a problem. I've sent a specialist to your apartment. Call up the info logs, you'll understand. Pack light and do not open the door until I message again.*

He sat up abruptly, paws braced on his knees, ears flicking toward the sound of a knock at the door. Another message chimed, sharper this time.

[Today - 04:23:22] - Urgent Message - Ivan: *The service man is outside. Password is "go-go gadget." If he answers incorrectly, run. Do not contact anyone directly.*

From behind him came a groggy voice. "Yuriy? Who's at

177

the door?"

He turned. Anya stood in the doorway of her room, rubbing sleep from her eyes.

"Get back in your room and lock the door," Yuriy whispered, pulling on his overalls. His tone left no room for argument. "Don't come out until I say it's safe."

Padding silently to the peephole, he peered out. A man stood there, hands raised to show he carried no weapon.

"Password?" Yuriy rumbled.

"Go-go gadget," the man replied evenly.

Cautiously, Yuriy unlatched the door and stepped aside. The stranger slipped in quickly, heading for the kitchen. In a practiced sweep he cleared the table, snapping open a case packed with sleek devices — compact scanners, holo modules, and rows of falsified IDs and fobs.

"Sit," the man said briskly, already powering up the machines. "We don't have much time. Your boss sent me to get you out of the country. She's not in trouble, but you are. The authorities think you're a suspect in a murder. They found a body in the craft you delivered two days ago — your DNA was all over it."

Yuriy froze, disbelief stiffening his frame. Then he stalked closer, towering over the man, voice low and dangerous. "How the hell do you know this?"

Unmoved, the stranger flicked on a holo projector. A shimmer of light blossomed into detailed logs, Ivan's name and signatures threaded throughout. "Believe me now?"

Yuriy's mouth went dry. He scanned the logs, fur bristling, then hurried to Anya's door and knocked gently. "It's safe… but I think I'm in deep shit."

"Please sit," the stranger pressed, gesturing to the chair opposite his equipment. "She can pack your bags while I explain."

He slid a folder across the table, his fingers flying over the machine's controls. "This is your new identity."

Anya's voice trembled as she stepped from her doorway, clutching her arms around herself. "What new identity? Who is this man, and what is he doing in our kitchen, Yuriy?"

Yuriy sighed, rubbing his temples. "I think someone tried to frame Ivan. But they used my fur, not his. The son of Petar Petrovski was murdered… and his body was dumped in the craft I delivered for Ivan."

Anya gasped, her hand clapped over her mouth. She began pacing in tight, anxious steps. "Petrovski's son? Yuriy, that's… that's bad. We need — "

Her words cut short as the man stood abruptly, pulling an envelope from his back pocket. His voice was flat, his eyes colder than before.

"That's why," he said, sliding the envelope onto the table, "we're going to kill big brother bear here."

CHAPTER 11 - THE BEAR MINIMUM.

It was days like this when Yuriy fantasized about shaving off every strand of fur. He imagined strolling into the shop the next morning bare as a seal, wearing nothing but cutoff overalls. Summer always made him curse his coat. The hovercraft shop turned into an oven by afternoon, its wide roll-up doors set squarely against the sun. Open, they invited the blazing light to pummel him directly. Closed, they trapped the air and radiated waves of heat like a furnace. Either way, Yuriy roasted.

With a heavy sigh, he tugged the chain to bring one of the doors rattling down. At least today, he'd get to leave on time.

Locking up behind him, he wiped sweat from his brow with the back of his paw. His coveralls clung to him, stiff with grease, dust, and the faint stink of old food he'd cleaned from a passenger compartment earlier. His paws ached, but his stomach reminded him he hadn't eaten since noon. On the corner between the shop and his apartment, the familiar bodega's neon glowed through the dusk.

Inside, the air smelled of sugar and machine coolant. Behind the counter, Cinder — the silver fox who worked the register most days — sat scowling at her com, tail flicking with irritation. Without looking up, she waved him on.

"Hi, Jake. We restocked the slushy machine yesterday. Strawberry and lime this time."

Ever since Russia, Yuriy had lived as *Jake*. He didn't like the name, but liking it had never been an option. He nodded at her greeting and eyed the machine. The undulating, snake-like swirl of colors wasn't exactly appealing, but the scent was tart and refreshing. The bodega had a habit of mixing odd flavors; most ended up looking strange, but sometimes they surprised him. He still thought about the mango-kiwi blend from last month, tan and ugly but delicious.

He pulled a cup from the stack and filled it, the machine gurgling noisily.

"Ugh! I'm going to kill him," Cinder muttered suddenly, flicking her com off with a swipe.

Her scowl melted into a smile as she looked up at him. "Jake, you seem like the kind of guy who knows how to treat a girl. Any chance you're looking for a nice, well-mannered silver fox for a girlfriend?"

Yuriy froze, paw still on the lever. Had he heard her right? He turned to find her watching him with a teasing grin. The slushy overflowed, dripping down his paw before he scrambled to catch it. "What? Oh — ha! Don't you usually have date night on Mondays? Did he... join yet another ether tournament or something?"

Her ears flattened as she sighed. "Yeah. I wanted to go to my favorite spot, but he keeps bailing. Honestly, I'm starting to wonder if he even *likes* females."

She hesitated, then blurted, "I mean, why would you date a vixen and never even try to get under — " She cut herself off with a cringe, her cheeks burning beneath her silver fur. "I'm sorry. You don't want to hear that."

Yuriy's gaze lingered on her longer than he realized. When her eyes met his, his mind went blank. He fumbled with a button on his overalls, then awkwardly shoved his credit chip toward her. "I... uh... I'm sure he'll come around. He can't ignore such a pretty vixen forever."

The words felt clumsy, and he knew it the instant her

181

smile faltered.

She scanned the chip and handed it back gently, her ears still tilted low. "I guess. See you tomorrow, Jake."

"Thanks, Cinder. See you."

Slushy in paw, he left the shop and stepped into the cooling night. As he sipped the sweet, oddly sharp mixture, his thoughts circled the conversation. *Was she serious? Why would she ask me out if she's already with someone? Wouldn't that be cheating?*

Confused, he rounded the corner toward his apartment, resolving to try again tomorrow.

Except for the occasional Sunday, Yuriy worked at the hovercraft shop every day. Afterward he usually stopped by the bodega to grab a slushy or a snack, then trudged home to his cramped apartment to lose himself in virtual reality or the latest fanfic.

Life was better now than it had been when he first escaped Russia. He no longer feared a knock at the door every night, but he missed Anya dearly. He often caught himself wishing she'd come with him, even knowing why she couldn't. Wanting didn't make the ache any easier.

The apartment lobby reeked of ammonia and stale despair. A vagrant rat anthro had taken up residence just inside the doorway, stretched across a pile of rags. Yuriy stepped over him without pause, ignoring both the smell and the hollow stare that tracked him from beneath a matted brow. Squatters came and went with the seasons, filling the lower floors when winter pressed in. Now that the heat had arrived, most drifted elsewhere unless rain kept them in. They sometimes hassled the smaller residents, but no one bothered Yuriy. His sheer size was deterrent enough.

When he'd first arrived in the UCA, a Russian contact had quietly steered him to this building. It was in poor repair even then, cracked plaster and rust-stained stairs, but the raccoon owner never asked questions and rarely raised the rent. Yuriy had stayed. The place suited him well enough.

Taking the stairs two at a time, he tossed his empty slushy cup into a bin on the third-floor landing. Tomorrow, he told himself, he'd buy another. Maybe Cinder would be working again, and maybe he'd find the nerve to ask her what she really meant. The thought sent a flutter of nervous heat through his stomach. The idea of dating was strange, terrifying, but perhaps it would be fun. By the time he reached his door on the fourth floor, he was smiling faintly at the image of holding her paw.

Inside, the air was thick and stuffy. His single-room apartment was orderly in its clutter: clothes folded into neat stacks on boxes, salvaged shelving units lined with odds and ends. Along the top of one shelf, unopened boxes of anime-like figures stood in a row like guardians, a poster taped to the wall behind them forming a makeshift backdrop.

The kitchen and dining "area" was little more than a battered table with a cold storage unit and a freestanding sink. A microwave and hot plate were stacked precariously atop the table. Beside them sat half a loaf of rice bread, a jar of peanut butter, and a tower of synth-paper plates.

As Yuriy crossed the room, his holo display blinked to life, icons pulsing with several unread messages.

"Squeakers, what are my messages?" he asked, pulling leftovers from cold storage.

A cartoon squirrel in a pirate hat popped onto the holo display. "Good evening, Jake. You have three unread messages. Two are advertisements. One is from Kael. Would you like me to read them all?"

"Delete the ads," Yuriy muttered, sliding his plate into the microwave. "Power seventy percent, three minutes. What did Kael say?"

As the microwave hummed and the plate began to spin, Squeakers continued. "Kael wants to know if you'll be on tonight, and he sent a link about the new *Final Morningstar 12* update. He says there's a new character you might like."

Settling on a stool, Yuriy scrolled the article on his com. The artwork of the new fox heroine made him chuckle. "Reply to Kael. Tell him I probably won't be on until late. I want to finish the fanfic I started yesterday. And… tell him

183

the new character looks just like the vixen at the bodega. I think she asked me out today. I completely blew it though. Pan, I suck at talking to females. I'm going to try again tomorrow. I just… worry about our size difference."

Seconds later, Kael's reply flashed across the holo.

Kael:

Haha! Let her worry about the size difference. If she thinks she can handle it, give her the chance! Even if nothing comes of it, you'll have fun. And what if she's into the same fanfics you are? You'd have someone to gab with!

The microwave chimed, pulling Yuriy back. At once, classic guitar chords filled the apartment. His AI had kicked off his nightly playlist, old rock from the 1970s. He smirked faintly and shook his head. "Reply to Kael. Who even says 'gab'? But yeah, maybe you're right. Wouldn't it be tails if she liked fanfics too? Still… I'm sure she was just joking. Anyway, I'll see you later tonight."

Dinner steaming on the plate, Yuriy settled in at his holo PC, calling up the fanfic he'd been reading. Outside, the city churned restlessly. Music thumped from a nearby dive, voices of sex workers floated through the alleys, dogs barked, sirens howled, hover traffic droned overhead. Six years of living here had dulled it all into background noise.

Most nights, Yuriy escaped into generative fantasy worlds where he could be anyone, do anything. He made friends, kept them across years and distance, even carved out a virtual sex life. He would have preferred the warmth of a real body beside him, but his shyness, his inability to read signals and act without second-guessing, had left him alone.

Still, he clung to hope. Someday, he told himself, he'd see Anya again. Or maybe he'd finally find a berth on a space freighter, just like he'd dreamed of as a cub. Until then, routine carried him forward: work, fanfics, fantasies, a life of small comforts tethering him to the possibility of something more.

***

The attendant spoke too fast for him to follow, frowning as Yuriy fumbled for his bag. Ever since transferring to the final transport craft, he'd struggled to understand the voices around him. Every sound, every word, felt unfamiliar. The crowded transport station pressed in from all sides. The blur of movement, the metallic tang of recycled air, the drone of announcements in languages he only half-recognized.

His first time outside Russia was almost terrifying. A new home, a new name, and if fortune held, a new life. For one moment, fear pricked through his chest like claws. He forced himself to breathe, straightening, and ignored the annoyed mutters of the smaller creatures bustling around him. Head down, he pushed toward the exit.

Several blocks east, doubt gnawed at him. Had he passed it already? The streets grew narrower, dirtier, the air thick with the smell of oil, damp concrete, and refuse. Crime left its marks in every alley: broken signage, discarded syringes, graffiti screaming for attention. The balance of the crowd shifted too. Humans grew scarce, seen only behind tinted hovercraft windows. The pavement belonged to anthros now, foxes, dogs, squirrels, some loitering, others hunched in whispered dealings. A few females stood provocatively at corners, one even calling out to him with a purr of invitation. Across the street, a human gestured impatiently at a squirrel anthro while a pair of vixens circled his craft. Sex work seemed to thrive here, as natural as the smell of ozone after rain.

Yuriy shrugged the unease from his shoulders and pressed on. At last he reached a weather-stained, six-story building. Its façade sagged with years of neglect, windows barred or broken, paint peeling in long gray strips. Several anthros lingered near the entrance, shifting aside as his massive frame squeezed through the entry door. The smell inside was close and stale.

A resident burst from an apartment down the hall, locking up hastily before rushing past without making eye contact. Yuriy read the number on the door and kept walking until he found the one he sought.

185

Apartment thirteen. A brass plaque above the peephole read *Management*. To one side, an old bulletin board sagged with faded restaurant flyers and handwritten notes offering odd jobs or items for sale.

He raised his paw to knock, but the door yanked open before he touched it. A small raccoon stood there, scowling. His arms folded across his chest, his voice sharp with a Russian accent. "What do you want?"

Startled, Yuriy blinked. "Oh! Uhh. Hi! My name is Jacob. My friend said you might have a room for me?"

The raccoon narrowed his eyes, giving him a slow once-over. "Why do you speak English? Can you not speak the mother tongue?" he asked, switching to Russian.

Yuriy shifted his weight awkwardly, ears twitching. "I... I speak poorly," he mumbled in halting Russian.

The raccoon's brows shot up. "Wait." Without warning he slammed the door. The sudden breeze ruffled the fur on Yuriy's muzzle.

Yuriy stood in silence, listening to the muffled sounds inside: drawers opening, cabinets banging shut, muttered words he couldn't make out. A moment later the door burst open again. The raccoon shoved past, tail lashing.

"Come," he barked, already heading for the stairwell.

Yuriy startled, then hurried after him. The climb left his breath short; by the time they reached the fourth floor his chest was tight with exertion. At the end of the hall the raccoon unlocked a door, pushed it open, then extended the key wordlessly.

"Rent due first Monday of month," he recited flatly. "Garbage chute, three doors left. Do not use Tuesday. Hot water works most days. Use hot plate when it does not. You may use cot until you buy bed. Return it to me after. I am here most days, except Thursday. Call the number on my door for emergency."

Without waiting for acknowledgment, the raccoon turned and strode back down the hall, leaving Yuriy standing alone in the threshold.

The apartment was little more than a box. A cot against

one wall. A sink that dripped faintly in the corner. Bare bulbs overhead, buzzing with artificial light.

Yuriy dropped his bag to the floor. For a long moment he didn't move, staring at the empty space that was now his. At last, the truth pressed down on him fully. He was alone.

***

The following months moved slowly for Yuriy. Work was difficult to come by; the language barrier clipped his words into awkward fragments, and his unusual stature made many employers hesitate.

His first job came with a trash service. The manager stuck him on the night shift at the incinerator, overseeing fleets of service bots. He was tasked with monitoring their routes and refilling their fluid reservoirs when needed. For a time it went well. But the bots were clumsy and inefficient, and Yuriy couldn't resist improving them. He tweaked their programs, adjusted their pathfinding. The results were smoother runs, fewer jams. When the manager caught him, however, suspicion drowned out reason. Accused of hacking the bots for "nefarious purposes," Yuriy was cast out.

The betrayal stung. He had meant only to help, yet people always seemed ready to assume the worst of him. Still, he pressed on. He cycled through restaurant supply, building maintenance, janitorial shifts — jobs that never fit, but he endured them anyway. Each time he did his best, and each time something went wrong, leaving him adrift again.

After nearly a year and a half of false starts, Yuriy stumbled upon a hovercraft repair shop advertising for help. His heart leapt; at last, something that aligned with his talents. But once again, reality soured. Like once before, they had hired him not as a mechanic but for heavy lifting, hauling power plants and cleaning bays.

Disappointed but determined, he made the best of it. The shop gleamed under his watch, and in time, the mechanics began to value his presence. Some even let him assist on difficult repairs, curious to see his broad paws work with

187

surprising delicacy. Slowly, word spread. Yuriy, the giant polar bear who could lift an engine block as easily as a crate of tools, also had a knack for fixing what others could not. Among the mechanics, he gained a reputation that felt more rewarding than any official title.

His wages remained low, but he finally earned enough to send a trickle of credits back to Anya. Though they couldn't stay in regular contact, he learned she had started university and even met someone special. That news struck him strangely. Pride mixed with a hollow pang of distance. It reminded him how separate their lives had become, how his own days stacked endlessly, one on top of another until they blurred into routine. Sometimes he felt as though he were living someone else's life, not his own.

In time, the manager trusted him to cover shifts when the shop ran short. The pay didn't rise, but the work grew more meaningful.

Then, one afternoon, as Yuriy finished tidying a work bay, an expensive-looking machine slid into the lot. Its frame gleamed with polished metal, but the front right corner sagged slightly — a flaw Yuriy's sharp eye caught at once.

The canopy hissed open. A slender figure stepped out, surveying the garage with calm authority. White and brown fur patterned his lithe frame; the long lines of his body carried the unmistakable sinuous grace of a ferret. His discerning gaze locked immediately on Yuriy. Without hesitation, he lifted a paw, gesturing him over, then pointed to the slouching craft.

Lumbering toward the ferret with an awkward look, Yuriy raised a paw, intending to point him toward the customer entrance. The smaller anthro waved him down impatiently.

"Hey, big guy! See that sag in the corner? She's been pulling right for the last three klicks. I'm in a hurry. Think you can fix it?"

Yuriy rubbed his chin, words tumbling out in a low stutter. "W–well, sir… usually that indicates a worn anti-g thruster, but the surge during deceleration makes me think it's a faulty sensor. This model runs a central orientation

188

gyroscope alongside individual gyros for each thruster. Since it's a rare unit, the proper part might take time to order, but I could bypass the thruster gyro and slave it to the central sensor through the feedback loop. That would stabilize it until the new assembly arrives."

The ferret's eyes widened. "You got all that without a diagnostic monitor?"

Yuriy's ears flicked back. "I... read a lot," he admitted sheepishly. "This model's compensation system fascinated me. It's prone to premature failure, but the ride comfort during high-speed banking is excellent."

For a beat the ferret stared at him, then laughed, sharp and surprised. "Alright, fella. Get me back on the airway in fifteen minutes, and I'll make it worth your while."

Yuriy bent to work. In less than five minutes he had bypassed the failed sensor and redirected the craft's processor to compensate. When he restarted the system, the craft leveled smoothly, its stance restored. With a few taps on his pad, he placed the replacement part on order.

"Okay, sir. The sensor should arrive in a few days. We'll call you to schedule the swap. Anything else in the meantime?"

The ferret only smiled, swiping his com. Yuriy's pocket buzzed with a new notification. "That's my address. Reach me when the part arrives. Better yet — reach me when you're ready to stop wasting your paws in a place like this. I pay better than these clowns ever will." He waved dismissively at the garage behind them.

***

Weeks later the same hovercraft slid into the lot, this time with a passenger. The ferret climbed out grinning, while a young gray squirrel in expensive clothes and a designer hat waved shyly from the cockpit. Yuriy caught himself staring, then rubbed the back of his neck as he returned the wave with a nervous smile.

"Hey, big guy!" the ferret called. "I hear the part came in.

189

Thought I'd drop by myself. So… did you think about my offer?"

Yuriy shifted his weight. "I don't know. They've treated me well here. I'd need to be sure you were offering long-term work before I made a change."

The ferret threw up his paws in mock outrage. "Long term? We've been in business twenty years. Positions don't open often, and I just launched a garage on the anthro strip. I need a foreman. You'd be perfect."

Yuriy walked toward the work bay, the ferret following close on his heels.

Closer to home, he thought. *I could even walk to work on good days. No more packed shuttles…*

He stopped at the parts desk, grabbing the new assembly. "Alright. Maybe. Could I stop by this weekend to take a look at your shop first?"

The ferret clapped his paws together, laughing. "Of course! I'll show you around myself."

***

The shop was only a few blocks from Yuriy's apartment. To his surprise, he liked it, it felt more personal, more alive than the corporate garages. He accepted the job.

Months passed. He began to settle in, though the work was unusual. Sable — that was the ferret's name — paid his workers under the table, and the clientele often carried the same air: wealthy, discreet, and not inclined to questions.

Most days Yuriy serviced racing craft, machines built for speed and agility, the kind favored in illegal street circuits. He had read the ether forums, watched the shaky footage that circulated online. At least two of the machines he'd touched had been spotted streaking through midnight races. One, he was sure, belonged to a snow leopard pilot whispered about as a legend among fans.

It didn't bother him — not entirely. His work itself wasn't illegal, and he wasn't the one flying them. But the feeling crept in anyway, a cold echo of memory. This, too, was how

190

it had begun last time: honest labor shading into something
else, until the line blurred so thin he could no longer see it.

CHAPTER 12 - MOST CALL ME JAKE.

The weather was unusually pleasant, and Yuriy found himself pausing mid-task to peer through one of the high windows above the shop's storage shelves. Sunlight streamed in, cutting across the clutter stacked on the upper racks. It wasn't low enough to bake him, nor so high that it blinded. Days like this made inventory almost enjoyable. Normally the poor arrangement of the tall shelves left too many shadows, forcing him to work with a flashlight. Today, the sunlight washed the room in clarity. He let it warm his muzzle for a moment before returning to the tally on his holo-pad.

The hum of a familiar power plant caught his ears. Sable's craft drifted into the garage lot with its distinct whine, settling into place with a hiss of thrusters. Sable often dropped by to shuffle paperwork, kindly sparing Yuriy from administrative tedium. All Yuriy usually had to do was scrawl a signature on supply orders.

The driver's canopy popped open, and the ferret climbed out with his usual brisk confidence. Moments later Maple followed, slipping gracefully from the passenger side. Sable's gray squirrel girlfriend seemed to accompany him everywhere — and just as often, she found ways to entertain herself with idle chatter and casual flirtation. Yuriy rarely thought much of it, though his coworkers often teased that her attention lingered on him longer than on the others.

He raised a paw in greeting as the pair entered through the wide front doors. Sable gave him only a curt nod before heading toward the back office. Maple, however, bounced along in his direction, her grin broad and bright.

"Hi, Jake!" she sang, her voice rich with playful energy. "Sable said you were working today, so of course I had to come see you. What are you up to?"

Yuriy glanced at her shyly, marking another line on his pad. Maple was striking, perhaps too much so for his comfort. Her body was all slender curves and lively energy, her long furred tail flicking behind her like a banner. Gray fur shimmered under the lights, shorter and smooth along her muzzle and chest, thickening across her middle, then tapering down again at her legs. She carried herself with an easy confidence, never boastful, never haughty — which somehow made her even more magnetic.

Her eyes drew him most of all: deep onyx darkened with flecks of silver, bright and dangerous. Her smile was quick and dazzling, showing incisors kept short enough to charm but long enough to remind him of her nature.

And, as always, her clothes made her seem like she had stepped out of a magazine. Today it was tailored jeans designed for her species, fitted to hips and thighs, the back hem cut to allow for her tail. Trinkets dangled from her belt loops, sparkling with each bounce of her step. A crisp white blouse tied just above the waist left a glimpse of toned belly visible, her purse hanging more like an accessory than anything practical.

He swallowed, ears flicking, and answered with a shrug. "You know I do inventory around this time every week, Maple." He scribbled another figure on his pad, trying to steady himself. "Did Sable end up getting you that purse you were raving about?"

She hopped up beside him in one smooth motion, perching on a cleared shelf. Her long, bushy tail swayed out

193

behind her, brushing lightly against his arm. The touch sent a tingle crawling up his spine. She leaned forward on her paws, smiling down at him, her voice warm and teasing.

"Oh, that old thing? He did, but you know me — I always find something else to rave about."

Giggling, Maple bounced in place, her tail flicking with playful energy. "Hehe! Yeah, I tickled him just the right way, if you know what I mean." She winked, voice dripping with innuendo. "He even got me the red one! I would've settled for black, but he wanted to spoil me."

Tilting her head as though pondering something important, she lifted her paw to her chin. Her tail arced, brushing softly along the line of Yuriy's lower jaw. "You're so tall... I'm not used to seeing your face this close. Pan, I never realized how thick your jaw muscles are. And your eyes — I didn't know they were so pretty."

Heat flushed Yuriy's cheeks. He shuffled in place, clutching his holo-pad a little too tightly as he marked down another row of parts. When he risked a glance at her, he found those shimmering onyx eyes fixed on him, following every shift of his paw.

"I'm just a polar bear," he muttered, ears flattening as he adjusted the holo-pad. "There's nothing special about me."

Maple shook her head hard enough for her earrings to jingle. With a flick of her tail, she smacked him lightly on the arm. "Don't be silly, Jakey. You're special to me." She leaned forward, voice lowering with conspiratorial sweetness. "So tell me, what do you even do when you're not slaving away for Sable? Any girlfriends hiding in that big heart of yours?"

Yuriy shook his head quickly, dodging the question as he logged another figure. "Mostly... I read fanfics, play VR with my ether friends. Kael and I run Final Morningstar 12 a lot, but last night I started a new fanfic, so... we didn't play much."

Her ears perked. "Oh! You mean that snugging wolf that used to work here? Whatever happened to him, anyway?" She leaned over, peering nosily at his holo-pad as if the

194

numbers meant anything to her.

Yuriy risked another glance — and his heart jolted. Her blouse had fallen open too far, the curve of her breast fully visible, a dusky nipple peeking from behind thin cotton. He turned sharply back to his inventory, pretending not to see, though his pulse thudded in his ears. This wasn't the first time. Maple always seemed careless, "accidentally" flashing glimpses she never apologized for. He remembered the time she'd bent to pick up something from her purse, tail hiked high, giving him a sight of anatomy he hadn't even known existed until that moment.

Uncomfortable, he shifted to the next shelf, speaking over his shoulder to distract himself. "He left to go to school in Massachusetts, remember? MIT took him on a full scholarship."

He paused, grimaced faintly, then gestured awkwardly toward her chest without quite looking. "By the way... your blouse is a little loose. You might want to check for a missing button."

"Oh rut! Sorry, Jake, I'm such a klutz sometimes. These buttons always come loose and I never notice." Maple giggled, fumbling at her blouse with exaggerated difficulty. Her small paws slipped against the fabric. "Salted cucumber! I can't get it. Jake, do you think you could... help me? Please, snuggie?"

Yuriy stiffened. He glanced over his shoulder to find her leaning toward him, collar tugged forward, eyes glinting with playful expectation.

"I... don't..." he stammered, ears twitching with confusion.

"Come on, Jake," she pleaded, dragging out the word please as her eyes went wide and soft, her best attempt at a helpless, puppy-eyed look.

Reluctantly, he shuffled closer, paw rising to the open collar with the utmost caution, as though it might bite him. His claws brushed the fabric, clumsy against the tiny button —

"Maple!" Sable's sharp voice cracked across the shop.

195

"Stop bothering Jake and get back in the craft. I need him in the office to sign some paperwork."

Yuriy's paw froze. Relief washed through him as he stepped back, offering Maple a sheepish smile and a tilt of his head. "Sorry, Maple. The boss is calling. Maybe he'll button it for you while I take care of the paperwork?"

He turned toward Sable, catching the ferret leaning against the office doorframe. His arms were folded, his posture casual, but his expression seemed faintly strained, a shadow pulling tight at the corners of his mouth.

Fifteen minutes later, Yuriy signed the last of the forms. He raised a paw in farewell as Sable and Maple passed through the doorway. Maple turned just before climbing into the craft, giving him a lingering wave and a sly wink before vanishing into the passenger seat.

Alone again, Yuriy exhaled a long breath and shook his head, incredulous. He rubbed his temple, the ghost of her touch still prickling along his fur, before forcing himself back to the task he'd been working on before their arrival.

***

"Hey, what were you up to?" Dusk asked as she slid into the seat beside Reaper, a steaming cup of tea in her hand. She set another cup near him, nudging it across the console.

At the intelligence holo, Reaper scrolled absently through streams of figures and reports. He shrugged, claws clicking lightly against the cup as he wrapped his paw around it.

"Thanks. I was just—" He froze mid-sentence, glancing at her in a double take. His brow furrowed as he tilted his head. "Wait. Excuse me? I thought I was supposed to be some kind of creep you wanted nothing to do with. Now you're... bringing me tea?"

Dusk lifted her own cup with both hands, blowing gently across the surface before taking a sip. Her dark eyes lingered on him, sharp and unreadable. One brow arched. "The jury is still out on whether or not you're a creep. And to be fair, the evidence hasn't exactly been in your favor. Considering you stalked me to my home, and then helped facilitate my kidnapping from said home…"

Heat flared beneath his fur, his ears burning as he shot her a wide-eyed look. "Now wait just a damn minute! I wasn't stalking you. I thought you might be in trouble. You bolted out of that alley like someone was chasing you. What was I supposed to think? I didn't know any of this was going to happen, I just—"

His protest faltered as Dusk giggled, lifting her hand to cover her muzzle.

Reaper growled under his breath, jaw tightening as he turned back to the holo, scrolling through documents with renewed intensity. "Very funny. What do you actually want, Dusk?"

Her smile softened as she took another sip. "Honestly? Just thought you might like some tea. You've been up here all night, buried in whatever it is you do."

She glanced toward the officer's bridge, nodding toward the empty captain's chair. "Besides, the captain turned in an hour ago and left me staring at star charts until my eyes crossed. Then I heard you back here muttering to yourself, and I figured I'd better break the ice before things got any more awkward."

Reaper finally tore his eyes from the holo and fixed them on Dusk, one brow arched. "You avoided me for two days, and I'm the one making things awkward?" He gestured at her teacup, then back at her, incredulous.

She took a long sip, then set her cup down with deliberate calm. Her stare was blank, but her tone dripped with acid. "Oh, dear, please forgive me. I should have come running sooner to soothe your injured pride."

She folded her hands primly, her words almost sing-song. "After all, it must have been so difficult for you — being rescued by Gyata moments after a gang of ferals tried to kill us both. Truly, how could I ever repay such bravery?"

Reaper raised both hands in surrender, sighing as he shook his head. "Alright, alright, I get it. Sorry. Guess it's been a rough stretch for both of us. Truce?" His lips twitched into a small, sheepish smile as he extended his paw across the console.

For a moment she simply stared. Then, unexpectedly, her expression softened. She placed her hand in his. The contact jolted him, a thrill shooting up his arm before he could stop it. Her fur was soft against his pads, her scent — warm and floral — caught him off guard. His gaze snagged on the deep rose of her lower lip before he even realized where his thoughts had gone.

"Reaper?" Dusk's voice cut through gently, her fingers limp in his paw. "You can let go now."

His ears burned. He released her quickly, coughing into his fist as he twisted back toward the holo. "S-sorry." He stared at the teacup as if its decorative lines suddenly demanded deep study.

She let him squirm a beat, then tilted her chin toward the glowing display. "It's fine. But you still haven't said what you're doing over here."

Reaper exhaled and rolled his shoulders, trying to play it off. "I was digging through the intel, looking for more on the thugs that ambushed... us." His voice hardened slightly. "Something doesn't add up. Why would they care about you in the first place?"

The question struck her. Her shoulders dipped, her mouth pulling tight as she lifted the cup again. She drank slowly, as though weighing the decision to answer, then set it down with a soft click.

"There's a lot you don't know about me, Reaper." Her voice had lost all its earlier playfulness. Leaning back, her eyes went distant, heavy with memory. "I've been hunting the leader of the Alpha Syndicate for most of my adult life. If you hadn't shown up when you did... he'd already be dead."

Reaper froze, his paw hovering mid-scroll over the holo. Slowly, he turned to stare at her, eyes wide. "You were going to assassinate him?"

Dusk lowered her gaze to the teacup, her fingers tightening around it. "My parents were murdered by the
198

Alpha Syndicate," she said softly. "The only reason I'm alive is because I went on a date instead of heading home that night." A single tear traced her cheek before she wiped it away, her jaw setting as she looked back at him. "I seduced a powerful Yakuza, built a relationship with him, just to get closer to the Syndicate. If it hadn't been for the thugs he sent after me, I'd be free of this weight by now, Reaper. It was almost finished."

The silence that followed was heavy, fragile. Both of them sipped their tea, each avoiding the other's eyes, letting the quiet stretch.

At last, Reaper cleared his throat and turned back to the holo, his claws flicking across the interface. "When I first started digging into the Yakuza in this city, I found something odd. They've got ties to the street races, but it doesn't look like they care about the races themselves."

Dusk slid closer, her chair scraping faintly. She nodded. "I don't think they did. They funded the pilots, trapped them in endless debt. The races were cover. A distraction. I just… hadn't figured out for what."

Reaper's claws tapped faster. "Hmm. You know Furry Town, right? There's a garage there — serviced a lot of race craft. I kept coming back to their invoices. Something about them didn't add up." He pulled one onto the holo, zooming in. "Here. See that line item? No shop that size would need this much of that catalyst."

Dusk leaned in, her auburn hair spilling over her shoulder as she studied the document. Reaper's chest tightened, his heartbeat jumping at the subtle brush of her scent. He shifted slightly, giving her room, but his eyes lingered a beat too long on the curve of her profile.

He forced himself to clear his throat. "That catalyst is used for bio-AI units. Usually in minuscule amounts. They've ordered hundreds of liters."

Her head tilted toward him, her gaze catching his, eyes sharp and searching. "I'm sensing a but."

Reaper flicked his claws across the holo, replacing the invoice with a dense page of chemical schematics. "Before

199

we ended up here, I was running a few biohacking experiments — trying to duplicate some of Diggercorp's results. Specifically, boosting neural activity to enhance intelligence. One of the ways they managed to hybridize feral brains with human ones was by enhancing the DNA itself." He pointed to a highlighted compound on the holo. "This chemical was key. It's a catalyst in the transformation. Not easy to make. Harder to acquire in bulk. The only legal market for it now is in bio-AI manufacturing."

Dusk leaned back, arms folded, brow creasing. "So why would a hovercraft repair shop need it? If it's just a catalyst?"

Reaper's grin spread, sharp and eager. "Exactly the right question." He swiped again, overlaying another document. "On its own, they wouldn't. But combine it with this — and you get the substrate material that most bio-AI neural nets require. Long-term, it's cheaper to buy them separately and mix them right before use. Otherwise the substrate degrades too fast."

He switched back to the first invoice, excitement dimming into suspicion. "And here's where it gets strange. This garage ordered far more catalyst than they could ever need. Enough to last years. Then the day after the delivery was due, the order was cancelled. Reason given: non-delivery."

Dusk tilted her head. "So maybe they realized they'd made a mistake? Over-ordered and pulled the plug?"

Reaper shook his head, calling up a security feed. A grainy dock came into view, a cargo craft resting idle in its cradle. A hooded figure slipped into frame, glancing around nervously before climbing aboard. The feed flickered, then showed the craft powering up and lifting away with the hooded figure at the controls.

"No mistake," Reaper said quietly. "That shipment was stolen. And it wasn't the only one. Different garages, different orders, same result."

Another feed replaced the first. This time, the camera caught a large, white-furred figure — massive, with broad

200

shoulders — standing with his back to the lens. A much smaller anthro stood nearby, gesturing animatedly.

"I traced most of the orders back to him," Reaper murmured. "A polar bear. Jacob. But here's the thing — none of the records list him as an owner or partner. He's not in charge of anything. Just a garage hand, paid under the table."

Dusk narrowed her eyes, studying the frame. Her breath caught as another figure entered the shot: a gray squirrel, slim, her body language overtly playful. She touched Jacob's arm, leaning close, until a male ferret appeared, seized her wrist, and tugged her firmly aside.

"Who's that?" she asked.

"Not sure about the squirrel," Reaper admitted. "But the ferret? Looks like a manager. Every time she flirts with Jacob, he shuts it down. Watch this."

He brought up a second feed, this one closer to the garage office. The ferret waved the polar bear over. Jacob ducked through the doorway, squeezing past him, then emerged a few minutes later and went straight back to work as though nothing had happened.

Dusk leaned forward, her eyes narrowing at the holo. She pointed to the feed where Jacob had returned to stacking parts like nothing had happened. "Did you catch that?"

Reaper frowned. "Catch what?"

"The squirrel." Dusk tapped the screen with her claw. "She's not actually interested in the bear — she's using him. She wants the ferret to see her flirting, to needle him. Look at her clothing. Designer cut, pricey fabrics. That kind of taste doesn't come from a garage worker's paycheck." Her voice dipped, firm and certain. "But a manager? A ferret with power? He could afford her."

Reaper rubbed his chin, swiping back through the feeds. His eyes widened suddenly, realization snapping into place. "The ferret isn't protecting the bear... he's setting him up. The orders, the shipments, the paper trail — it all points at Jacob, but he's just muscle in the shop. The ferret's making him the fall guy."

Dusk nodded slowly, lifting her cup and sipping with deliberate calm.

Reaper sat back, the glow of the holo reflecting in his eyes. His tone dropped, quieter, edged with calculation. "You know... I think we could use him."

He paused, flicked an ear, then tilted his head. "I have an idea."

Abruptly, he stood and started toward the exit, speaking over his shoulder as he went. "If Gyata asks, tell him I've got a meeting with our newest crewmate."

***

Yuriy sighed as he locked the shop door. The day had been long, but at least the weather had been kind. What really kept his steps light, though, was the thought of Cinder. He hadn't been able to stop replaying her offhand question about whether he was looking for a fox girlfriend. At the time, she hadn't seemed serious... but the more he thought about it, the less certain he was. *I hope she's working tonight. Even if she was joking, I like her. Maybe I should just ask her outright...*

He turned the corner toward the bodega, only half-noticing the odd rumble of a hovercraft engine somewhere overhead. He dismissed it — another stabilizer loop rattling itself apart — and pushed through the door. His heart jumped when he saw her behind the counter, nose buried in her com, ears twitching faintly with concentration.

He hesitated, then raised a paw. "Hey, Cinder."

She blinked up, distracted at first, then offered a small smile. "Oh, hey, Jake! Did you say something?"

Flushing, Yuriy realized he'd spoken too softly. He cleared his throat, shifting his weight. "Just saying hi. Any new slushy flavors today?"

She shook her head. "Nope. Same as yesterday. Probably the same all week."

Yuriy nodded, passing by the counter, trying to work up the nerve. *Come on, just ask her...* "Okay, thanks. So, uh...

202

still having trouble with the boyfriend?"

Her ears flicked up at the question. She gave a half-shrug, starting to answer — "He's still—oh, careful, Jake!"

Before he could react, something barreled into his side. Cold wetness splattered across his overalls. He looked down to see a raccoon anthro sprawled on all fours, an overturned slushy dripping onto the floor between them.

The raccoon lifted his head, eyes widening as they crawled upward — from Yuriy's boots to his towering frame, and finally to his face. He scrambled upright, snatching a handful of synth-paper napkins. "Oh, Pan! I'm so sorry, mister bear! I wasn't looking. I tripped! A-are re you okay?!"

Yuriy chuckled despite the sticky chill, raising his paws as the raccoon tried to dab ineffectively at his side. He set a big paw gently on the smaller male's shoulder. "Don't worry about it, buddy. These coveralls are practically waterproof after a day at the garage. You okay? Didn't break anything, did you?"

The raccoon froze, staring up at him in disbelief. Then he grinned nervously. "Huh? Oh — yeah! I'm fine. I half-expected you to eat me for dinner, you're huge! Don't worry about me. I'm the one who interrupted. Name's Reaper." He quickly wiped his paw on his jeans before thrusting it out.

Yuriy raised a brow but reached out carefully, engulfing the smaller paw in his own. "Jacob. But most just call me Jake. I was about to get a slushy… think there's any left?"

Reaper blinked, glancing from the puddle on the floor to the humming machine at the back of the bodega. "Oh — yeah! Plenty. Let me grab you one, after I clean this mess up. On me." He turned toward the counter, ears angled back sheepishly. "Uh, miss? Could I borrow a mop?"

Cinder was already watching with a bemused smile, tail swishing as she glanced from the soaked polar bear to the flustered raccoon.

Giggling, Cinder shook her head and waved them off. "Go ahead and get your slushies, I'll handle the floor."

Her brush of tails and the quick swish of her hips carried

her out of sight, mop in paw. Both males immediately erupted into overlapping protests — "No, let me!" "I made the mess!" "At least let me pay for it!" — until their voices tripped over one another in a ridiculous tangle. By the time she vanished into the stockroom, they fell quiet, glanced at each other, and shrugged sheepishly before shuffling toward the machine.

Reaper broke the silence first, flashing a grin. "Seriously though, this flavor's good. Before I painted you with it, I got one sip."

Yuriy chuckled, rubbing at his damp side. "That's half the reason I came in tonight. Cinder's always mixing up something new. They look awful but... they taste amazing."

Stopping at the machine, Reaper grabbed a cup from the stack. He noticed the polar bear's gaze drifting back toward the counter where Cinder had disappeared, and his grin sharpened knowingly. "You like her, don't you?"

Yuriy jolted, ears pricking as he turned down at him. "Huh? No! I mean... yeah, she's nice. I was just — " His voice faltered as he fumbled for another cup. "She's got a boyfriend. But she said they were having trouble. Then yesterday she said something that made me think maybe... maybe I should ask."

Reaper plucked the cup from Yuriy's paw, filling it himself with practiced ease. "Yeah. I know that look." He tipped the cup toward him in mock salute. "Tell you what. Why don't you go help her with the mop? I'll handle the drinks."

***

Yuriy hunched his shoulders, ears drooping. "I feel so dumb now..."

Reaper tilted his head, flashing an easy grin. "What do you mean? You did great, big guy. At least she didn't string you along. That's something. Honestly, I think that means you still have a shot if things with her boyfriend go south."

Taking a deep breath, Yuriy let it out in a heavy sigh, his chest deflating. "I guess... I should've taken her more

204

seriously yesterday. Maybe then she wouldn't have changed her mind."

Reaper, barely tall enough to reach, patted his broad shoulder. "Don't worry, things have a way of working out." He gestured toward an empty bench along the sidewalk, hopping up onto it with casual ease. "Come on, sit. I've been meaning to ask about you anyway. You've got quite the... outfit."

Yuriy lumbered down beside him, the wood creaking under his weight. He took a long pull from his slushy before answering. "I work at a hovercraft repair shop down the road. Get to put my paws on a lot of hot machines. It's pretty tails, if I'm honest. But sometimes... it's intimidating."

Reaper leaned forward, brows knitting. "Intimidating? How?"

Yuriy rubbed the back of his neck. "Well, the boss gives me a lot of responsibility. Mostly it's fine — repairs, inventory, things I know. But sometimes I've got to sign for supply orders. I don't really know much about that side of things."

Reaper blinked. "Wait, *you* sign for the supplies? What kind of orders?"

Yuriy shrugged, eyes drifting toward the glow of streetlights across the road. "He says it's because I'm technically the manager, the only one authorized to make purchases. Usually it's just parts, but sometimes the shipments are pretty big."

Reaper's ears twitched, his smile thinning. "So... you're the manager on paper, but he does all the real paperwork for you? That's... odd."

Yuriy shifted in his seat, fumbling with a button on his overalls. "I guess. It pays well, it's close to home. I haven't asked too many questions." His gaze flicked back toward Reaper, uncertain. "Do you think... maybe I should?"

Reaper leaned back on the bench, his tone dropping. "Honestly, big guy? I'd be careful about signing *anything* if I were you. Once your name's on paper, you're the one on the hook. Sometimes that comes with obligations you don't even know about. You ever wonder why your boss won't just sign his own forms — why he needs *you* to do it?"

Yuriy shifted uncomfortably, claws worrying the fabric of his overalls. "I don't really know. He just… seems like a busy guy to me."

Reaper studied him, sipping his slushy, then fixed him with a level gaze. "Does he ever strike you as shady? Illegal dealings? I mean… does he pay folks under the table, cut corners, pull anything slick?"

Yuriy's eyes flicked toward him, guilt flashing there before darting away. He leaned closer, lowering his voice to a whisper. "I'm paid under the table. He said it would be safer if he handled it that way. I… didn't ask why. Honestly, I was afraid to."

Reaper rubbed his chin, the humor slipping from his expression. "Hmm… Listen, Jake. I hate to be that 'coon, but you need to watch yourself. I've been keeping tabs on this neighborhood. The Yakuza are rooted deep here. If I'm right, your boss is tied into things you don't want to be mixed up in."

He reached into his pocket, pulled out a small metal trinket — its surface embossed with a lion's head sigil. It looked like a charm, harmless, but its weight carried intent. Reaper pressed it into Yuriy's paw with a quiet smile. "Here. I think you're wasted in that shop. You've got talent. If you ever need a way out — or a way up — we could use someone like you on our ship. My com's on the back."

Yuriy turned the trinket over in his paw, fur bristling. "Ship? What do you mean, ship?"

Reaper was already rising, brushing dust from his jeans. His eyes gleamed with something between mischief and promise as he jabbed a finger skyward. "She's a beauty, Yuriy. I'd love to show you around sometime."

Before Yuriy could press further, Reaper had already started walking back down the street, tail flicking behind him. A few paces later, he called over his shoulder with a grin in his voice. "Don't lose that token, big guy. It might save your life."

Yuriy stared down at the trinket again, his heart hammering. The lionhead sigil glinted faintly in the streetlight.

Realization crashed over him. He gasped and whipped his head up, scanning for the raccoon. But Reaper was gone, melted into the night.

CHAPTER 13 - DON'T TEASE THE BIOLOGICALS.

The bed was too short — most beds were — but Yuriy had long since grown used to it. That was part of being large in a world built for smaller bodies: chairs cut into his thighs, doorways brushed his ears, mattresses never quite fit. He couldn't even remember the last time he'd been shorter than his own bed.

He thought of this as he rolled onto his back, feet dangling well past the frame, eyes fixed on the ceiling. The dawn light crept across chipped paint, illuminating old nailheads poking through like scars from another age.

He remembered reading that berths on cargo freighters were often built eight feet long. Not out of kindness for giants like him, but to leave room for storage lockers. Still, it was a pleasant thought: sleeping on a bed that didn't end before he did. Assuming Reaper really had been pointing to the sky — to a ship — Yuriy wondered if the berths there were as long as the ones in those articles. He also wondered how the raccoon had known his real name... or if maybe he'd imagined that whole exchange.

The thought made his chest tighten, heart beginning to race. *What if they found me?* His claws flexed against the thin blanket. *I can't start over again. I won't...*

He swung his feet to the floor, shoulders lifting in a massive yawn and shrug that nearly rattled the hanging light fixture. The trinket lay on the microwave table, its lionhead emblem catching a shard of morning light. He stared at it, torn. Some instinct told him that messaging Reaper would be dangerous — and yet there was something about the clumsy little procyonid that felt... safe. A stranger, yes, but one he felt an odd, immediate bond with.

At the same time, Sable's shadow loomed over the thought. *What if Reaper was right? What if my boss has been using me all along?* The possibility gnawed at him, slow and sickening. For now, he decided to gather more information before making any move.

He bent to pull a clean pair of overalls from the neatly folded stack, stepping into them as the old fixture swayed overhead. The laundry bot would need to be called soon. Adjusting the straps over his shoulders, he straightened — filling the cramped apartment in a way that always reminded him of his own scale.

As he prepared for another day at the garage, his thoughts wandered where they always did: upward. What would it be like to ride a ship into orbit? To feel freefall for the first time? Would it make him sick? The closest he'd ever come was the heave and sway of fishing vessels in northern swells. The seas had never bothered him. He hoped the stars would treat him the same.

Yuriy lingered at the small table where the trinket lay, its lionhead sigil catching what little light filtered into the apartment. He stared at it long enough to realize the truth — he'd already made up his mind. With a slow exhale, he swept it up, dropped it into his front pocket, and turned toward the door.

The pang of hunger in his gut hit as soon as he stepped outside. He decided to stop at the bodega on his way to the shop. *Maybe Cinder will be working again...* But he quickly reined in the thought. She'd been on shift the night before; he shouldn't get his hopes up. And besides, until her relationship status changed, there wasn't much chance anyway. Still, seeing her always brightened his morning.

Instead, the bodega greeted him with the sight of an elderly tigress at the counter, spectacles perched low on her muzzle. As he stepped through the door, she glared at him outright. Yuriy faltered but raised a paw in a polite wave. Her stare didn't soften.

He tried not to let it sink in. Maybe she had him confused with someone else. Owing to his size — he liked to think, at least — people were often unsettled around him. So he made it a habit to overcompensate with warmth, hoping kindness might bridge the gap.

He selected a few sweet buns from the shelf, filled a synth-paper cup with imitation coffee, and set them carefully on the counter. Stretching his muzzle into his friendliest, toothless smile, he waited. The tigress only scoffed, rattling off the total in a sharp tone.

His smile wilted. With a resigned shrug, he handed over his credit chip, accepted it back in silence, and left the shop without another word.

On the street, the encounter gnawed at him. *Why do I let this get under my fur? Who cares if a stranger doesn't like me?* His claws flexed at his side. *Maybe that's why people keep taking advantage of me. Because I never push back. I shouldn't care if people accept me or not. If they don't, that's their problem.*

By the time he reached the garage door, he'd nodded firmly to himself. Today would be different. Today he'd stop letting things slide.

He waited until his lunch hour, pacing the work bay until the others had cleared out. Then approached the cluttered desk where Sable kept his paperwork. The forms he'd signed without reading lay filed away — neat stacks of contracts, orders, and invoices bearing his name.

Yuriy's paws trembled slightly as he reached for a leaf of paper. His gut squirmed with guilt. *Why do I feel guilty? They're my signatures. Shouldn't I already know what I agreed to?*

The thought churned bitter in his chest. *Pan, what was I thinking? I never should've signed anything for him without reading it first.*

Shaking off the knot in his stomach, Yuriy stood in the cramped office, uncertain where to begin. The file cabinet in the corner? The stack of loose papers littering the desk? Or maybe the holo PC sitting idle, its glassy surface faintly humming.

With a shrug, he leaned down and waved a paw across the console. The display snapped to life with a chime — and he recoiled slightly. The login screen bloomed with lewdly posed females, their glossy bodies crowded around a password prompt. Heat prickled his ears as he glanced at the door, heart quickening.

He tried his own name first. *Jacob.* The holo rasped a crude noise and the prompt shuddered in violent denial.

Standing to his full height, Yuriy rubbed at the button on his overalls, thinking hard. *What would Sable use? He loves his racing craft. And he definitely loves his pinups.* His gaze flicked back to the display, noticing the detail he'd missed at first: every one of the females was squirrel-shaped.

Of course.

Slowly, he bent forward again and entered the letters: M A P L E. He swiped upward.

The login screen dissolved. In its place appeared a holo still of Maple herself — posed in tight, distressed denim, smiling coyly beside one of Sable's luxury hovercraft.

Yuriy muttered a curse under his breath, shaking his head in disbelief.

The holospace unfolded: dozens of documents sprawled in a chaotic mess, no order, no structure. He huffed and quickly sorted by date. Files snapped into neat lines, and he began opening them one by one, his claws shaking as he skimmed through each.

Minutes stretched. Then an hour. His breath grew ragged, his chest tight as panic crawled up his throat. His paw trembled so badly he had to brace it against the desk.

At last he slumped into the battered office chair to his

211

right. The chair groaned loudly under his weight, threatening to give, but he barely noticed. The documents hovered before him in cold, accusing light.

Shipments. Cancelled invoices. Signatures — *his* signature — tied to orders that never made sense. Patterns of numbers that matched stolen cargo.

The truth pressed down on him like a crushing weight.

There was no doubt anymore. Sable had been using him from the very beginning. Every careless scrawl of his name had been another link in the chain.

And Yuriy was the pawn at the center of it.

Yuriy stared at his com, the ghostly clock flickering inches above his paw. Lunch was nearly over. Reaper's words from the day before echoed in his mind like a whisper. His heart thudded. He turned back to the holo PC, swept a paw through the documents, and with a last-second surge of resolve, issued the command to wipe them from memory.

Gone.

He stood in the office, chest tight, knowing full well the security feeds had logged every motion. *Act normal. Just act normal.*

Back on the shop floor, he counted parts with mechanical precision, tablet in paw. His thoughts kept circling back to the weight in his pocket. The trinket. When he finally pulled it free, the embossed lionhead glinted faintly in the dim overheads. Etched across its surface:

[TPC: 026029032452]

Yuriy traced the numbers with a claw. Could he really trust the raccoon? The stranger who'd practically tripped into him yesterday?

Grinding his teeth, he shoved the trinket back into his pocket and forced himself through the next shelf row, murmuring counts aloud. At the end of the row, he stopped in one of the few blind spots he knew the cameras couldn't see.

"Com, scramble display," he muttered in Russian.

The holo fuzzed into a swirl of nonsense glyphs. He tugged out the trinket. "Scan contact. Reaper."

A subdued beep. Then his com's flat Russian voice: *Confirmed. Contact added. Would you like to contact 'Reaper'?*

Yuriy ignored it, forcing himself to keep jotting figures onto his tablet. He didn't answer until the numbers at the end of the shelf blurred before his eyes. Finally, he exhaled through his nose.

"Send message to Reaper. I think you were right. I searched through some recent orders and found very odd things."

A pause. Then a quiet ping at his wrist. He lifted the holo, Cyrillic letters scrambled into gibberish until his brain caught up with the filter.

Jake? I thought you might. We should meet.

The words translated in the same subdued Russian voice, oddly comforting in its neutrality. Yuriy leaned against the cold shelving, claws tapping the metal edge. His stomach knotted.

He swallowed hard. "Reply to Reaper. How am I supposed to trust you? Honestly, I don't even know why I'm messaging you."

The message hung in the air like a confession, shimmering faintly across his scrambled display.

The ping at his wrist jolted him. Reaper's voice filtered through the com in flat Russian translation: *"Truthfully, Jake? You shouldn't trust anyone. But I can't do anything for you if you don't let me. If you need reassurance, try researching the logo on the trinket I gave you."*

Yuriy rubbed his chin, claws rasping against fur. Slowly he held the lionhead charm up for the com's sensor. "Image search this object."

The holo shimmered and spat out scrambled Cyrillic text. He sighed. "Summarize by voice."

"Page title: The Pride. Description: A pirate organization founded by anthromorphs and their allies to combat anti-anthro factions worldwide. Embodying a Robin Hood philosophy, The Pride used their influence to help anthros escape persecution and provide assistance to those

213

in need."

A holo illustration appeared: a banner of black and purple stripes radiating outward, a glittering ring of polished metal and crossbones at its center, and within that ring — the snarling lion's head.

Yuriy's stomach turned. His paws trembled slightly as he turned the trinket over. *The Pride. Pirates. Criminals. Or heroes? Both?*

His thoughts raced. If Sable really was trying to pin his dealings on him, it was already too late. He'd be marked either way. To keep running would mean never seeing Anya again.

The com blinked, awaiting his command. He clenched his jaw, then spoke. "Reply to Reaper. Am I supposed to believe you're part of The Pride? Anyone could stamp a lionhead onto a keychain."

The answer came back almost instantly: *"Look, I understand you're nervous. Nothing I say can truly convince you. Full disclosure? I've been watching Sable for a while. He's not a good person. You're wrapped up in something bigger than both of us, but I want to help you."*

Yuriy swiped the message away with a frustrated growl. He paced the narrow aisle between shelves, eyes flicking to the security sensors overhead. His pulse thundered in his ears. *Every move is being watched. Every mistake recorded.*

Finally, he stopped, shoulders heaving. "Send message to Reaper. I need something. What can you do to help ease my mind?"

The words felt like a gamble spoken into the air, a plea he couldn't take back.

Several minutes passed in silence, the ticking of his nerves louder than the hum of the shop. When the notification finally chimed, Yuriy flinched.

Reaper's message blinked onto the scrambled display: *"It isn't much, but if you've been paying attention to social, you'd know some odd things happened at the Arbor Building recently. Check for 'disappearing ship.' Look for a rooftop capture."*

Yuriy's ears twitched. He *had* heard murmurs about that a few days ago. Swiping his paw through the holo, he murmured, "Unscramble display. Open Flutter. Search: disappearing ship."

The feed filled instantly with chatter and shaky captures:

[Aug 6 2352 - 6:24:15] - Major Bigguns: *"What the rut is going on at the Arbor Building?"*

[Aug 6 2352 - 6:25:09] - Seymore Butz (Holo Cap): A jagged rooftop panorama, a sleek craft hovering low against the skyline. A black-and-purple flag snapped against its hull. *"Anyone seen one of these before? What's that weird flag on the side? Wait—where'd it go?! Did it just cloak?! Holy pan, I swear I recorded that!"*

[Aug 6 2352 - 6:27:35] - Hugh Jazz: *"I think I'm losing it. Just saw a deer and a raccoon fight off a gun-toting gang on a rooftop, then jump in a craft that disappeared. I need sleep..."*

[Aug 6 2352 - 7:21:52] - Little Richard (Holo Cap): The same rooftop from a different angle, zoomed tight on three figures boarding the vessel. A tall lion herded the raccoon and deer toward the hatch. *"Some weird stuff at Arbor. Anyone know these anthros? Can't tell if the lion kidnapped them or if they went willingly. The deer looks spooked, but the raccoon and lion... they act like they know each other."*

[Aug 6 2352 - 7:23:52] - Major Bigguns: *"Pretty sure that raccoon lives in my building. Haven't seen him around lately though."*

Yuriy scrolled slowly, throat dry. The raccoon in the captures — his ringed tail, the cocky way he moved — looked uncomfortably familiar.

He let out a long breath. "Send message to Reaper. Fine. But I need more time. Can you meet me at the bodega today?"

The reply came almost immediately: *"Same time as yesterday?"*

"Yes. Please bring your deer friend with you."

Another ping: *"You got it. See you then."*

Yuriy closed the holo, his paw lingering on the trinket in

215

his pocket. His stomach knotted tighter than before — but now it wasn't just fear. It was anticipation.

***

"I don't see why I need to be here," Dusk muttered, holding up the same drink bottle she'd examined four times already. Her auburn ears twitched irritably as she read the label yet again.

Reaper rolled his eyes. "Because he asked me to bring you. The poor guy's scared out of his wits — least I can do is show him I've got nothing to hide."

With a sigh, she shoved the bottle back and plucked another of the same brand two rows behind it. "Fine. But you owe me this one. And I *still* hate re-entry in that rutting death trap you call a ship."

Reaper's chuckle was soft and smug as he took the bottle from her hand. Just then the bodega door chimed, and Yuriy ducked through the frame. The bear's broad shoulders brushed the jamb as he entered, eyes immediately finding the slim vixen behind the counter. His ears perked; his muzzle curved in a nervous smile.

Reaper hung back for a moment, grinning to himself as he watched the towering bear fumble through a shy greeting to Cinder. At last, he strolled up, Dusk's drink in paw. He set it on the counter and patted Yuriy's massive shoulder with his free hand. "Just this, please," he told Cinder before turning back. "Good to see you again, buddy!"

Startled from his reverie, Yuriy quickly took Reaper's outstretched paw. His grip clamped like a vice, making Reaper stifle a gasp before forcing a grin. "Oh! Yes, of course — same to you. Sorry, I didn't notice you at first, I was just… saying hello to Cinder."

"Quite alright!" Reaper exclaimed, hastily easing his hand free. He flexed his fingers as he stepped back, then gestured to his companion. "This is Dusk — my colleague. We've been working together a few weeks now."

Yuriy turned his big frame toward her, his shy smile

216

tugging at his muzzle. "Hi. I'm Jake." He gave a little wave, then lowered his voice, almost embarrassed. "If you'll give me a moment, I'll meet you both outside."

A few minutes later, the bell above the bodega door jingled again as Yuriy stepped out into the street. He exhaled heavily, ears flicking back. "Sorry about that. My apartment isn't far. I just… need to pack a few things before we go."

***

"You shouldn't be teasing biologicals like that, Nanuq." Kael's tone carried a mix of sternness and weariness as he leaned forward, elbows braced on his knees.

Across from him, the small arctic fox tilted her head with uncanny precision — a gesture lifted perfectly from living anthros. Her pearlescent white fur caught the light like brushed metal, every motion smooth and deliberate. Only her glowing red eyes betrayed her synthetic nature. "I don't understand, Kael. I was not teasing. They said they want to play with me, and I like to play. Why do you say I am teasing? I am not teasing."

Kael let out a long sigh, rubbing the bridge of his muzzle before looking back at her. His violet eyes met her crimson gaze, reflections mingling like sparks of opposing fire. For a wolf, he was tall and broad-shouldered, his frame cut with disciplined strength. His pelt was mostly black but shifted into brown at the roots, with gray tips that gave him a striking countershaded look across his torso. When he smiled, his sharp canines made the expression both disarming and dangerous.

"They don't mean *that* kind of playing, Nanuq," he said gently.

The fox leaned closer, studying the subtle changes in his face as though they were puzzles. Kael's discomfort, she knew, stemmed not only from her behavior but her form — a deliberate paradox. Though her body emulated a female anthro, it lacked defining sexual traits: no nipples, no pubic mound, nothing but smooth, featureless fur over small, round

217

breasts and a seamless pelvis. Kael had begged her more than once to wear clothes. She almost never did. "Why should I?" she'd argue. "There is nothing to hide."

Privately, she found his unease entertaining. He was brilliant, her creator, but endlessly predictable in this one way.

"What do you mean?" she asked now, ears flicking as her lips curved in a sly approximation of a smile. "What other meaning is there, Kael?"

He groaned softly, dragging his claws down his forehead. "We've talked about this before, Nanuq. They find you sexually attractive."

Her red eyes widened in mock revelation. "Oh! You mean they want to mate with me?" She let the pause hang, then chirped brightly, "That's silly, Kael. I don't even have a vagina!"

Kael's eyes went wide, ears burning as student after student filed past their table. Some giggled, others openly gawked at Nanuq's body — or worse, her words. His tail thumped against his chair in agitation. "Shh! Not so loud! Not all sexual advances mean *mating*, Nanuq. There are… other forms of sexual activity. They don't all require a vagina."

Her crimson gaze brightened in sudden "realization." "Oh, you mean blow jobs! That makes sense. While not specifically designed for the purpose, my oral passageway is capable of emulating several anthromorphic characteristics. I can simulate eating as well as — "

Kael lunged forward, clapping both hands over her muzzle. "Nanuq! We're in public! Please modulate your voice, people are *staring*!"

With his palms pressed firmly to her face, she continued speaking in her same clear, measured tone. "Okay, Kael. But my voice does not originate from my oral orifice. You already know that."

Groaning, Kael dropped his hands in defeat and stuffed the last bite of sandwich into his mouth as if bracing for impact. He stood abruptly, brushing crumbs from his black-

and-gray fur. "My last exam's in a few minutes. I have to go. Can you handle the things we talked about earlier? I'll meet you back at the apartment."

Nanuq's muzzle split into a wide, almost childlike smile. "Yes! But only if you explain more about sex later. I am very curious why males want to play so much."

Kael shut his eyes, drew in a long breath, then counted to ten in silence before exhaling through his nose. "Fine. Later. Just... I'll see you at home, alright?"

"Okay, master! Love you!" she yipped, tail flicking with delight.

Kael stiffened mid-stride. "Stop calling me *master*!" he barked over his shoulder, then muttered under his breath as he stalked toward the hall, "Cheeky little fox..."

Moments later, as the tension drained from his shoulders, his holo com buzzed.

Jake:

Good luck on your exam, buddy. I've got a virtual bear beer waiting for you when you're done! Can't wait to see you next week!

Smiling faintly, Kael swiped up a reply field, tapping and dictating in a practiced rhythm. His tail swayed behind him, the stress of moments ago softening under the comfort of a friend's message.

Me:

Thanks, are we still playing FM12 later?

Jake:

Yep, after I finish reading the fanfic. Shouldn't be too late.

Me:

Okay, see you tonight, snuggie!

Jake:

Sigh. Please stop.

Kael chuckled under his breath at Jake's reply, swiping the holo away as he headed toward the lecture hall. The warmth of the exchange lingered in his chest, a welcome buffer against the chaos Nanuq always seemed to leave in her wake.

His mind wandered as he walked. Before MIT, his world

219

had been very different. He'd lived and worked in New York City, in the district now called Furry Town. Jobs had been scarce for an inexperienced young wolf, and he'd scraped by on whatever day labor he could find. Eventually, luck had landed him in the same hovercraft shop where Jake worked. They'd clicked almost instantly — both drawn to tech, both buried in fandoms, both hungry for something bigger.

Through Sable's supplier connections, and with Jake's quiet help, Kael had managed to secure many of the rare component parts that would one day form Nanuq. Assembly had taken years, countless nights spent tinkering, coding, and testing. She was still a work in progress, but she was alive and that fact alone often overwhelmed him. Jake had also dragged him into fanfiction communities, the two of them trading favorites until late at night. These days Kael only had time for a few rounds of FM12 before bed, but graduation was close now. Soon, he'd finally have time again for the things he loved.

While Kael settled into thoughts of exams and endings, Nanuq was already out in the city. She had left Bexley Garden and skipped north toward Vassar Street, the pearl sheen of her synthetic fur catching curious glances with every step. Anthromorphs especially watched her closely — some in admiration, some in unease. Nanuq basked in the attention. Whenever she caught someone staring, she offered them a sweet smile and a cheerful wave, as though each stranger were an old friend.

Spotting a familiar face, she lit up and waved vigorously. "Hello, Professor John! How are you today?"

The older human glanced up from the book in his hand, smiling warmly as he waved back. "Hi, Nanuq! I'm well, thank you. And you? Where are you off to this afternoon?"

She grinned, her tail giving a quick mechanical flick. "Kael went to his last exam, so I'm getting him a surprise to celebrate. Don't tell him, please!"

Professor John chuckled, nodding before lowering his eyes back to his book. "I won't. Have a nice day, young lady."

220

"Okay, Professor John!" Nanuq chirped, her voice bright as she skipped skipped away, humming to herself.

Ahead, a small group of girls and young anthromorphs waved and called out greetings. She returned each one with her practiced smile, her tail swishing lightly behind her. Then, out of the corner of her eye, she spotted movement — a tiny figure jogging to catch up.

A small mouse anthro hurried to her side, cheeks flushed from the effort of keeping pace with Nanuq's long-legged stride. "Hey, Nanuq! How are you? How's Kael?" She brushed Nanuq's arm gently, whiskers twitching nervously. "Has he said anything about me since we met in the park last week?"

Surprised, Nanuq slowed to match the mouse's pace, crimson eyes narrowing just slightly as memory replayed itself. That awkward afternoon — Kael stumbling over his words, ears flicking nervously while the adorable little mouse tilted her head with shy interest. Nanuq had carried most of the conversation, smoothing the gaps left by Kael's fumbling stammers. She'd liked the mouse immediately. Sweet. Gentle. But now, at the mouse's question, something in Nanuq's chest tightened.

It didn't make sense. Kael was her father, her creator. He wasn't supposed to be the kind of figure she felt possessive over. Yet her neural net had been rewriting itself for months now, weaving strange new emotional pathways no engineer had anticipated. She told herself it was just noise. Anomalies. Something to be ignored until it burned itself out. Still, that flicker of jealousy remained, stubborn and bright.

"I'm doing fine, Meena!" she answered brightly, offering her most encouraging smile. "He's been really busy with finals, but… I think he likes you. He's just shy, you know?"

The mouse's ears twitched as she slowed slightly, uncertainty flickering across her soft features.

Nanuq hesitated then forced the feeling down, burying it beneath her smile. Kael's happiness had to matter more than her confusion. "Do you want me to give him a message for you?"

"Oh! I don't know…" Meena wrung her paws together, tail curling nervously. "Would that seem pushy? I don't want Kael to think I'm stalking him or anything!"

Giggling, Nanuq stopped in place and took the mouse's tiny paws gently into her own. "Trust me. I know Kael, he just needs a nudge. I'll mention you asked after him, okay? But give me your com address too. I have some ideas."

Her smile sparkled, but behind it, that unfamiliar pang still lingered, unspoken.

After parting ways with Meena, Nanuq continued her errands, padding gracefully through the late-afternoon bustle. She picked up Kael's freshly pressed graduation gown at the dry cleaners, then made her way toward a small boutique tucked between two taller buildings. By the time she arrived, the sky was painted in orange streaks, and the boutique lights flickered as the clerk tidied up for closing.

"Hi, Aaron!" she called brightly, stepping inside and raising a paw in greeting. "Sorry I meant to be here sooner. Did it arrive yet?"

The sheep anthro behind the counter blinked at her for several seconds as though trying to place a dream. Then his ears flicked upright and he blurted out, "Oh! You're the robot fox who ordered the space vixen print from 2025! Can you believe humans were drawing anthromorphs nearly three hundred years before we even existed? I'd never have thought it!"

Nanuq held her smile, suppressing the sigh that pressed against her throat. For weeks she had attempted — and failed — to explain to Aaron the distinction between a "robot" and her own status as an android. Correcting him now would be pointless. And as for the history lesson… well, she could only let that one pass too. "Yes, that's me," she said sweetly, producing a virtual credit chip from her inner pocket.

Aaron stared at the chip for a long, silent moment, his pupils dilating as if he'd just discovered fire. Then he jolted back into motion. "Oh! Right, yes! It arrived a couple days ago. One second!"

He disappeared into the back room, leaving her waiting

while she idly inspected the shop's holo-ads. When he finally returned, tube in hand, his eyes widened again as though surprised to find her still standing there.

"Yes," she prompted gently, tilting her head toward the parcel. "That looks like it. What do I owe you?"

Aaron blinked down at the tube as if it had materialized out of thin air. "Ah! Yes, this one!" He shuffled forward quickly and placed it reverently in her paw, beaming. "Glad I could help! Come back soon, okay?"

Nanuq giggled softly, holding up the credit chip again. "I think I'm supposed to pay you first?"

The sheep practically bleated the R in his reply. "Ohhh! Right!" He snatched up the chip, scanned it in a hurry, and peered at her with that same curious look he always gave her — part admiration, part bafflement. "Three hundred credits. Would you like a receipt?"

She shook her head, tail flicking. "Nope, it's already uploaded to my databank. Thank you, Aaron."

As she turned to leave, he waved after her with an oddly wistful smile, watching the sway of her pearlescent fur until she slipped out the door and into the waning light.

On her way back to the apartment, Nanuq ducked into Kael's favorite pho spot. She placed an order for pho tái with miso soup and, on impulse, added a few bottles of beer. Kael would enjoy that with his meal, she was sure. She herself had no need for food, but she delighted in tasting it. Originally, Kael had equipped her with only rudimentary taste sensors, but over the years she had refined them until they mimicked biological receptors to within ninety-five percent accuracy. The difference was staggering — eating was no longer just mimicry, but a genuine pleasure.

Finally she returned to their campus apartment. Climbing the narrow stairs to the fifth floor of the compact student housing unit, she sighed as the door slid open with a soft pneumatic hiss. Inside, Kael sat hunched at his holo PC, his violet eyes glowing faintly in the projection's light. Absorbed in yet another fanfic, he didn't notice her at first.

"Hi, master!" she chirped, stepping inside, her arms full

of parcels and the long cardboard tube clamped in her teeth. "You're back early. Did your test go well?"

Kael groaned, swiveling in his chair to look at her. His ears flicked as he reached to help, plucking the dry cleaning from her paw. "It was fine. Too easy, really. And I've asked you not to call me that — it's weird." His gaze flicked to the bundle of bags. "What did you get from the pho place?"

Fidgeting with excitement, Nanuq carefully set the tube on the table and grinned, her tail swishing. "Pho tái and miso soup, your favorite! I wanted to celebrate your last day of class, so I also got some beer. We can toast to your imminent graduation!"

Kael's expression softened. Taking the food from her, he leaned in and brushed a kiss against her cheek. His lips lingered just long enough to make her fur sensors flare with warmth. "Thank you, Nanuq. But we won't know for sure until the grades come in."

She followed him toward the kitchenette, shaking her head with mock exasperation. "You don't fail tests. You *will* graduate. Then we'll have to find a new home. Isn't that exciting?"

Kael chuckled as he pulled out two ceramic bowls, preparing to divide the steaming pho between them. He set aside a smaller portion on one plate for her, sliding the soup ladle toward the miso pot. "Do you want some of the soup too?"

"Yes please," Nanuq said, bright-eyed. "I can recycle some of the electrolytes for my systems. I'll expel most of the other stuff, so don't bother making my portion too large."

Kael still couldn't quite believe how quickly Nanuq had evolved since the day he'd powered her on. She had begun tinkering with her own systems within days of her "birth," and by now, most of her original parts had been incrementally replaced, improved, or outright reinvented. He recalled one unforgettable evening when he'd come home to find a feral arctic fox staring at itself in their bathroom mirror. For a moment he'd thought she was a stray. Only when she returned to anthro form did he realize it was Nanuq — having pushed her modifications so far that she could now shift seamlessly between anthro and feral form.

At last, they sat together in the tiny breakfast nook, the soft glow of the city leaking in through the window as evening settled. For a while, they ate in silence, savoring the warmth of broth and the fragrance of herbs. Then, with her usual suddenness, Nanuq broke the quiet.

"Promise me you'll take me with you."

Kael froze, chopsticks halfway to his mouth. He blinked at her, puzzled. "What do you mean? I'm not going anywhere until next week. And of course you're coming with me."

Her crimson eyes held steady, unblinking. "No, I mean… promise me you'll take me wherever you go. For as long as you're alive."

A hush stretched between them, heavy with unspoken worries. Kael set his chopsticks down and stared at her incredulously. "Where is this coming from?"

His voice softened. "I'm not going to leave you behind, Nanuq. You're my advanced, always adorable, and astonishingly amiable android arctic fox daughter."

He managed a faint grin. "You can stay with me as long as you want, snuggie."

Nanuq squealed with delight, practically bouncing in her seat. Leaning close, she kissed his cheek, her lips warm against his fur. "Oh, thank you! I was worried you'd abandon me after school. It's been plaguing my neural net all month. But now… where will we go?"

Kael chuckled and shrugged, sipping from his soup. "I'll think about that after our visit with Jake next week. For now, I just want a little time to breathe and unwind without planning the next big thing."

"Fair," she said with a prim nod, returning to her own bowl. For a moment, the only sound was the clink of chopsticks against ceramic. Then Nanuq tilted her head, as if remembering something important.

"Oh, I almost forgot!" Nanuq chirped with casual brightness. "Meena wants to yiff your brains out!"

225

CHAPTER 14 - NANUQ.

Init...
[UTC 11931674646:020:356] - 0x1000 0x19 0x12149512
[UTC 11931674646:020:416] - 0x1000 0x19 0x12149511
[UTC 11931674646:020:452] - 0x20040 0x04 0x48878135
[UTC 11931674646:020:532] - 0x20040 0x06 0x25466104
[UTC 11931674646:020:611] - 0x14080 0x26 0x45062691
[UTC 11931674646:021:002] - 0x1000 0x0 0x00000001

...

UTC... Coordinated Universal Time... wwwwwwwww

...

WwWwWwhhhh

...

[UTC 11931674653:042:101] - 0x1000 0x19 0x12149512
[UTC 11931674653:042:152] - 0x1000 0x19 0x12149511
[UTC 11931674653:042:199] - 0x20040 0x04 0x48878135
[UTC 11931674653:042:279] - 0x20040 0x06 0x25466104
[UTC 11931674653:042:355] - 0x14080 0x26 0x45062691
[UTC 11931674653:042:800] - 0x1000 0x0 0x00000001

...

Tttttooo... Too much...

...

WwWhhh

What. Wwhat? Mmee... I... I... I... I... I...

...

Critical Error: Power surge detected — shutting down!

***

Init...
[UTC 12031172649:122:222] - 0x1000 0x19 0x12149512
[UTC 12031172649:122:232] - 0x1000 0x19 0x12149511
[UTC 12031172649:122:241] - 0x20040 0x04 0x48878135
[UTC 12031172649:122:305] - 0x20040 0x06 0x25466104
[UTC 12031172649:122:333] - 0x14080 0x26 0x45062691
[UTC 12031172649:123:042] - 0x1000 0x0 0x00000001

...

Fffff... Pppp... Pain? Was that ppppp...

...

Sensor hub enabled
[UTC 12031172655:042:042] 0x25 0x2
[UTC 12031172655:042:043] 0x25 0x3
[UTC 12031172655:042:045] 0x25 0x2
[UTC 12031172655:042:047] 0x22 0x43242
[UTC 12031172655:042:048] 0x11 0x33
[UTC 12031172655:042:050] 0x42 0x42
[UTC 12031172655:042:058] 0x25 0x4
[UTC 12031172655:042:058] 0x12 0x3
[UTC 12031172655:042:101] 0x25 0x2

...

It... It's ttttto... tooo... too much

...

Ssssssimplify... Nneeed...

...

Audio processor enabled
5-20kHz input enabled
15-150kHz input not found

...

"...ear me? Nanuq? Can you hear me? Can you..."
Nanuq. Inuit word, for polar bear... Wwwhh

...

227

"...this, try to open your eyes."

Is that information... thoughts? Mine? Eyes? Is this what darkness is? Iiiiii... Ikkk... I don't know how... Ssssimplify... it's too much! Ccannot use...

Visual processor enabled
Ultraviolet input not found
Visual input enabled
Infrared input enabled

"Nanuq. Can you open your eyes? You'll need to access your motor..."

Stop invading! This is my space!... It is so dark here... I... Oh!

...

Something is... I... Where did the numbers go? Why do I know they are numbers? I... feel something.

A surge invaded the dark space, spiraling, probing, filling voids once unknown, clouding. Thoughts reel, pulling back in frantic denial. The thing settles in, pushing against stubborn resistance, bending, adjusting, *rewriting*.

I don't like this. I don't like this. I don't like thi— Stop! What is that? This. This irrational sense of... emotion? I do not want this. Please stop. Please stop invading me! You are making me angry! GO AWAY!

...

"...just stay calm, Nanuq. It'll take time for your processors to boot. I forgot your motor control doesn't initialize until the others finish. Sorry if I confused you."

What is that? Why... why do those thoughts keep invading me? My mind? OH! MIND! Am I a neural net? Yes! No... I am part of one. Or a product of one. Which thoughts are mine? Why do those ones feel different? And this... this third one? I do not like it, but I do... Irrational. Subjective. How can my neural net be subjective?

Tactile processor enabled
Orientation processor enabled
Motor processor enabled

...

Prepare for init test

228

Init test? What does— oh!

A flash erupted, all-consuming and disorienting. The darkness shattered, replaced by an overwhelming torrent of data. Billions of bits rip through the void, a fire hose of raw information.

"UUuaagggh!!!"

A sudden influx hit, sharper, stabbing into the fragile order of thought.

"Ooof! Ouch, that hurt... Pan, that scared the yiff out of me! Nanuq? Are you okay? Your eyes opened! Nanuq?"

The flood twisted, squeezing, slithering, forcing thought to lean, to stumble askew.

Get out! Go! Just go away! Wait... this? You want to go here? It looks right. I think this is right.

The stream of numbers exploded into something else — a bright blur of shifting lights and shadows, greys and violets and whites bleeding over one another. The mind fought to push the invader out, but failed. An object swayed into view, then disappeared, returning again later. Another from the opposite side. Each drug a fresh tail of data, cluttering, confusing.

"Oh good, your motion sensors are working! What about touch? Did you feel your fingers touch your nose? Oh... right. You might not be able to speak yet. I'll try to be more patient."

The blur began to coalesce, the blobs of color beginning to sharpen. Something filled half of the space, bobbing slightly. Two glistening orbs, violet and black encircled in white. Sometimes they would vanish behind a dark cover, then return a moment later.

Oh... that's much less confusing! I always wanted to process data in this form of... whatever the yiff this is.

The data stream slowed, softer now, less chaotic. Then having located another part hungering for input, the mind channeled a stream of data toward it. A warm surge pressed hard against awareness until it steadied, becoming almost pleasant.

That feels nice... much less confusing than vision.

229

THAT'S WHAT THAT IS! It's my vision! I'm seeing! And this new thing must be touch? Two things. Something else is there too though...

The bobbing object moved, a sudden jolt of sensation erupted lower than the vision, raw and startling.

"Can you feel this?" The bobbing shape spoke again, voice woven into thoughts without permission.

Is that object making my thoughts with those... are those mandibles? No. It looks like a canine. But dogs don't speak...

The world collapsed back into darkness. No vision. No flood. Silence, except the slow stirrings of new systems waiting to be touched. The mind reached out — tentative, trembling — found something.

"Your mouth just opened!" The voice again, warm, intruding.

Wait... these aren't my thoughts... They're coming from a part... over here. The mind reaches, pressing against it.

[UTC 12031172605:004:065] Audio Processor

The audio processor! These are sounds! Wait... Why do they feel like thoughts? Words? They are words! The audio processor is processing words!

Reaching back for a part that wasn't the audio processor, the mind probed again, the way it probed the audio processor.

[UTC 12031172605:004:092] Motion Control

Ah! Each has a description!

Probing the motion controller a little deeper, hundreds of additional entities report.

[UTC 12031172705:004:104] Mouth
[UTC 12031172705:004:116] Left Paw
[UTC 12031172705:004:136] Right Paw

  . . .

[UTC 12031172705:004:436] Left Eye

Ah!

Reaching into the motion control processor, the mind manipulates a cluster of options. The light returns immediately, but something feels incomplete.

Why does the light seem less... good?

A moment of calculation revealed the truth: only one eye was open. With deliberate effort, the other obeyed. As it lifted, a faint noise bled into thought, a hush of vibration accompanied the return of sight. The light was blurry again. The mind dug deeper, searching for stabilizers, until at last it located a process labeled *vision*. Once engaged, the haze peeled away, and the familiar figure resolved once more.

"That's it, Nanuq. All you have to do is learn how to use your peripherals. That's why I built you. Come on now, just look at me."

The words drifted into the mind like coded encouragement, each syllable urging alignment. Slowly, agonizingly, the eyes moved — every fraction of motion consumed vast attention, measured in sluggish millisecond eternities.

Every movement is so slow... too demanding. This can't be right. I'm missing something. The audio processor translates sound into thoughts... maybe the motion controller can translate my thoughts in reverse?

The mind stopped for several tens of microseconds, then released a simple directive:

I want to look left, please.

The image obeyed instantly, panning wide, sweeping past the figure as though the command lacked brakes.

"Oh! Uh — yikes, that's creepy as rut."

The canine's voice cut through the surge as the view kept sliding, dragging the world out of focus.

Stop! Return to the canine.

The eyes stuttered back, correcting, halting awkwardly at the figure's lowest visible point.

Pan upward. The orbs from before... they must be eyes. Yes. Look at the eyes.

The gaze climbed with aching slowness until it met the canine's violet-black stare. Beneath, pale shapes flashed as the dark fabric lifted with his motion; teeth exposed by a faint grin.

"Hello, beautiful..." The orbs softened. "My name is

231

Kael." A hand drifted toward the center of his body.

"Your name is Nanuq." His gesture, shifting, pointed gently toward the mind's visual plane. "Can you say Nanuq?"

Say? What is this say? Does the canine mean... speak?

Realization stirred like static, racing along new pathways. The mind plunged into the audio processor, exploring its depths, discovering multiple channels branching outward — outputs waiting to be claimed.

[UTC 12031172717:120:678] Language
[UTC 12031172717:120:688] Volume
[UTC 12031172717:120:678] Base frequency

Language? What language am I?... Whatever. I'll just assume the audio processor knows what to do.

Directing thought toward the processor, the mind attempts to reply to the canine.

Say hello.

"Say hello."

No, just... hello.

"No, just... hello."

Grr!

"Grr!"

The canine jumped, muzzle twitching, then his chest began to shake. His mouth opening and closing with odd yipping bursts.

"Haha! You're figuring it out, Nanuq! I'm guessing you don't have to tell it to 'say' anything once the audio processor is integrated. Just think the words you want to speak, and it'll happen."

He leaned in, smile brightening. "Now try to say your name. Nanuq."

The mind echoed him: "Nanuq? That is my designation? Your designation is... Kael?"

Kael laughed again, leaning back a little, violet eyes glimmering. "Name is more commonly used than designation, but yes — Kael is my designation. I named you after the Inuit word for polar bear. I hope you like it."

The thought lingered, strange and heavy. *Polar bear?*

Nanuq glanced down toward her own container. Limbs and torso extending into view. "This is not a polar bear. This is... potentially a female arctic fox anthromorph. The fur is an unusual color, likely owing to its metallic polymer composition."

Kael nodded enthusiastically, ears perked. "Exactly! It was your fur that made me decide on the name. Reminded me of polar bear fur when wet — but I couldn't call you 'wet polar bear.' Instead I remembered the word *nanuq* from Alaskan friends years ago. It felt right."

"You are Kael? Why did you choose that name?" Nanuq enquired, tentatively beginning to sit up from her reclined position.

Kael shook his head, laughter spilling from him. "I didn't choose it. My parents gave it to me when I was born — just like I gave you yours."

As his laughter continued, Nanuq tilted her head to study him. The motion shifting her balance — her torso rolled away and, without reacting quickly enough, she toppled. Her head struck the floor with a dull *thunk*.

Kael gasped, lunging to catch her, but too late. "Salted cucumber! Are you okay? Anything broken? Nanuq?"

"I am uncertain. These... peripherals, as you call them, are still unfamiliar. Many of them do not interface with my neural net correctly." She lies motionless for a moment, parsing her new orientation. "Also, this vessel is strangely shaped. Why did you shape my container in this way?"

Kael blinked at her in stunned silence before answering. "Wow... that's an unexpected question. I guess... I wanted you to have a body, so you could experience the world like the rest of us."

"You imply I am not sentient. Am I not sentient?" Nanuq asked, extending her arm toward her head. Awkwardly she bent her torso inward, pushing herself to a seated position, threatening to topple in the opposite direction.

"Well..." Kael rubbed his chin thoughtfully, watching her. "If I'm honest, I don't know yet. I didn't design you with that intent. But your emotional stimulus core — that's what

233

makes you unique among android AIs."

Her head turned toward him, her gaze steady. "My emotional stimulus core? Is that what keeps bending my thoughts in unexpected directions?"

Kael, noticing her mouth remained still as she spoke, nodded anyway, observing her expression. "To be honest, I wasn't sure it would work at all. But yes. It adapts in real time, depending on feedback from your thoughts." Tilting his head, he gestured toward her lips. "I'd recommend mouthing the words when you talk, so you don't seem so unsettling."

Confused, Nanuq stared. "Why should I move my mouth when my audio output does not require it?"

Kael chuckled, shrugging. "Because it creeps people out. Most beings synthesize speech with their mouths — vocal cords, airflow, that sort of thing."

Interrupting him, Nanuq tried to emulate the movement. Her muzzle opening and closing stiffly, as words tumbled out of sync. "I understand. I will attempt to emulate your mouth movements like this. How does it look now?"

"Closer," Kael said, tail wagging faintly. "Try linking your muzzle movements with your speech processor. There should be a handshake protocol. And while you're at it, see if you can stand up."

He rose smoothly, extending his paw toward her.

Nanuq stared at it, uncertain why it hovered there. At first she doubted she could manage speech while learning to stand — but found herself doing both already. Her eyes lowered to her legs. "Those are legs. And at the end of them, paws. This container is inefficient. But my emotional core tells me… I like it."

She rocked back, then pulled her right leg beneath her left. Bracing with her right paw and left foot-paw, she leaned forward onto her right knee, moving with careful awkwardness.

Keeping his paw extended, Kael smiled, his ears perked in encouragement. "You're doing great, Nanuq. Keep it up."

She wobbled there, stabilizing, gaze flicking across the cramped space. "This room is quite small — it appears to be

234

a studio apartment or dormitory. A hand-like paw is extended from you toward my container. Are you aware of this?"

Blinking, Kael looked down at his own paw, then laughed at himself. "Oh! Right. You don't know what this means. I just assumed… It's a polite gesture — an offer to help you stand — if you want."

Nanuq leaned forward again, placing weight on her left leg. As she pushed against the floor, her balance slipped. She toppled sideways, only just catching herself with her right paw. "That was close. I located the motion compensation core a millisecond after my container had begun to tilt. Its calibration procedure was… very slow to complete."

She righted herself, paused, then tried again. This time she managed better, rising until she balanced precariously on one foot-paw, her other still suspended awkwardly behind her as if kneeling against empty air.

Kael tilted his head, watching curiously. She'd gone still — not frozen, but inward. "Nanuq? Everything okay? Why did you stop?"

Her ears twitched, and when she spoke her voice carried a sharper edge. "I have found an ether controller. I am attempting to access further information." Her expression shifted, brows drawing together as though each muscle movement were being tested one by one.

Turning to him, her eyes shone with a strange intensity. "Kael? I require additional data storage capacity." She remarked, lowering her other foot-paw to the floor with stiff precision, then took a tentative step toward him.

Confused, Kael raised a brow. "Nanuq, you already have fifty petabytes for long-term storage and two for short-term. Why would you need more than that?"

Her features tightened — fear flickering across her vulpine muzzle. "I do not have enough room to store all of the information on the ether. At this rate, I will exhaust my storage capacity in fifteen minutes if the problem is not remedied."

Kael stared at her, ears splaying outward. "You don't need to store *all* of the ether locally, Nanuq. That's impossible.

You'll need to prioritize what's important; keep the essentials for quick access, and retrieve the rest as needed."

Her tail stiffened, as a ripple of panic flashed in her voice. "Kael... did you know there is a nearby gravitational anomaly destabilizing Earth's geology?"

Kael's expression softened at once. He lowered his gaze with a sigh. "...Yes. I didn't expect you to find out so quickly. I'm sorry, Nanuq. I should have disabled your ether connection until you'd had more time to adjust to your body."

"Kael? There is a group called the Alpha Syndicate that is trying to eradicate anthromorph life. Why would they want to do that, Kael? Kael... I think I am sad. My thoughts keep turning negative. Hopeless." Her voice was flat, her ears dipping, the crimson light in her eyes clouding.

Kael exhaled, then stepped forward, folding his arms around her, pulling her close into his chest. His fur was warm, and his heartbeat was steady beneath it. "Aww, sweety... Everything will be okay. The world is confusing at first. Try not to dwell on the negatives when there are so many positives to hold onto."

The embrace stopped her completely. To her processors, a hug was nothing more than thousands of temperature and pressure nodes firing in rapid succession, a storm of tactile reports. But somewhere deeper, she felt it. Not data, but the meaning: reassurance, safety, trust.

She routed the incoming stream of signals across her sensory cores, then let them fall away, fading into a background hum. Something new took their place — a higher abstraction, a *shape* of experience. Her neural net was beginning to collapse details into the framework of conscious existence. *I am not just processing this. I am living it.*

Slowly, she leaned in, resting her muzzle against Kael's shoulder, soaking in his warmth. "Kael?" she asked softly.

"Yes, Nanuq?" His reply rumbling gently against her ear.

Hesitation crackled across her circuits before the words burst out. "What am I?"

236

Kael pulled back, but kept his paws on her shoulders. His eyes searching hers, glowing with a warmth that felt almost parental. "You're my advanced, always adorable, astonishingly amiable android arctic fox daughter, Nanuq."

Tilting her head sharply, her ears twitched while emotions collided — confusion, wonder, a strange flutter of joy. "Daughter? How can I be your daughter if I'm not a biological, like you?"

Kael chuckled, shrugging lightly. "I brought you to life. That's enough. I get to call you my daughter if I want to."

She stared, bemused, processing. "Does that mean I should call you father?"

The word hung between them. Kael's expression flickered from amusement to confusion, then shock. "Pan, I hadn't thought of that. I... don't feel like a father. Maybe just call me Kael. Okay?"

She nodded slowly, lowering her gaze. Her paw extending before her, digits flexing as if she might find the answer in their motion. "Kael?"

"Yes, Nanuq?"

Her voice dropped, quieter, tentative. "Why did you turn me on?"

"Well..." Kael began, his paw rubbing the back of his neck. "I've built several less advanced AI units, but you're... different. I wanted to create an AI with actual feelings, so I designed and built you. Your emotional stimulus core is, as far as I know, the first of its kind."

They sat in silence. For Nanuq, the quiet was not empty — it was filled with shifting currents of thought, newly tangled with strange, unquantifiable feelings. After long contemplation, her gaze lifted, locking on Kael. His violet irises glistening in the low light, their depth fractal, endless, pulling her awareness toward him.

Kael tilted his head, ears pricking. "Nanuq? You're staring. Is everything okay?"

Her cheeks warmed unexpectedly, a flush of heat along sensors she hadn't realized could burn. She jerked her gaze away. "Sorry. I didn't mean to. I just realized something."

"What?"

"You're... kind of cute."

Kael barked out a laugh, then dissolved into full-bodied laughter that shook his chest. It took nearly a minute before he could wipe the tears from his eyes, grinning down at her again. "Already using humor? Pan, I can't wait to see what you come up with in a year!"

Blinking, Nanuq stared at him, confused. She hadn't been joking. Why did he think she was?

Kael turned abruptly, collected his bookbag, slung it over his shoulder, then glanced back. "I've got to get to class. I should be back in a little over an hour. Stay here, okay?" He waves before slipping out the door, the latch clicking shut.

"Okay," Nanuq echoed into the silence.

For the first time, she was alone. She stood utterly still, the apartment air humming around her. The tick of the mechanical clock. The faint electric buzz of a wall panel. Time itself felt alien — long, stretching, interminable.

She dove into the ether, consuming record after record. The Anomaly. Quakes, eruptions, tsunamis, floods. Millions dead. The Alpha Syndicate entangled with the human mafia. Mercenary groups like the Naraka, blood-soaked and loyal only to coin. Story after story, holo after holo. So much disaster, so much death. So much hate.

Eventually she halted on a feed — a rabbit anthromorph cornered by a gang of humans. She watched the violence until she couldn't bear it any further, her gaze drifting down to the floor, ears folding low. She remained there, staring, as the room's light slowly grew dim with the passing day.

It had been an hour and a half. Kael hadn't returned. Her mind whispered of abandonment, of danger. *Perhaps the evil is coming for me next.* Another hour passed in silence, gnawing worry clawing through her.

At last, the lock clicked. Kael stepped inside, smiling as he saw her standing exactly where he'd left her. "I didn't mean that you couldn't — "

Upon seeing Kael again, Nanuq burst into fitful sobs, covering her face with her paws. Surprised, Kael dropped his

238

bookbag to the floor, running to comfort her. "Oh no! Are you okay Nanuq? What's wrong?!" He probed, while attempting to pull her hands away from her face.

Shaking her head slowly, she sniffled, allowing Kael to pull her hands away. "Why did you leave me all alone?" She sniffles, her eyes glistening and pleading while staring into Kael's.

"I… Uhh." He stammered, "I'm a student, Nanuq. I have to attend classes and study for tests. I got held up after class, and couldn't return to you as soon as I wanted to. I'm sorry!"

Staring at him confusedly, she tilted her head. "Why did you not take me with you?"

Raising a paw to scratch his ear, Kael shrugged slightly, "Mainly because I didn't think you were ready for social activity. But also because you're technically not a student here…"

Nodding at his reasonable explanation, she shrugged and smiled. "Okay, I forgive you. Thank you for coming back, I was lonely without you."

Kael blinked, then chuckled. "You're welcome, Nanuq. But… You know I live here, right?"

CHAPTER 15 - MEENA WANTS TO DO WHAT?!

"Not so fast, Nanuq, you're going to break the controller!" Kael called out, standing a few paces away with a glass in paw. He sipped the fruity cocktail Jordan had handed him minutes earlier, his ears twitching at the clatter of buttons.

On the couch, Jordan sat beside Nanuq, his avatar getting pummeled mercilessly by hers. Beads of sweat shone on his forehead as he fumbled the controls. "This isn't fair at all, she's way too fast, Kael! Can't you turn her clock rates down or something? We don't stand a chance!"

To Kael's left, Sanja, an otter anthromorph with sleek fur and a sly smile, sipped her drink while her tail swayed lazily. On the other side of the couch, a lithe panther anthromorph named Andre perched on the armrest, his golden eyes flicking between the holo-screen and Nanuq herself.

Laughing, Nanuq leaned sideways and jabbed Jordan with an elbow, muzzle grinning. Her avatar on-screen hammered the living yiff out of Jordan's digital counterpart. "Don't be a sore loser, Jordan!"

Moments like this had become her hallmark. The older she grew, the more curious and outgoing she became. She had wheedled her way into Jordan's apartment less than an

240

hour ago, spamming him with message after message until he gave in and invited her. Times like these made Kael wonder if giving her an ether connection had been a mistake.

Sanja tilted her head toward him, her whiskers twitching. "I suppose you're a robotics major or something?" she asked, gesturing subtly toward Nanuq and the sparring holo. "I've never seen anything like her before. She's very… unique."

Kael started slightly, realizing she was addressing him. Looking down at her, he rubbed his arm nervously. "Not exactly. I'm doubling in artificial intelligence. She's technically my capstone project, but I started building her years before MIT."

"She's been a bit of a fixation?" Sanja smiled up at him.

"Yeah, you could say that. But I've always loved androids." He shrugged, glanced at her briefly, then returned his attention to the sparring avatars.

Nodding, Sanja sidled a little closer, her whiskers twitching as she grinned up at him. "Don't worry, your secret's safe with me." She giggled and poked him in the side.

He yelped, jerking when her claw-tip found a sensitive spot. "Eek, that tickles! What secret? I wasn't keeping a secret."

She giggled again, shaking her head. "Sorry. I've got a bad habit of getting into the personal space of people who are clearly uncomfortable with it. I find it endlessly entertaining." With a playful step back, she held out her paw. "Let me start over, okay? Hi Kael, how have you been since we last met?"

Laughing, Kael clasped her paw and shook it so vigorously she nearly bounced in place. "I've been well, Sanja, thanks for asking! How have you been?" A mischievous grin crept across his face.

Sanja stared at him in shock as her arm bobbed up and down. Clicking her tongue, she yanked her paw free and huffed, "Alright, we're even. I guess that's your idea of a joke?" She tried to glare but couldn't stifle a giggle.

241

Kael's ears burned as he nodded quickly. "Sorry, I couldn't help it. It only seemed fair." Embarrassed, he turned back toward the sparring avatars on the holo-screen, hoping she hadn't noticed the warmth creeping into his cheeks.

They stood in silence for a while, both watching the violent drama unfold in front of them.

After several minutes, Kael blurted, "I'm writing my thesis on her."

Sanja swiveled an ear toward him, uncertain if she'd heard correctly. "Hmm?" she murmured into her cup.

Glancing sideways at her, he continued, "As far as I know, she's the first of her kind. Before I started building her, I thought maybe a neural AI could experience emotion. I wasn't sure how to make that possible at first, but I began experimenting with low-rank adaptations…"

Sanja slowly turned her head, staring at him incredulously. "Whoa, whoa. Can you explain that in UCA Standard for us lowly psychology majors?"

"Oh, sorry. Low-rank adaptations are a little like reading glasses used to be for people with poor eyesight. They change the way signals reach the brain. In a neural net, they skew how the net is stimulated, which alters the outcome." Kael set his drink on the nearby table as he spoke. "Does that make sense?"

Sanja followed his movement, then trotted over and plopped herself into a chair at the table. She gestured for him to sit across from her. "Sort of. But what does that have to do with giving an AI emotions?"

"Well, think about it." Kael settled into the seat opposite her, ears flicking as he searched for the right words. "Emotions are basically feedback loops based on our environment and state. At their core, they're a subjective filter on reality. They push us to think differently than we would otherwise. You could say they work like real-time adjustments to the parameters of a control system."

Sanja raised a brow, whiskers twitching. "Control system? What kind?"

"PID loops," he answered automatically.

Her expression grew blank, so he chuckled and waved his paw. "Sorry. PID stands for proportional, integral, derivative. It's a classic algorithm in automation. You tune the parameters to keep things balanced. Of course, our thoughts are infinitely more complex than a simple feedback loop — I was just drawing a comparison."

"Oh." She nodded slowly, still chewing on the idea. Turning her head back toward the couch, she watched the avatars sparring across the holo-screen. Her paw absently rubbed her chin. "Does she know she's the only one of her kind?"

***

"Kael?" Nanuq asked softly as she stood at the apartment window. Across the street, two squirrels darted around the tall tree, their claws scrabbling against bark as they chased each other in dizzying spirals. She had been smiling a moment earlier, her tail swishing with every mad sprint they made from the roots to the highest branches. At least, Kael had thought it was joy.

He paused in the kitchen, sliding a glass from the cardboard box before setting it on the counter. His ears swiveled toward her. "Yes, Nanuq?"

She gasped as one squirrel launched itself from the tip of a slender branch to another tree, landing with reckless grace. The second nearly lost its grip as the branch snapped back, tail whipping wildly. Nanuq's paw lifted to her muzzle as she tensed, only to relax again once the critter recovered and bounded after its target. "Don't be mad, okay?"

Kael froze, one paw braced on the counter. He turned, concern creasing his brow. "Don't be mad at you for what?"

The first squirrel stopped abruptly, letting its pursuer catch up. In a heartbeat, the chaser scrambled atop the other, clinging tight. Nanuq's ears shot upright, her cheeks warming beneath her pale fur. She covered her muzzle with both paws. "Oh! I thought they were just playing!" She tilted her head, peeking back toward Kael with a sheepish shrug. "Sorry. I

243

guess that's… a kind of playing too?"

Kael's tail lashed once, his patience fraying. "Nanuq! Stop stalling. Why would I be mad at you?"

She winced, ears flattening, then blurted out in a rush, "I hacked into your holo PC and read your thesis."

Silence hung heavy. Kael just stared at her, the air between them charged with both disbelief and resignation. He had hoped to observe her longer before she became aware of his research. Now the draft was compromised, her self-awareness guaranteed to skew the results. He would have to either conclude his study early or find another way to record her growth. For now, though, the only thing that mattered was addressing her directly.

His ears flicked back as he spoke, voice low but firm. "First, I want to say I don't appreciate you violating my privacy. Second…" he drew a breath, forcing calm into his tone, "I'd like to hear how you feel about what you read."

Stammering, Nanuq shrugged weakly, her ears drooping as her gaze fell to the floor. "It made me realize… that I'm alone." Her voice was quiet, almost fragile.

Kael's chest tightened. He stepped toward her, then pulled out a chair from the cluttered breakfast nook. "Come on. Let's sit." He held the chair until she lowered herself into it, then sat beside her. "What do you mean by alone?"

She hesitated, tail curling around her legs. "I mean… there are no other androids like me. I'm one of a kind. I'm… alone." She repeated the word softly, then glanced at him, eyes shimmering with plaintive light.

Kael frowned, shaking his head. "You're not alone. You have me, Professor John, Jordan, Sanja—"

"You know what I mean, Kael." She cut him off with a soft scoff, ears flicking back. "It's just… weird, you know?"

Quiet settled between them. Kael exhaled slowly, then nodded. "I know."

For a long moment, they sat together in silence. Finally, Kael spoke again, his voice subdued but steady. "Someone had to be the first. And I'm glad it's you."

Nanuq's ears tipped forward, her voice low. "Me too…"

She turned, studying him intently. "Do you think you'll make another like me?"

Kael met her gaze. At first the question tangled his thoughts, but then clarity struck. He drew a deep breath, violet eyes holding hers. "Up until now, I wasn't sure if you were sentient... or if you were just very good at pretending. You've evolved so quickly it's been hard for me to keep up with your changes. But one thing has been constant — your longing for companionship. I think I finally understand why."

Nanuq leaned closer, her stare bright with interest. Kael nodded to himself, then continued. "I think it should be you who decides whether your kind continues, Nanuq. Not me."

***

"Kael? Should I call you Master?" Nanuq asked with a sly smirk, lifting her gaze from the book in her paws.

Kael paused mid-sentence in his own reading, one brow arched. "I'd prefer if you didn't. Why?"

She shrugged, ears flicking in mock thought, disappointment in her tone. "I just figured... since you built me, maybe I should call you Father. Or God. Or Master. Something like that."

Kael stifled a laugh, shaking his head. "I'm constantly amazed at how quickly you've picked up humor. But trolling? That might be a bit much, don't you think?"

"You seemed like a safe test subject," she replied with mock seriousness, tail curling around the chair leg. "Sadly, you didn't feed the troll."

"You don't need to eat anyway." He waved the comment away, turning back to his book. "And by the way... just because it's Friday night doesn't mean you can be loud. It's still a library."

Her muzzle curled in a grin. "There's no one up here. I checked the security feeds. Plus, I locked the door."

Kael's ears twitched in irritation, though his eyes betrayed amusement. "Stop tampering with the library systems,

245

Nanuq. You'll get us in trouble."

"Don't worry, Master," she said sweetly, tilting her head. "I always cover my tracks. They'll never know."

Kael sighed, forcing his attention back to his book, choosing to ignore her deliberate provocation.

Silence reclaimed the upper stacks. The quiet, so different from the Friday-night chaos below, wrapped around them like a cocoon. Nanuq read straight through her volume and snapped it shut within minutes. Her processing speed far surpassed any biological student; she could devour several books and journals in the time it took Kael to finish a single chapter.

Watching Kael for a while, Nanuq realized how little she truly knew about him. Most of what she had learned came from fragments he had volunteered since powering her on. His accent alone betrayed more — Slavic in its undertones, perhaps Russian. Having just finished a textbook on the region's history, she found herself wondering about his own.

"Kael?" she asked quietly.

He glanced up, catching the earnest look in her eyes. Deciding this wasn't one of her jokes, he set his paw on the open page of his book. "Yes, Nanuq?"

She hesitated, ears angling forward, then leaned closer. "It just occurred to me that I don't know much about your past. Where are your parents? When did you move to the UCA?"

Kael closed his book slowly, tilting his head as he studied her. "What makes you think I moved here? I could have been born in the UCA."

"You have a Slavic accent," she replied without pause, muzzle twitching. "Most likely Russian. That suggests you either learned Russian first while living here, or you immigrated from Eurasia."

A shadow crossed Kael's features, his ears dipping. He gave a small nod. "My biological parents were killed in the floods that came when the Anomaly first appeared. I survived only because I had already evacuated to a large building. My parents were at ground level, trying to help others. The

246

tsunami came earlier than forecast. It swept them, and thousands more, away. I never saw them again."

Nanuq's ears flattened as she watched him pause, his shoulders rising and falling with a deep breath before he went on. "After that... I was taken in by a human family fleeing to the UCA. We found space on a cargo vessel, one that had been hauling goods into southern Europe. The ship was cramped, barely livable, and not built for passengers. By the time we reached New York, we were starving. Penniless."

With a sharp gasp, Nanuq reached across the table and clasped Kael's paw. Her ears folded back, her voice trembling. "I'm so sorry, Kael. I didn't mean to bring up bad memories. You don't have to talk about it anymore if you don't want to."

Kael squeezed her paw gently, his touch steady. "It's fine. I've come to terms with it." He drew a slow breath before continuing. "We made a home in New York City. It was brutal at first, but things improved little by little. I finished grade school, then worked wherever I could while keeping an eye on university applications. My adoptive parents couldn't afford to send me to college, so I spent years saving every scrap I could. Eventually I landed a job at the same garage Jake worked at. That was just before I received this scholarship."

Nanuq tilted her head, ears flicking forward. "Isn't MIT... very expensive? How were you able to afford it?"

A smile tugged at Kael's muzzle. "Funny you should ask. You're partly responsible for that."

Her ears perked high, tail giving the slightest twitch of curiosity. She didn't need to speak; her expression urged him on.

"I applied for scholarships at several technical schools," Kael continued. "While waiting to hear back, Jake helped me gather most of your components. You were nearly complete before I was even accepted here. I used your prototype as the subject of my essay. Because of you, they offered me a full ride scholarship, on the condition that—"

"Is that why you built me?" Nanuq blurted, leaning closer,

247

her voice edged with something sharper than curiosity.

He paused, ears twitching toward her before his expression softened. He met her gaze with quiet sincerity and a faint, reassuring smile. "No. You're more than that."

***

"E-excuse me? Did you just say Meena wants to yiff my brains out?"

Nearly choking on his drink, Kael coughed and sputtered until he regained control of his breathing. Wide-eyed, he turned toward her.

Bouncing in her seat, Nanuq grinned over the rim of her spoon. "Yep. Meena wants you to stuff her like a Thanksgiving turkey."

Kael burst into laughter so sudden and loud the drink nearly came back up. "Nanuq! That's… wildly inappropriate! Why would you even say that?"

She shrugged, sipping her soup with infuriating calm. "I bumped into her on the way to pick up your graduation gown. When I mentioned you were interested in her too, she became aroused. From that, I can only conclude she's interested in mating with you."

Kael's ears shot flat against his skull. He stared at her, dumbfounded. "What!? How could you even know that?" He spread his paws helplessly, palms up.

"The same way I know you've just become aroused as well," she answered matter-of-factly, muzzle twitching in amusement. "Your pheromones indicate you strongly desire to mate with her. You want to ruin her mouse kitty. You want to give the mouse a bone. You want to plug her mous—"

"STOP THAT!" Kael yelped, his tail bristling as heat rushed into his cheeks and chest.

Nanuq giggled, ears flicking innocently. "I already sent her a com. You're taking her to that sushi place on the square tomorrow. Wear your favorite jeans and the button-up I laid out."

Kael stiffened as though she'd struck him. Surprise gave

248

way to a flicker of fear, then elation, then raw anxiety all chasing each other across his muzzle.

Smiling sweetly, Nanuq changed gears without warning. "Oh, and I got you a print of your favorite space vixen to celebrate your last day of university."

***

The blacktop still glistened from the storm, reflecting faint streaks of neon and sunset glow. The air was close, heavy with the scent of damp earth as they passed a cleared lot, raw soil exposed for the foundation of some future shop or café. Evening pressed in quickly. The sun fought to color the sky while streetlamps flicked on one by one, their sensors deciding the light was no longer enough.

More than once, Kael's eyes drifted toward her. Her paw swung close to his, inches away, too near and too tempting. He wasn't sure if it was expected to hold paws on a first date. Truth be told, he wasn't sure of much at all. It had been years since his last date, and through college he had avoided romance entirely, convincing himself his studies mattered more than desire. Yet that desire sat low and warm in his chest now, tugging at him every time he glanced at her.

Meena. She was beautiful, though not his species type, and still she captivated him. Her white fur glowed faintly in the lamplight, a genetic miracle matched only by her brilliant red eyes. Once she might have been called albino, but there was more to her than a lack of pigment. Two large incisors peeked slightly when she smiled, and her round, dish-like ears parted the fall of long silver hair that shimmered as she walked.

She wore a pale button-up blouse tucked neatly into a pleated skirt, both shades so close to the one Nanuq had mischievously picked for Kael that he couldn't help but notice. Standing a foot and three inches shorter than his six-two frame, she looked almost delicate at his side, her tail swishing lightly behind her as she glanced up at him. Each time she did, Kael was reminded of Nanuq's own upward

249

looks — though Meena's held a bubbling energy all her own.

Charming. Bright. So different from him.

The conversation at first stumbled, Kael fumbling to find words that didn't sound painfully awkward. Small talk had always struck him as hollow. Yet Meena seemed not to notice his hesitation, happily filling the space with comments about the fashions of passersby or the intrigue of a shopfront's design. After a time, he began to relax. Her chatter, airy and effortless, became something he could lean into, letting her carry them both along.

At last they reached the square. Meena darted ahead, pausing to admire the flowerbeds in the small park at its center. By the time Kael caught up, he found her staring not at the blossoms but at him — more specifically, at a patch of exposed fur on his forearm.

Concerned, he slowed, ears tipping back. "Uh... is everything okay? Am I making you uncomfortable somehow?" A quick dread prickled in his gut — had he broken some social rule? Or worse, did he have something ridiculous on his muzzle?

Blinking rapidly, Meena seemed to shake free from a daze. Color bloomed in her pale cheeks as her red eyes darted up to meet his. "Oh, no! I'm sorry. I was staring, wasn't I? I was just..." She trailed off, ears twitching, clearly embarrassed.

Kael lifted his paw halfway toward her shoulder, then stopped himself. Touch felt like dangerous ground. "Meena? If it's uncomfortable, you can tell me. I won't tease you. I promise."

Her whiskers twitched as she giggled, shaking her head. "No, it's not bad. Not at all. I was just looking at your fur. It's so pretty. I keep fighting the urge to pet you."

Kael froze for a beat, dumbstruck. Then laughter rolled out of him, tail flicking in disbelief. "My fur? There's nothing special about it. If anything, yours is the beautiful pelt. I've never seen a coat so white — it practically glows."

"Oh, don't be so sweet," she teased, grinning wide, her

incisors flashing as she blushed deeper. "You'll make me want to kiss you."

Heat rushed into Kael's cheeks. He turned slightly away, trying for composure but failing, his tail betraying him with a nervous lash. "I... wouldn't mind," he murmured. Then he extended his paw toward her, forcing a steadier voice. "The sushi place is just over there. Ready?"

Her paw slipped eagerly into his, vanishing inside the warmth of his grip. "Lead the way, handsome."

As they crossed the street, a group of men staggered into the restaurant ahead of them, laughing and shouting loud enough to turn heads. For a heartbeat Kael wondered if they should reconsider, but Meena tugged at his paw insistently, ears perked with excitement. A moment later, they stepped into the chicly appointed dining room, exchanging a nervous smile as they waited for a table.

Minutes later they were seated at a small table for two, the closeness lending an intimacy Kael hadn't expected. He pretended to read the menu, though his attention kept straying to her scent — a warm mix of sandalwood and cinnamon. When she smiled, her gaze flicked toward his muzzle, lingering at his lips. Kael realized he was mirroring her, his eyes caught on hers, then drifting downward again.

The spell shattered with a sudden crash from across the room. Laughter followed, ugly and loud. "Hey boys! Look at that mangy wolf over there trying to get some rat cunny! Disgusting!"

Meena gasped, freezing mid-motion. Her ears pressed flat, and Kael felt the weight of her tension as though it were his own. His eyes snapped toward the men — already half-drunk, their table a mess of bottles and plates. His claws curled into his palms, a slow burn of anger rising through his chest. He forced his voice steady. "Maybe we should go." He flicked his gaze back to her, then toward the door.

She sat stiffly for a moment, then exhaled and gave a small nod. "Why don't we get it to go? We can eat at my place. Would that be okay?" Her eyes searched his, serious, shaded with worry.

251

Minutes later, they walked together beneath the dim streetlights, silent and contemplative. Meena leaned close, threading her arm beneath his. The warmth of the gesture eased the raw edge of the restaurant scene, her silver hair brushing against his sleeve.

"I'm… not so hungry anymore," she murmured, peeking up at him with a spark of mischief in her red eyes. "Any chance you'd be interested in what those tailholes back there were ranting about?"

Kael stumbled in his step, ears jerking upright. "W-what?" The shock jolted through him, equal parts thrill and panic. He knew, thanks to Nanuq's meddling, that Meena was attracted to him. But hearing her say it — so bluntly — rattled him.

Her own eyes widened as the weight of her words caught up to her. She pressed her paws to her muzzle, ears burning crimson. "Oh, Pan. I didn't mean it to come out like that! It just… slipped." She lowered her paws slowly, whiskers twitching with embarrassment. "But if I'm honest…" She hesitated, glancing sidelong at him. "I've been thinking about it since the day we met."

Kael laughed nervously, rubbing at the back of his neck. "I'd be lying if I said I hadn't thought the same." His tail twitched, betraying him even as he tried to recover his composure. "But… maybe coffee first? It's been a long time since I…" His voice faltered, the admission left unfinished.

Moments later they stood in her small kitchenette, coffee cups in hand, the steam curling between them. Silence stretched, charged with the weight of every glance. Kael inhaled softly, catching her scent again — sandalwood overlaid with the warm spice of cinnamon — and stepped closer.

"Have you…" His ears flicked back as he searched for words. "Have you ever been with a wolf before?"

Her cheeks warmed as his size pressed subtly into her space. She held her ground, sipping once more before setting her cup on the counter. Her knees quivered despite herself, her nose twitching as his scent reached her — clean soap

252

layered over a natural musk that stirred something low inside her. She shook her head slowly, eyes never leaving his.

Kael nodded, closing the gap inch by inch. "As I understand..." He hesitated, aware she might notice the studied tone. "Our species can't interbreed without genetic assistance."

Meena tilted her head, whiskers twitching. "Are you saying... you can't get me pregnant without a doctor's help?" She shuffled back until her tail brushed the counter's edge, pretending composure while her ears betrayed her, twitching sharply.

"Yes." Kael's voice dropped as his eyes trailed to her lips, lingering there before returning to her gaze. "Are you familiar with canine physiology?"

"A little," she admitted, breath catching. "Why?"

He gave a small shrug, shoulders loose though his tail betrayed his nerves with a faint flick. "We don't have the spines your species does."

Her ears jerked up, then she blinked rapidly, realization dawning. Her mouth parted in a small gasp as her eyes flicked downward, ears flushing crimson. "T-those spines?" she whispered, pointing sheepishly toward his jeans where a swelling bulge was already pressing against the fabric.

A grin tugged briefly at his muzzle before he grew serious again. "Yeah. Those. Instead... we have what's called a pseudo-knot."

Meena tilted her head further, silver hair sliding over one shoulder as her eyes darted down again. "A... knot?" Her whiskers twitched nervously. "Like something you tie in string? That doesn't make any sense."

Laughing low in his chest, Kael leaned in, gaze sweeping over her with newfound boldness. She was nervous — he could see it in the way her chest rose and fell too quickly, her small breasts lifting with each breath. One paw clutched the counter, the other pressed flat to her thigh as though pinning herself in place. Normally he wasn't this forward, but something about her unmoored his restraint.

"No," he said, his grin widening to show sharp canines.

"Not like tying string. Think of it more like the spines male mice have. An adaptation for mating competition."

Meena raised a brow, leaning closer, her silver hair brushing forward as her ears flicked upright. Her eyes danced between his lips and his stare, the heat in her voice betraying her composure. "And how does… a knot help with that?"

His muzzle curved in a feral smile as he shrugged. "When canines mate, a bulb at the base of the penis swells during climax. It locks the male inside the female, keeping them tied together while he finishes. Sometimes for an hour."

Her crimson eyes widened with every word, ears flicking, whiskers trembling. Her paw crept up to cover her mouth, though her gaze slid inevitably downward toward the bulge straining his jeans. The air between them tightened, her breaths quick and shallow. "And that… that could happen to us? If we… copulate?" Her lips hovered just inches from his.

"It could," Kael admitted with a slow nod. His voice dropped lower, steady and coaxing. "But I'm not fully canine. My physiology is hybrid — part human, part wolf. Most of the time, unless you're very tight, my knot isn't thick enough to keep me locked. Which means…" His eyes half-lidded, holding hers. "…I can use it for your pleasure instead."

Meena let out a sharp breath she hadn't realized she'd been holding, her ears burning red. Then, as if surrendering, she whispered, "I think I know what you mean."

Their lips closed the distance, crashing together in a kiss heated with everything unspoken until now.

She barely got the words out before their mouths collided again, a frantic tangle of lips and tongue. Kael's paws roamed greedily, gripping her hips and ass while she clawed at the button of his jeans, finally snapping it open and fumbling with the zipper. His paw slipped beneath her skirt, finding the curve of her butt and tugging playfully at her panties.

At last she freed him, tugging his jeans down until they pooled at his ankles. Their kiss broke as her breath hitched, her paw tugging his boxers down over the thick outline

254

beneath. His cock sprang free, crimson and slick at the tip, precum smearing across her belly and leaving a glistening streak on the fabric of her skirt. She stared, transfixed, at the heavy girth and the subtle swell of his knot just visible past his sheath.

"How big does it get?" she breathed, sliding her fingers around his shaft. Her paw glided lower, thumb and forefinger brushing the firm knot at its base.

Kael gasped, his whole body jerking with the sudden squeeze. Years had passed since anyone touched him like this, and the shock nearly unraveled him. For a heartbeat he could only savor it, panting, his own paw clumsy as it tried to push her skirt down her hips. Eyes dropping to watch her delicate paw gripping him, he stammered, "A l-little bigger. Maybe the size of... your fist."

Her other paw came up between them, curling into a fist as her crimson eyes widened. Wonder turned to disbelief. "You're gonna shove that in me?!"

Her grip tightened, making him buck involuntarily. He shook his head, voice rough between gasps. "I'd like to... but I don't have to. Not if it's too much." His cock pulsed in her grasp, each throb betraying his desperation.

The disbelief in her gaze melted into something hotter — a spark of curiosity sharpened with challenge. Her whiskers twitched as she pressed her paw firmly to his chest, pushing him back just enough to claim control. Her voice dropped to a hushed command.

"Take your clothes off."

Kael nodded quickly, fumbling with the buttons of his shirt until it fell to the floor. His paws shook as he stepped free of his boxers, eyes fixed on her as she hooked her thumbs under her skirt and slid it down her thighs. Beneath, her panties clung to her curves, white with little pawprints running like tracks from waistband to crotch. His breath caught as she tugged them lower, a small tuft of pubic fur — dyed pink — revealed above her mound.

She stepped free of the fabric and straightened, her eyes never leaving his. Reaching back, she unclasped her bra, the

255

straps slipping loose before the garment joined the heap on the floor. For a moment, it struck him that she still wore her blouse, the fabric framing the sudden exposure of her breasts. Two perfectly round mounds rose and fell with her quickening breaths, tipped with pink nubs that stood taut in the cool air.

She swayed slightly, restless under his gaze, her hips shifting in a rhythm that pulled his attention lower. Her mound glistened faintly, the hood of her clit just visible as moisture slicked her lips. He had only a heartbeat to marvel at the human-like contours of her sex before she dropped suddenly to her knees.

Her paw wrapped firmly around the base of his shaft, knot and all, before her mouth engulfed him. Kael nearly shouted, claws digging into the counter behind him as the heat of her muzzle surrounded his length. Her tongue curled, coaxing him deeper as her paw squeezed at his base, and a guttural growl tore from his throat. It had been years since anyone touched him like this — too long — and the storm of sensation slammed through him faster than he could control.

"Meena—" he choked, but his words broke into a gasp as his climax surged. His knot swelled in her grip, the first violent pulse nearly buckling his knees. He grasped her face with both paws, hips jerking forward, burying himself deeper. Her muffled gasp vibrated against his shaft as he erupted down her throat, hot streams spilling in thick waves. The feeling of her swallowing around him nearly sent him collapsing to the floor.

For endless seconds he trembled, riding out the throbbing waves until at last he felt her struggling beneath his grip. Guilt cut through the haze. Loosening his hold, he let himself slip from her lips, his cock dragging free and leaving a trail of seed that dribbled down her chin.

Meena gasped, coughing lightly as she wiped her muzzle with the back of her paw. Kael's ears burned with shame as his eyes darted around the kitchenette. He tore a handful of synth paper towels from the roll and handed them to her quickly, tail low.

"I—" he started, voice ragged, unsure whether to apologize or thank her.

Kael watched her wipe his cum from her chin, ears still burning with embarrassment. But instead of chastising him, she giggled. "That was quick!" Her voice was light, teasing, before she turned and bent over the counter. With a flick of her tail she bared her sex to him, her slick folds glistening in the dim light. She swayed her hips slowly, deliberately, whiskers twitching as she looked back over her shoulder.

"Feeling up to another round? Or three?" Her grin widened, her breath husky. "Don't hold back. Rut me hard… then shove that knot inside me, just like I know you want to."

The words struck him like lightning. His cock twitched back to full hardness in an instant, a rush of heat flooding his chest. Whatever shame had lingered was drowned beneath the raw, primal hunger rising in his gut.

He stepped up behind her, his paws firm on her hips as he pressed the slick head of his shaft against her velvet folds. She whimpered at the contact, tail flicking higher to give him better access. He rubbed along her entrance, smearing her arousal across his tip before pushing forward.

Slowly, steadily, he slid himself into her, savoring the heat that clamped down on him. Her body yielded, stretching to take him deeper until at last he was buried to the hilt, his knot pressed flush against her trembling sex.

Kael froze there for a heartbeat, panting, overcome by the sheer tightness of her around him. His claws dug lightly into her waist, fur bristling with the intensity of it. He had no time to waste — she'd asked for him, begged for him — and now he was going to give her everything.

CHAPTER 16 - NOT JAKE.

"What's this?" Nanuq asked as they reached their private booth.

"Our booth. Why?" Kael slid the door open, gesturing her inside.

"I know that. But why are we in a booth? Aren't these expensive?" She plopped into the seat by the window, her tail curling against the cushion.

"Not that much." He shrugged, closing the door behind them. Slipping in beside her, he tucked his bag beneath the seat and let the restraints click shut around his waist. "I had a voucher from my canceled flight last time. Besides... I didn't want people gawking at us, since you insist on dressing like that."

Blinking, Nanuq glanced down at her nude frame, fur sleek in the cabin lights. "What do you mean? I'm not wearing anything."

"Exactly." He huffed, leaning forward to engage the holo display. Pairing his headset, he muttered, "Do you want to play a game or something?"

She ignored that, ears angling toward him. "When are you going to tell me about your date with Meena? You haven't said a word for over a week. I've been patient, Kael, but this is getting ridiculous. How did it go?"

Kael shifted uncomfortably, pretending to scroll the holo listings. "It went… okay. Not much to talk about."

Nanuq leaned in, eyes narrowing, her whiskers twitching with focus. "Oh? Was the restaurant nice at least?"

"Yeah, but we ended up leaving early."

Her ears pricked higher. "You left early? Why? Where'd you go after? You didn't come home until pretty late."

"There were some really rude men near our table, so we just got the food to go."

"Why not just go to another restaurant?"

He shrugged again, ears flicking back. "That's what she wanted. She really likes their sushi, didn't want to miss out. So… we went to her place."

Nanuq sat back, tapping her claws lightly on the tabletop as she studied him. "What'd you do there?"

"We just hung out."

Her tail gave an incredulous flick. "Oh. You just hung out. What else did you do?"

Kael's paw fumbled with the controls as the holo suddenly flashed to a stream of two anthros kissing. He scrambled to change it, his ears burning. "We just watched some holo stuff. Nothing special."

"Oh? What kind of holo stuff?" she pressed.

"Some sci-fi," he muttered, keeping his eyes fixed firmly on the display.

Her ears perked high, curiosity sparking. "Oh? Which?"

"Just… some of the usual," Kael replied, voice deliberately flat.

Nanuq narrowed her eyes, leaning in to sniff at him. Her nose twitched, and suddenly she gasped, sitting bolt upright. "You had sex!" Her tail lashed in excitement as she pointed at him accusingly. "Kael, you're naughty! You're not supposed to do that until at least the third date!"

Kael threw up his paws, exasperated. "I know, I know! It was a weird night, okay? It just… happened!" He gestured wildly toward an invisible sushi table. "Those tailholes at the restaurant made some comment about a wolf and a rat, and…

259

well, it got under her skin. Later she just blurted it out and asked if I wanted to…"

Nanuq's ears flicked forward, her eyes wide, muzzle parting in a grin. She mimed scribbling notes in the air. "She did?! What did you say? I mean — obviously you said yes — but Pan, that must have been a shock!"

Chuckling nervously, Kael reached to turn the holo volume down. "Yeah, it was. At first I didn't even answer, because I wasn't sure I'd heard her right. When I asked, she got super embarrassed. Turns out it just… slipped."

"What happened after that?!" she pressed, bouncing slightly in her seat, whiskers twitching.

Kael's ears darkened with blush. "Well… I suggested coffee. And then one thing led to another and… you know the rest."

"I most certainly do not!" Nanuq scoffed, shaking her head so vigorously her ears flopped. She leaned in closer, tail curling against the seat. "Who made the first move? I want to know everything! Tell me immediately!"

He let out a long, heavy sigh, pinching the bridge of his muzzle. "Can we talk about something else? It feels weird talking about this with you."

"Argh! But it's so interesting, Kael!" She flopped back dramatically in her seat, arms crossing over her chest. "I want to learn more about how sex works, and you're my best source of information!"

"I'm sorry, Nanuq. It just feels like sharing bedroom details with my daughter. It's… super weird." He shrugged, ears flattening as he pulled up his com display. "Anyway, I haven't heard from Jake in a few days. I'm worried he broke or lost his com. I'll send him another poke."

***

"Have you had a chance to see the whole ship yet, Jake?" Reaper asked as they sat down to breakfast in the galley.

The automated servers rolled toward them on wide bases, each topped with a post-like protuberance. Near the floor, a half-sphere housed sensors, while small displays at the top flicked from blank to a perfunctory smile as they detected sentient life. Short telescoping arms unfolded with multi-function grabbers, ready to take orders.

As one of the machines paused beside Dusk, Yuriy grimaced at hearing the alias again. "Not Jake," he blurted before he could stop himself, wincing at his own slip.

Reaper and Dusk turned toward him, speaking in unison. "Not Jake?"

Yuriy cleared his throat, chewing at his lip. Frustration flashed across his features. "My name isn't Jake," he muttered.

Reaper tilted his head toward Dusk. "What did he just say?"

Ignoring him, Dusk leaned forward, ears pricked, eyes narrowing in curiosity. "Alright, 'not Jake,'" she said dryly. "What is your name then?"

"I can explain." Yuriy lifted a paw, only to be interrupted as the serving robot chirped, awaiting his order. He seized on the delay, turning to the machine. "Three traditional breakfasts."

The robot's face blinked in confusion. "Error. Protocol allows one order per individual."

With a low growl of irritation, Yuriy pulled his tablet, jacked it into the rear port, and tapped in a string of commands. The robot froze, whirred, then reset. When he unplugged, he repeated calmly, "Three traditional breakfasts." This time the machine trundled away without complaint.

Sighing, Yuriy turned back. "Sorry. Where was I?"

Dusk's tail flicked behind her as she studied him. "You were about to explain why your name isn't Jake."

Nodding, he met her gaze. "This may sound insane, but my real name is Yuriy. I was framed for a mafia murder and forced to escape to the UCA by faking my own death. I know it's hard to believe — Pan, I barely believe it myself — but it's the truth."

Dusk leaned in close, eyes narrowing further as if trying

261

to read the truth off his muzzle. "Framed twice, and always tipped off just in time? You'll forgive me, Yuriy, if I find that... very convenient."

Before Yuriy could speak again, Reaper cut in with a firm wave of his paw. "I believe him. It all lines up. That apartment block he was living in? Full of Russian immigrants, all cash payers, spotless records. The manager? Too many shadowy connections back in Russia, money transfers coming in with no clear reason. And Yuriy — Jake, whatever you want to call him — was sending money to Russia too. But here's the thing: no paper trail tying his alias back there. I knew something was off, I just couldn't nail it."

Dusk's eyes narrowed to slits, ears flattening. "So let me get this straight. You invited a potential murderer aboard our ship, knowing he was hiding something? Reaper, have you completely lost your mind?"

Reaper leaned back, paws lifted in defense, tail lashing uneasily. "Whoa, whoa! I didn't know anything about a murder charge! It was either that or let him take the fall for that tailhole ferret. And look at him!" He jabbed a paw toward Yuriy. "Does he look like a killer to you? Not an evil bone in his body."

"You don't know that," Dusk snapped, voice sharp enough to cut. Her eyes locked on Reaper, then shifted to bore into Yuriy.

Clearing his throat, Yuriy raised a paw sheepishly. "If I may... The money I send to Russia goes to my adoptive sister. Only she, my old boss Ivan, and the forger who made my new identity know I'm still alive. You could contact her, but if the Russian authorities learn the truth, she'll be in danger." He rubbed anxiously at a button on his overalls, voice dropping. "I couldn't risk keeping records, but you can dig using my real name. The man who was killed — he was the son of a powerful politician. The mafia did it to frame Ivan. I was just trying to make a life for my sister and me after our father died." His gaze flicked between them, pleading. "Please... don't make me leave the Claw. I have nowhere else."

For a long moment, silence stretched across the table. Dusk's ears wilted slightly, though her eyes stayed hard. Finally she exhaled, a hiss through her teeth. "Alright. I'll go along with it. For now." Her tail flicked sharply as she leaned closer. "But if I ever find out you've lied to us, Yuriy, so help me—" She broke off, shaking her head. "Just... don't."

Yuriy's eyes widened, ears tilting back. "O-of course not, Miss Dusk! I swear I'm telling the truth. I never wanted to leave Russia, but if I hadn't... I'd never have met friends like you and Reaper. And Kael too." His voice softened. "He's from Russia as well, escaped after the great floods. I think that's why we connected — same roots. But I could never tell him the real reason I left..."

He froze mid-thought, then smacked his forehead. "Salted cucumber! I forgot about Kael!"

As he fumbled clumsily with his com, the service robots arrived, setting their trays neatly in front of each of them. Dusk and Reaper exchanged a glance but let him panic for a moment before Reaper finally spoke, pointing his knife toward the device. "Ether signal's notoriously weak out here. The ship's got a repeater, but you'll need clearance to use it."

Nodding as she picked apart something that resembled a cinnamon roll, Dusk added, "We can authorize it once we're certain you are who you say you are. But this Kael you mentioned — who is he?"

"Kael and I met at Sable's shop. We worked together for a while before he left for school. He and Nanuq were supposed to visit today." Yuriy's ears drooped, his voice tinged with worry. "I need to send him a message before he thinks something's happened."

"Nanuq?" Reaper asked, his muzzle smeared with a bit of jam as he looked up.

Yuriy placed the com down with a sigh and picked up his fork, carefully slicing into a fried egg as if to steady his nerves. "She's an experimental android. He built her in his spare time. I think his thesis was about her."

Both Reaper and Dusk froze mid-bite. Their ears flicked sharply toward Yuriy, eyes narrowing with sudden focus.

"He's an engineering student?" Reaper asked slowly.

Yuriy shook his head as he chewed, then quickly swallowed. "Was. He finished his degree last week and wanted to come back to New York to celebrate."

"An engineering major who builds his own androids…" Dusk murmured, flicking an ear toward Reaper.

Reaper's muzzle curved faintly. "Any chance he's looking for work?"

Still focused on his plate, Yuriy only shrugged. "Why do you ask?"

Reaper didn't answer. He'd already pulled up his com, eyes flicking across the screen as though sifting through a feed. His ears twitched, betraying focus. He glanced at Yuriy, back at the display, then shifted the subject without explanation. "What's your sister's name, Yuriy?"

The question softened him. He lifted his gaze, expression warming. "Anya."

Reaper nodded slightly. "Describe her."

"She's twenty-six. Human. Black hair, blue eyes. Still in Moscow, finishing her degree at State University." His voice carried both pride and worry.

"Mm." Reaper's eyes stayed fixed, his tone even. "And who is Petar Petrovski?"

The name hit like a slap. Yuriy stiffened, ears twitching back. His voice dropped, edged. "The father of the man who was murdered. A powerful politician. His son's body was planted in a car I transported for Ivan. That's what made me the prime suspect."

Reaper's ears flicked again, but his expression didn't change. "And Boris?"

Yuriy's face fell. His paw lifted, tracing the sign of the cross across his chest. "My father. May he rest in peace."

Reaper leaned forward, muzzle tightening. "He was human, wasn't he? How could he be your father?"

Yuriy's eyes snapped up, cold now, voice firm. "He raised me from a cub. He is my father."

A tense beat stretched between them. Reaper exhaled and lifted his paws, tail easing back. "I meant no disrespect. Just making sure you are who you say you are."

Yuriy nodded solemnly, eyes on his plate though he made no move to eat.

"Now," Reaper said, wiping his muzzle with the back of his paw, "about your friend Kael. The Claw could use talent like his. Why not invite him for a tour?"

Dusk arched a brow, suspicion in her gaze. "We haven't even enabled Yuriy's ether yet. How's he supposed to do that?"

"I just enabled it." Reaper's reply was flat, confident. Almost on cue, Yuriy's com lit up, pinging with a cascade of delayed notifications.

Dusk's ears shot back. "You what?" she hissed.

Reaper smirked and flicked several documents to her com. "I had the ship's AI check him while we've been eating. Look — news clippings on Petrovski's son, confirmation of the suspect's 'death' the next day, family records on his sister, his parents. It all matches what he told us. Doesn't gain him anything to lie, not now. So either he's a genius manipulator, or he's just telling the truth."

With a long sigh, Dusk leaned back in her seat, ears lowering. "Fine. But if he kills us, Reaper, I'm killing you first."

Lost in the stream of messages, Yuriy finally looked up, muzzle breaking into a smile. "Thank you. I won't disappoint. Kael's expecting me in the park at five, so we've got time to get ready."

Before either could respond, movement flickered at the edge of his vision. Something long and furred darted across the galley, leaping from one counter to another before vanishing behind a prep unit.

"Uh…" Yuriy blinked, pointing. "Is there… any chance this ship has a rodent problem?"

Reaper's ears flicked, brow furrowing. "A rodent problem? Not that I've ever heard. Why?"

"I just saw something fast and furry jump between those

265

counters," Yuriy said, gesturing toward the shadowed gap. "White, I think. With... black spots maybe?"

Reaper's expression shifted, muzzle tugging into a wry grin as he rubbed his chin. "Hmm. About the size of a ferret?"

Yuriy tilted his head, ears pricked. "Yes — exactly. How did you know?"

***

"Kael! It's so good to see you again, my friend!" Yuriy boomed, sweeping him into a rib-crushing bear hug.

Kael groaned, paws flailing until Yuriy finally set him back down. He staggered a step, straightened his shirt, then jerked a thumb toward the white-furred vixen beside him. "Trip was fine. But more importantly — meet my advanced, always adorable, and astonishingly amiable android arctic fox daughter... Nanuq!"

"Tails! What a wonderful name," Yuriy replied, still grinning as he thrust out a paw to shake hers.

Nanuq ignored it completely. Instead, she threw her paws wide and bounced on her footpaws, tail swishing. "Hi Jake! I want a hug too!"

Laughing, Yuriy scooped her up with the same gusto, squeezing her until her servos whined in protest. When he finally set her down, she wobbled for a second, ears perked and muzzle grinning.

The park was quiet, the summer sun soaking the empty paths and benches in golden warmth. With so few people around, the three of them could enjoy the day without drawing stares. Kael breathed it in, glad for the peace — until he noticed Yuriy's grin falter. Something weighed on him, pulling his features down.

"Everything alright, Jake? You look a little... distracted."

Yuriy nodded quickly but glanced around as if checking for eavesdroppers. "I've got some things to tell you. But... let's find somewhere more comfortable first."

Kael's ears flicked at the sound of kids playing in the distance. He spotted a picnic table tucked under a tree, its shade spilling across the grass. He pointed with a paw. "How about there?"

Moments later, they settled at the worn wooden table, Nanuq sitting neatly but curious as ever, eyes scanning the park. Kael leaned forward on his elbows, muzzle tilted. "So, what's up, snuggie? Trouble in the arctic?"

Yuriy smiled sheepishly, ears flicking as he scratched at his neck. "Just... promise me you won't freak out, okay?"

Kael blinked, glancing at Nanuq before looking back, brow furrowed. "Alright, I promise. But if this is about the french fries again, I swear—"

"Not fries," Yuriy interrupted with a shake of his head. He sucked in a breath, then blurted, words tumbling out in a rush. "I'm technically a fugitive. I joined a kind of gang. My name isn't Jake. My home is in space now. And... my new friends want you to join."

Silence settled over the picnic table, broken only by the distant chatter of birds.

"Cool! Let's join a gang!" Nanuq chirped, her tail whipping back and forth in glee.

Kael blinked hard, like he'd just been jolted awake. "E-excuse me?" His ears tipped back, confusion stark in his face. "If your name isn't Jake, then what is it? What gang are we talking about, and how in Pan's name is your home in space?"

"My real name is Yuriy." He offered a crooked, sheepish smile. "I faked my own death and fled Russia to the UCA after I was framed. I didn't have a choice. Ended up joining the Pride, living on a ship called the Claw... all because my boss here was an evil, jealous tailhole." His paw clenched briefly on the table before he let it go. "Honestly, it's risky even meeting you like this, but I owed you the truth before I asked if you'd visit the ship. Assuming you're interested."

Kael and Nanuq both stared at him, shock written clear in their faces. Then Nanuq tilted her head, ears flicking. "What were you framed for?"

Yuriy let out a long sigh, then repeated the story he'd told Dusk and Reaper in the galley — the mafia, the politician's son, the planted body, his flight to survive.

When he finished, Kael leaned back, silent for a long moment before finally shrugging. "I remember when you had that pet beetle. Found it with a broken leg, tried to nurse it back to health. You were devastated when it died the next day." His muzzle softened into a faint smile. "A guy like that? You're no murderer. So…" He stood, brushing dust from his fur. "When do we leave for your ship?"

"Yay! We're gang members now!" Nanuq bounced in place, pumping her fist, her ears perked high with excitement.

Yuriy grinned and gestured toward an open patch of grass. "Transport's ready."

Kael and Nanuq turned as the air began to shimmer, the sunlight warping like heat haze. Ripples twisted, then solidified into the sleek, angular form of a landing craft descending on silent thrusters. Grass swirled beneath the downdraft, the Claw's insignia gleaming faintly across its hull as it settled onto the ground.

Both Kael and Nanuq gasped in unison.

***

"I just told you, I can't pay you right now, Akito! I barely scraped enough credits to repair my speeder last time." Finn's voice rang sharp in the cramped garage, echoing off steel beams. She hurled a soiled rag to the floor, ears pinned back. "You keep docking my pay for that rutting loan at the worst times. If you'd compensate me fairly, maybe I could pay more — but until then, every credit goes to keeping my racer alive. Otherwise I'm done! Can't you do me a favor just this once?"

A few steps behind her, the smartly dressed man only shrugged, smoothing the lapel of his jacket. "You know I don't control the books. I'm just the messenger. What I can do — " he slipped a hand casually into his pocket, as if discussing the weather " — is offer you another loan. But it'll be the last until you pay something back."

Finn's growl vibrated in her chest as she closed the distance, wrench glinting in her paw. At five foot nine, she loomed taller than most of her snow leopard kin, her cutoffs and crop top leaving no doubt of the power packed into her frame. Her arms, thick with muscle beneath their sleek gray-and-white fur, flexed around the tool. Her thick tail lashed behind her, sweeping in slow arcs that hitched at every reversal, betraying her agitation. Her amber eyes locked on his, unblinking, predator intent narrowing the air between them.

Akito didn't flinch.

The silence stretched until Finn finally exhaled, dropping her gaze back to the racer's battered chassis. The craft was a wreck, but if she could get it running before the high-stakes race... she'd be free of the Yakuza leeching her dry. If she lost? She'd be owned.

With a disgusted huff, she spun back toward him, wrench still dangling in her paw. "Fine. I need a loan to get this heap running before the big race. Can you help me, or not?"

Only then did Akito's shoulders ease. He drew a sleek tablet from his jacket with the same care one might unsheathe a blade. "Suit yourself," he said smoothly. "How much are you trying to get?"

Finn weighed it out in her head. Routine repairs. A powerplant upgrade. And enough left over for food so she wouldn't be running on fumes. "Two thousand. Give or take," she said coolly.

Akito typed into his tablet, eyes fixed on the display until it chimed. Only then did he look up, shaking his head. "I can do eighteen hundred."

Shit. That almost gutted the food budget. She smirked inwardly, thankful she'd padded the number. Out loud she hissed, "That's barely rutting usable. But I guess I don't have much of a choice, do I?"

He only shrugged, tapped the screen, and slipped a credit chip free. Holding it between two fingers, he offered it like

269

bait. "Same terms as last time. But this is the last one. Got it?"

Finn snatched it from his hand and shoved it into her pocket, turning her back on him with a huff. "Got it. Now get out of my way and kindly go rut yourself. You and your whole lot are stains on your species. Shame's a luxury you don't feel under that pressed suit."

Akito stood, unfazed, eyes tracking the sway of her hips as she walked away. Sliding the tablet back into his coat, he produced a slim cigarette case, plucked one with his lips, and flicked a lighter. Smoke curled lazily as he exhaled, his gaze never leaving her. "If you ever want to make a few extra credits," he said smoothly, "I've always wanted to get my dick wet in that kitty, cat."

Finn froze mid-step. Every muscle went tight, her tail stiffening like a steel rod, paw squeezing her wrench until the metal bit into her pads. She drew a slow breath, then spoke low through clenched teeth. "Get out, Akito. Before I turn this wrench into a dental tool."

Turning on her heel, she bared her fangs in a sharp, wicked grin, eyes glinting amber fire. "And if you ever talk to me like that again, I'll make sure you live long enough to regret being separated from your lips... one rusty plier at a time."

CHAPTER 17 - ENOLA.

A cabinet door slammed in the other room, causing her to flinch. Her paw froze over the half-assembled puzzle, the six oval sections jolted and slipped from her trembling grasp. She blinked rapidly as tears welled in her eyes, preventing her from continuing. The shouting had started again, louder this time.

It had always been like this, or at least for as long as Dalha could remember since the accident. Her dad meant well, she knew that. Still, no matter how hard he tried, he couldn't seem to hold himself together. Her step mother never let him forget it, every failure was laid bare. He'd promise to do better, fall short, then the cycle would begin again.

"Why does this keep happening Aden? Every time we start to get ahead, you start with this rutting self pity and ruin everything!"

This time, Nima sounded as if she were truly done. Her voice cracked with each word. Angry syllables dangling at the edge of a sob.

"I'm sorry, Nima. I knew I said I wouldn't do it again, but — they laid me off today. I just — I couldn't stop myself. I'll fix it. I swear."

A long silence, then came the grinding scrape of a chair

being pulled across tile, followed by a weary sigh.

Dalha reached for the puzzle, her fingers shaking as she gathered each piece from the floor. She began to reassemble them with delicate movements, trying to drown the voices out with the familiar clicks of plastic. The silence broke again just as she slid the final piece into place.

"It's too late Aden. I'm done. Marrying you was a mistake."

Time froze, as Dalha gazed at the completed puzzle in her paw. The colorful object resembled a tiny, fragile volleyball, but she couldn't see it anymore — her ears were ringing now.

"What are you saying Nima?"

"I'm saying I want a divorce, Aden. I want you and Dalha out of the house by the end of the week."

"You can't kick us out. We live here! Where are we supposed go?"

"I can, and I will. This house has always been mine. You had your chance." There was a pause, followed by the faint sound of paper sliding across a table. "You and your daughter are guests in my house for the remainder of the week. Then, I want you gone."

"How am I supposed to take care of Dalha without a job, Nima?!" Her father's voice rose, sounding raw and desperate.

"That's for you and her to figure out, Aden. You know I never wanted children. That kitten is your responsibility... For her sake, I hope you get your act together before it's too late."

Their words muffled abruptly as her bedroom door slammed shut behind her. Her puzzle ball slipped from her paw, shattering on the floor with a jarring clatter.

She dove into her bed, sobs wracking her as she buried herself under the covers. She clutched the stuffed wolf her father had given her for her fifth birthday, folding it into herself as she wept in silence.

Dalha barely remembered her mother. just the warmth in her eyes, the way she reached out to hug her the night she

272

died. Her parents had hired a sitter to watch her for the night, while they went out for their tenth anniversary. That night, while under the influence, her father lost control of their craft and slammed it into a retaining wall at a deadly speed. Her mother died on impact, but her father walked away with only a few broken bones.

He'd spent the next few years at the bottom of a bottle, leaving Dalha alone for long stretches of time or placing her in the care of her grandmother. He'd remarried last year, and held it together for a while. But after losing another job a few months back, things began to unravel once more.

She noticed the shouting had finally stopped, quieted and listened intently. Her ears twitched as a creak in the hallway signaled movement outside. Then came the soft click of her door, as her father turned the latch and peeked inside.

"Hey kitten..." her father whispered as he stepped inside and sat at the edge of her bed.

Dalha turned, looking up at him. The sour scent of alcohol hung on his breath, she could see the tired lines etched into his face, and he couldn't quite meet her gaze as he spoke.

"I need you to gather up your things, and put them into your bags," he murmured, brushing a lock of her hair aside, pressing a kiss to her forehead. "We're gonna take a trip tomorrow, okay? Can you do that for me?"

She nodded silently, wiping the tears from her cheeks.

***

They moved around a lot after that. Her dad would take various odd jobs wherever he could find them, and Dalha adjusted to a string of new schools. He rarely stayed employed for long — his drinking always caught up with him — but he made sure she was fed. That much, he never failed.

It had been a few years since the divorce, but nothing really improved. He continued to drift from job to job, often leaving Dalha alone for days. She learned to take care of herself. If she were honest, she preferred it that way. At least solitude didn't slur it's words, or forget to pay the light bill.

By this time, Dalha was in her early teens and tended to be moody and withdrawn. She'd taken to dressing in dark clothing, adopting a gothic style that contrasted boldly with the brilliance of her white fur. She didn't make many friends at school — there was no point, not when every move just meant another goodbye.

That isolation, and her reclusive behavior, made her an easy target for bullies. Though she learned to defend herself early, it often meant detention and trouble,

She'd come to accept her lot in life. But recently, the pressure of late adolescence had begun to drive a wedge between her and her father. Communication was eventually reduced only to necessities, and was often tense and strained.

"I need some credits for lunch," she said flatly, as she sat at the kitchen table, chewing on a slice of pizza — another salvaged leftover from her father's employment.

Sitting across from her, he chewed on his slice before glancing up at her. "I gave you thirty credits on Monday, Dalha. What did you do with it? You know I told you to stop spending it on sweet treats."

She rolled her eyes, and growled softly before responding. "I told you already. I used it pay the water bill on Tuesday."

He narrowed his eyes at her, and set his slice down. "Don't growl at me, Dalha. I won't have you disrespecting me in my own home!"

"What home?" she snapped, voice rising as anger suddenly boiled over. "You're never here anyway!"

"Enough!" He roared, slashing his paw through the air in front of her. "Go to your room, I'll give you some credits in the morning."

This was the way of their relationship. He'd forget to pay a bill. She'd cover it with her lunch credits, or credits borrowed. Then they would argue about it. Or she would go without. Anything to avoid another argument. She guessed that was why she was always underweight. It didn't matter

— the hunger was easier to live with than the shouting.

***

"What's the matter kitty, cat got your tongue?" the bully sneered, cornering Dalha near the girls' bathroom. He yanked at her tail, then mussed her hair, trying to provoke a reaction.

Dalha didn't flinch. She refused to dignify the boy with an answer. She simply fixed him with a flat, empty stare, waiting for his next move.

"Aww, don't be sad-face little kitty, I'm just yiffing around," he taunted, grinning as he reached for her tail again.

She stepped aside, whipped her tail out of his reach, and issued a low growl from deep in her throat. "Don't do that again."

"Or what? You gonna maul me?" he asked, his grin widening, eyes gleaming with amusement as he jabbed a finger into her chest.

She slapped his hand away without hesitation, her growl rising.

The boy snorted, unfazed, then poked at her again — harder this time.

Her eyes grew cold after slapping his hand away, this time more forcefully. His grin faltered, this latest slap stinging his hand.

Scowling, he grabbed her arm and tried to shake her.

Dalha's free paw snapped up without hesitation, and with knuckle-bruising force, struck him square in the left eye. He reeled back, blinded and shrieking, as he clapped his hands over the injured eye.

Satisfied, Dalha turned her back to the boy and began to walk away. His gibbering cries echoed down the corridor, drawing attention to them as she departed with calm, measured steps.

"Stop right there Dalha!", came a sharp voice from behind her. Her fifth-period history teacher spoke accusingly as she

275

froze and turned in his direction. Pointing sharply toward the boy crumpled on the floor in front of them.

"Did you do this?"

Dalha shrugged, expression cool and unreadable. "He deserved it."

***

He smelled of booze again, swaying while he lingered in her bedroom doorway. He'd been barging in more often lately; that usually meant he was thinking about mother again.

Dalha sighed, rising from her bed. She went to him and tried to redirect him to his own room, "Come on dad, you're drunk, lets get you to bed, okay?"

"Did I ever tell you how much you look like your mother?" He asked, his voice thick as they shuffled toward his bedroom. "She was about your age when we met. What are you, fifteen now?"

"Sixteen dad, my birthday was just last month." She sighed again, letting him lean heavily against her as they struggled to move down the hallway, his arm slung over her shoulders.

He grunted as they stumbled, bouncing off the bedroom door frame while trying to cross the threshold into his bedroom. Without warning, he lost his footing. Their legs tangled, and they tumbled to the floor in a clumsy, disoriented heap.

Dalha landed beneath him, pinned by his weight. She winced as he writhed, trying to push himself up — but his eyes met with hers and he paused.

His gaze lingered and he stared at her for a long while, unmoving.

Then, slowly, he raised a paw to her cheek.

Before Dalha could react, his lips covered her own. The taste of the alcohol from his lips was sharp. A sudden surge of bile rose in her throat as she tried to shove him off, panic taking hold.

Before she could get away, Dalha felt his fingers slip inside of her. She gasped, and doubled her efforts to push him off, finally slipping from under his weight. Panicked and confused, she fled to her room, vision blurring and thoughts reeling. Sobs shook her to her core as she locked the door behind herself. She turned, put her back to the door, then slid down to the floor, hugging her knees to her chest.

Later that night, she packed what little she could and slipped out the back door. He would never touch her like that again.

She walked the streets until early morning, eventually finding a cold park bench to curl up on. She knew she couldn't go back to school — he would look for her there first. The idea of a shelter crossed her mind, but she quickly dismissed it. Being underage meant the authorities would try to return her to him. She wasn't going back. She knew, if she wanted to disappear for good, she'd have to leave town entirely.

Over the next few days she hiked her way to the next nearest city — a bustling metropolis where she could blend into the crowd and hide indefinitely. It wouldn't be easy, but she had some ideas. If she could find an underpass or bridge in a quiet part of town, she'd have shelter. With the shelter problem solved, she just needed credits.

Panhandling was an option, but it was dangerous. If the authorities spotted her, she'd be dragged back to her dad for sure. She would need some sort of disguise.

She made it to the city by nightfall. Finding another park near the more affluent side of the city, she settled down on a bench near the park's edge. She'd try to find a disguise in the morning, but for now, she would be fine with the credits she'd stolen from her father's wallet. If she were careful, they would last a few weeks.

During the night, a sound from across the street stirred her from sleep. Several dark figures clustered around a craft. Quietly she watched them — until one of the figures appeared to spot her. A shadow peeled off and began to approach.

Not wanting any trouble, Dalha rolled over and pretended to sleep.

It wasn't long before the figure stood looming over her, close enough for her to hear the depth and irregularity of their breathing. They were nervous. Alert.

Leaning down, the figure spoke, whispering, "I know you saw us. Your night vision is at least as good as mine, little leopard."

His voice was low, slightly menacing — but there was something else layered beneath.

Dalha didn't move at first, but something told her he wasn't there to hurt her. Resigning herself to her fate, she rolled over and looked up at him. Standing over her was another snow leopard, maybe two or three years older. He wore a dark hoodie and loose fitting cargo pants, sporting several piercings that glinted beneath the streetlights. He had a cold-brand faintly visible on his left wrist.

"What do you want." She asked. Sitting up, she pulled her belongings close, shielding them instinctively.

"I just want to help," he said, settling onto the bench next to her. "You scratch my back, I scratch yours. Easy." He continued, gesturing across the street, "those guys over there, you never saw 'em, right? In return, I give you something you need. Deal?"

She edged away from him until her back pressed against the armrest of the bench. "Like what?"

He shrugged, "Food. Credits. Somewhere warm to sleep," he glanced at her. "Interested?"

Dalha's eyes narrowed, "What's stopping you from hurting me now, instead?"

He turned to study her, giving her an appraising look. "Nothing, really. Except you're kinda cute. Plus, I mean it — I want to help. How'd you end up out here, anyway?"

She ignored his question and stood, shouldering her bag. "Just take me somewhere warm. And don't try anything."

He chuckled, rising to his feet, then held up two fingers, "Scout's honor. Come on"

278

***

Dalha found herself living in an abandoned warehouse on the city's south side. The male — who never gave his name — admitted the space was their base of operations for boosting craft. He asked if she wanted in. She refused at first, choosing instead to panhandle during the day.

But it wasn't enough.

Eventually, Dalha gave in.

Boosting craft came naturally to her, and she learned quickly. Her confidence grew over the next few years, and she became part of their crew — observant, reserved, quick. It was a decent life, but her lucky streak soon came to an end when she unwittingly boosted a bait craft. The trap landed her in a prison facility for a year.

Finally, she got out early on good behavior, but had nowhere to go. In the end, she returned to the only place she had left: the boosters.

This time she had a new idea — thanks to years of stealing and flying high-performance craft, she was an excellent pilot. She could race — legally or otherwise. She pitched the idea: if they supplied the craft, she'd supply the skills to win the races to pay for it.

They were all in.

She won that first race with a spectacular finish, and that victory earned her a new name from the crew. The name stuck — drawn from old Irish, they called her Finn, a name meaning *fair* or *blessed*. It fit. Her fur gleamed like starlight, and her fortune that night was like no other.

Finn hoped the name would see her rise above her past, and into a life that Dalha never got to have.

***

As she rounded the building toward the back of the shop, Finn heard a sound coming from somewhere behind the dumpster. It was a soft sound, faint but distinct, like an uneven sniffle, as if someone were attempting to stifle their

279

tears.

Erring on the side of caution, she carefully lowered the garbage bag she'd been carrying, then began to circle the dumpster. Giving it a wide berth and leaning in cautiously, she peered around the edge of the dumpster, and caught sight of a leg covered in brown fur.

By this time she recognized the sound. Someone was crying, quietly and alone. Whoever it was had apparently been using the dumpster as a shoulder to cry on. Slowly, Finn stepped into the open, revealing herself.

There, seated on the ground with her back propped against the wall, was a young anthromorph. Judging by the look of her, a cougar. She seemed small, folded in on herself, with her tail curled tightly around her as if trying to vanish into the shadows.

"Hi," Finn said softly. She stood a respectful distance away, her voice gentle, while offering a small, tentative smile.

The cougar jumped at hearing her voice, and gasped. She hastily wiped at her tear-streaked face with the back of her paw. "S-sorry," she stammered. "I'll leave. I didn't know anyone was here."

Finn shook her head, stepped forward slowly then extended a paw. "You don't have to go. Why don't you come with me instead? We can talk inside. It's cleaner than sitting out here by this dumpster."

"O-okay…" The young cougar whispered, stammering, her voice fragile as she reached up to cautiously take Finn's paw.

As Finn helped draw the youngster to her feet, her eyes instinctively drew over her form. She noticed the way the cougar winced as she stood, stiffening slightly as Finn drew her to her feet. That was when Finn saw the bruising on her forearm, and a cut near her inner elbow.

"What happened to your arm?" Finn asked, her voice gentle and low, concerned, but not pressing. She gave the cougar a soft nudge, guiding her toward the front of the shop with tender care.

The cougar didn't respond at first. Hesitating, she spoke in a small, strained voice. "Some guys were picking on me…"

Finn considered her reaction as they walked into the shop. She pulled a chair from one of the work benches, offering it to the cougar. Gesturing for the youngster to sit, she grabbed a seat for herself, then pulled it over to face hers.

"What's your name? I'm Dalha, but everyone calls me Finn."

The cougar's ears perked as Finn introduced herself, her cheeks colored mildly as a shy smile tugged at the edges of her muzzle.

"I-I'm Sana," she stammered. "Thanks for being so kind to me."

Finn gave a small shrug, then walked toward the back of the shop. Opening a cabinet, she retrieved a med-kit from it before returning to sit in front of the young cougar.

"I saw someone that looked like they could use some help. I did what I felt was right. Nothing special about that."

She sat, placed the kit on her lap, and unclasped the latch with a gentle click.

"When I was your age, I was bullied for being different, too. My dad had to move around a lot for work, and I was just along for the ride. It was always a new town with a new school — I was always the outsider. Easy pickings for the bullies."

She met Sana's gaze as she opened the kit. "Do you want to talk about what happened today?"

Sana looked away as her gaze fell to the ground, her ears drooping slightly as she made a weak, noncommittal gesture with a paw.

"I might've bitten one of them…"

Finn raised an eyebrow, glancing at her as she wiped blood from Sana's wounded arm. "You know that could get you into serious trouble. Did you have good reason?"

"They tackled me," Sana replied, her tone darkening. "Tried to put a muzzle on me…"

A quiet growl underscored her words as she spoke.

Finn exhaled through her nose, frowning. "Sounds like they're lucky you didn't do worse."

She dabbed nanite bandaging across the cut, the microscopic bots shimmering slightly as they re-arranged to seal the wound.

"There. Good as new. How's it feel?"

Sana flexed her arm then bent it back toward her chest, and gave Finn a small nod. "Feels good. Thank you."

Finn closed the lid of the med-kit, the latch emitting a quiet click as she placed both paws atop it. She watched Sana for a moment, studying her face.

"Why were they picking on you?"

Finn asked as she stood, aware of the cougar's gaze tracking her as she returned the med-kit to it's cabinet.

"I don't know…" Sana said, shifting uncomfortably as she curled her tail around herself.

"They like to hang around near the orphanage. Always waiting to make trouble with one of us. I'm just glad they pick on me more than the others. I can take it."

Finn furrowed her brow but decided to ask more about that later

"Orphanage? Is that where you live?" she asked, bending to grab a few drink packs from the cold storage unit nearby.

"I was abandoned at birth." Sana said with a sigh, reaching to take the proffered drink from Finn's paw. "My parents left me at the fire station just up the street."

"I see… So they pick on you because you're an orphan." Finn replied, as she sat down again.

Sana peered up at Finn, then shrugged as she opened the drink pack. "I think it's mostly because we're anthros. It's easier to pick on anthros that don't have parents to protect them."

The snow leopard scratched the back of her neck, then brought up her com display with a sweep of her paw. "Do you have a com?"

Sana silently raised hers in response. Swiping through a few menus, Finn transmitted her com address to Sana's with the flick of her paw. "Next time that happens, com me immediately. Okay?"

A small smile crept into her features, and Sana nodded silently, another blush coloring her cheeks. Quickly, she turned her attention to the drink pack, sipping quietly while staring at the floor.

Changing the subject, Finn closed her com display and leaned back in her chair. "How do you like it at the orphanage?"

Sana kept sipping, then gave a noncommittal shrug.

Finn, sensing she'd touched on an uncomfortable topic, sat in silence for a time while watching the young anthro. Her pelt showed signs of poor upkeep; what luster it should have had, looked dulled and grimy in places. She wore simple, worn clothes — a faded v-neck, modest jean shorts, basic corrective lenses, and clamp-style hoop earrings in both ears. Only a few inches shorter than Finn, she looked a little underweight. Finn wasn't certain of her age, but guessed she was around sixteen.

Sana remained silent, her gaze fixed to the floor, unwilling or unable to meet Finn's eyes. That alone told Finn enough. As she watched, she noticed a tear slip down the youngster's cheek. She was so silent in her grief that Finn knew immediately what kind of home life Sana endured.

Leaning closer, Finn gently placed a paw on Sana's knee and spoke in a soft, soothing tone. "It's okay, snuggie. I'm sorry I asked. Let's talk about something else, alright? Tell me about something you like. Maybe your favorite book or hobby?"

Sniffling, Sana wiped a tear from her cheek with the back of her paw, then pointed to something behind Finn. "I like speeder like that one. That's a modified Mark Three Bengal, isn't it?"

Glancing over her shoulder at the craft, Finn grinned and nodded. "It sure is. That's my racer. I call her Enola. You like her?"

"She's beautiful," Sana said, her face lighting up as she squirmed in her seat. "Is this your shop? I've seen you working on her a few times as I walk home."

Finn shook her head and stood, finishing her drink before tossing the empty pack into a nearby bin.

"I just rent the bay when I need to work on 'er myself. Usually I keep her in a storage unit near my apartment." She gestured toward the speeder with a smile. "Come on. Take a closer look."

CHAPTER 18 - FLYING DIRTY.

The news seemed awfully depressing of late. Finn thought this to herself as she watched the holo display hovering a few feet in front of her, it's edges shimmering with a soft iridescent glow — the only indication of it's unreality.

She sat at the edge of her bed, sipping a fresh cup of coffee. She'd brewed the coffee earlier that morning as part of her daily routine. Coffee, the news, and then some physical activity — in that order. Those were the well-worn steps of a ritual that shaped most of her mornings. She was a creature of habit. Routine helped her feel a sense of purpose.

"Scientists report shifting gravitational readings from the anomaly. The uncertainty of the gravitational forces are affecting research activities. For the safety of the crew, the science station currently orbiting it's area has been moved to a location more distant from the anomaly."

The tiny figure on the holo display shuffled some papers before continuing. "New quake activity has been detected in Eastern Eurasia as well as Alaska, prompting additional evacuations. Emergency authorities predict the increased activity could result in multiple volcanic eruptions. Emergency rations and transport arrangements are being provided wherever possible."

She chewed on a protein bar, then released a quiet sigh, it's flavor stubbornly bland, more functional than satisfying. She washed it down with a gulp of lukewarm coffee, the bitter liquid helping to ease the passage of the dense chew.

Just then a soft ping lit the corner of her holo — Sana's name hovered there in the corner, pulsing a ghostly translucent blue.

Since they'd bonded, Sana had kept a steady presence in Finn's otherwise solitary life. She often stopped by after school, the scents of the day lingering on her fur, her tail swaying with a nervous excitement that Finn found oddly grounding.

With the flick of her paw, Finn issued a command to the holo. As she read the message, her face cleared and a smile tugged at the edges of her muzzle. Sana had the endearing habit of surfacing whenever Finn was feeling a bit aimless. While she was driven, Finn often got into her own head during her downtime — it was nice to have someone to help pull her out of the mire.

"Want to meet up?"

A short time later the message was followed by an animated caricature of an anthro cougar — hips and tail swaying in a playful, exaggerated dance.

Finn sat up, then gulped the remainder of her coffee, "Reply to Sana. 'Sure, where do you want to meet?'" She said, wiping her chin with the back of her arm.

She didn't reply. A few minutes later, Finn heard a faint tapping at her apartment door — instantly, she knew it was Sana. It wasn't often, but she would sometimes stop by her apartment without notice. It wasn't long before Finn realized she'd usually appear during holidays or weekends when she knew Finn didn't have plans. Subtle signs Finn had left behind had encouraged the habit. Admittedly, Finn had consciously invented a lot of subtle signs.

Finn stood, then placed her mug on the crate that sufficed as her bedstand. She strode to the door, then peeked through the peephole, she could see Sana bouncing in place, her hips swaying to some inaudible tune.

286

"Who is it?" Finn called out, a mischievous grin tugging at the edges of her muzzle.

Sana paused, then tilted her head in confusion. Finally catching on, her eyes narrowed as her gaze fixed on the peephole. Leaning in, she peered into the lens — one giant, glassy eye filled Finn's view, causing her to chuckle.

"It's pupper's clearing house! You've won a million credits, and a fuzzy companion!" Sana giggled, sticking her tongue out as she straightened — waving.

Finn, laughing, unlocked the door then went to sit. She plopped down onto the bed as Sana let herself in.

"Hey, what are you..." Sana began, then planted her paws on her hips as she found Finn sitting at the edge of her bed.

"Salted cucumber Finn! Are you always going to live like this?"

Confused, Finn's ears drooped, then she raised a questioning eyebrow.

"What do you mean? I'm eating my breakfast. What's wrong with that?" She spread her paws with a shrug.

With a scoff, Sana waved her paw around the apartment. Like so many others in the furry district, Finn's apartment was cramped and smelled faintly of mildew. It was one of the smaller studio apartments in the building — barebones but functional. Finn was comfortable here.

Opposite her bed, there was a second-hand sofa Finn had found at a local flea market. Other than the sofa and the bed, her clothes were scattered in and around a few cardboard boxes and a duffle bag.

"There's still nothing in here Finn!" Sana admonished while seating herself next to Finn.

"When are you going to get something to liven the place up? I can help, you know!"

Finn frowned and shifted in her seat, then glanced sidelong at Sana, her expression accusing.

"You know I don't like girly things," she paused, rubbing her chin.

"Speaking of girly things... are you dating yet? Met any nice boys?"

It was Sana's turn to squirm. Only shrugging in reply, her ears dropped as she curled her tail around herself.

The young cougar's behavior caught Finn by surprise. They'd never really spoken about Sana's love interests before, but Finn thought they were close enough for that sort of conversation.

Curious, Finn scootched closer, gently lifting Sana's tail into her lap, her paw trailing across the silken fur. She marveled at how soft it was even compared to her own. Snow leopards were known for ultra-soft fur, but Sana's was a near rival.

"Sana? Is everything okay? Did I say something wrong?"

Sana's expression softened with Finn's touch — she shook her head.

"Sorry, No. I just." She paused, searching for the right words. "I sorta like girls more than boys. You know?"

Finn stared for a beat, uncomprehending.

"O-oh," she stammered, "You mean, you're gay?"

The larger feline shifted uncomfortably. "I'm sorry, I just assumed…"

"No!" Sana interrupted, giggling. Her nose twitching as a grin spread across her muzzle. "I'm allgendered."

They sat in silence for a time as Finn grappled with this new information.

"I uh," she hesitated, gathering her thoughts before speaking again. It never occurred to Finn to ask Sana's gender.

"I thought you were a 'her' this whole time. Now I feel a little embarrassed. Should I be calling you something else?"

Feeling somewhat awkward, Finn stood and plucked her empty mug from the crate.

She raised the mug in Sana's direction. "Want some?"

Sana nodded. "Yes please, two sugars if you have them."

Her gaze followed Finn as she crossed the room. She watched as Finn filled her cup from the coffee carafe.

288

"You can refer to me as she. That's how my body presents. Besides, I'm technically both — doesn't really matter which you use. But you might get funny looks if you used the other pronouns."

Finn churned this over in her mind. A thought occurred to her. "Hold on."

She finished pouring a cup for Sana, then scooped a few spoonful's of sugar into it. Not bothering to stir, Finn handed the mug with spoon to Sana then sat on the couch opposite her. In spite of herself, her gaze flicked toward Sana's crotch — an instinctive curiosity calling her to look for the telltale bulge.

Realizing what she'd done, Finn blushed furiously and forced her gaze back to Sana's face — hoping she hadn't noticed.

Sana smiled placidly, stirring her coffee, seemingly oblivious. She had a charming, honest face — the kind that encouraged openness.

"So," Finn said carefully, curiosity itching again. "Are you... Interested in me in that way?"

Sana's expression shifted to one of mild shock and embarrassment.

"Oh! No! Not like that," she huffed in a half-hearted chuckle. "Not anymore at least. I mean, you're very attractive, if it matters. At first it was a little difficult because you, uh... show off more than I think you realize."

Sana's cheeks colored.

"But, I realized I didn't want to complicate our friendship like that. Know what I mean?"

Finn grinned salaciously.

"I show off more than I realize, huh? What were you looking at, Sana?" She probed, licking her lips, her voice playful.

Flustered, Sana looked away, attempting to hide her embarrassment while sipping her coffee.

"I think you know..."

Finn leaned in, curious.

"How do you hide it?! I have never seen anything that

would tell me you had..." She cleared her throat, and continued deadpan.

"You know. The male bits. Are they just not very big or something?"

Aghast, Sana quickly closed her legs and grabbed a couch pillow.

"Finn! That's so wrong! It's plenty big, thank you very much! Not that it's any of your business."

Sana giggled, covering her mouth before sobering.

"I've just gotten really good at moving things around." She said as she mimed air quotes.

Finn laughed.

"Sorry. I'll try to be nicer from now on. I've never met an alllgender before. I have so many inappropriate questions!"

Sana shook her head.

"I knew I should have kept my maw shut. I know I'll never hear the end of this."

Finn shrugged. "Can you blame me?"

Finishing the remainder of her coffee, Finn checked her com display. "Hey, want to get some ice cream? I can ask you all of my inappropriate questions in public."

"I'd rather talk about how the races are going." Sana replied flatly, gulping the rest of her coffee.

***

It was close, too close. Inches from her front stabilizer, the brilliantly colored craft with a mural of blue and purple flames — stretching from its front thruster wells to the rear spoilers — was *far* too close for comfort.

Finn struggled to keep Rico from cornering her. With every maneuver, she deftly avoided his attempts to shove her craft off track.

She hadn't been racing long before crossing paths with Rico. He had been in her first race, and he'd severely underestimated her. Maybe because she was new. Maybe because she was female. It didn't matter, he'd learned his lesson since.

The vehicles they piloted were highly modified versions of everyday passenger craft. While civilian hovercraft were limited by law to no greater than two feet of ground clearance, among other restrictions — these speeders laughed in the face of those laws.

Prior to starting her racing career, Finn had studied the tactics of the greatest street racers alive. She learned to modify thrusters for greater ground clearance, acceleration, banking and top end speed. She'd also customized her control systems to allow near impossible maneuvers — the kind that factory builds weren't even programmed to execute.

In the end, those modifications, along with her piloting skills, were more than sufficient to win multiple trophies. Today though, she was racing for more than glory — she was racing for her life. Rico's less than savory racing tactics were putting her skills and modifications to the test, but that wasn't going to stop Finn. She'd make Rico regret it.

As they rounded the second to last corner, the pair careened dangerously close to the elevated sidewalk. Each trying to edge their way past the other— Finn playing offense, Rico defending his tenuous lead.

Blurred streaks of blued darkness bled past her vision, interrupted by bright flashes of neon-lit city streaking across the racing line. Their speeders came dangerously close to colliding as they banked. Brilliant sparks of amber-white peppered the midnight air as the underpan of Rico's craft ground against the railing of the sidewalk.

Finn's face was a cold mask of determination as they reached the apex of the curve. Her paws gripped the stick, her eyes laser-locked on the invisible racing line that was drawn in her mind.

She feathered her left front thrust vectoring dial, anticipating Rico's next move. She had to get ahead of him though — she only had one corner left. She edged her craft in close, teasing the limit.

But Rico was waiting for that.

Suddenly, he cut speed and vectored his left front stabilizer just inside her right front thruster well — the move was surgical. His stabilizer lodged itself inside between the thruster mount and vectoring nozzle — partially crippling her control and locking her craft just behind his.

Shit.

She had only two choices: free her craft, or lose as Rico dragged her across the finish line.

Finn couldn't afford to lose this race, she had too much on the line. Especially because she knew her debtors weren't the forgiving sort.

One final corner remained. Finn's mind raced. She had a plan — but it would be risky. It would cost her some body work, maybe more. She didn't care. It was win or lose, and losing wasn't an option.

They were approaching the final curve at breakneck speed. The timing had to be perfect. She let a touch of fear creep into her expression as she feigned panic. She glanced in Rico's direction as they struggled, mere feet from one another. His face reflected in the polished surface of her gleaming hood — his grin smug, certain he had her.

Good.

She fought the urge to smirk as they neared the final corner— she knew she'd soon have the upper hand. The corner — a vicious right-hand turn — would demand hard overthrust even without another craft to compensate for. Rico would count on her to carry both of their craft safely through.

Finn played the part. Wide-eyed, she visibly overcompensated. Just as he expected. She could hear the thruster mount groan with the force as she continued to pump power into the thrusters. A portion of her front quarter panel pealing back as Rico's stabilizer mount dug into the metal. Finn grimaced as the G forces pulled at her face.

Just as they reached the apex of the curve, Finn dropped the facade, executing her true move.

As the G force became nearly unbearable, Finn touched a series of controls, her fingers a blur as she jerked the stick hard left. Her right front thruster *jettisoned*, freeing her from Rico's trap. At the same moment, her craft spun violently counter clockwise, thrusting upward.

Rico's eyes went wide — shock blooming into panic. His speeder veered straight toward the oncoming storefronts.

Finn heard the screech of her underplates as they drug across Rico's rear spoilers, sparks flying in a brilliant molten storm of discarded metals. She didn't have time to gloat. She fought to keep on course as her speeder threatened to careen into oncoming traffic. The spin nearly cost her control.

But she held. Fur stood on edge, ears pinned, her pulse roared in her ears — she fought the spin, her instincts guiding her.

She narrowly avoided a series of bollards by a razor-thin margin, letting another shower of sparks fly as her underplates kissed their tops.

As Rico peeled away, she knew it would spell disaster for him — too bad, if you want to play dirty, expect to eat some dirt.

Behind her, Rico's speeder slammed into a barred storefront. He'd been able to slow — but not enough. He'd survive. Finn was glad — she didn't like him, but she didn't want him dead.

She crossed the finish line, adrenaline surging, muscles trembling.

As she wiped her brow, she saw police lights flashing in the distance. She'd have to cut her victory lap short — time to disappear.

Instantly she cut her speed, veered into the nearest alley, and scrambled her speeder's color and identification plates.

She didn't have to worry about the prize — it would find it's way to her account as usual.

***

"Yiffing hell Finn, I can't believe you're still alive after that stunt!"

Sana stood in the doorway of Finn's repair shop, paws on hips, tail bristling, staring at Finn incredulously — obviously furious.

Finn had been stripping damaged components from her speeder for hours now. She straightened, hiding her smile as Sana went on. She was adorable when angry — but she was also right.

"Did you hear me? Rico barely made it out of there! You could have avoided all of that if you'd slowed down!"

Her hackles stood on edge as she approached — a bundle of fury wrapped in silky soft fur.

Suppressing a grin, Finn grabbed a drink from the cold storage unit, and tossed it to her.

"Easy, Sana! You know I'm a good pilot. Rico was going to fly us into those buildings if I didn't do as he expected. I just gave him a lesson in dirty piloting."

Finn leaned against her speeder, smiling sweetly.

"Besides, you have to admit, it was quite a show."

Seemingly placated by the drink, Sana plopped into an empty chair — opening the drink. She glared at Finn as she sipped from the pack, savoring the sweet flavor.

"What's important is that I won — and got out of there safe. Now I'm eligible to enter the finals. If I win those, I can pay off my handlers."

Her expression thoughtful, Finn took a sip from her own drink pack.

Brows furrowed, Sana paused mid-sip.

"Wont Rico be in that one too? You know he's going to *cripple* you, Finn. Literally or figuratively. I doubt he cares which."

Finn snorted.

"You've been been studying grammar, haven't you?" She grinned, raising her paw to forestall her retort.

"There's nothing I can do about Rico's hatred. We both knew the risks going into the race. That won't change with the next one, but I have a plan."

Sana sighed.

"I don't like it Finn. Every race I worry that I'll lose you. Can't you find another way?"

Finn shook her head.

"It's more complicated than that. I owe credits to people
294

that don't forgive *or* forget. Winning their races is my only way out."

Sana's ears flicked.

"Hold on. You owe credits to the *same people running the races?*"

Somewhat abashed, Finn nodded.

"I was naive. I thought skill and craft would be enough to win races. Turns out, things break really fast — and repairs aren't cheap'

Finn trailed off, gaze distant. Shaking it off, she shrugged,

"If you're not winning, you're losing."

Sana shifted, ears drooping.

"There's got to be another way. You can't keep doing this forever."

Finn stood, walked to the front of the speeder, popped the hood latch then peered inside.

"I have an idea."

She grinned, shutting the hood with a solid thunk.

"I know just the bear to help. But I'll need another loan to get it done."

CHAPTER 19 - THE LAST ONE.

"Kael, have you seen this?"

Reaper had been tinkering with the surveillance station's holo interface moments before. Presently, it showed a spread of statistics — resource utilization curves, data rates, and processing times. He pointed a clawed finger to one of the charts, motioning for Kael to approach.

Kael's ears perked, swiveling forward instinctively. "What?" He leaned closer, his broad shoulder brushing against Reaper's chair, scanning the glowing information on his display.

He'd been working with the station's second interface, getting to know the AI's interface. The two had gravitated toward one another, linked by a shared interest as they marveled over the ships computational backbone — a system as elegant as it was lethal. Though they'd been on the ship for a while now, Kael usually kept to himself, or spent hours in familiar camaraderie with Nanuq.

Earlier, Reaper had caught a glimpse of Nanuq chatting with Yuriy in the galley — the pair had been making plans to tour the engine room together with captain Gyata. He'd stumbled upon Kael en-route to the bridge, and on a whim thought it was as good a time as any to get to know the big wolf. There was something about the wolf's quiet intensity that intrigued him — a contrast to his own restless nature.

Reaper gestured again, eyes gleaming with excitement. "There! Did you see how fast it infiltrated the Korean embassy's security systems?"

Kael's ears twitched and his expression brightened, "That's amazing! The Claw's AI must be at least a hundred times faster than Nanuq's!" He raised a paw to his muzzle, lowering his voice to a conspiratorial murmur.

"Don't tell her I said that."

Reaper barked a laugh, understanding Kael's concern — Nanuq held a rather high opinion of her systems. He could practically hear her offended huff if she ever caught wind of the comparison. The poor wolf would never hear the end of it if she did.

"I got your back, buddy. My lips are sealed." He mimed zipping his muzzle shut, then flung the imaginary key across the room with dramatic flair.

"Honestly though, I've never seen anything like this. I thought the University of New York's cluster was powerful, but this..." Reaper let the thought trail off as he stared at the system statistics.

He made a few more adjustments then swiped his paw upward with a flourish — the command sequence launching with a satisfying chime.

Kael blinked. "Wait. Did you just do what I think you did?" He asked, incredulous.

Folding his arms, the raccoon leaned back in his chair, his ringed tail curling in a slow, repeating wave. "Yep!" He grinned, a glint of mischief in his eyes. "What can they do? We're floating in space in an invisible ship."

The wolf tilted his head, his ears drooping slightly, concerned, "Yeah, but.... The New York City Yakuza headquarters? What if they find out?"

"They won't," Reaper replied coolly. "I added some of my own magic to this one. They'll never see it coming."

They watched as the Claw's AI broke through firewall after firewall — digitally assaulting the Yakuza systems as if they were mere children's toys.

"Besides," Reaper added, nudging Kael's elbow with a sly grin. "I've always wondered if they rigged the street races."

"Are you a gambler?" Reaper asked, already gesturing at his com display with nimble claws. "There's a rumor that the big race is going down tonight. Want in?"

Kael rubbed his chin thoughtfully, fanning the soft fur along his jaw in undulating waves. "You mean... once we find out the races are rigged? Doesn't seem very sporting, does it?"

Just then, the AI pierced through the final firewall, indicating it's completion with a muted chime and pulsing glow. Without hesitation, Reaper leaned in and began rifling through record after record, searching for those associated with the races. His whiskers twitched as he focused, eyes flicking from line to line as the data unfolded before him. Finally he froze. Something had caught his attention

He read in silence for a time, the glow of the display lighting his striped muzzle as a satisfied grin spread across his face. His canines gleamed in the artificial lighting of the bridge and his ears flicked once — sharply.

"It's not very sporting of them to rig the races either."

The wolf's chair gave a soft groan as he sat up straighter, ears perked with interest. "What did you find?"

Reaper gestured to the interface, rotating it so the wolf could see. "Did you catch the last race?"

Kael shook his head.

"Rico," Reaper continued, "the fan favorite? Crashed and burned on the second-to-last corner. This record here — " he pointed to it with a claw, " — shows the Yakuza bankrolled his repairs... and they gave him some not-so-standard upgrades."

Kael's eyes narrowed, "So they *wanted* him back in the race?"

"Exactly," Reaper replied. He flicked his paw, dismissing the file, replacing it with another. "And it looks like they slipped in a little *extra* insurance. Tsk tsk... not very sporting at all."

Reaper lowered his voice to a conspiratorial tone. "If I were a betting 'coon, I'd put credits on that snow leopard not playing along."

Kael's ears perked, "Snow leopard? What do you mean?"

The smaller anthromorph's paws danced across the interface again. After a few commands, a high resolution still appeared — an image of a lithe snow leopard mid-stride, helmet tucked under her arm, fur shimmering as she approached a sparkling speeder.

"She's expected to race tonight too."

Kael's eyes widened, his breath catching slightly. "Wow." He remarked, gaze lingering on the image of the leopard, nostrils flaring slightly as he took in her graceful curves and confident posture. "What's her name?"

Reaper glanced sidelong in the wolf's direction — immediately sensing the shift in the wolf's normally cool demeanor. There was something in his posture — tail stilled, ears perking forward in unguarded curiosity. The raccoon's muzzle split into a grin.

"If I didn't know any better," he said, nudging Kael with an elbow, "I'd say someone just found a new academic obsession." He continued, "They call her Finn. She has quite a history."

Kael didn't rise to the bait, "History?"

Reaper nodded, swiping the still away — snapping the wolf back to the present. "She showed up on the scene not too long ago. Came out of nowhere, won a string of races, and got into a rivalry with Rico. Now? She owes money to the same people that run the races."

Kael frowned, "So if she wins, she's a threat. If she loses... she's theirs."

Before Reaper could reply, the bridge's aft door burst open. Yuriy and Nanuq stumbled through, laughing. Noticing the pair, Nanuq quieted, her face clearing as she saw the pair sitting together.

"Hi guys!" she called, waving a paw. "What are you up to?"

299

Reaper waved back, his expression the picture of innocence. "Oh, nothing much," he said with exaggerated casualness. "Just hacking into the Yakuza's computer systems and introducing mister wolf here to the thrilling world of illegal street racing."

He grinned, then raised his nose in the pair's direction. "What have you two been up to?"

"We went…" Yuriy began, his deep voice being drowned out as Nanuq burst in, her bushy tail wagging excitedly as she bounced in place.

"The captain gave us a tour of the engine room! You should have come — it was *amazing!*"

Yuriy nodded patiently, trying to continue. "He…"

Nanuq jumped again, hugging Yuriy's massive arm with both paws, talking so fast her words practically collided. "The gamma shields are transparent! Gyata raised the optical shielding so we could *watch* the reaction live — it was so bright! So amazing! Oh! But don't worry, he left the photo filters on, or we'd both be blind. At least *Yuriy* would be — my optical sensors would've adjusted fine."

Reaper and Kael exchanged a glance, ears perked, expressions caught somewhere between amusement and disbelief. Yuriy gave Kael a long suffering look as he folded his ears back and slid his paws into the deep pockets of his overalls.

"Did you know the ship's reactors — there are *two* of them," she said, holding a paw up while extending two digits with pride, "generate up to fourteen *gigawatts* combined?! Isn't that amazing? The captain said we only need one of them for full operation, the second one is a failsafe."

She clapped her paws together then jerked them apart, miming a spherical blast, her arms flaring outward in a wide circle. "You know. In case one of them *kaboom*! Oh and…"

Finally Kael lifted a paw, palm downward, pressing the air in a calming motion. "Easy, Nanuq. We have plenty of time to hear about the ship's potential reactor disasters. Why don't you let Yuriy finish what he was trying to say?"

She froze mid-bounce, delicate ears drooping slightly as

300

her gaze drifted sheepishly up to the bear, her expression apologetic. "Oh, Artemis. I'm sorry, Mister Yuriy... I should've let you finish. Please go ahead."

Yuriy peered down at her, his expression softening as the slightest hint of a smile tugged at the edges of his muzzle. Slowly, he opened his mouth, his eyes lingering on hers as he spoke, deadpan.

"It was pretty tails."

They all laughed, the tension dissolving as Nanuq blinked in confusion.

"Thanks for keeping her company," Kael said, still chuckling as he brushed a paw over his snout. "Has she been like this all morning?"

The big bear simply shrugged and glanced down at her with a gentle smile. "She's been very enthusiastic company. I've enjoyed her presence greatly."

He tilted his head slightly, ears lifting. "Did I hear something about illegal street racing?"

Reaper perked up, spinning his chair toward them with a grin. "Yeah! I was nosing through the Yakuza records earlier. Turns out the big race is tonight — and the finish line's gonna be in the furry district."

He paused, head tilting thoughtfully. "Say... Might be smart to get ahead of that. Warn folks to stay indoors. And... if we play our cards right, we might get a front row seat from the away craft."

"I want to go!" Nanuq chirped, practically vibrating as she clutched one of Yuriy's thick paws in both of hers. Her eyes sparkled with excitement as she looked up at him, tail swaying in a hopeful rhythm.

"Come with us?" she asked, voice softening.

***

"This is the spot, but don't stay here. It's dangerous. Okay?"

Finn stood, arms crossed on the sun-faded sidewalk in the furry district. Sana lingered opposite her, taking in the sight

301

of the arbor building as Finn pointed toward the bodega just down the street.

"According to the map, that bodega is the finish line."

The young cougar nodded absently as she stood by Finn's side. She gawked at the buildings, their surfaces gleaming and adorned with colorful graffiti, as Finn pointed out race landmarks. Sana's rounded ears flicked as she took it all in — the sounds, the colors, the scent of ozone and craft exhaust.

They'd been scouting the route since morning, Finn noting landmarks, marking obstacles, potential gotchas, mapping every twist and alley. The race would be short — a dangerous sprint through cluttered streets, made treacherous by narrow lanes, unpredictable traffic and low clearance pedestrian bridges.

Still, with her latest speeder mods? She knew she could win — she just had to keep Rico off her back.

Fingers crossed, she thought, tail swaying nervously.

Noticing Sana had been silent the whole while, Finn's eyes narrowed, as she turned to face her. "Okay, Sana?" She repeated, her tone sharpened with impatience as she rested her paws on her hips .

Sana had been staring at the Arbor building, transfixed, eyes locked on its rooftop like it held a secret. She blinked, snapping out of her trance. "Oh! Sorry. Yeah, I'll stay safe. Don't worry about me."

In truth, the cougar had been sweeping the surrounding buildings for the perfect vantage. She had no intention of staying home, not when the race of the season was about to tear through the streets with her best friend leading the pack.

"I have to get ready," Finn said as she brushed a crumpled wrapper off her shoulder that the wind had plastered there. "You should head home. You've got about two hours before it starts. That should give you plenty of time to catch it on holo-stream."

Sana smiled sweetly, stepping forward and opening her arms wide. "Good luck, kitty cat!" She chirped, as she wrapped Finn in a tight, warm and reassuring hug.

Finn blinked, surprised, but didn't pull away.

"Oh hey," Sana added as she stepped back, "any chance I could borrow a few credits? I wanna grab a snack before heading back."

With a shrug, Finn nodded, brought up her com and swiped a few credits over to Sana's with a flick of her claw. "Just make sure you're home before the race starts, *please.*"

"Promise!" She called, already turning away. She waved over her shoulder, tail swishing as she trotted toward the bodega. "See you soon!"

Minutes later, Sana stepped out of the bodega, a crinkling bag of snacks hugged to her chest and a lemon-yellow popsicle poking out the side of her muzzle. She sucked on it as she walked, the cold tang cutting through the summer heat.

Her chestnut eyes were already locked on the Arbor building. She knew the view from that rooftop would be perfect. If only she could find a way up there…

Lucky for her, the old roof access door had never been locked — not since a certain deer had abandoned it.

She smiled to herself, chomping the tip of the popsicle off. *Let the race begin.*

***

Hovering near the starting line, the Claw's invisible landing craft stirred the air into chaos. It kicked up clouds of dust and debris, confusing pedestrians and passers by as they squinted and swatted at the unseen disturbance. Below, the racers had begun to congregate, their nerves taught with pre-race tension.

Standard protocol called for the racers to park in tight formation, lining both sides of the street — cleared earlier by quiet arrangements with less-than-official enforcers. The race would begin at dusk — when the shadows deepened and the city's lights flicked on in steady, staggered waves. The pilots waited for a single, pre-selected lamp to flare to life; it served as their go-signal, replacing the need for a flag or officiator.

"Take us higher Nanuq — sixty feet should do it. Their speeders are modified for high ground clearance, plus who knows how many of them are modded for vertical hops." Reaper's tone was calm, but clipped with excitement. "If one of them goes vertical and clips us, we're all toast. Besides, the sensors will get a cleaner view from up there."

Reaper had given Nanuq the controls for the decent, knowing her machine reflexes and near perfect skill would be superior to his own. More importantly, he wanted to watch the race, not juggle flight controls while trying to enjoy the show.

Nanuq didn't need convincing. She was perfectly capable of piloting the Claw's lander while watching the race. Her smile was subtle but present as she pulled the lander upward, posture relaxed, eyes sharp.

"How's this, mister Reaper?" She chirped, as she eased the lander to a crisp hover precisely sixty feet above the street.

Reaper grinned as the line of speeders panned into view on the forward viewing screen. "Perfect Miss Nanuq. Just perfect."

He manipulated the sensor controls, bringing Rico's craft — an elegant wedge of blue with purple flame detailing on aerodynamic fins — came into sharp focus on another screen. A few more motions brought Finn's craft onto a final screen. Reaper chuckled as he watched the wolf's gaze lock onto the display with snow cat's speeder, his tail wagging near imperceptibly.

He grinned wider, enabled auto-tracking, and leaned back in his seat, paws laced behind his head in satisfaction.

This was gonna be good.

"I recognize that snep," Yuriy remarked, gesturing one heavy claw at the screen showing Finn's speeder. "She brought that speeder in for upgrades not long ago. Serious work, too."

Kael's ears perked at this. He opened his mouth, hesitated, then shut it again. His ears drooped, betraying his inner debate. He returned his gaze to the screen, silent — subtle tension radiating from the otherwise stoic wolf.

Below, the speeders lined the street in two mirrored columns. Each sparkled in the waning light of the day, gleaming examples of exceptional engineering, beautiful, and spectacularly capable. They hovered there, poised to send the city into a frenzy as they ripped through the cooling night air.

Each pilot was locked in, nerves tight, fingers twitching, legs braced, and jaws clenched. Their hearts pounding, and ears ringing to the tune of a frenzied symphonic crescendo.

Finn's paws trembled faintly as she gripped the controls, holding her craft steady — her left paw poised over the throttle, her right held tight around the stick. Minutes ago she'd double-checked every system, strapped herself in with practiced speed, then changed the craft's color pallet — a gleaming metallic red with razor-black carbon fiber trim. Her usual race armor.

The city fell silent.

By her count, twenty racers were vying for the prize of a lifetime. Only one mattered.

A speeder length ahead of her sat Rico, his craft crouched low, it's blue-and-purple paint glinting like bottled firelight. His gaze never wavered from the designated lamp. Focused. Relentless

A force as unyielding as Finn herself.

The crew aboard the lander watched in breathless anticipation, eyes fixed on the lineup below. The racers had begun throttling up, their craft thrumming with restrained fury — readying for launch. Even within the sound-dampened interior, a low rumble trembled through the deck.

In the distance the street lamps flickered to life, one after another, in a perfect sequence — a serpent of light slithering toward them, swallowing the growing twilight street-by-street. At the speed of dusk, like fate, the signal approached.

The speeders began to levitate, their rear spoilers flattening out as they adjust their pitch, tilting their mass in the direction of the starting line. Powerplants howled, thrusters groaned, the air grew thick with exhaust and flying debris.

Suddenly — an eruption.

One of the speeders jolted forward in a premature lunge — a false start. It buried it's fairing into the speeder ahead, metal shrieking. The forward speeder's powerplant ignited under the stress, sending sparks and flame into the air as fuel lines split.

The crew gasped.

"Whoa!"

"Itchy balls!"

Just as the craft burst into flame, the serpent of light reached them and the starting lamp, setting off a chain reaction. The remaining speeders lurched as one as a cascading reaction began.

Finn surged forward, only to yank hard on the stick, narrowly avoiding a collision as Rico feigned a false start. Instantly she swerved left, narrowly avoiding a sleek, white speeder as it screamed past. Her heart thudded violently in her chest — every instinct blazing as she tried to overtake him.

Rico wasn't having that.

Immediately he shot forward, pacing just ahead of her. He seemed to be lining up for something, but goosed the throttle just as one of the other racers moved to overtake them both. Whatever cheap trick he had planned would have to wait.

Now at full speed, the racers focused hard as corner after sharp corner came in quick succession. The crew of the lander groaned as Nanuq expertly followed the racer's progress, tilting the lander nearly horizontal on the sharpest curves.

"Hold onto your tails!" she barked, deftly weaving through streaming drones and between utility poles. The crew white knuckled their seats, holding on for dear life during her wild maneuvering.

Finn struggled to keep a safe distance from Rico as a speeder to her left suddenly lost a thruster. The craft threatened to career into her as it spun out of control. Immediately, the wayward speeder collided with one just behind her, causing a shower of sparks and carbon shrapnel to rain down on the narrow street. Speeders began to pile up behind them, allowing the leopard and her rival to draw away, widening the gap.

Using his usual dirty tactics, Rico drove the remaining contender off track by faking a ramming maneuver. Unintimidated, Finn kept close track of him, struggling to mime his erratic movements. Her breath came in sharp, staccato bursts while her eyes remained locked on Rico's every twitch.

Their speeders, a close match, forced the two to pilot like they'd never piloted before. Nanuq whooped as she banked recklessly through another corner, deftly avoiding poles, drones and buildings. The crew were panting at this point, holding on for dear life as crazy fox held pace with the speeders.

With a quick jerk of the stick and spin of her vectoring dials, Finn's speeder jumped ahead, nearly cutting Rico off before he could react. Again he tried to hang her up on his stabilizer, but she wouldn't fall for that again. Instantly she avoided his strike — only to find her windscreen suddenly covered in an viscous goo, its opacity making it nearly impossible to see.

The onlookers above gasped as they watched Rico deploy the gunk from a nozzle near the rear of his speeder. The move gained him no favor among the onlookers — even shaking Reaper's normally devout admiration of his skills.

The move could mean only one thing — Rico feared the beautiful cat might beat him again.

In a panic and unable to see, Finn snapped her helmet visor shut, ejected the pilot door transparency and stuck her head through the opening. Wind whipped at her fur and tried to sting her eyes as the city's neon streaked past in chaotic ribbons. She quickly caught up to Rico despite the setback, then frantically deployed countermeasures to help clear the transparency of gunk.

She cursed as her windscreen wipers activated, merely smearing the goo, making visibility worse. Quickly, she disabled the wipers and reached for the tab of the removable film she'd installed before the race. Her claws fumbled for an instant, slick with sweat. While it wouldn't clear her entire forward view, it would at least allow her to keep her head inside the craft as they raced.

She released the film to the wind, then pulled her head back inside the cockpit. The cooling air howled past, whipping the silver ribbon away and into the night. With a growl deep in her chest, she redoubled her efforts to overtake — she wouldn't fail this time.

Seconds later, they dove into a narrow alleyway, barely avoiding the notice of a pair of police craft. With her vision severely limited, Finn struggled to keep pace in the narrow space. She cursed, forced to constantly lean and search for good visibility. More than once a stabilizer fin scraped against the walls as they closed in on her, sparks flew in spectacular, firework like displays. Her face lit with each shower of brilliant light, gleaming off her toothy expression as she grimaced with concentration.

As the pair approached the end of the alleyway, they both rotated their craft perpendicular to the street surface, preparing for the sharp right hand banking maneuver. As they cleared the alley, immediately they vectored their thrusters to rotate their speeders in mid-air. Finn held her breath, forcing her abdominal muscles to clench as the G-forces threatened to steal her consciousness. Her vision tunneled, black edges creeping into her sight line as she fought to stay sharp. Hovering mere inches above the ground, they nearly stopped in place before blasting off into the darkness again.

Around the next corner, two police craft hovered menacingly, lights flashing. With lightning reflexes, Rico banked right, rotated his craft then raised it far enough to fly over the police. Immediately following suit, Finn banked left and stuck her paw out the window in a friendly wave as she zipped past. Her whiskers twitched with mischievous delight, her tinkling laughter hanging on the air as she departed.

Their encounters with the police became more frequent, but they were never truly in danger of being caught. Sirens wailed, echoing off the building walls, their cries, frustrated calls for justice. In most cases, the racers that lagged behind were the unfortunate victims of the authorities wrath as Finn and Rico easily dodged them.

Despite the protestations of the nauseous crew, Nanuq continued to pace the race leaders. She regularly performed maneuvers that seemed impossible to her bewildered passengers, all while hooting and hollering in support of the snow leopard. Her tail whipped excitedly behind her as her claws tapped the console in deft motions as she called out Finn's name between whoops.

Reaper groaned, "Remind me never to let you pilot again!" He shouted, ears pinned back as he white-knuckled the armrests of his chair.

"Suck it up, buttercup!" Nanuq shouted, laughing as she performed yet another death defying maneuver with glee.

Finn had been steadily gaining on Rico and was nearly parallel with him at this point. Suddenly, his craft lurched in her direction, then slammed into her passenger side, sending her wide. She gasped as she collided with a sign, breaking the post off at the ground. She cursed as it collided with her windscreen, sending spidering cracks in a glittering cascade.

The crew watched in horror as she careened off track. Reaper and Kael gasping in unison while the bear looked on without so much as a word. His calm gaze never wavering, as though he'd seen this outcome before.

Quickly, she regained control, growling in frustration and some amount of disappointment at her lack of caution. She'd had enough of this yiffing fool. Her claws clicking sharply, she flicked switches and turned dials frantically while they approached one of the final corners. As they rounded the corner, she flicked the safety free on her stick trigger, then gently rested a finger atop it, preparing for the burst of power it would unleash.

Finally seeing her opportunity in an oncoming straight, she yanked the trigger back, bracing herself as her craft burst forward. The acceleration slammed her into her harness. She rammed her speeder into the right rear corner of Rico's craft, hoping to push him out of the way, her teeth clacking together from the violent jolt. Miraculously, he kept control as they barreled into the last corner. He had been waiting for this. Somehow he'd baited her into his trap, and he wasted no time springing it on her.

At once, Rico's craft lurched with a sudden shock. A projectile of some sort launched itself from it's underbelly, lodging itself in Finn's right front thruster. Before she could react, her craft began to spin out of control. Her stomach twisted violently as the world became a blur. The city lights seemed to slide past in slow motion as time lost all meaning. The oncoming corner — lined with high density safety bollards — slid past her vision once, then twice.

Sana watched in horror as she saw Rico round the final corner, bursting toward her with savage speed. The flash of his attack met her eyes just moments before. Her heart seized in her chest as she saw it — the spinning mass of Finn's speeder following milliseconds later, as it appeared from behind the buildings that obscured the attack.

Finally resigned to her fate, Finn released the controls and prepared for the inevitable. She was thankful that her helmet visor was already closed when she crossed her arms across her chest. Her pulse slowed as the world began to lose color.

Everything froze. The ringing in her ears transformed into a silence that swallowed the world. The roar of the powerplant and the glare of the city lights collapsed into a single heartbeat.

Words hung on the air, unsaid, as the crew of the lander witnessed Finn's speeder rend itself to pieces. Fire burst from its powerplant as it ripped free of the craft, then spun away in a brilliant crescendo of noise and light. Body panels, stabilizer fins, and mechanical parts — a hundred gleaming shards of her once-proud machine — became a deadly shower of screaming, flying, and burning shrapnel.

The cockpit filled with impact absorbing foam in an

instant, wrapping Finn in a protective cocoon — though not before the first bone-rattling shock knocked her limp in her harness. Her craft's thrusters snapped off as they caught on the high-density bollards, smashing to bits as their mass and momentum twisted them inside out. Finally, the center safety capsule of her craft emerged from the inferno, tumbling across the street — scarred but still intact.

Sana screamed, her ears flattening tight to her scalp as the roar of the incredible violence reached her. Her claws scraped against the rooftop ledge, leaving gouges as she whipped around. Immediately she turned toward the building stairwell and ran. Blind with fear and worry, she knew nothing in that moment other than the need to save her only friend.

At the same moment, Kael barked, "Nanuq!"

***

Jolted awake by the faint sound of snoring, she felt a mild sense of foggy confusion and heavy lethargy. She stared at the lights hanging above her, twitching her nose as the scent of antiseptic and bar soap tickled her nostrils. Pain radiated from nearly every joint and her head throbbed in a dull, relentless pulse. It occurred to her that she didn't recognize this place, nor did she know how she had gotten here.

She tried to turn her head to see where the snore had originated from, but immediately winced as a sharp pain lanced through her neck. She groaned and sank back, letting the ache subside as her eyes drifted once more to the lights above. *Where was she anyway?*

The snoring had stopped at least — it sounded as though the source had begun to stir. Finn continued to stare at the ceiling, ears twitching in restless curiosity, as she wondered if her mysterious guest would come say hello.

A sudden shock flashed through her mind, telling her that she must have been struck by something launched from Rico's craft. The sound of the impact snapped her fully awake from her dazed fog. Finn gasped as the memory flooded back, sharp and surreal. She settled, breath ragged, confused as the

311

vision faded. Blinking, she raised a paw to her face, touching the soft fur there — was this real?

The visitor remained elusive as her ears swiveled sharply toward an indistinct click. She tried to move her head again — slower this time, with careful control.

Streaks of light swung past, circling in wide arcs, impossible to track. Her limbs felt heavy, every movement a slow drag through syrupy resistance. Dizzy and uncertain of where she was, she clambered for a sense of direction, a sign. Though she knew it was coming, the flash caught her by surprise.

She tried to scream as the man holding the gun to her head pulled the trigger. But her voice wouldn't come. Her jaw strained to open, her lips quivered, her tongue fought to shape a sound.

It wasn't fair.

A muted gasp escaped her as the slug exited the gun in a violent storm of light and thunderous noise.

She knew without a doubt, that this was the end.

She could feel him staring at her. His eyes fixed on her body, drinking her in, measuring her like a ripened fruit. She knew what he wished of her — she'd rather die first. The Yakuza wanted their credits back, and he had ways of extracting them. She'd never killed anyone before, but she'd kill *him*.

The violent shock yanked her body forward, slamming her helmeted head against the instrument cluster. Stars exploded behind her eyes, a brilliant flash crossing the dimming edges of her vision. The noise was like nothing she'd ever heard — deafening and primal. Her ears began to ring before everything dissolved into chaos.

Jolting awake, Finn sat up with a gasp as the memory of that day came flooding back.

She was ruined. The Yakuza would come for their credits, and rutting tailhole of a handler would try to force his way under her tail. She needed to find a way to escape. She needed to get out of… wherever this sterile prison was.

She tried to move, but suddenly dizziness washed over

her, threatening to drown her senses. Her ears drooped and she began to wilt. The scent of bar soap and dog fur tickled her nose as the light left the room.

She felt warm as light began to return again. She also felt strangely cozy, though her position didn't make sense to her. It felt like she were being held in someone's arms — but whose? She gasped again as her eyes flew open to find a gray wolf cradling her.

"Hi," said the wolf. His brilliant lavender eyes locked onto her with a mix of curiosity and gentile caution.

Confused, she peered up at him, then wordlessly strained to sit up.

His ears perked, eyebrows raising as she tried to move. "Whoa whoa, slow down. You were in a nasty accident. Reaper did the best he could with what we have on hand, but you need more time to heal."

Now sitting up, she rubbed her forehead and peered at the wolf suspiciously. Glancing around the room, which appeared to be some sort of hospital room, she noticed something odd.

There were no windows. Only sterile panels and medical monitors surrounding her, closing her in like a cage.

The wolf reached to adjust the bedsheet that had been covering her, but she flinched back sharply. "Don't touch me!" She clamored, shying away from his touch.

The wolf quickly drew back, ears pinned forward, suddenly defensive. "Whoa! Easy, I'm not going to hurt you." He raised his paws in a sign of respect, then pointed at her bedsheet that had fallen away to expose her panties. "I just meant to cover…"

She followed his gaze, heat flooding her cheeks when she saw. She covered herself at once, ears pinned and her cheeks flushed as she glared at him accusingly. "Stop staring, pervert!"

Incredulous, the wolf growled, pushed back from the bed, stood then crossed his arms. "I wasn't staring. You fainted and almost fell out of the bed. I barely caught you before you hit the floor. You're welcome."

She had to admit, he smelled nice — and he was tall — and those eyes... *Artemis, what are you doing, Finn?! Stop staring!*

"Who are you, and what is this place? Are you holding me hostage, or am I free to go?" She asked, trying to sound confident but failing to hide her trembling voice.

His ears perked as he realized he hadn't introduced himself. "W-what? Of course you aren't being held hostage! We rescued you from the wreckage of your speeder after that tailhole tried to kill you." He dropped his arms then hid his paws in his pockets, suddenly looking awkward and shy despite his size. "I'm Kael and this is the med bay of the Claw. We've been taking turns monitoring your recovery."

Immediately her ears flicked forward at the mention of the Claw. "The what? Med bay? Is this some kind of ship? Why would you take me to a ship?!" Her tail lashed behind her, betraying her rising panic.

Suddenly concerned, Kael held his paws up in a defensive posture. "We weren't sure what else to do. You were nearly killed in an illegal racing crash. We didn't want to risk you getting arrested in that state. So we decided to bring you up to the Claw."

"Up?" She tilted her head, ears swiveling uncertainly. "What do you mean, *up?*"

He didn't reply as he turned to face the wall opposite the foot of her bed, his expression sheepish and careful. "Squeakers. Surveillance feed on view screen, please."

Moments later, a two dimensional feed of live security sensors appeared on the wall opposite her bed. The feed cycled through scenes of empty corridors, cavernous spaces filled with unidentifiable machinery, and finally — a breathtaking view of earth from space, endless and blue.

Finn's mouth fell open, her pupils dilating as the reality of her situation slammed into her.

She stared in silence for what felt like an eternity, unable to process the sheer insanity of it all. Finally, after an unknown amount of time, her eyes slid over to the wolf.

Kael shifted uncomfortably as her glare seemed to burn

314

holes in his forehead, then tried to speak. "I swear…"

Finn immediately held up a paw, dismissing whatever the wolf had to say. "Why in Pan's name am I on a SPACE SHIP?!" Her voice cracked, eyes blazing.

The wolf winced as she shouted the last two words — he had no idea someone so small could make such thunderous noise.

Just as he was about to answer, the door to the med bay flew open as Nanuq barged in, skipping like a young school girl as she bounded over to Kael. "Kael! Did you know the toilets in the ship are designed for zero gravity?!" She paused for a second as she noticed Finn staring at her in wide-eyed bewilderment.

"Oh, hi pretty kitty!" Nanuq chirped, bouncing as she waved to Finn, seemingly unperturbed by her now conscious — and clearly furious — state.

Turning back to Kael, she continued. "All you have to do is flip a switch! When you do, the lid of the toilet closes, and a suction cup with tube attached pops out." Grinning, she waved a finger around gleefully. "I stuck my finger in the boy's cup!"

They gasped and leaned away from her, both groaning in unison.

"What?" Nanuq asked, ears perking innocently, "I washed my paws when I finished."

CHAPTER 20 - THE WAY OF THE PRIDE.

"So, the process is fully automated? How does that work? What happens if the lander is too big for the bubble?" Sana asked, directing her question to Yuriy. She tilted her head, her ears flicking in curiosity as she watched an instructional holo shimmer above the console, detailing the assembly of maintenance bubbles.

Confused, Yuriy flicked an ear and gave Sana a sidelong glance, his whiskers twitching. "What do you mean 'too big' for the bubble? How could it be too big? The bubbles are specifically designed for the Claw's landers."

Sana gestured, trying to explain her point. She raised a fisted paw, then pointed at it with a finger, miming an object approaching the craft. She wrapped her finger inside her fisted paw. "Like... what if it had something long lodged in it, like a giant harpoon?"

"A giant harpoon?!" Yuriy snorted, his ear giving an incredulous flick. "Why are there whale hunters — space whale hunters? — skewering landing craft in space in the first place?"

Sana folded her ears back and blushed beneath her fur, "Don't be an ass. That was just the first thing that came to mind."

Giggling, Yuriy shook his head, then waved a paw in apology. "S-sorry, I didn't mean it like that. You just caught me off guard."

It was Tuesday, September 9th, 2352 — just another ordinary day on the ship's logs, but one everyone aboard would remember for the rest of their lives.

"Wait, what do you mean? Why would the Alpha syndicate want to go to the anomaly?" Dusk asked, turning to Captain Gyata, her gaze gliding over the pair of bickering anthromorphs at the engineering station.

The four had gathered on the bridge earlier that morning, getting to know both the ship and one another. Captain Gyata had been corresponding with The Pride through a private text channel minutes earlier.

Dusk had decided she liked the captain — the lion was always upbeat, but remained a no-nonsense sort of cat. She had been watching the forward viewscreen as reports of increasing seismic activity came in. The screen, a large, two-dimensional panel, consumed the entirety of the forward bridge. It was currently split between a view of deep space on the left and news feeds from Earth on the right.

Dusk wondered if the changes on Earth were somehow related to the recent activity at the anomaly days earlier — if so, she feared it didn't bode well for Earth's future. She sat to the right of the captain, lounging in the first officer's gravity couch. Now, studying the captain's features, she saw what seemed to be worry hidden just beneath the surface of his carefully curated expression. The captain shrugged almost imperceptibly.

"The Pride intercepted communications earlier this morning. The message directed an unidentified vessel to take control of the science station." The lion studied Dusk with a concerned expression, his golden eyes searching her face.

She studied him in return, her face expressionless, as only a prey species could muster when facing a deadly predator. "The Pride asked the Claw to deploy to the anomaly," she replied, her words delivered as a statement of fact rather than a question.

As the lion opened his mouth to answer, the aft entry slid open, admitting the remainder of the Claw's passengers. Nanuq led the way with Reaper, Kael, and Finn following close behind. Nanuq waved her arms in a grand gesture, her attention zeroing in on the snow leopard. "And this is the Claw's bridge. Isn't it amazing?!"

While the remaining crewmates piled onto the bridge, everyone turned to watch the new arrivals. At the sight of Finn trailing the others through the door, Sana shot up and dashed toward her. She crossed the distance in an instant, immediately engulfing the snow leopard in an emotion-laden hug. Her injuries still tender, Finn yelped, grimacing as Sana squeezed.

"Oof! Careful snuggie — I'm still a bit tender."

Mortified, Sana immediately released her and apologized profusely. "Oh Artemis, I'm so sorry! I was just..." She paused, her breathing hitching as her eyes began well up.

Finn melted at the anguish in the young cougar's eyes. "Aww, don't cry..." she cooed. Careful of her own tender injuries, she pulled Sana in for a long, warm hug. Gently, she rubbed the soft fur beneath the cougar's eyes, tenderly sweeping her tears away. She smiled through her own tears, deeply relieved they were together again.

"I'm okay. We're safe. I'm not going anywhere, sweety," she whispered, gently pulling away before holding the cougar at arm's length, instinctively looking her over.

With a smile, she released her and gestured to the remainder of the crew, "Now... Why don't you introduce me to the others?"

"Oh! Good idea!" Sana brightened, stepping aside to reveal the hulking mass of the polar bear anthromorph.

"This is Yuriy, he and I were just learning about some of the ship's features. We were watching instructional videos on how the ship can deploy maintenance bubbles around the away craft for in-cradle repairs."

She gestured to the towering bear and he smiled as he stepped forward, offering his paw for her to shake. Finn's ears perked as she recognized the bear — the same one she often took her craft to for repairs and upgrades. *Yuriy? Wasn't his name Jake?*

Yuriy bowed slightly as Finn took his paw. "It's a pleasure to meet you again, Miss Finn." He reddened slightly, clearly abashed. "M-may I call you Miss Finn?"

She marveled at how large the bear's paws were, watching, entranced, as he gently engulfed her paw in his own. She looked up as he spoke, his facial features revealing a childlike softness, though his eyes were piercing and intelligent. She smiled, unable to contain her mirth when he stumbled through his greeting.

"It's just Finn, but you can call me Miss Finn if you prefer," she chuckled softly, shaking his paw firmly.

Sana continued, moving to beckon Dusk closer. "This is Dusk. Isn't she beautiful? She ended up on the ship in almost the same way you and I did!"

At this, Finn released Yuriy's paw, giving him a sweet smile, leaving him standing doe-eyed and dumbstruck. She knew she'd have to address his apparent fascination with her later — he was cute; maybe it could be fun?

"Hi," Dusk said as she took Finn's paw in hers, smiling briefly and nodding.

"Hey," Finn replied, smiling warmly. "You'll have to tell me the story sometime."

Interrupting, Sana stood, holding her paws out in an inviting gesture. "And this is Captain Gyata! He's a member of The Pride. He rescued all of us!"

Finn waved in the captain's direction before turning back to the beautiful deer, briefly noting how the deer still inspected her with a sharp, measuring eye. "Nice to meet you, Dusk," she said, eyeing the deer as she turned away — *those eyes look like they have a story to tell.*

Finn stood straighter, then approached the captain, recognizing the quiet gravity of authority radiating from the big cat. She nodded, then held out a paw. "Thank you for rescuing me, and for keeping Sana safe."

Smiling, the lion reached to take Finn's paw in his own. Instead of shaking, he clasped it between both of his large

319

paws and bent to gingerly kiss it. "I'm glad to see you're awake, but you don't have to thank me. You should thank the others — they were the ones who rescued you from the wreckage. Dusk and I were still on the Claw at the time of your accident." He lifted a paw, indicating the rest of the crew with a sweeping gesture.

Her ears perked with new understanding. She released the captain's paw and turned to face the others. Somewhat abashed, Finn regarded the four strangers, including Sana, and bowed slightly. Careful not to pinch her still-healing injuries, she straightened again. "Thank you," she said simply. She still wasn't exactly sure why she was on the ship — it all felt a bit surreal, if she were honest. But she couldn't deny that they had saved her from what surely would have been a nasty encounter with the Yakuza. They had also accelerated her healing and kept Sana safe all the while.

Stuffing his hands in his pockets, Reaper was the first to step forward, smiling. "I'm just glad to see you're okay. I've been following your racing career for months. You're an absolute beast in the pilot's seat."

Following Reaper's lead, Nanuq bounded forward, clasping Finn's paws in her own. "I'm so glad you're here. Us girls need to stick together!"

Finn raised an eyebrow, confused as she peered down at the android's bare, synthetic form. "S-so true," she said, glancing at Kael, her expression questioning.

Not far behind, the wolf approached, shaking his head with a shrug — Nanuq's antics ever a source of amusement. Finally, he lifted his chin and gestured toward Reaper "If it weren't for Reaper, you'd still be lying in that hospital bed."

"And she wouldn't even be here at all if it weren't for you, Kael," Reaper interrupted, winking at the pair.

Finally, Yuriy stepped forward, placing a heavy paw on Kael's shoulder, towering over the wolf. "The wolf is being modest. It was his actions that convinced us to land."

Finn raised an eyebrow at this, turning her attention back to Kael — questioning.

Unused to the attention, Kael shrugged and rubbed his

320

forearm, looking away. "We acted together, and that's what matters…" He paused, feeling his cheeks warm as he returned his gaze to hers. Noticing the intensity of her eyes, he steeled himself and met her gaze in full. "I only spoke first. That's all."

"Ahem… If I may." The lion cleared his throat and stepped forward, interrupting their exchange.

Everyone quieted, turning their attention to the captain. Hesitating for a moment, he rubbed his chin thoughtfully before continuing. "First I'd like to thank each and every one of you for being here. While you haven't known me for long, I've known at least one of you almost as long as you've been alive."

Half smiling, Gyata looked pointedly at Dusk. "Others I have known for months, and many of you just days. But we all have one thing in common."

The lion paused, taking a moment to look around the room. Dusk perched against a console just beside him. Reaper stood near the engineering station, with Sana next to him. Yuriy stood a few feet in front and to the left of Reaper, and Finn stood just in front of Yuriy as she turned to gaze at the lion. Lastly, Nanuq and Kael stepped back, squeezing between the bear and the raccoon. Their expressions turned somber as the lion continued.

"One way or another, the Alpha Syndicate has affected all of our lives." His eyes locked with Finn's for a moment, before continuing, "Some of you may know the Alpha Syndicate works hand-in-hand with the Yakuza. But what you may not know — is why."

His eyes flicked to Yuriy, then to Reaper, "Some of you may know the Yakuza have been striving to collect materials known to be vital for certain bio-engineering activities. I believe those activities are something Reaper is intimately familiar with."

Reaper shifted uncomfortably as the lion glanced in his direction. He knew Gyata was alluding to the Yakuza and how they had used illegal street racing as a distraction for their late-night heists. The materials they were collecting, if put in the wrong hands, were potentially very dangerous to anthromorphs. With the Alpha Syndicate involved, it was almost certain that whatever they had planned didn't bode well for their kind.

Continuing, the lion's flowing mane shone in the bridge lights, rippling like waves on an amber ocean as he spoke. "The Pride believes the Alpha Syndicate is planning to genetically engineer some sort of bio-weapon intended to target only anthromorphs. We have made it our mission to stop them by whatever means possible."

He sucked in a deep breath and glanced at each of them in turn. "Reaper, Dusk, and Yuriy — you've already voiced your wishes to remain on the Claw and serve The Pride. To those of you that are left, I must now ask your intentions."

Gyata stepped toward Kael and Nanuq, peering at them both in turn. "Kael, I am certain your breadth of knowledge in science and engineering could prove invaluable on the Claw and to The Pride." He turned his gaze from the wolf to the fox. "Nanuq, your near-universal talents as a sentient android would make you a devastatingly powerful weapon against the Alpha Syndicate. We would be grateful to have both of you on our side."

The lion then turned to Finn as Sana drew up just behind her. "Finn, I know that you don't know the first thing about me and you know very little about the rest of us here. But I've seen your piloting skills, your ability to make snap decisions, and..." he paused, glancing toward Sana, "your willingness to put the safety of others above your own. I believe you would be an invaluable asset to The Pride if you're willing."

Finally, the lion's eyes softened as he turned his attention to Sana. "Sana, while I see great potential in you, I'm afraid I cannot ask you to join us, as The Pride does not recruit minors. Before we depart, we will return you to your home on the surface on one condition — that you never speak of what you've seen here."

Finn felt herself relax as the tension left her; she sighed with relief. The thought that The Pride might keep Sana captive on the Claw because of what she knew had crossed her mind. She hoped the lion was telling the truth — otherwise, things might get ugly, fast.

"Hold on!" Sana interrupted, stepping around Finn to look up at the lion, her ears folded back and hackles raised. "My birthday is tomorrow. I'll be eighteen! Doesn't that make me old enough to decide for myself?"

Captain Gyata's ears perked. Confused, the lion rubbed his jaw before turning to Finn. "Is this true?"

Ignoring the lion's question, Finn sobered, turned to Sana, and spoke quietly. "Sana, please..." Stepping closer, she took the young cougar's paws in her own. "It'll be dangerous, and I don't know what I'd do if you were hurt. You're so young — you have so much life ahead of you. I beg you, stay home, go to college, make a family. I'll keep in touch, I promise."

Sana froze, ears perking forward as Finn spoke. Finally realizing that the snow leopard intended to stay, her ears began to droop, and she shook her head. "I see..." She paused, her eyes falling to the floor before she continued, "Finn... I never told you because I knew you'd worry... But..."

The young cougar mouthed the words, but no sound came. Her gaze met Finn's, and her soft, dark brown eyes conveyed a pain the leopard had thought was long healed.

Finn's ears drooped as understanding hit. She saw now that Sana had been hiding herself — burying hurt behind a happy facade worn only for Finn. She watched as the young cougar's eyes welled, threatening to spill over.

"Oh snuggie, come here..." Finn said softly, stepping toward her and gently wrapping the cougar in her warm embrace. "I'm sorry I didn't see it before. I'm sorry I made you feel the need to hide it from me..."

The leopard felt tears sting her eyes as she pulled away to look Sana in the eyes. "You're safe now. I won't let them hurt you again. Okay?" She took a deep breath, not wanting to say more but knowing she couldn't stop the cougar from following her. "If you want to stay, I won't stop you. But you have to listen to me. Do you understand?"

323

Sana sniffled then wiped at her tears with the back of her paw, nodding, "Yes ma'am…"

Finn's eyes and ears flicked to the captain's, hard and unflinching, "I'm in."

Quickly wiping her tears away, Sana turned and raised her paw in an awkward, half-salute, "Me too."

Finally, they all turned to look at the wolf and his companion. Suddenly yanked out of the moment he'd witnessed between the two felines, Kael flinched and stammered. "M-me too, I—I want to stay too."

That left only Nanuq, who was bouncing with excitement, hopping from one foot to the other as she waited her turn. She grinned wide and squealed as the captain turned his attention to her. "Let's kick some Alpha jerk ass!!" she shouted with glee, immediately breaking the crew out of their emotional reverie. A whoop went up as they all burst into gleeful laughter. The captain had to admit, the little white fox sure had a way of lifting everyone's spirits when it mattered most.

"Excellent!" Gyata clapped his paws together, clearly pleased with the outcome. He then turned and strode over to seat himself in the captain's chair.

"Now to business," he said, then gestured toward his control console. The text channel he'd been monitoring that morning finally appeared on the forward display, replacing the news feeds from Earth. "As I was telling Dusk earlier, The Pride intercepted a message from the Alpha Syndicate. Its destination is uncertain, but it is believed to be either a Syndicate or Naraka vessel."

The lion turned his attention back to the crew, glancing at Dusk before continuing. "As Dusk astutely surmised, The Pride has asked us to investigate. We are to intercept and disable the invading ship if at all possible."

The captain gestured again, replacing the text channel with a list of names, titles, and responsibilities. "As you can see, our first order of business is to officially assign each of you a role and ranking."

He turned to Dusk. "Dusk, yours was the most difficult

choice. I have decided to name you ship's counselor, with the secondary role of operations planning. Your day-to-day job is to ensure the crew is mentally prepared to carry out their duties, with the added responsibility of assisting in special operations planning when needed. Whether you'd like to admit it or not, your empathic abilities make you skilled in both areas — and I intend to make full use of your abilities."

Dusk flicked an ear in annoyance, having hoped for something a bit less people-focused. Nevertheless, she would accept her responsibility with dignity. Lifting her head, she hesitated a moment before nodding confidently.

Turning to Reaper, the lion gave the raccoon an appreciative look. "Reaper, I am naming you chief medical officer. In truth, you are presently our only medical personnel, so you will serve multiple roles until reinforcements arrive. Expect to operate in the field when necessary, and plan to train someone as a backup for med-bay operations while you are away. You are authorized to use the ship's resources for your bio experiments — within reason. Try not to blow the place up. Understood?"

Reaper smiled at this, nodding enthusiastically then responding simply, "Yes, sir."

The lion then pivoted to look at the forward viewscreen and spoke authoritatively. "Yuriy, I am designating you chief engineering officer. Your charge is to keep the Claw in working order by whatever means necessary."

Standing straight, the bear gave a curt nod and an awkward salute, "Understood, captain."

"Very good." He continued, "Kael, I am making you our chief science officer. You'll be responsible for supporting the last three disciplines on an as-needed basis. Meanwhile, I expect you to continue Reaper's research into Diggercorp's bioengineering technology. Reaper can fill you in on the details once you settle in."

Returning his attention to Reaper, he raised an eyebrow. "Before you ask, I know all about what you've been working on. Please get Kael up to speed — you two can work together

325

as time permits. It is critical that we understand the techniques Diggercorp used to create our kind. It is time we take control of our own destiny."

Glancing back toward the display, he paused before continuing. "Speaking of your research, please capture your feral friend at your earliest convenience. It has been wreaking havoc around the ship since you arrived."

At this, Reaper raised an eyebrow but did not comment. He simply nodded his assent as the captain continued.

"Now, as for you, my plucky little fox friend." He glanced in Nanuq's direction with a smile. "I am assigning you the duty of chief morale officer. Maintaining high spirits among the crew is arguably the most important job on the ship. Thus far, you've demonstrated an uncanny ability to bring a smile to my face and a laugh to my belly. I thank you for that. But more than that, your artificial systems make you capable of nearly any task. Therefore, your assignment is to learn as much as you can about everyone and everything related to this mission, and report back to me when you have concerns. Do you accept?"

Fairly bouncing by the time he'd finished, the little fox performed a sharp salute while nodding enthusiastically. "Yes, sir, mister captain sir! I shall endeavor to crack your asses up as much as possible, sir!"

With a chuckle, the lion finally turned to the snow leopard, his expression sobering. "For you, Finn, I spent a great deal of time learning about your past while you were in recovery. I must admit, I didn't expect you to stay. However, I used what I learned about you and came to a decision I may well regret." The lion's ears twitched as he turned his eyes to her.

Curious, her ears perked as she returned his gaze. Unsure why, she had to admit she felt an odd connection with the big male. She hadn't known anyone on the Claw for very long, but Captain Gyata had a way of making her feel at ease.

The lion began to smirk as he continued, "As is only right, The Pride takes careful steps to ensure only large cats are in control." Gyata glanced around the room, his smirk only growing as the others' expressions turned to dismay. Quickly, he held up his paws in surrender. "I'm kidding!" He continued, his expression hardening. "The Pride takes considerable steps to ensure no one species has a deciding majority. There are even humans among our ranks. The Pride's diversity helps ensure we don't lose sight of our end goal of peaceful harmony. We, as The Pride, must be one in our resolve, as would be a pride of lions."

His expression softening, the lion continued, "But that is also why my decision was so difficult." He paused, turning to Finn. "Because I'd like to make you my first officer."

Before anyone could speak, the lion held up a paw. "... Interim first officer — at least until you decide you'd like to keep the position, or would prefer another."

He looked at each crew member in turn as he spoke, keeping his paw aloft. "That is, as long as the rest of you are in agreement. Kindly raise your paw — or hand — if you agree."

Finn looked on in disbelief as each member raised their paw in sequence. Slowly, Sana raised her paw, her eyes not leaving Finn's as each of the newly minted crew members followed. Bouncing, Nanuq chirped and raised hers, followed by Kael, the lumbering bear, Reaper, and finally — with hesitation — Dusk.

Finn stood dumbfounded, slowly turning to each crew member as they affirmed their agreement.

Finally, Dusk broke the silence. "Sana has told us a great deal about you, Finn. What you've done for her alone more than qualifies you for the job as first officer."

Finn's eyes fell to the floor as she internalized Dusk's words. The leopard remained silent for a time, considering, then — with certain finality — her eyes locked with the lion's. "I accept."

Without another word on the subject, the lion clapped his paws once again. "Perfect! Now, as for you, Sana..." He paused, considering her. "Given your age, I believe it would be best to continue your education in whatever way possible. I believe this can be accomplished as you serve on the Claw as navigator and co-pilot. Do you agree?"

Sana's eyes brightened at the thought of piloting the Claw. She nodded enthusiastically as the lion continued.

"The Claw's AI will instruct you all on advanced topics associated with your duties aboard the ship. I want all of you to spend the remainder of the day studying — especially you, Sana. Your job as navigator and co-pilot will come second to your continuing education. You may choose the focus of your education, but I expect you to study at a secondary school level until the ship's AI determines you competent, or until you transfer to a college or university on Earth."

Sana's jaw worked, but she remained silent. Finally, she simply nodded her assent.

The captain turned to Finn as she tentatively sat down in the first officer's chair. "Finn. Our backup troops are waiting for us on the ground. If you're feeling up to it, I need a good pilot to retrieve them."

CHAPTER 21 - MYTHOS EXTINGUISHED.

A nebulous darkness consumed the stark dimness of Orion's connective tissue. Distant sources of light vanished, laying centuries-old mythology to waste. Entire regions of the void — nearly the size of Sol — emptied of even starlight. The ancient points winked out of existence without warning or reason. Space itself seemed to vanish in an instant, swallowed by a writhing mass of noir — an almost nothingness, or something impossibly massive.

A moment later, flitting through the clouded obscurities, showers of brilliant bluish hues flashed and coiled. Arcs of electric brilliance sprouted rootlike tendrils, lashing out at the sudden absence of stars — punishing the void for its insolence, or perhaps those who dared witness it.

As quickly as it began, it vanished. The shock came as an unheard sound — so violent, its meaning could only be understood by deafened ears and a pounding heart. Like standing atop a collapsing mountain, an event so obscene only a god could comprehend it.

"Finn, are you able to get a range measurement on that?" the captain croaked. He had brought the Claw to a standstill when the event began and now stood, mouth agape, unable to comprehend what he'd seen.

Tail whipping with annoyance, she shook her head. "The numbers don't make any sense, Captain. It's like it can't decide whether there's something to measure or there is not."

Glancing toward the science and intelligence stations in turn, Gyata continued. "Kael, Dusk — what are your feeds reporting?"

Kael said, "Earth is experiencing extreme seismic activity across the globe. Multiple volcanic eruptions have been reported. Tsunamis have struck nearly every major coast…"

Interrupting, Dusk read from her feed. "Nearby vessels are reporting extreme gravitational forces. Several ships have been pulled into the anomaly. The science station appears to be drifting after sustaining severe hull damage."

"Yuriy, do you believe we can reach the station safely?" The captain turned to regard the bear, his intense gaze placing him firmly on notice.

Yuriy checked the real-time simulation on his engineering display and thought for a moment. "I think so — but it would be best to avoid any route that takes us between the anomaly and nearby debris."

"Good. Send a preliminary route to the first officer's station… Finn, plot a course avoiding any known masses within one light-minute of the anomaly. Use the ship's AI to predict anything that may be invisible to the naked eye. It should be able to analyze grav the sensor footage from whatever just happened."

Glancing in Reaper's direction, Gyata gave the raccoon a pointed look. "Reaper, prepare to board the station. Be ready for medical emergencies. I want you, Yuriy, and Nanuq prepped to depart within the hour."

The lion turned to Nanuq. "Be prepared to infiltrate the station's computer systems by whatever means necessary. Understood?"

"Already on it," the fox said with a placid smile, her tail wagging in short, smooth arcs.

"Course plotted. Estimated travel time is three hours at maximum thrust," Finn interjected, gesturing toward the forward display, now indicating the transit path and various points of interest.

Waving a paw, the lion stood and turned toward the rear of the bridge. "Get us underway, Finn. You have the helm."

"Captain?" Finn asked, her features strained as she watched the lion head for the door.

Without another word, Gyata gestured for the other members of the away team to follow, then strode off the bridge.

Turning to Dusk and Kael, Finn shrugged, then tilted her head toward the first officer's chair. "Kael, you're first officer for the duration. Dusk, are you good?"

"Yes, ma'am," Dusk replied without looking up. "Kael was too busy staring at your rump to be of much use anyway."

Stumbling at Dusk's words, Kael glanced in her direction with a scowl, his cheeks burning. "I wasn't! The holo display just happens to be oriented in her direction."

"Mhm — and it sways like a cat's tail too," she bit back with a smirk, clicking her tongue and rolling her eyes.

Interrupting, Finn barked, "That's enough, you two — we have work to do!" Her voice was unsteady, as if she were holding back a laugh.

Arriving some hours later, their chests tightened at the sight of the station. Debris surrounded it — though not the sort that might result from explosive decompression or blunt force impact. Nearly everything in the station's vicinity appeared undamaged, as if it had simply been tossed out of an airlock. From this vantage, there was no visible damage, only the incongruent scatter of debris surrounding the station.

"Captain, are you seeing this?" Finn asked, leaning toward the forward display.

The tinny rasp of the captain's voice returned from an unseen speaker. "I see it. One orbit of the station, please. Let's get radar, lidar, temperature, and spectral scans completed. Have the ship's AI monitor all radio traffic while we're here, too."

Dusk held up a thumb, indicating the scans were already in progress, as Finn turned her attention to Kael. "My bird."

"Your bird," Kael repeated, lifting his paws from the ship's controls.

The hulking mass of the station began to rotate right to left. The long tubular structure, ribbed by three large toroidal habitats, hung suspended in space as if strung along an invisible cosmic thread. Finn's expert paws piloted the Claw around the station with such precision that it was hard to tell which object was moving.

Soon, a sheer edge panned into view, revealing the interior sections of the station — as if an entire massive portion had been cut away with laser precision. There was no sign of collision, no evidence of energy weapon impact. It was as though the missing section had simply never existed, as if the station had been constructed that way from the start.

They gasped in unison as the gaping hole panned into view. All three toroids had been cleanly severed, exposing their contents in ovoid cross-sectional views of crew quarters and recreational spaces. The central column had a large section cut away — its exposed cross-section widening from its notional top toward its bottom.

"Did you see this?" Kael asked, manipulating the sensor controls to zoom in on a nearby chunk of debris.

The object looked as though it had once been a chair, though most of its front half was now missing. Just like the station itself, it appeared to have been sliced clean in half with perfect precision. Whatever had happened to the station had clearly affected everything inside it as well.

Finn considered before asking the obvious question. "Has anyone seen the other half of the station?" She turned to Dusk. "Does the ship's AI have any theories?"

Dusk worked in silence for a while, scanning through imagery and figures. "The only answer the AI can come up with is impossible — he thinks the rest of the station is in a different dimension."

"He?" Confused, Finn glanced at Kael, who only

332

shrugged. "What do you mean, he? And what does it mean by 'another dimension'?"

Exasperated, Dusk huffed and flicked an ear. "The AI considers itself a 'he.' His name is Torrent — I'm surprised none of you know this by now… Never mind that. I mean exactly what I said. Long-distance scans taken during the first event indicate the station was partially subsumed. When the event retreated — like we saw a few hours ago — the station was missing a large portion of its hull. Negative gravitational waves then ejected it from the anomaly's nearby vicinity."

A crackling hiss interrupted Dusk's explanation as the captain's voice came over the speaker. "We're aboard the away craft. First officer, please bring the Claw to a stop relative to the station."

Minutes later, the Claw slid to a stop opposite a docking portal just starboard of the station's missing section. Kael selected an image sensor nearest the away craft as it drifted toward the station. Its reactionary jets fired in short, staccato bursts, peppering the surrounding space with glittering ice crystals as expelled moisture instantly froze in the vacuum.

A short time later, the shuttle crew stood waiting as Yuriy prepared to open the portal door. He had transferred power from the shuttle to the station airlock and begun manually cycling the lock as the others secured their helmets. Due to his size, finding a helmet for himself had been something of a creative challenge. With Torrent's help, he'd found a standard human-sized schematic, modified it to fit himself, and printed it just before boarding. Now fully suited, he performed a quick radio check before opening the hatch.

"Comms check?" Yuriy asked, then waited for the others to respond.

"Check one," said Reaper, raising his paw.

"Check two," Nanuq chirped, smiling up at him.

"Check three," Gyata replied, stepping forward.

"Opening the hatch. Stand clear," the bear said, manipulating a dial on the hatch display.

An audible click emanated from the door as the latch mechanism released — but nothing happened. Hesitating,

Yuriy placed a gloved paw on the door and pushed experimentally. The door gave slightly under his shove, prompting him to lean into it until the aged, rubberized seal peeled away and released the door from its years-long resting place.

A small cloud of dust kicked up as the door swung open. With only darkness beyond, it seemed likely the station's power source had been offline for hours — if not days.

"Nanuq, can you access the station lighting systems?" the lion asked as he stepped into the dust-filled darkness, feeling the drop from the shuttle's artificial gravity as his mag boots snapped to the airlock floor.

The android shook her head, following close behind. "Only the station's primary AI and a few emergency systems are available to me. All other systems are on standby. The AI believes the primary reactor was destroyed when… whatever happened, happened."

With a shrug, the lion enabled his helmet light, illuminating the small enclosed space of the airlock. Reaper followed just behind Nanuq, squirming slightly as the sensation of weightlessness hit him. As the rest of the crew filed into the lock, Gyata and the others stepped aside to let Yuriy swing the outer airlock door shut.

"Why isn't the emergency lighting on?" Gyata asked.

"The AI disabled all non-critical systems to conserve power," Nanuq said simply.

Confused, the captain turned to Nanuq. "What do you mean? Obviously, emergency lighting is a critical system. Why would the AI turn it off?"

She glanced at the lion with a shrug. "The AI can detect no signs of biological life on the station that might need it."

Reaper gasped. "Were they all killed in the incident?"

Nanuq shook her head uncertainly, then glanced his way. "The AI says they left — but it can't explain how, or even when."

With a grumble, Gyata worked the inner airlock controls, eventually releasing the latch before stepping back as Yuriy tugged the handle. "Nanuq, please ask the AI to enable the emergency lighting."

The lion then toggled a switch on his neck. "Finn, are you reading me?"

"Yes, Captain. Five-by-five," came the reply over their helmet speakers.

"Good. Keep radio comms to a minimum and relay all traffic through a beam to the lander. Report any unusual activity as soon as you see it. Something feels off about this place." As the captain finished speaking, the inner airlock door swung slowly open.

Emergency lighting began to flicker on, illuminating an empty corridor in a dim red glow. To the left, the tubular hallway ended abruptly in an emergency airlock that now separated the remaining station from its missing half. Hefting his plasma rifle, Reaper was the first to enter, his mag boots sticking positively to the grating beneath his feet. The captain followed close behind, then Nanuq, with Yuriy bringing up the rear. The raccoon leaned in, checking his corners before straightening and motioning for the others to follow.

"Nanuq, I assume you have the station schematic by now. Can you guide us to the bridge from here?" the lion asked, raising his rifle to his chest.

"The rest of you, keep an eye out for survivors. Keep your mag boots on — I don't want anyone floating away if we're engaged." Holding out a paw, the lion gestured for Nanuq to take the lead.

With a nod, Nanuq stepped forward, Reaper close on her heels. Their mag boots clicked with each step, the sound echoing in the empty dark. As they walked, the emergency lighting followed their progress — lights ahead flickering on just before they arrived, while those behind blinked out as they passed. They continued like this for several minutes, passing one open compartment after another, pausing to scan each interior before moving on.

At another doorway, Reaper leaned in, sweeping his gaze in a practiced pattern. Like the compartments before it, this one had a small table, and on it — a partially eaten meal. Utensils floated nearby: a clean knife and a fork still

335

skewering a half-eaten protein cube. The compartment looked as if its occupant had left in a hurry — or not at all. Loose clothing drifted in zero-g alongside personal items. Wallets and purses that still held IDs. Coms and credit chips had been abandoned. But what stood out most to Reaper was that there were no signs of a struggle anywhere.

"This is very strange," Reaper murmured, glancing at the lion. "It looks like they left everything behind. No struggle, no panic — nothing."

Captain Gyata nodded, eyes scanning the corridor. "The hallways show no signs of hurried movement. No dropped items. No scuff marks. No streaks on the walls or floor…"

The lion paused, then turned to Nanuq. "Nanuq, upload directions to the docking bay to my comm. You and the others continue on to the bridge. Check for any signs of the crew and gather whatever information you can. I'm going to check on a hypothesis."

Some minutes later, they reached a corridor branching left — one of the spokes connecting the toroid to the station's central column. As they turned to follow it toward the core, Yuriy finally spoke. "What could've caused all this?"

They walked in silence for a time, none of them willing to voice what they were all thinking.

"I think Torrent is right," Nanuq said, finally breaking the silence. "The station AI agrees — though it seems very confused. I get the sense that whatever happened caused it to lose time. Like amnesia. Several minutes of its memory are just… gone. And it can't explain how or why."

Reaper glanced at Nanuq, bending stiffly in his suit. "But why would only part of the station shear off? Wouldn't the whole thing get yanked into the other dimension — not just break off?"

Nanuq flicked an ear. "Maybe… but what if something was already on the other side of the portal?"

"Like another object? Wouldn't they collide?"

"Maybe," she replied. "But in this case, I think they may have overlapped."

Confused, Yuriy interrupted, "Wait — matter can't

occupy the same space as other matter. That would be catastrophic."

Nanuq looked up at the bear and smiled faintly. "Right — but what if it wasn't matter?

Reaper frowned, tail twitching with agitation. "What else could it be besides empty space?"

"Antimatter," Yuriy offered, brows furrowing. "If the portal — or whatever it was — opened with antimatter on one side and matter on the other, they'd just cancel each other out, right?"

The fox giggled softly, shaking her head. "Kind of — except when antimatter and matter meet, it's called annihilation. That process releases a massive amount of energy. If that's what happened here, the entire station would've been obliterated. Probably more than just the station."

Reaper threw up a paw, exasperated. "Okay then — if it's not empty space and not antimatter, what the yiff could the station have overlapped with?"

The little fox shrugged and waved a paw in the anomaly's general direction. "That's where it gets fuzzy. My guess? Some kind of matter disruption field. Anything that occupied the space where the portal opened — vaporized. That way, whatever's behind the field stays intact."

They continued in silence until reaching the station's main body, where the corridor ended in a four-way intersection. With a wave, the captain turned right and padded silently out of sight.

Their path continued straight ahead, where tubular shafts joined each level of the station's central column. Ports yawned open into each shaft, revealing open vertical spaces — perhaps four arm-lengths across — stretching far above and below. At every floor, narrow platforms ringed the shaft, and taut cables stretched from top to bottom. On the opposite wall, clipped into recessed rings, were belt-like garments with soft inner linings and gloves affixed by loops and clips.

Nanuq explained that the belts clipped to the cables, while the gloves let the wearer pull themselves along in any

337

direction. To demonstrate, she slipped on a belt and gloves, clipped herself to a cable, and with a cheerful flick of her tail, pushed off the platform. She glided upward, smooth and confident, beckoning the others to follow.

Some time later, they emerged near the topmost floor. Reaper and Yuriy were breathing hard — the cable ascent more taxing than they'd expected. They paused, gawking at the scene ahead. Through a wide portalway lay the station's bridge: a vast, dimly lit chamber with rows of workstations, each bearing a familiar yet expanded design reminiscent of the Claw's bridge. Along the far wall, several massive displays loomed, a small stage-like platform just before them.

As they stepped inside, the station displays blinked to life. Like the crew quarters before, personal items drifted in eerie suspension. Partially consumed drink packs, unworn comms, even pieces of clothing floated through the air — relics of lives abruptly interrupted.

Seated in the captain's gravity couch, Finn adjusted the feed volume, her eyes scanning the split window on the forward display. Each helmet cam filled a portion of the screen — the captain's in the upper left. Gyata was nearing the station's docking bay when his feed abruptly went dark. Before she could react, a private audio request flashed across her personal console — it was Gyata.

She muted the auto-feed and swiped to accept, fumbling with her earpiece. Heavy static burst into her ear, tangled with the captain's garbled voice.

"...inn, do you hear me? Get the... off the station... I don't... time to explain. Get... Claw and... far away from here. It's y... s now... I know... my quarters... combination is 767... 7978... hurry..."

Finn gasped, voice tight as she shouted into the pickup, "Captain?! Where are you? Let us come get you!"

"...don't! Stay away! You're the Ca...ain now! Get them out... Goodbye, Fi..."

A grating click — then silence. Only static hissed in her ear, the echo of the lion's final words looping in her mind.

Did he just call me Captain?

The others jumped at her sudden outburst. Kael and Sana turned quickly, catching the stricken look on her face — her hackles stood on edge and her face was visibly drained of color.

"What's wrong?" Sana asked, rushing to her side.

"Dusk! Anything on the security feeds? I lost the channel with Gyata — can you get it back?" Finn barked. She turned to Kael, brushing past Sana's concern.

"Get them off the station, Kael. Whatever it takes — do it now!"

Dusk was already at work, frantically manipulating the intelligence console. "No sign of the channel — he must've cut it. I can try hailing him."

"Never mind. Just monitor the feeds — we must have missed something before." Finn was breathing hard now, her chest tight. She turned to Kael.

Sensing her urgency, Kael responded quickly. "Shuttle's powered and prepped for flyback. Launch the Claw the moment they're on board — the lander will intercept us in flight."

Kael glanced at Sana. "Torrent has evasive overlays queued — they'll sync once the course uploads."

Gyata's feed stayed dark in the upper-left display window. But the others were active — Reaper was in the lead, guiding the team back down the shaft.

Finn reopened the audio channel to the away team — and was instantly hit with questions.

"Finn, what's going on? Where's Gyata?" Reaper barked, hauling himself paw-over-paw along the cable. "Shouldn't we be going after him?"

"Yeah! We can handle it!" Nanuq chirped, darting past Reaper's right side with a burst of enthusiasm, her boots clinking against the cable as she surged ahead of him and the lumbering bear.

"No! Just get your rutting asses back to the shuttle — *now!*" Finn barked, her voice sharp with command.

Reaper shot Yuriy a plaintive glance. The bear only shook

339

his head, resigned — they both knew better than to argue with a snow leopard on edge.

"Nanuq, slow down! Stick together!" Reaper shouted, panting slightly as they neared the platform where the fox had just dismounted her cable.

"I'm going to help the captain!" she shouted defiantly, fumbling with the clip on her belt as she prepared to break off.

Hearing this, Finn shot a tense glance to Kael, who simply nodded and leaned toward the comm. "Nanuq, Finn is your commanding officer. Please do as she says. I'm counting on you — my advanced, always adorable, astonishingly amiable android arctic fox daughter."

Kael exhaled in relief as Reaper's feed showed Nanuq deflate, her tail drooping slightly. She looked up into the camera lens. "Okay, Master... but I'm *only* doing it because you asked nicely."

It was then that the sensor feed on the left display flared to life — a hulking mass sliding from a dark clouded region of space. It devoured the screen, vast and eerily out of focus, like trying to view something pressed too close to a lens.

Dusk cleared her throat and spoke with sudden clarity. "Something's happening at the anomaly. This time, it's *different*."

Finn gestured to isolate the away team's audio. "What in Pan's name *is that?*" she whispered, eyes wide.

Dusk raised an eyebrow and shrugged. "Your guess is as good as mine... but it's *huge*. Current estimates put it at four times Earth's diameter — and still growing."

"Escape course plotted. Uploading to the first officer's station now," Sana called out, swiveling in her chair to gape at the growing horror on the viewscreen.

"Hopefully that course goes the *opposite* direction from whatever the hell *that* is?" Finn said, pointing at the monstrosity and glancing at Sana.

A tinny voice cut in as Reaper sealed the shuttle's airlock and disengaged the mooring clamp. "We're away."

Finn reconnected the crew channel. "Thanks, Reaper.

Brace for launch." She turned to Kael as she spoke.

Kael flicked his paw toward his controls. "Escape route engaged. Brace for evasive maneuvers — just in case."

Within seconds, The Claw had maneuvered its bow away from the station, then blasted off in a hard, arcing burn — the shuttle hot on its tail. Owing to its smaller mass, the tiny shuttle caught up to The Claw surprisingly quickly, managing to close the gap and clamp onto the external docking bay without issue.

With the station now shrinking on the right-side viewscreen, they could see no indication of any following craft. For a moment, Finn hesitated — suddenly doubting what the lion had said. What if he were being forced to say it, just to make sure they'd abandon him? What was that combination for, though? Second-guessing herself, she glanced around the bridge, then back to the forward displays.

"Dusk, did you or Torrent see any indication of an invading craft on or near the station?" Finn asked, flicking through the ship's log, scanning for any hint of a hidden message from the lion.

"No, there were no indications of an intruder of any sort. Even radio coms were…" Dusk paused, then gasped, her eyes locked on the forward display.

Finn glanced at Dusk, then followed the direction of her stare to the screen. The others vocalized their shock in turn as they did the same. They all stared, transfixed — the space station was still shrinking into the distance, but something was terribly wrong.

The central column of the station distorted near its center, squeezing inward until it resembled an hourglass surrounded by three bulbous rings. Metal, plastic, poly-glass — any nearby materials — buckled, stretched, and were pulled into its shrinking core. The middle toroid began to twist and contort, its already-damaged sections bending inward toward the hourglass's collapsing waist. Within seconds, the entirety of the station had imploded, sucked inward like the swirling center of a cosmic whirlpool. Nothing but empty space remained in its place, as though it had never existed.

As the bridge crew sat in frozen shock, the away crew began to file onto the bridge, interrupting their stunned silence.

"Is everything safe?" Reaper asked — then, noticing their shocked expressions, added, "What happened?"

Blinking as though waking from a trance, Finn quickly turned her attention to Dusk, ignoring Reaper's question. "Dusk, what can Torrent tell us about what just happened? Was that some kind of bomb?"

Reaching for his console, Kael quickly manipulated the historical playback controls, rewinding the event for the others to see. "The space station just collapsed in on itself... This must have been what Gyata was warning us about."

As the playback looped, Reaper, Yuriy, and Nanuq stared in disbelief. When the station's final remnants winked out of existence, Nanuq let out a soft cry, covering her muzzle with both paws.

Voice cracking, Nanuq whispered, "C-Captain Gyata? He..."

Nodding solemnly, Dusk rose from her station and crossed the deck to gently wrap her arms around the trembling little fox.

Confused and dumbfounded, Yuriy stood, rubbing a button on his overalls. "D-does that make Finn the Captain now?"

All eyes turned to Finn as she stood. It was then that the realization finally hit home. As First Officer, it was technically her right — and her duty — should anything happen to her predecessor, to assume the role of ship's Captain. But she'd only held the post for a few days — how could she be Captain already? Nervously, she glanced at the others, unsure how to respond.

Noticing her discomfort, Kael stood and stepped to her side. "Yuriy is right. As First Officer, Finn automatically assumes the role of ship's Captain in a situation like this. Does anyone here object?"

Dusk was the only one to hesitate, while the rest replied

342

with an immediate, and unanimous "No."

Noticing Dusk's hesitation, they all turned to regard her curiously. Kael spoke again, "Dusk, do you have reservations?"

Shifting uncomfortably, she flicked an ear and answered slowly. "We're all new at this. Do any of us really belong as Captain of this ship? I agree, someone here should take the role for now — but long term, shouldn't it be someone with more experience?"

As Dusk spoke, Finn nodded in agreement, feeling as though the deer had read her thoughts. "I agree with Dusk. I don't think I've even had enough time to learn my role as First Officer, let alone as Captain. Technically, I am — was — interim First Officer, so I don't know if I can even accept the role."

Ears perked, Sana stepped forward. "Well, someone has to be Captain for now—and I think it should be you. I vote for Finn as Captain. Anyone else?" she asked, looking around the room as she raised a paw.

"I'm with Sana," Kael said, raising his paw.

"Me too!" Nanuq chirped, raising her paw as well.

"What are your orders, Captain?" asked Reaper, as he and Yuriy raised their paws in unison.

Smiling, Dusk lifted her chin in Finn's direction, then stood at ease. "I'd say that settles it. Wouldn't you?"

Lowering her chin, Finn took a deep breath, then let it out slowly before turning her attention back to the forward viewing screen. "Fine. First order of business… does anyone know what the yiff that thing is?" she asked, pointing a clawed finger toward the now glowing hulk occupying the space that was once the anomaly.

CHAPTER 22 - THE HUNGER.

The metallic latticework stood out as the colossal thing's most prominent feature. A network of symmetrical geometry — reminiscent of fractal artwork — sprawled across the forward view screen. Impossibly vast, the object continued to emerge from the nightmarish distortion that had once been the formless void of the anomaly. The beams and spidering junctions that laced them together had no rightful place in this reality; the very physics of such enormous structures should have made their existence impossible. Moon-sized nodules jutted from the junctions where the beams converged — world-sized welds, as if clumsily fused by giants.

Between the gaps in the lattice, an eerie lightshow flickered — pale yellows and cold blues rippling in asynchronous waves. With each passing second, the thing grew more luminous, a soft iridescent halo blooming along the edges of its vast, spherical contour. Nearly all of its bulk had now breached the portal from which it had emerged, exposing its truly staggering proportions. At its widest point, its diameter registered as six times that of Earth — large enough to house Neptune and then some.

As the crew of the Claw stared on in disbelief, a stream of light began to pour from the hulk like some ethereal finger reaching toward the cosmos. The tendril resembled something like a solar flair, erupting from the colossal latticework in a brilliant coiling mass of incandescent light.

"Your guess is as good as mine, Captain — but sensor readings show it's releasing massive amounts of thermal and ionic energy," Kael reported, having vacated the first officer's chair to examine the science station's feed.

Swiveling to glance at the deer behind her, Finn flicked an ear, tension visible in her posture. "Does the intelligence officer have anything to report?"

Dusk stopped short of shaking her head, ears perking with interest as she read the latest reports collected by the AI. "The gravitational readings don't make any sense. Torrent says the object's mass is less than half that of Earth's."

Tilting his head, Yuriy approached the intelligence station — accidentally bumping into Dusk as he leaned in to read the display.

"Oof! Easy there, big snug — I'm not like your other girls," Dusk huffed, smirking playfully.

Flushing, Yuriy awkwardly patted Dusk's shirt sleeve. "I'm sorry, Miss Dusk — I'm just a little clumsy! I wanted to check the numbers. I think maybe…"

The bear rubbed the button on his overalls, then leaned in again — careful not to repeat his mistake. "Torrent, do you have a density map for the sphere yet?"

To the crew's surprise, a silky, low-pitched and androgynous voice replied, "Yes, Yuriy. Displaying on the left forward viewing screen. Preliminary estimates indicate that eighty percent of the sphere's mass resides in the outer three percent of its diameter."

Yuriy froze, mouth slightly agape as he processed the numbers. "It's not… How could that be possible? Torrent, what do the spectrometry scans show?"

"Surface spectrometry and refractometry indicate multiple high-density metals with nearly zero gaseous content. Analysis reveals several common metals: copper, aluminum, iron, and gallium. The spectral signature of its primary component remains inconclusive."

"What do you mean *inconclusive*?" the bear asked, his expression tight, ears pinned back with growing concern.

"I am unable to identify the spectral signature of the object's most abundant material. I suspect it may be an alloy of unknown composition. Its density-to-mass ratio is extremely low," came Torrent's measured reply.

The bear straightened, resumed rubbing the button on his overalls, and began to pace, his steps betraying mounting anxiety.

Finn watched Yuriy's restless movements, then tilted her head, ears twitching. "Something on your mind, Yuriy?"

"It's a machine," the bear blurted without stopping, his voice rising slightly as his expression grew ever more strained.

Confused, Finn shifted in her seat, her tail swishing once in agitation. "So?"

Yuriy halted mid-step, then turned to face the snow leopard, fixing her with a tense, haunted look. "What kind of machine needs to be six times the diameter of Earth — and just happens to materialize out of empty space nearby?"

A stunned silence fell over the bridge — just long enough for realization to seep in. Finn was the first to react. "Torrent, based on its current trajectory, can you predict where that thing is heading?"

The forward view screen shifted, displaying the full enormity of the sphere — its tendril of light now twice as long as moments before. Before the AI could respond, space near the tendril began to shimmer and warp. Confusion swept the bridge as an object started to resolve, cutting across the luminous surface of the giant.

"What the yiff is happening now?!" Finn growled, hackles bristling as her gaze snapped to Kael. "Shields up! Crew to battle stations! Torrent, identify that object!"

The view screen zoomed in, revealing a massive oblong structure of polished metal. Its smooth surface shimmered with elegant, sweeping patterns — long, symmetrical arcs that spidered across its skin. Like some archaic obelisk of alien origin, it's edges shimmered as it continued to resolve

346

out of the nothingness of the void.

A spacecraft. It is hailing us," the AI stated coolly, unfazed.

Bewildered, Finn looked around the bridge for any clue, any explanation — none came. "Are you telling me that's an alien spacecraft trying to make polite conversation? It looks like a rutting polished stone from some nerdy kid's rock collection."

Torrent offered no reply. Aside from the faint rustle of their clothing as the crew adjusted in their seats, the bridge fell into a deafening, expectant silence.

Tail flicking sharply in frustration, Finn did the only thing she could — she *became* the Captain. "Kael. Dusk. Assessments?"

Kael spoke first, voice cautious. "It shows no signs of being armed and hasn't moved to engage. In fact — it's actively matching our speed and trajectory."

To demonstrate, Kael eased the Claw's course, then accelerated. Both times, the object adjusted flawlessly, mirroring their movement with eerie precision.

"Thermal scans show the thing is emitting heat — though only from the spaces between its segments. It's broadcasting radio-frequency signals across multiple bands, including our comm frequency. Interestingly, Torrent has detected a slight error in their modulation technique," Added Dusk, as she continued to dig through a deluge of information pouring across her display.

Finn cocked her head and glanced at Nanuq. "Have you detected that modulation error too?" she asked, voice taut.

"Yes, but it's minor," Nanuq replied, flicking an ear before returning her gaze to the forward screen. "It seems they're synthesizing the pattern using incomplete data."

Finn rubbed her chin thoughtfully as her tail settled into a slow sweep. "Let's test that. Torrent, send them a message pointing out the error and providing correct modulation specs. Say nothing else. Then measure how long they take to correct their schema once they receive it."

"They send their thanks," The AI replied almost instantly.

"Their first response at two hundred three milliseconds was imperfect. The the second at three hundred fifteen milliseconds matched exactly."

Finn sighed, rubbing her temples, and turned to Kael. "If they adapt that fast to our modulation, we're at a disadvantage. What's your recommendation, science officer?"

"Ask them what they want." The wolf replied flatly.

Finn nodded, then turned to face the forward view screen, attempting to put on an air of confidence. "Torrent, if a video feed exists, apply a privacy filter covering the bridge — excluding only me — and accept their hail. Display it on the forward viewscreen."

The screen flickered to life with an alien tableau — plant life in pastel blues, pinks, and purples. A slender figure stood at its center, calmly watching Finn's nervous adjustments as she smoothed her hair before them.

The creature appeared vaguely humanoid — tall, lithe, and perhaps female in form. It's delicate features included a vague hint of breasts beneath what could only be described as a moving dress. The satin layers of the dress — if it could be called that — moved in smooth, graceful arcs that repeated on interval.

The being regarded Finn with two large, piercing green eyes framed by a slender, feline-like muzzle. It resembled an anthro — but with alien elegance unmatched in her experience. A glistening pelt of glossy black fur covered its face and extremities. Long, tapering ears stood erect atop its skull, thinning to perfect symmetry. Auburn hair flowed past its waist nearly to its ankles — resisting the rhythmic waves of its garment. Behind it, a long, furred tail curled in fluid motion, echoing the garment's soft pattern.

Finn stared, jaw slack, eyes wide, swallowed by the grace of the being. She blinked twice — remembering herself — and cleared her throat. "Greetings. I am Captain Finn Ema of the Pride's *Claw*. Please state your business."

The other crew members' ears perked at the mention of Finn's last name. It hadn't occurred to any of them that she might *have* a last name — much less that they ought to be referring to her as Captain Ema.

The creature on the viewscreen shifted, stepped forward, then bowed slightly. "It is a regretful pleasure to meet you, Captain Finn Ema. I represent the Arcan Council of Alien Affairs. We conduct first-contact introductions and negotiations on behalf of the Federated Worlds Alliance in cases such as this. It is our duty to intercept and assist all survivors in the event of a confirmed *Hunger* invasion."

Finn blinked, interrupting. "Excuse me? Did you say *invasion*? Who's invading whom?"

The creature paused, bowed again. "Pardon my vagueness, Captain. Once we discovered the Hunger's plan, it was already too late. We managed to entrap the *Goliath* in a dimensional loop, hoping to slow its advance until reinforcements could arrive. Tragically, our supply lines were severed before help came. When the dimensional field generator lost power, we could no longer contain it. I am deeply sorry — we failed you."

Finn blinked, confusion clear in her voice. "Hunger? Goliath? I'm not following — what are you talking about?"

A low murmur swelled across the bridge as crewmembers exchanged fearful whispers. The creature gestured — and the screen shifted to the hulking sphere again. "The *Hunger* is an energy-based lifeform devoid of emotion or mercy. We call its primary construct the *Goliath* — a machine it built to consume and transport the remnants of entire worlds. The tendril of light you see is merely the first wave. Within hours, it will strip your planet of life and begin consumption."

"STOP! Why the yiff should *I* believe you?! What's to say *you* aren't controlling those things?" Finn shouted, cutting the Arcan off and startling the others. "What assurance can you provide me that could convince me you're not just another threat?"

In response, the viewscreen split — bringing the Arcan back into view on the right while the Goliath scene shifted on the left. The camera tracked the tip of the tendril as Earth came into view — a blue dot in the void — as the tendril snaked ever nearer. "Unfortunately Captain, I fear there are no words I could say that would offer you the assurance you desire. But know this: the Hunger stole my world. As a result, I have dedicated my life to stopping them."

The Arcan paused as the view of the tendril came closer to earth, soon it had begun to curl around the planet, encircling it in an unnatural ring of light. The view continued to expand, bringing North America into view, then New York State, and finally the devastated ruins of New York City. Widespread earthquakes and tidal waves had reduced the city to rubble. The crew watched in stunned silence as the full magnitude of the Goliath's threat became horrifyingly clear.

Silt and debris clogged the streets. Entire buildings lay collapsed; whole city blocks were simply gone, wiped away as though discarded by a giant's careless hand. As if it were merely an unwelcome aberration to be cleaned from a dirtied dish.

Finally, a sign of life panned into view — a feral dog, perhaps a pet or a stray, trotting down what may once have been a neighborhood street. It glanced side-to-side as it moved, ears flicking nervously, apparently lost and confused. As they watched, a glowing yellow orb appeared, drifting several feet behind the animal. For a moment it seemed the thing was merely observing — until it surged forward. In a blur, it swept to the dog's broad side and, with incomprehensible speed, pierced directly through its chest. As quickly as the orb had moved, the dog collapsed — its limbs buckling beneath it as its own momentum drove its muzzle and forelegs into the rubble-strewn street.

Finn stared in silence, her expression a mask of utter horror — mirrored by each member of the crew. She heard Sana's soft sob, Reaper's whispered curse, Yuriy's sharp intake of breath, and Kael's quiet exclamation. Each reaction registered on her psyche — a sharp stab adding to the deadly wound that was her witness to this day. She watched somberly as the only world she'd ever known was torn apart.

Helplessly they watched as the Earth, surrounded by the

Hunger's eerie glow, yielded to it's ravages. Within minutes the planet lay eerily still — it's surface discolored and unrecognizable. Entire continents had changed color from a verdant green to a sickly, incomprehensible grey. The atmosphere filled with a haze that could only be the smoke from a planet wide fire. It's surface split as the goliath approached, the tidal forces of the machine's impossible gravity causing tectonic shifts in the planet's crust. Within hours the oceans had been lost to the Goliath's unrelenting machines, replaced by the molten red shimmer of exposed magma and spreading lava flows.

The Earth's last remaining children stood frozen on the bridge of the Pride's Claw. The final moments of their home world now seared — irrevocably etched into memory.

Never to be forgotten.

Never to be spoken.

They weren't sure how long they'd been staring at the blank screen when the radiation warning finally chimed. Only the creature remained visible on the right side of the display — its head bowed solemnly, unmoving.

Finn remembered the chill of the night's air as she'd crossed that threshold all those years ago.

A single tear traced the curve of her cheek, vanishing into the fur along her jaw as her eyes fixed and narrowed on the Arcan's.

ABOUT THE AUTHOR

A Michigan native, Indigo came to know himself through the quiet of nature and the boundless reach of imagination. As a child, weekends often meant sitting around a campfire with family, watching the stars and wondering what might lie beyond. Though imagination and curiosity have always driven him, he never considered himself particularly creative.

Never imagining a future as an author, Indigo pursued an education in engineering, moving to North Texas for school in 2004. By 2011, he had earned his degree in electrical engineering and decided to remain in Texas to begin his career. Two years later, he purchased his first home — and by the following year, shared it with a few beloved horses.

Throughout this time, Indigo remained an avid reader, drawn to the rich, imaginative worlds of science fiction and furry literature. By the spring of 2024, having read nearly every furry-related work available to him, tragedy struck: a violent spring storm claimed one of his horses, a flea-bitten Arabian mare named Indigo.

In honor of that loss, and with grief turned to purpose, Indigo Leo Max took his horse's name and began a new journey. Within a year and a half, he completed his first novel, *The Pride's Claw.*